PASSION'S PROMISE

He was urging her back, down on the soft, yielding moss, and suddenly her flimsy chemise was no longer protecting any part of her body. Soon his hands were touching her. Rough, male hands, not smooth and pampered like her own, frightening in their bold demands, but delighting, too.

"Oh, my darling," she whispered, "I love you so much! I will always . . ."

"Shh—" Jeremy touched his lips lightly to hers, just enough to still her. "No promises, *petite*. Not when I can give you nothing in return."

"Nothing . . . ?"

He laughed softly. "Nothing but a small lesson in lovemaking . . . and how it feels to be a woman. If that is enough."

"It is enough. . . ."

FLEUR-DE-LYS

Susannah Leigh

AN ONYX BOOK

NEW AMERICAN LIBRARY

A DIVISION OF PENGUIN BOOKS USA INC.

ONYX TRADEMARK REG. U.S. PAT. OFF. AND FOREIGN COUNTRIES
REGISTERED TRADEMARK—MARCA REGISTRADA
HECHO EN DRESDEN, TN, USA

SIGNET, SIGNET CLASSIC, MENTOR, ONYX, PLUME, MERIDIAN
and NAL BOOKS are published by NAL PENGUIN INC.,
1633 Broadway, New York, New York 10019

First Printing, May, 1989

1 2 3 4 5 6 7 8 9

PRINTED IN THE UNITED STATES OF AMERICA

PROLOGUE

Lorient, France, 1731

The sky was clear, but a biting wind swept across the wharves, giving the early-spring morning a wintry feel. The rigging of the single ship at anchor creaked and groaned. Even on shore, sharp slapping sounds could be heard as men tugged the canvas sails into place.

On the dock, a young woman sat quietly on the weathered piling, worn smooth by ocean squalls. She was hatless, and the wind had loosened wisps of hair, which glowed like a red-gold halo around her delicate features. The softness of her face in repose went beyond beauty; there was about her an almost ethereal quality, more angelic than real. Only her mouth was worldly, full lips, parted unconsciously, a little too vivid with color. Her mouth and her eyes, a deep, mysterious emerald green, framed by long lashes darkened in the shadows.

A sound from the ship caught her attention. Looking around, she saw one of the Gray Sisters struggling up the unwieldy gangplank. The wind gusted sporadically, whipping skirts and plain, modest petticoats around the good nun's legs, and she clutched with both hands in a futile attempt to hold them down and hang on to her bag at the same time. Behind her came a girl clad in a simple dress and dark hooded cloak, threadbare, but clean and neatly mended. The last of the girls to arrive, no doubt, for the docks were now still except for a few men scurrying to take care of last-minute chores, and no more carriages could be seen hurriedly pulling in, or wagons laden with passengers and cargo.

Les filles à la cassette—that was how they had already come to be known. The casket girls, for the small trunks in which they carried everything they owned in the world.

7

Two dresses, two petticoats and chemises, six headdresses, and various other carefully counted articles of clothing and household linen—all this had been provided by the Mississippi Company in exchange for the decent, hard-working, God-fearing daughters of humble farmers and impoverished middle-class families. "Send me wives for my *canadiens*; they are chasing after Indians in the woods," had come the word from the French territory of Louisiana, and young women had been traded for a casket of clothes and a promise of a better chance in life . . . and of course, in some cases, the sheer relief that came from getting rid of another female of marriageable age with no prospects and no dowry.

The young woman on the dock watched pityingly as the other girl reached the top and paused, her head bowed against the wind. What was she thinking now? Was she glad to be getting away from whatever it was she was leaving? Or was she nervous at the thought of the long sea voyage ahead, and the unnamed man who would be waiting at the end?

Only a short time before, she herself had been like that girl. She glanced down at the trunk beside her, with its coats and shirts and headdresses that made her just like everyone else. Barely two weeks before, she had been riding in a coach with one of the Gray Sisters as chaperone, thinking the same thoughts the other girl must be thinking today. Now . . .

"I am sorry, *mademoiselle* . . ."

A boy appeared awkwardly at her elbow, a scrawny creature, barely fourteen. He stammered slightly as the full force of those green eyes turned on his face.

"I . . . I am sorry, but the captain says he cannot wait any longer. We will be weighing anchor in a few minutes."

The girl smiled vaguely. She had already explained to the captain that she would not be sailing with the others, but he had barely listened. Obviously he thought she was indulging in a girlish fantasy, and he had sent the cabin boy rather than deal with it himself.

"It's all right," she said calmly. "I understand."

"He says I have to, uh . . . ." The boy looked unhappily at the casket at her feet. He had not failed to notice the celestial effect the sun created in her hair, and he hated to disappoint her, but there was nothing he could do. The captain was a harsh master, and he expected his orders to be obeyed. "I have to make sure everything is on board. I could, uh . . . carry it for you. If you like."

The girl reached out, laying her hand for a second on top of the trunk, then waved it away. It didn't matter, after all. Those things belonged to the Mississippi Company really, not her. And clothes that were meant for a farm wife would hardly be appropriate where she was going.

Besides, Roger would take her as she was.

"Yes, thank you. I would be very grateful if you would do that. Please . . . carry it for me."

She was aware, as the boy picked up the trunk and glanced back, that he was looking at her much as she had looked at the girl on the gangplank before. She turned for a moment, her ear picking up some slight sound in the distance; but when she listened, there was nothing, and she looked back again. He pitied her, and he felt sad . . . but she did not need his pity. Soon Roger would come, as he had promised, and carry her off on his magnificent black stallion with the wind whistling all around them and sunlight drenching the earth.

She smiled to herself as she thought of that first time she had met him . . . if indeed "met" was the way to describe it.

There was nothing about that particular afternoon that had set it apart, except perhaps that she was more tired than usual. The succession of coaches from Normandy to Paris, then west to the seaport of Lorient, had grown progressively cruder, and the roads were so bad, the weather so uncertain, they were frequently bogged down in mud. Only that morning, the wheels had been so badly mired, everyone had had to get out, and while the coachman waited for reinforcements for their team of twelve horses and twenty-one oxen, the rest of the party had gone on on foot. The coach had not reached them until well after noon, by which time poor Sister Xavier had been so spotted with whitish mud that she looked like a barnyard hen.

Not that I look much better, the girl had thought as she squeezed in gratefully between the nun's plump body and the wall. Though she had tried, surreptitiously, to wipe the mud off her cheeks and lashes.

The carriage jolted, eliciting a grunt from the man

opposite her. She glanced up with distaste. Only two men
were in the seat across from her, riding forward; the third
had been wedged in next to Sister Xavier. One was a
tight-lipped man, courteous, but distant, who spent most
of his time staring through the window. The other, though
he did not speak, was hard to ignore. He was solidly
built, and the cape he had wrapped around himself, while
mud-spattered, was lined with velvet and obviously well
made. Probably a gentleman of some standing, she thought.
Clearly he believed he was, for he plainly disliked having
to share his coach with those more humbly clad.

The girl let her eyes drift toward the window, trying
not to think about what lay ahead, but unable to avoid it.
It had seemed such an adventure, just a short time before, when she had left the small village near Caen where
she had been living for three years, since her parents had
died so tragically within months of each other. Homes
had been found easily for her younger brothers—masculine
hands were always welcome on a farm—but she had been
taken in grudgingly by an uncle and his wife, and not a
day had passed of all the time she spent with them that
she was not reminded she was a burden. What little
money Papa had left, they said, had gone for her daily
care, and while she knew it was not true, she did not
blame them. They had three daughters of their own to
find dowries for. Every spare penny, naturally, went for
that. So when the priest had explained that wives were
needed for settlers in La Louisiane, it had seemed a
perfect solution.

But now . . . She stared out at the passing scenery,
aware for the first time of the magnitude of what she was
doing. It was still early spring, but a warm spell had
brought out the first wild roses by the roadside, and
splashes of red showed against the muddy snow. Tears
blurred her eyes as she thought of the beauty of this land
she was leaving. Louisiana was French too, they said, but
it was French in language and government and culture.
The land about her would not be French, the feel and the
smell and the sights would be different, and she knew a
part of her heart would ache for home.

She did not even notice when they pulled to a stop,
they had stopped so many times that day. When she
finally did, she thought only that they had reached another impasse and were going to have to get out and walk

again. But when she looked up and saw the expression on the face of the man opposite her, she knew something was wrong.

She did not have to stick her head out the window and crane her neck to see what it was, for just at that instant the door flung open and a man came into view. A man with a black mask that covered most of his face—and a pistol aimed at the coach.

A highwayman!

Her heart thumped wildly, mostly from apprehension, but from excitement too. She had had so little in her life that went beyond the ordinary, and tales of bold robbers waylaying stages on the open road had always seemed the height of glamour and romance. Now she was actually confronted with such a man—and he was not a disappointment. As she descended from the carriage with the others, she could not tear her eyes off him, he was so exactly what she would have imagined.

He was a tall man, and fashionably slim, with a kind of easy grace that seemed deliberately accented by black clothing, simple, but not plain, for there was no lack of rich fabric here, or the skillful use of the tailor's art. She did not need to see his face to know he was handsome. He carried himself like a man who was sure of his looks and the way they would be received by others. A man who knew that few men would look on him without envy, and very few women without at least a faint quickening of the pulse.

He seemed to sense what she was thinking, for he turned slowly, meeting her gaze with the bluest eyes she had ever seen. And in that instant, suddenly, without knowing how or why, she realized that this handsome, unlikely sorcerer had cast a spell over her. There was no reason for it—heaven knew, it was beyond all rhyme or sense—but in that one reckless moment she had fallen hopelessly in love. Perhaps it was just her youth, perhaps the despair that had swept over her before when she realized how dark her future looked, but she knew absolutely, undeniably, that a part of her would belong to this man forever, if only in her heart.

He made short work of the task he had come to perform. The men, including the driver, were lined up against the carriage and relieved quickly and efficiently of their possessions. The one with the velvet-lined cape was even asked for a small case which he had shoved under the seat, and she noted with a little twinge of satisfaction that he seemed to mind it greatly. Even Sister Xavier was forced to hand over her watch.

"The church is rich enough to afford a little donation for my pocket," he said, his voice edged with something that could have been amusement. "Some poor swine of a peasant will mortgage his farm to tithe it back again."

He turned to the girl, and she felt herself tremble, not, she had to admit, wholly from alarm. She knew she ought to be terrified—hadn't she heard stories of highwaymen murdering their victims so no witnesses would be left behind?—but somehow she couldn't bring herself to be afraid of those beautiful blue eyes.

Her hands gripped a little leather reticule in which she was carrying the small amount of gold the Mississippi Company had given as her dowry. She thought for an instant he was going to reach out and take it. But something in his face seemed to soften, and while his mouth didn't move, she could have sworn he was smiling.

"What is your name, *petite*?"

She was too startled not to reply. "Lili-Ange," she said. Then, hearing a sharp intake of breath in her ear, and realizing Sister Xavier had been shocked by the familiarity, she hastened to add: "Fleurie. My name is Lili-Ange Fleurie."

"Lili-Ange . . . Fleurie." The smile came out then, clear and surprisingly gentle. "A whole heavenly garden in your name, and a very French one at that. Lily-flower . . . the *fleur-de-lys*. You must be of royal blood, then."

She tried not to, but she couldn't keep from smiling back. "My family is not of royal blood at all," she said, careful to avoid what she knew must be Sister Xavier's disapproving frown. "We are not even aristocratic, though we were at one time, I believe. Originally the name was *de* Fleurie, but that was a long time ago, and we are plain and poor now."

"Poor perhaps, but never plain, *mademoiselle*." He saw the handbag she was clutching and reached out, taking it from her with a brief, magical touch that was worth every piece of gold she would ever have in her life. Instead of putting it in his sack with the others, however, he took some of the cash he had stolen from the heavyset man and slipped it inside, returning the reticule to her.

"You say you are poor—and he is very rich. I'm sure the
gentleman would prefer *you* to have this, rather than
some lawless brigand on the highway." Laughter danced
in his eyes as he dropped her a courtly bow. Strangely, it
did not seem incongruous with the mask or the gun in his
hand. "Good-bye, pretty Fleur-de-Lys. May *Dieu et la
vie* be kind to you."

He backed slowly over to his horse, the pistol still in
one hand as he flung the bag over the saddle with the
other and mounted in a swift, fluid motion. On impulse,
just as he was whirling around, he swung down and,
snapping off the prettiest of the red roses, held it out to
her.

"It should be a lily—should it not?—but this is the best
I can do. Take it, *petite*, and remember me."

Then he was gone, leaving Lili-Ange to stare after him
until a kind but distinctly unnerved Sister Xavier pressed
her back into the coach. She did not even mind too much
when the man with the velvet cape helped himself to the
money the bandit had given her. He tried to take her few
gold coins too, saying he had lost considerably more than
that, but the thin-lipped man gave him a sharp look, and
apparently he decided it wasn't worth a fight. Not, she
noticed as her fingers tightened around the rose, forgotten now by everyone else, that he offered to share it with
the others who had also suffered losses.

She was still wrapped up in her own thoughts several
hours later when they pulled into the cluttered yard of a
small rustic inn shortly after nightfall. It was not a particularly comfortable place, nor did it look clean, but it was
much too late to go on. There was one large room in the
back, to be shared by whatever male travelers showed
up, but the only place for the women was a cramped attic
chamber, reached by a rickety ladder which probably
wouldn't have borne Sister Xavier's weight even if her
well-padded hips could have squeezed through the opening at the top. In the end, after much grumbling on the
part of the innkeeper, a bed was made for the nun on a
lumpy couch in the parlor, and Lili-Ange went to the
attic herself.

In a way, she was glad. The room was damp and filthy,
with the only bed a pile of straw on the floor, but a clean
breeze came through the window when she pried it open,
and she was grateful for the privacy. When she was a

child, she had had a tiny room of her own off the kitchen in her parents' house, but then she had gone to live with her uncle and she had never been alone again. Now it was good to be by herself, especially with the confusing thoughts that were whirling around in her brain.

Never in her life had she seen a man quite so dashing. She sat down on the straw, her knees up to her chin and her back to the window. Or so generous! He thought nothing of stealing from others, yet when he saw how little she had, he had been ready to share his booty with her. And he had been so chivalrous, too—the way he bent and plucked that single rose. She knew it was foolish, letting herself think about him, *care* for him so much, yet she had the feeling no man would ever treat her so gallantly again.

With a little sigh, she picked up the poor wilted rose she had set beside her and tucked it into her hair. It was so unfair! She was young and pretty, and she wanted a handsome young man to love her back. And all she would ever have was some middle-aged farmer or shopkeeper who would, if she was lucky, at least be kind to her.

She had not expected ever to see her unlikely cavalier again—it was the last thought in her mind—yet when she heard a sound behind her and turned, she already knew a split second before what she was going to find at the window.

She recognized him instantly, even without the mask. His eyes were bluer than she had remembered, and light-brown hair streaked with gold tumbled on the brow of a face that was every bit as handsome as she had known it would be.

"*Mon Dieu*—what are you doing?"

The sharpness in her voice made him laugh. He eased his shoulders through the window, coming to rest for a moment on the sill. Moonlight caught in his hair, throwing his face into such fantastic shadow that Lili-Ange thought for an instant she must be imagining it. Then his voice broke the illusion.

"What? Profanity—coming from such a lovely mouth? And here I thought you were a sweet little thing, too well-brought-up for that."

It was a deliberate challenge, and floods of pink rose to the girl's cheeks. She *had* been well-raised. Ordinarily she never said anything like that. "I would have been more discreet, *monsieur*, if you had been discreet yourself."

"You think it's indiscreet of me, climbing up the vines on the side of the house to tap at a lady's window? Which I had every intention of doing, by the way, except I found it already open." He flung his legs over the sill and came boldly into the room, bringing a gasp of alarm to Lili-Ange's lips. "And here I thought I'd been the *épitomé* of discretion—and stealth."

"You are absolutely mad!"

"I've been called that before," he admitted easily. "But how is it madness to long to see a beautiful woman who has set the blood coursing hot through my veins?"

"It is madness if they are looking for you—and you know they will be!" She lowered her lashes, trying not to see the way his eyes were caressing her, lingering on each sweet girlish curve with an ardor that was only half teasing. Strangely, she was more frightened for him than for herself. "We have not yet reported what happened, but surely you are known in the area. I may not be well-acquainted with the ways of highwaymen, but I'm not naive enough to think that this afternoon was an isolated occurrence. Even now the king's men must be searching for you. If someone saw you climb up that vine—"

"No one saw me. I made sure of that, more for your sake than mine, *petite*—and no one is looking for me."

"But you are a dangerous highwayman—"

"Hardly that." To her surprise, he sat back on the sill again, this time from the inside, as casually as if he had just come to pay a social call. "Dangerous perhaps, but not a highwayman—unless you count one reckless act of recovering what was mine."

"What was . . . yours?"

He leapt up, laughing as he swept her a courtly bow, like a handsome *chevalier* with a plumed hat in his hand. "Roger de Courbet Montaigne at your service, *mademoiselle*." Then, seeing the look of surprise on her face, he added, "And that unpleasant-looking man with the case under his seat was my second cousin—who had made himself rather too free with some family jewels which had been entrusted to my care."

"You mean he stole them? But he looked so affluent."

"Oh, he didn't do it for the money, though he's not averse to cash, or anything that can be turned into cash.

He took the jewels to discredit me because they were in my keeping. There's a certain rivalry between us, which, incidentally, neither of us will win. The bulk of the family fortune is beyond us both. But I gave him a bit of his own back today—and made him hopping mad besides!"

Lili-Ange stared for a moment, studying him in the light of the tallow candle that was the only illumination in the room. He looked almost like a little boy, so thoroughly pleased with himself. "And yet," she said quietly, "you took from the others too."

"Not really. They'll wake up to find their goods safely returned at the foot of their cots. I even gave the nun's watch back, though it was against my better judgment. The church is so much richer than the peasants it serves. But she had a kind face, and she looked concerned about you."

He looked concerned too, Lili-Ange had to admit. His eyes were touching her with more than teasing passion now, and she felt suddenly confused. "Really, you . . . you shouldn't be here. In my bedchamber like this. It isn't proper . . . or safe. Sister Xavier will be retiring soon, and—"

"Sister Xavier has already retired." He laughed gently, enjoying the modesty that put roses in her cheeks to match the drooping rose behind her ear. "Have you forgotten, I've already slipped the watch back in her pocket. And there are no other women staying here. Don't you think I checked on that before I came?"

"*Monsieur* . . ." She hesitated, even more confused now. His voice was soft, but there was no mistaking the tremor in its depths, and she felt herself turn hot and cold all at the same time as she realized belatedly what was going on in his mind. "Surely you don't think . . . you cannot believe I would ever consider doing something like *that*. I may be poor, but even a poor woman has her virtue. I would never—"

"I know that." He reached out and touched her very lightly on the arm, then drew his hand back again. "I knew that the moment I saw you. Just as I knew I must make you mine."

"But you said . . ." She felt her breath catch in her throat.

"I said that I knew you would never give yourself carelessly, for the pleasure of a single night. I said that I knew you were the kind of woman who would require a promise of marriage before surrendering to a man. . . . And I am ready to give it."

"You are ready to promise to marry me?"

"I would promise anything to have you, *petite* Fleur-de-Lys. I *will* promise—anything you want." His voice was husky, deepening in his throat. "Are you sure you aren't a royal princess in disguise? I have always had a weakness for pretty princesses."

"No." It was hard to focus when he was standing so near like that. "There is nothing royal about me, nothing in my background a man like you would want to marry."

"It's not your background that interests me, *chérie*. Even young as you are, and no doubt inexperienced, you must realize that. Are you going to tell me you don't believe it's possible to fall in love at first sight? Because if you are, you're wrong. I saw you, I wanted you, and I loved you—in exactly that amount of time."

Lili-Ange shook her head, unaware that she was smiling dreamily. How could she argue when that was just what had happened to her? "But marriage is not always the natural end of love, *monsieur*."

"Roger," he prompted as he took a step closer. She was so near that he could feel her body begin to tremble, and he knew a moment before her that he had won. "You cannot continue to call me *monsieur* if we are going to be married. I don't pretend it will be easy. I am a younger son, and my branch of the family is not well-to-do. I am expected to marry for money. My parents may disown me, they may refuse to have anything to do with you—but if you love me, we will manage somehow."

If she loved him? What a foolish thing to say. She had barely laid eyes on him a few hours before, but already loved him more than life itself, more than the air she breathed. She would give up anything, do anything, to be with him. He was closer now, their bodies were touching. She knew she ought to push him back, ought to tell him he would have to wait until the vows had been spoken, but she loved him so much . . . and part of love was trust.

"You are sure?" She needed the words, the reassurance, one last time. "Very sure?"

"I am sure . . . as you are."

The night wind blew through the window, cold against

the heat of her cheeks, and the smell of something sweet
was in her nostrils. At first she thought it came from
outside; then she realized it was the rose in her hair.
Raising her hand, she touched it tentatively with her
fingers. The rose he had given her, the first wordless
token of his love.

Then his hand was there too, and he was taking it
gently out of her hair. And her hair was loose suddenly,
floating over her shoulders, and he was easing her back
on the bed. . . .

The sun reflected off the water, dancing in little golden
shimmers along the shore. White sails bobbed in the
distance as fishing boats glided back and forth. The air
was brisk, but it felt warm when the wind died down, and
Lili-Ange could feel beads of perspiration forming on her
brow.

She raised her head again, listening, still not hearing
anything. She had been a little surprised the next morning when Roger had kissed her, tenderly but firmly, and
told her they would have to part for a while. She had
wanted to protest, but his lips had been too sweet on
hers, and besides, the explanations he had given sounded
so reasonable.

It would be wiser, he had told her, if he approached
his family alone. If he couldn't persuade them to accept
her, of course, they would run off and be married—and
the devil take the consequences! But wouldn't it be easier, and more practical, if he could get their blessing?
Lili-Ange, who had just had an excellent example of his
powers of persuasion, could hardly disagree. And where
better for her to remain in the meantime than under the
excellent protection of Sister Xavier?

Now it was two weeks, two long weeks since she had
seen him.

She let her hand rest briefly on her stomach, a little
surprised at how flat it felt. She did not know how she
knew—she was essentially ignorant of such matters—but
there was no doubt in her heart that that one enchanted
night had left her carrying his child. The sun seemed to
grow warmer, and she tilted her face up to catch its rays.
She would have something to tell him now, when he
appeared on his beautiful black stallion . . . or later,

perhaps, when they were alone and discussing their marriage plans. And wouldn't he be pleased? And proud.

A figure appeared at the top of the gangplank, and Lili-Ange saw with a sinking feeling that it was the captain. Before, when it had been simply a matter of fetching her trunk, he had sent the boy. Now he was coming himself. That meant they would be sailing soon.

Just for an instant she felt herself waver. Would she dare stay there, all alone on the dock, with Roger still nowhere in sight . . . or would she be forced to go on? What if she were wrong after all? What if he had forgotten all about her? Then she remembered the way he had looked, regret misting his eyes the morning they had parted, and she knew nothing could ever make her leave him. He had said he would come, and he would. She would wait forever if she had to.

At last her ear picked up the sound she had been waiting for, the faint but distinct drumming of hoofbeats on the hardened earth around the wharves. She laughed out loud with relief. What a fool she had been, doubting him, even for an instant. Of course he hadn't forgotten! Hadn't he sworn to love her forever? Picking up the cloak, which had slipped from her shoulders, she tossed it over her arm and started forward to greet him.

But the rider who came into view was not Roger.

Lili-Ange stopped for a moment, uncertain. He seemed to be a young servant, simply but rather finely clad, as if he came from an elegant household. And he was heading straight for her.

"*Mademoiselle* . . ."

She glanced up, puzzled. She had never seen him before in her life, she was sure of that. Yet he seemed to know her.

"You are looking for me?"

"I believe so, *mademoiselle*." He reached under his belt, pulling out a small parcel. There was no expression on his face as he handed it to her. "This is for you." Before she could say a word, he had turned and trotted off, and Lili-Ange was alone on the dock again.

Bewildered, she looked down at the package in her hands. There was something hard, wrapped in what appeared to be a handkerchief of the most exquisite white linen. Slowly she unpeeled the layers of fabric to discover that she was holding several large gold coins. More money than she had ever seen in her life.

For just an instant she thought the messenger had made a mistake, though it seemed an oddly careless thing to do. He hadn't even asked her name before he gave the package to her. He must have been looking for someone else. But then she glanced down again and saw the mark on the handkerchief—a delicately embroidered *fleur-de-lys*.

Roger. The coins were from Roger.

I would promise anything to have you, he had said, and in that at least he had been telling the truth. He would promise . . . but oh, he would not keep his promises. Tears of disappointment stung her eyes, and she forced them back. He had no intention of marrying her. He had *never* intended to marry her. He did not love her, he only wanted her, and the coins in her hand were his way of soothing his conscience.

He would not be coming.

She turned slowly to where the captain was still standing, surprisingly hesitant at the top of the stairs. She could have sworn he was not a patient man. But then he had seen the messenger, and he must have known, as she did, that there were no choices for her now. Head held high, she started toward the gangplank, taking care not to look in his direction. She could not have borne the pity in his eyes.

Thus it was that the first Fleurie woman to be remembered in family history departed for the New World . . . and the legend of the curse began.

New Orleans, 1808

1

The handsome four-wheeled carriage rolled down Royal Street, turning right at Toulouse. It was the morning of Mardi Gras, and the unpaved lanes that crisscrossed the old section of the city were more crowded than usual. The sun was bright, and cabriolets trotted by with their tops folded down, while on the narrow wooden *banquettes*, housewives in neat muslin dresses with baskets of produce and fresh fish balanced on their hips paused to haggle with the hawkers or call out laughing greetings to friends across the street.

Lili Santana's eyes sparkled as she leaned over the side of the open carriage. Festivity was in the air, and it was hard not to catch the special excitement that came over the city once a year as the people of New Orleans prepared for their most cherished holiday. A modishly dressed man on a prancing bay kept pace with them for a short distance. In spite of herself, she could not resist glancing over. He did not miss the look, for he touched his fingers to the brim of his hat, flashing an impudent grin, and Lili—very much aware of the disapproving frown of her chaperone—hastened to drop her gaze, dark lashes fluttering with a show of innocence against her cheeks.

The gesture fooled no one, not the stranger, and certainly not the nursemaid who had tended her from the day she was born. Lili Santana was much too young—and too high-spirited—to conceal her feelings well. And right now she was feeling distinctly flattered by that masculine expression of approval.

Not that the man would be likely to call her beautiful. Lili sighed as she leaned back, letting the wind blow through her hair, which for the first time in ages she had been allowed to wear loose, without the proper white veil Creole ladies wore on the street. "Striking" was more the word for her, and in a society with rigid standards for feminine modesty, "striking" was not always a compliment. Once, when she was a little girl, she had overheard one of a long string of governesses saying that the *petite mademoiselle* was "perhaps a bit too vivid," and even then she had known the woman was right. Somehow, she had assumed that age would have a softening effect, turning her into a vision of loveliness, like all those elegant ladies in family portraits in the hall. But then she had turned seventeen, and eighteen, and just recently nineteen, and still her mirror was telling her the same things.

Her features, for one thing, were all wrong. Lili resisted the temptation to run her fingers tentatively along the line of her chin. It would still be too strong, with just a touch of squareness, her cheekbones still too high, her nose finely but firmly chiseled, as if there were more than a little Spanish mingled with the French in her veins. Which, of course, might be the case, since her background was, at best, questionable. Then there was her coloring. Her hair was dark, but it wasn't the pure raven-black that was so admired in New Orleans. It was more a chestnut hue, with too much curl of its own and a disconcerting way of flashing sudden shimmers of red, and her skin showed definite ivory tones, even when she stayed out of the sun. And her eyes . . .

She laughed as they rounded the corner into Chartres and the coachman picked up speed. Her eyes were the one feature with which she was truly satisfied. Curly coal-black lashes, with not the slightest need for artifice, framed wide circles of luminous hazel, an unusual color that turned brown sometimes in the shadows, or almost catlike yellow, as now, when caught in the rays of the sun. They were exotic eyes, eyes that a man would notice, as the man on the bay had noticed before, and she sensed he would not forget them soon.

But he would be disturbed by them too, and Lili had already come to realize that men didn't like to be disturbed, except by passing fancies. Eyes like that would have made things hard for her—even if it hadn't been for the legend.

"Do you think it's really true?" she said impulsively.

"That there's a curse on all the Fleurie women? Generation after generation, till the end of time?"

"*Ma foi*, what nonsense!" The elderly woman opposite her scowled, readjusting her considerable bulk on the leather-upholstered seat. The weather was unseasonably warm, and dark spots of moisture showed on the bodice of a serviceable gray dress. "That's what comes of letting you play with pickaninnies in the kitchen. All that gossip in your ears has turned your brain soft! You should have outgrown such *folie* years ago!"

"But how can I outgrow it," Lili said, lips twisting puckishly at the corners, "when it concerns my own family? The curse, if it exists, applies to *me*." Technically, of course, she was not a Fleurie, she was a Santana. But she was well aware that if it hadn't been for Don Andres, her dear papa, and the passionate love he had borne for a beautiful woman who was already carrying another man's child, she would indeed have been a Fleurie, and illegitimate like the others. "They say every woman in the family is destined to love the one man she cannot have, and to bear a child by him. Always a daughter, too—have you noticed?—as if to perpetuate the curse."

The older woman rose to the bait, as Lili had known she would, though perhaps a bit more vehemently than usual. It did seem that she had grown touchier about the subject in past weeks.

"They say, they say, they say! Servants, all of them, and gossiping when they ought to be working. It was all well and good, believing such things when you were a child. But you're a young *demoiselle* now—you ought to have more sense! Don't you know they're just stories the kitchen maids make up to amuse you? Like the fairy tales I used to tell when you were a baby, to help you go to sleep."

"I'm not a baby any more, M'mère," Lili said softly, using the affectionate nickname that had begun with her mother years before. It never occurred to her to wonder where it came from. Perhaps it was a corruption of "Grandmère," or perhaps simply the French equivalent of "Mammy," which was essentially the woman's position in the household. "And fairy tales aren't real. I know that. But the stories I've heard about the Fleurie women are."

"The stories, maybe," the other conceded grudgingly. "But stories are just a bunch of happenings strung together. What you make of them is your own doing. Imagining curses and all that silliness is something in your head!"

"You really think so?"

"What I think is that your papa should never have allowed you to hear such things in the first place! He ought to have forbidden any mention of them in his house."

"He did try, you know," Lili reminded her gently. "I used to hear him sometimes, telling the servants—in his sternest voice—that they were never, *never* to speak of it again. Only, the more he told them, of course, the more they went on doing it!"

Perhaps if she had had a mother to watch out for her, things might have been different, Lili thought as she rested her arm against the side of the carriage. Or an ample-bosomed black mammy to storm into the kitchen after those little pickaninnies and tell them to "hush yo' mouth!" But her mother had died when she was almost too little to remember, and M'mère, who considered the colored servants beneath her dignity, spent as little time in the back quarters as possible. As a result, Lili had been raised on forbidden tales, and she had never tired of hearing, over and over, about the first of the Fleurie women, whose name was so much like her own, only with an "-Ange" on the end—how she had fallen in love with a daring highwayman with a black mask on his face and streaks of gold in his hair, and how she had come alone to the New World, carrying his child in her belly.

The good sisters at the Ursuline convent must have been shocked when she arrived, a fact which Lili could appreciate as she grew older, since the casket girls had been specifically chosen for virtue and piety. But they had decided—after some rather un-Christian debate, no doubt!—to find a husband for her anyway. She was a pretty little thing, and except for that one regrettable lapse seemed innocent enough . . . and at least she had proved her fecundity. So they had paraded her along the ramparts with the others, where the men could look them over and make their choices. But when the offers had come—and come they did, for there was an air of sweetness and vulnerability about her—she had surprised everyone by refusing to wed. She loved the man who had ruined her, though she was not blind to his faults, and if

she could not have him, she would have no one. In the
end, as it turned out, it had not mattered, for she died in
the convent, giving birth to her infant daughter.

And from that day forward, not a one of the Fleurie
women, right down to Lili's own mother, the sad, beautiful Cybèle, had ever prospered in love.

"Four generations—that's a long time." She glanced
teasingly at M'mère, saying it mostly to get a reaction. It
wasn't that she believed in the curse herself—not really.
Still, it *was* funny, the way things kept happening again
and again. "And you have to admit, it's wonderfully
romantic."

"Romantic? Bah!" The old woman spat the words out.
"Romantic to you maybe, but not to me! The curses,
they are terrible, *tragique*. They ruin people's lives, eh?
What's so pretty about that? Besides, there's no such
thing as a curse. It's a lot of made-up nonsense!"

Lili bit her lip to keep from laughing. Dear, predictable
M'mère. Railing against curses and denying their exis-
tence in the same breath! "Confess it now—the truth.
You *do* believe in the curse, don't you? Just a little bit?"

"I don't believe anything of the sort," the woman
grumbled, though Lili noticed her hand twitched super-
stitiously, as if she had been about to cross herself. "And
neither should you! You're too old to listen to foolish
gossip."

"But you're much older than I, M'mère, and you listen
to gossip all the time! And you love it. You know you do!
Why, just this morning I caught you on the front stoop
whispering with the sweetmeat vendor about the new
smuggler—or is he a pirate? The one they call the Blaze,
who's supposed to have been such a terror on the Natchez
Trace. And you were fascinated, too, and all because the
silly girl claimed she had actually seen him!"

"I may listen, but I don't believe everything I hear,
and that's the difference." She threw Lili an unexpectedly sharp look, fixing her with dark, slightly narrowed
eyes. "These things, they are not *les choses sérieuses*, you
understand? They are only to distract you for a little
while . . . that is all. You are not to take them seriously."

Lili looked away, feeling a little guilty. It was so easy
to tease M'mère, especially this morning, when she was
being *sérieuse* herself, but it really wasn't fair. Her only
fault was that she doted too much. For some reason, the

legend of the curse seemed to upset her, though that was odd, for she had always rather enjoyed it before. Maybe it was just that Lili was getting older and men were starting to smile at her on the street.

"You are right, M'mère." She turned back, trying, but not quite able to keep a glint of mischief out of her eyes. "There is no such thing as a curse on the Fleurie women. I will fall madly in love with the handsomest, most dashing man in the world, and he will sweep me off my feet and marry me."

"You will do no such thing." The elderly woman looked genuinely shocked. "I have never heard such talk in my life! You will marry the man your Papa chooses for you, of course. And he will be kind and decent and provide for you and your children."

And bore me to tears, Lili thought rebelliously, though she was careful not to utter the words out loud. Something in M'mère's face told her the woman was not enjoying their usual banter. And it was much too nice a day to quarrel.

"As you say, M'mère. I shall be a dutiful child and do exactly as I'm told."

They had just reached the Place d'Armes, which like everyplace else that day was thronging with people. The weather had been unusually dry the past week or so, and a thin film of dust settled over the square, coating the wrought-iron fence with its intricately worked gates and muting the spring foliage on rows of young maples. Out of the corner of her eye Lili caught sight of a flagpole in the center, with the Stars and Stripes flapping in the wind. As usual, she was aware of a flicker of irritation. She had been barely fourteen that day, five years ago, in 1803, when her father had brought her to view the ceremony that marked the sale of the territory, but even then she had felt a seething anger inside as she watched rough hands lower the beloved French tricolor for the last time and run up the American flag in its place. She had vowed then, as others around her had vowed—some in whispers, some boldly out loud—that she would never accept these boorish, uncouth intruders whose very presence defiled their gracious city.

Papa, strangely, had not seemed to mind so much. To Lili's shame, he had even, in the years that followed, begun to have business dealings with them, which, she had to admit, had prospered nicely. At least—thank heavens!—he had had the taste not to invite them into his home, so she had not as yet been forced to associate with them herself.

The coachman pulled up along the levee, drawing to a stop between two waiting carriages, and Lili forgot everything else as she prepared to climb down. It was an unexpected treat, being allowed to come out with M'mère for this bit of last-minute shopping. Ever since she had grown up, she had been expected to remain at home like a proper young lady and not mingle with the riffraff in the market. Even the few times she had wheedled permission to come along for the ride, M'mère had always insisted on bringing one of the black girls to do the actual shopping, for her arthritis was so bad she could barely make it to the top of the levee, much less up and down the long crowded rows of the old French Market. But today, it seemed, all the girls had been needed elsewhere and Lili had been sent in their place.

"Are you sure you have the list?" M'mère fussed, looking worried now that Lili had jumped down to the street and was brushing the wrinkles out of her skirt. "You haven't forgotten where you put it? You are always careless, n'est-ce pas?—especially about things like that."

"Don't worry." Lili patted the old-fashioned pocket that had been sewn into her new white muslin dress, a compromise with fashion, for the bodice, while snug, was decidedly high-necked, and the thoroughly petticoated skirt came almost to her instep. It was a pretty garment, and wonderfully flattering, though much too frothy to wear to market, and she had been a little surprised an hour or so earlier when it turned out to be the only thing the laundry maid had ready. "I haven't forgotten. It's right here." Not that she would need it. There were only two items on the list, a bouquet of early-spring flowers for the table in the front hallway, and a paquet of filé, the green powder ground from dried sassafras leaves that was used to thicken gumbo. Even if she were as scatter-brained as M'mére claimed, she could hardly forget two things!

"Get the flowers last." M'mère's voice came after her as she started up the levee. "Roses—there is a girl who always has them, but be sure to bargain! And mind you, stay on the levee. I don't want you running into the market, where I can't keep an eye on you!"

Poor, darling M'mère! How she did fuss—and how she knew her charge! Lili laughed openly as she made her way through the crowds up to the top of the broad earthen dike that extended as far as she could see in either direction. In fact, she would have loved to sneak into the market with its fantastic display of food and flowers and vividly colored birds. But M'mère would have been out of the carriage before she even reached the entrance, and then she would have had to feel guilty about all that arthritic pain she had caused. And wouldn't M'mère have reminded her, too!

She stopped at the top of the levee to catch her breath and look around. As long as she could remember, it had always been one of her favorite places. When she was a little girl, Papa had brought her here sometimes while he met a business associate or chatted with neighbors who had come to watch the ships being unloaded, and she had thought that all the magic in the world must be centered in that swarming, steaming, colorful, boisterous spot.

As always, the river was busy, a beautiful semicircle of water with perhaps as many as a hundred ships anchored along the banks, from France and Spain and England, from Port-au-Prince and Vera Cruz, Baltimore and Boston and New York. Flatboats loaded with ham and corn, or furs perhaps from inland trappers, or great rough casks of whiskey crowded the docks, while on the levee itself almost everything imaginable could be seen at some time or other. Lili detected a pungent odor, mingling with sweat and wood and the smell of the river, and she knew that a nearby stack of barrels contained tobacco, though others would be filled with sugar from the plantations along the river, ready to be hoisted onto seagoing vessels and carried off to Europe and the north. Great bales of fabric were wedged haphazardly between mounds of coal from Pittsburgh and piles of paving stones that must have come all the way from Liverpool.

The waterfront had a resonance of its own, and she paused for a moment, listening to the sounds that came from all around. The people were as varied as the merchandise disgorged from all those keelboats and tall ships, and her ear picked up the garbled cacophony of many languages. French, of course, and Creole, and Spanish and English, but she thought she caught traces of Portuguese too, which she recognized, although she did not understand the words, and Indian, and Greek and Italian and even Chinese. Sailors from all over the world brushed elbows with local businessmen, and the sons of the idle rich made way for middle-class housewives out doing their daily shopping. From somewhere in the background came the plaintive singing of black longshoremen, their lilting African dialect beating out a rhythm as they tossed heavy bales back and forth or rolled their barrels along the levee.

Lili could have stood there for hours, absorbed in the colors and noises and smells, but she remembered suddenly that M'mère was waiting, no doubt impatiently, in the carriage. Glancing around, she looked for a place to make her two small purchases. The first was easy enough, for there was an Indian on the ground a short distance away, wrapped in a filthy blanket—and probably not much else, which made it hard to know where to put her eyes—with good-size portions of *filé* powder tied in scraps of month-old newspaper. The girl who sold the flowers, however, had moved to another section, and it took several minutes to locate her.

Even then Lili was disappointed, for the early roses were small, and most had begun to wilt on their stems. Why M'mère insisted on roses was beyond her, for the buds were coming out in their own garden, and any day now the sun would coax them into blooms much prettier than these. But roses she had stipulated, and Lili, knowing better than to argue once M'mère had made up her mind, picked out the deepest, reddest dozen and haggled over them with a shrewdness that would have done the old woman's thrifty French heart proud.

She was feeling rather pleased with herself as she turned away. Not that there was any need for thrift in the Santana household; they were one of the wealthiest families in the city. But it was a principle she had learned as a child, like ciphers and lessons in geography, and she saw nothing inconsistent in bargaining pennies off small items in the bazaar, then turning around and spending a thousand times that much for imported metallic lace to trim a ball gown. It was all part of the game, and it was a game she played well and thus enjoyed.

She paused impulsively, burying her face in the bouquet. The flowers might not look like much, but they had a strong, sweet smell, and she drew in a deep breath,

throwing her head back suddenly and laughing out loud.
Not for any reason. Just because she was young and it
was so much fun being on the levee . . . and New Orleans in the spring was the most wonderful place in the
world!

The burst of laughter brought startled glances from
passersby, and Lili, her high spirits piqued, was tempted
to call out an impish comment or two—which would
surely have brought even more startled looks. But if she
caused a commotion, M'mère would be certain to see,
and Lili could just imagine what she would have to say to
that!

She had just started back to the carriage when she had
the sudden eerie feeling that someone was watching her.
Not amused, as the others had been before, but oddly
intense, almost brooding. Curious, she turned, searching
the area with her eyes, but she could make out nothing—no
one—out of the ordinary. Just for a second, peeking out
from under the shadows of a pile of old packing crates,
she thought she saw a pair of dark trousers and the toes
of dusty black boots. But then they were gone again, and
there was nothing there.

Strange. Little prickles ran up and down her spine, not
apprehension exactly, more like a heightened sense of
awareness, as if something were happening and she couldn't
figure out what it was. Tossing her hair back from her
shoulders, she started toward the carriage, but try as she
would, she couldn't shake the feeling.

What a ninny you are, she told herself irritably, jumping at shadows like that! She was imagining things, that
was all. It was silly, letting herself get worked up over
something that wasn't even there.

But the prickles wouldn't stop, and in spite of herself
she had an odd feeling of *déjà vu*, as if she had been in
the same situation before, only she couldn't remember
where it was.

Then, all of a sudden, it came back.

It had been five or six months ago, the first cool
autumn afternoon, and she had been allowed to take the
carriage for a ride as long as she promised not to get out.
There had been a deep pothole filled with rainwater on
the northwest side of the Place d'Armes—several coaches
had already gotten stuck—and the driver had just been
detouring around the other end of the square, coming

alongside the levee, when she had caught sight of a man abusing a puppy. Too angry even to think, all promises forgotten, she had been out of the carriage in a flash. Racing up to the man, she had grabbed the puppy in one hand, the stick he had been using in the other, and given him as sharp a tongue-lashing as he had likely ever received in his life! What he had thought, she had no idea, but she must have looked like an avenging fury, eyes blazing, hair flying wildly around her face. It had all been over by the time the anxious coachman got there to rescue her . . . and it had happened in almost the exact place where she was standing now.

It hadn't been until later that she realized how foolish her actions had been. She was never in any real danger, of course—people had crowded in from all directions, and the man wouldn't have been able to do anything even if he hadn't been too startled to move—but it could have been unpleasant. A business associate of her father's, a youngish man who worked in a bank, a Monsieur LeClerc, she thought his name was, had escorted her home, looking shocked and disapproving, especially when she had insisted on cradling the puppy in her lap. Papa, of course, had been furious when he heard, but not so furious he hadn't let her keep the dog, which by now had grown into its enormous feet and was the terror of the stables. She would probably have forgotten the entire incident if . . .

If she hadn't had the same feeling that day too. If she hadn't thought then—if she hadn't been *sure*—that eyes were boring into her. And when she had turned, she hadn't been able to see anyone.

She started down the levee, more shaken than she cared to admit. It did seem an uncomfortable coincidence —if that was what it was. Of course, she had been standing in almost the same spot. Perhaps that had triggered the memory. Yet the feeling had been so intense.

"It's the funniest thing," she started to say as she climbed into the carriage, then caught herself in time. If M'mère took her story seriously and really believed someone had been watching from the shadows, she would never be allowed alone in the streets again. "I thought that, uh . . . that the market would be more crowded. With all the Mardi Gras parties tonight and everything. I didn't find nearly as many people as I expected."

M'mère eyed her suspiciously. "It looked crowded to me."

"Yes, it did, didn't it? I thought the same thing myself—when I was in the carriage. But really, there was hardly anyone on the levee at all." She stared pointedly at the place where the rough boards of the *banquettes* met the street, as if they were truly fascinating, and when she heard nothing from behind, she decided, relieved, that for once she had put something over on M'mère.

It was almost noon, and carriages filled the streets, slowing traffic at the corners as businessmen returned home for lunch, and idlers, of whom the French Quarter had more than its share, ventured out to find their clubs and favorite coffeehouses. Every vendor in the city seemed to be there, stepping out into the street when the wooden sidewalks became too crowded, and their colorful garments looked like banners weaving back and forth among the constant parade of horses and carriages. One in particular caught Lili's eye, a tall, swaying woman with a basket on her head, not young, but still lithe enough to look sensual, her beautiful *café-au-lait* skin accented by a brightly patterned red gingham dress and vivid orange madras *tingnon*. Years ago, it was said, all the quadroon women wore elaborate headdresses, decorated with plumes and jewels and such flattering satin ribbons that the white women had been jealous and a law had been passed ordering them to tie their hair up in simple kerchiefs, "in the style of their Negress mothers." The law had not been an unqualified success, for an artfully knotted *tignon*, far from looking plain, actually enhanced its dusky wearer's charms.

Lili leaned back, smiling to herself. She used to think, when she was little, that she was really a quadroon herself—or perhaps an octoroon, for those lovely *gens de couleur* with their ivory complexions were frequently fairer than many a Creole belle.

It was not a totally outlandish idea, for her great-grandmother, Lili-Ange's daughter, who had taken the flashily dramatic name La Fleur when she went on the stage, was reputed to have had a love affair with a notorious runaway slave, not a mulatto either, but pure African, a giant of a man and black as the blackest jet. Years later, she had learned that it could not possibly be true, for the man in question had been captured and killed

when La Fleur was only eleven, but by that time the idea
had taken hold with all its forbidden appeal. Of course, it
was a much pleasanter fantasy here, in a place like New
Orleans, where blacks had a right to earn their freedom
under the Code Noir of the French and were sometimes
quite comfortably well-off, with a number of slaves of
their own.

Besides, Lili thought as she looked out of the carriage,
that beautiful quadroon on the street, with neither escort
nor chaperone to tell her where she could go and what
she could do, was in many ways freer than any Creole
woman would ever be.

She was laughing when they reached the house a short
time later and the coachman pulled the carriage through
a rear gateway into the walled yard. M'mère, her good
spirits restored, had been regaling her with stories of the
old days when she had just arrived from France and was
working as a servant in the old Ursuline convent on the
other side of town, and the sunlight was so pleasant that
Lili decided to stay in the garden for a while. She had
completely forgotten what happened in the market until
she picked up the roses, which were lying next to her on
the seat, and the smell brought everything back.

She *was* being silly, she thought as she handed them to
one of a pair of new maids who had just been hired, and
started inside to fetch the light cashmere shawl that she
had left carelessly draped over a post on the upstairs
landing. She had been right before: she was letting her
imagination get out of hand. Still . . . She paused for a
moment, looking back into the shaded yard, empty now,
for the coachman had taken the horses to the stable.

It *was* strange, the way she had been sure someone was
watching her.

2

Five minutes later, having found her shawl, Lili was back in the yard. The sun was warmer than she had expected, and the smells that drifted over the wall had an almost summery feel: the familiar odor of dust, intensified by the heat and sweaty horses and sewage from the open gutters that lined the streets.

The house itself was relatively new, an austere but graceful structure with intricate wrought-iron balconies and an Italian tile roof. The original Santana home, which had miraculously survived the fire of 1788, had been destroyed six years later, in 1794, when a second great conflagration had broken out in a courtyard where some children were playing with flint and tinder, and swept with devastating force throughout the city. Lili had only the sketchiest recollections of that terrifying day, with ashes and burning cinders falling like rain, for Papa had taken her away the instant the alarm went up, and they had spent the rest of the winter and all summer at their spacious country villa on the shores of Lake Pontchartrain. When they had come back, the new house had already been there, bigger than the old one, and more elegant, with a lighter, airier feel and considerably more land to accommodate the separate kitchen and other outbuildings.

Only the narrow garden in the side yard was the same, with the same stone fountain or an excellent copy in the center, and Lili had often wondered if that was because it was the one place in the house her mother had loved. She had been so little when Cybèle had died—and she had had so little contact with her even then—that her memories were vague and hard to pin down. The only image that was clear was a picture of her sitting by that same fountain in the garden, a beautiful sad-faced woman with the roses in full bloom behind her and sunlight catching on dark-gold hair.

The heady smell of early-spring flowers greeted her as she opened the creaking side gate and stepped inside. The garden had grown in the years since it had been planted. The sapling in the corner was now a tall black oak, giving generous shade, while masses of climbing roses, just beginning to blossom, softened the drab stone walls. Lili shut the gate behind her and was just going over to the fountain when she heard a voice.

"There you are! What took you so long? I thought you were never going to get back—I've been dying to talk to you!"

"Simone?" Lili turned to see her cousin, two years younger, barely visible in the deep shadows under the oak. "What on earth are you doing in the shade? You must be freezing, even with that silly *mantelette* over your shoulders. Why don't you come out in the sun where it's warm?"

"You know we aren't supposed to sit in the sun," the girl replied primly, though Lili noticed she came over readily enough to join her by the fountain. "Especially at midday—even when it's cool. M'mère has told us that over and over. It isn't good for our complexions. If we don't watch out, we'll turn as dark as little pickaninnies."

"What a goose you are, Simone," Lili said, more in affection than exasperation. Now that she was grown up and had long since gotten over the fits of jealousy she had suffered when the orphaned girl had been brought into their home, she had almost come to like her, in a protective sort of way. Not that Simone was exactly lively, or fun to be with, but there was a gentle sweetness about her, and she could be faithful as a slave to someone she adored. And she obviously adored her elder cousin. "You couldn't get dark if you sat in the sun every day for twenty years. Your skin is pale as milk, and quite your nicest feature, now that it's stopped breaking out in those dreadful red spots."

"Do you really think so?" Simone looked up, so wistfully that Lili felt a little guilty. In fact, she didn't think so at all. A bit of color might be unfashionable, but at least it

would have given some life to that plain heart-shaped
face.

"Of course," she said hastily. "Milky skin is very much
in favor. You're lucky I don't have an envious nature, or
I'd be quite horrid to you. My skin is nowhere near as
fair. Come on, now, let's treat ourselves, since lunch will
be late. I'm going to order some chocolate, with extra
sugar and lots of cinnamon, Spanish style. Or do you
want your eternal cup of consommé?"

"Consommé, please." Simone sat down at a small table by the fountain, painly determined to obey at least
one of M'mère's dicta, though this time, Lili had to
admit, with more reason. She was already showing a
tendency to plumpness, and though the last splotches had
disappeared from her face some months ago, sweetened
chocolate would probably be tempting fate.

"Very well, *comme tu veux*." She clapped her hands
briskly. A little black girl appeared almost immediately,
and Lili ordered the refreshments, turning back with a
curious glance to her cousin. "You said you wanted to
talk to me—no, you said you were *dying* to talk to me.
What about?"

Simone's small face lit up, making her look almost
pretty. "Did you see that carriage when you came downstairs? The elegant one, with four wheels like ours—which
your papa always says is unusual in New Orleans. Only I
think this one might be even grander. I peeked at it
through the parlor window, and it has the most exquisite
upholstery. All silvery gray leather, so soft it looks like
velvet."

"No, I didn't notice." Lili sat opposite her, suppressing
a yawn as she waited for the girl to bring the chocolate.
Leave it to Simone to get excited about a carriage in the
street! "Why should I? Papa has business associates calling all the time. I'm sure many of them must be quite
rich. And they all have carriages."

"Not like this one. You'd know if you'd seen it. Besides, it's parked in front of the house. When Don Andrés
has business callers, he receives them in his office—and
they always go in by the side door."

"True," Lili admitted, vaguely curious in spite of herself. "But perhaps the occupant of the carriage wasn't
coming here at all. Maybe he was going down the street,
and it was too muddy to get through."

Simone shook her head. "It hasn't rained for two weeks. And anyway, I'm positive he's here. The carriage arrived right after you came back—while you were still upstairs—and I heard the front door a minute later. I'm not sure, but I think it's the man who was here yesterday."

"Yesterday?" Lili frowned. She had been out most of the day, having final fittings on the gown she was going to wear to whichever of the many Mardi Gras balls she chose to attend tonight. Naturally, she was not allowed to go to public dances, even the exclusive subscription balls, but there would be plenty of private soirees. And as the daughter of the wealthy, influential Don Andrés Santana de la Vega, she had been invited to all of them. "You didn't say anything about a man coming here while I was gone."

"I didn't say anything because . . ." Simone broke off, a pink flush rising to her cheeks. "Because I knew you'd laugh! Oh, Lili, he was the handsomest man I've ever seen! He was young, and quite tall, with black, black hair. And when he saw me, he · . . . he smiled! I don't know how to explain it, there was something about him that was, well . . . different somehow. The way he moved, or acted, or looked. I think he might be an American, but I don't care! He was just so handsome!"

"An American?" Lili snorted, disgusted. Whatever interest she had had in the man was gone now. Simone might be at an age when she was beginning to notice the opposite sex, but she wasn't showing any signs of being discriminating. "Really, you have no taste at all—but then, I guess that shouldn't surprise me. This morning, when M'mère was out gossiping with the sweetmeat vendor about that smuggler from the Natchez Trace, you practically crawled on the parlor table to get closer to the window. Your ear was glued so hard to the glass, I thought we were going to have to call the surgeon to remove it."

"Well, you were listening too!" Simone shot back with an unexpected show of spirit. "And why shouldn't I be curious? He does sound wonderfully exciting. His hair is brown, they say, but there are streaks of yellow where it's been bleached by the sun. And his eyes are supposed to be the most fascinating color. Do you know, they call him the Blaze?"

"And you think he's going to come blazing into your

life and sweep you up on the front of his saddle and carry you off into the sunset. Really, you *are* a goose. What makes you think a man like that would look twice at you?

"Actually, I don't think he would." Her voice was quiet, but her face had an odd, pinched look. "He wouldn't even see me. He'd be looking at someone more like you. But I can dream if I want to—and no one can stop me!"

Nor should anyone, Lili thought later as she sat alone in the garden, sipping her chocolate and regretting the impulse that had made her tease her cousin that way. What on earth prompted her to say such a cruel, thoughtless thing? Simone was not Don Andrés' kin, but her own, the daughter of her natural father's sister; there would be no fortune waiting for her when it came time to wed. What man indeed would look even once at a girl with neither beauty nor dowry? In a city where marriages were arranged for family and status and wealth, a poor relation could look forward to nothing more than endless years as an old maid, living off someone's charity—and no one knew that better than Simone. All she had, poor thing, was her dreams, and she was right to cling to them.

The noonday warmth in the garden was soothing, and Lili wandered back to the fountain, sitting on the edge and running her hands through the water. The thick walls blocked out noises from the street, and all that could be heard was the droning of the bees, a low, monotonous sound as they buzzed among the roses. Even the city smells were gone, as if somehow that little plot of earth had been transported far away to a make-believe land where the air was perfumed with fragrant flowers and new green leaves.

Perhaps that was why her mother had loved it so much.

Lili looked up at the pure azure sky, wondering, as she had so often in the past, about the Fleurie women and the curse that sometimes seemed so real. Not that some of her ancestresses hadn't brought their troubles on themselves. La Fleur had been notorious for her many love affairs after the one that had supposedly broken her heart. Hadn't M'mère hinted darkly, more than once, that she was "no better than she ought to be"? And Fleurette, the next in line, had run off with some terrible

ruffian to the Swamp, the most infamous slum in New
Orleans, where M'mère had had to go—at great risk to
herself, as she never tired of pointing out—to rescue the
little daughter. But that daughter, Cybèle, Lili's own
mother, had had a heart that was good and gentle and
pure—and she had suffered like the others.

Lili knew her mother only from the stories that had
been told her, but those stories were, in their own way,
as real as any memories. Cybèle had been just seventeen,
a postulant at the convent, about to take her final vows,
that afternoon when she had gone out to fetch washwater
from a nearby well and met the two men who were to
change her life. One was darkly handsome Gabriel
Dubois—Gabriel of the woods—young and moody, with
melting brown eyes that had stared into hers and driven
all thoughts of the nunnery from her heart.

The other was Don Andrés, an older man, still handsome in a rigid Spanish way, but no match for the more
dashing Dubois. Though he had fallen deeply in love
with the beautiful girl in the veil, right from the beginning he had known she would never be his.

He had tried, at first, to be her friend, but even as a
little girl Lili had understood that friendship was not
always possible where the heart was involved. The more
deeply Cybèle had become entangled with Dubois, the
more suspicious Don Andrés had been, liking nothing
about the man, not his name, which seemed too common, nor the vagueness of his background, nor the mysterious wooded plantation he had renamed in honor of
the woman he was to marry. Half out of jealousy, half
from true concern, he had set out to investigate the other
man, and his investigations had borne fruit . . . but not
before Cybèle had surrendered to her lover's entreaties
and become his wife in everything but name.

Lili still felt the same sadness all over again when she
thought of the pain her gentle mother must have suffered
when Don Andrés told her Dubois was already married.
It had been an arranged marriage, not an affair of the
heart—and he had shipped his hopelessly insane wife
back to relatives in France the day he met his true love—
but he was still married in the eyes of God and the rest of
the world, and any ceremony with Cybèle would have
been empty mockery. Dubois had gone to her, they said,
tears in his eyes, begging her to run away with him,

someplace where no one knew them and they could start all over again. But the girl who had been raised in the convent could not live with the shame, and they had parted bitterly, never to see each other again.

It was only later that Cybèle had learned she was pregnant. With no place to go, no other choices open to her, she had done the one thing she could. She had married the suitor who loved her enough to want her no matter what.

Lili got up, wandering restlessly over to the wall and snapping off one of the new buds. She had always had an affinity for roses, perhaps because it was a rose in the hand of a masked highwayman on a country lane in France that had started it all. Poor Papa. It could not have been a bargain for him, that one-sided marriage, though she had never heard him complain. But his heart must have ached, watching his beautiful wife in the garden, her spirit broken, sitting there day after day, smelling the sweet perfume of the roses, and waiting quietly to die.

Was that what would happen to her one day too? When the Fleurie curse claimed its next victim?

Lili looked down, staring at the red blossom, just opening to the sunlight, in her hand. For the first time, she had an inkling of what M'mère must have felt earlier when she refused to discuss the subject. *Was* that what fate had in store for her? One brief moment of passion, then the disillusionment that must inevitably follow . . . and a life of quiet regret?

But no, even as the thought crossed her mind, she knew it could never be. The curse, if it existed, would have to take a different form for her. She was high-spirited whereas her mother had been gentle; she would have fought, whereas Cybèle had surrendered.

And though it made her vaguely uncomfortable to think about it, she had the feeling there wasn't quite the same degree of piety in her heart.

"I think she *should* have run away with him," she had blurted out once, after the story had been told her for perhaps the hundredth time, at her own request. "He was handsome, and he loved her. What difference does it make what people think?"

She had expected M'mère to be shocked. But "Hush,

child," was all she had said. "You don't know what you are talking about. It would have been a mortal sin."

"But they could have gotten married later, if his wife died first. Do crazy people live a long time? Then they could have gone to confession with someone nice, like Père Antoine, and everything would have been all right."

"Hush," the woman had said again, her voice gruffer than usual, but Lili had had the feeling she was laughing inside, and she wondered if M'mère hadn't used the exact same arguments with Cybèle, all those years ago. She was French, and Catholic to the core, but being French, she was practical too.

What would her mother's life have been like, Lili wondered, if she *had* run off with her lover? And, more to the point, what would her own life have been like, in a different home, with a different man as her father?

The sun was hotter, and she threw the shawl from her shoulders, wishing as she tossed it on a chair that lunch hadn't been pushed back to make sure she wouldn't be faint from hunger by the time the buffet was served at the ball that evening. She had never been particularly curious about her natural father. She had always known of his existence—Don Andrés' rigid sense of honor had required that she be told the truth at an early age—but he had never been "Papa" to her, never the man whose business meetings she had interrupted when she fell down and scraped her knee, or teased into taking in another stray puppy when the stable was already full of dogs, and she had never really wanted to know about him.

She had seen him only once, and that was after he was dead. Papa had awakened her in the middle of the night, and they had gone together on his horse to darkly beautiful Bellefleur in the midst of thick forests on the banks of the river. *He* had been there then, lying still like a wax dummy on a long table in the parlor. The first gray hints of dawn had filtered through the windows, muting the light of slender white tapers, hissing and sputtering in silver candelabra, and a faintly floral fragrance filled the air.

Lili had recognized instantly that she was a part of this man. Her coloring was his, that same faintly golden tinge to the skin, though his hair was slightly darker; his nose had the same French sharpness, the jutting cheekbones under those closed eyes the same aristocratic flair. But there was no feeling to go with the resemblance, no sense of a bond, however tenuous, between them. He was only a man in stories she had heard—somehow he had seemed more real when he wasn't there—and she had been bewildered and glad when Papa had taken her away.

A sudden chill came over her, like the chill she had felt that morning as she stood on a little stool and looked down at the man whose dark passion had shattered her mother's soul. Perhaps, after all, M'mère had been right. Curses *were* intriguing—from a distance. But there was no romance in tragedy when you had to see it for yourself and feel the pain and emptiness of lost love in your own heart.

She shook her head impatiently, annoyed with herself for the moody turn her thoughts were taking. She had called her cousin a goose before, but it was she who was the goose now. She had been mostly teasing, this morning in the carriage, when she provoked M'mère by pretending to believe in the curse. It was only a game, after all; she had been playing it for years. It would be silly to take it seriously.

She went back to the table where she had left her unfinished cup and picked it up. The chocolate was cold, but still sweet and richly spiced with cinnamon, and it tasted better now that she was not feeling quite so guilty about the way she had treated Simone. Still, she thought as she drained the last thick dregs from the bottom, she did owe her, if not an apology—that would have been contrary to the nature of their relationship—at least a little flattering attention.

If she had had to bet on it, she would have sworn she'd find her cousin at the parlor window staring out at the mysterious carriage that had intrigued her before. And she would have won the wager. In fact, Simone was so engrossed, she didn't even hear Lili enter.

"I see it's still here," Lili said, laughing as Simone turned with a jump. "Your four-wheel coach with the velvety silver upholstery."

Simone looked a little sheepish, but she didn't seem upset, and Lili dared hope her tactless remark had been forgotten. "Yes, but *he* hasn't come back. If it's him at all, and not someone else."

"Which is a distinct possibility." Lili brushed the curtain aside to look out herself. The carriage was indeed still there, every bit as imposing as Simone had promised, though its elegance came more from understatement than ornament. It was quite large, but so perfectly proportioned it appeared more modest, with black paint polished to a high sheen, and what looked like a crest on the door. Not the ostentatious sort of crest most people of aristocratic origin in the city affected—bold splashes of color from handle to hinge—but a small insignia, rather like a monogram in one corner, as if its owner were sure enough of his status and heritage not to need the display. "I must admit, it's most impressive, little cousin. You weren't exaggerating when you told me it was grand."

"It is, isn't it?" Simone glowed with pleasure, and Lili, remembering how she had behaved before, had the grace to squirm a little. It was so easy to make the child happy. What would it hurt to go out of her way more often?

"It is indeed, and I'm sure the man who brought it here is every bit as handsome as you say, even"—she took a deep breath, crossing her fingers the way she had when she was a little girl and about to tell a lie—"even if he is an American. But you said yourself, it might not be the same man . . . and if we stay here, we'll miss lunch. You know Papa always eats in the office when he has someone on business, so Cook won't delay for him."

To her surprise, Simone did not offer an argument. "You know, I've been thinking. I didn't see the carriage yesterday, so it probably *isn't* the same man. Besides, I smelled roast chicken stuffed with sausage when I went by the kitchen . . . and a wonderfully peppery gumbo to start. I don't know about you, but I'm starving."

"So am I. I could eat a whole horse all by myself." Lili slipped an arm around her cousin's waist as they headed toward the door. "Well . . . maybe a pony. Let's go."

3

Don Andrés Santana de la Vega leaned back in the well-worn leather chair behind a massive carved oak desk in his office, the only room in the house he had decorated in his native Spanish style. Flinty gray-black eyes narrowed as he took a moment to study the visitor opposite him.

The man was tall and well-proportioned, lean but not gaunt, with a certain muscular grace that women would no doubt find attractive. He had been pacing before, restlessly, almost catlike, as if he wanted to keep moving; now he paused, half-sitting, half-leaning against the broad polished window ledge. A seemingly careless gesture, but it put his host at a disadvantage, for the light, coming from behind, threw his craggy face into shadow. Don Andrés, who was fond of a gesture himself, did not fail to appreciate it.

"You're not having second thoughts?" The man's voice was deeply resonant, edged with a faint hint of amusement. Don Andrés raised his glass, taking a sip of the excellent sherry he had poured a minute before.

"No," His brows went up a fraction of an inch, matching the tone in the other's voice. "Are you?"

The man laughed easily. "No, I took care of my last doubts this morning. That's why I insisted on seeing her again, to make sure. This is not a step I take lightly. But then, you already know that, or I wouldn't be here drinking your finest Amontillado."

"No . . . but I can't say I'm happy with that little scene on the levee. You might have picked a different way to go about it, you know. The whole thing was, uh . . . unorthodox, to say the least."

"Ah, yes." The amusement was still there, coming out in a slight drawl. "And you, of course, are always orthodox."

Don Andrés shifted uncomfortably in his chair. There were very few men who were able to make him squirm. He was inclined to respect one who could.

"Perhaps not—and certainly I didn't object to your wanting to see my daughter again. I think, all considered, it was probably wise. But, good God, man, couldn't you have seen her in her own home? Or some proper place, like at the soiree of a mutual friend? Why did you choose such an unnatural setting?"

The man grimaced slightly, or seemed to, though with the shadows it was hard to tell. "You think *that's* not unnatural? A 'proper' social setting, with all its conventions and affectations? Forgive me if I disagree." He leaned back, stretching long legs out in front of him. "I wanted to see her in the sunlight, with people around, and color and action, things she could respond to—naturally—without worrying about what she was saying and how she was behaving . . . and who was taking her measure."

"And, of course," Don Andrés added thoughtfully, "that *was* where you first saw her."

"Of course." Even with the glare from behind, Don Andrés saw the man's face break into a grin. "And what a sight she was! You should have seen her, Santana. She leapt out of the carriage as if she had wings on her feet and raced up the hill, hair coming out of its pins and flying all around, with flashes of red in the sun. That bastard tormenting the dog never knew what hit him! She grabbed the stick out of his hand and waved it in his face, calling him names I'll wager you didn't even think she knew. And he just stood there, mouth open, gaping at her!"

"And you stood there yourself—watching. I don't suppose it occurred to you to go to her aid."

"I didn't have to. The poor devil was no match for her, even if there hadn't been plenty of men around, much closer than I. I wouldn't have put a stop to that show for anything in the world!" He paused, moving away from the window, his face clear now, with a deliberation Don Andrés sensed was planned. "The man was never any threat to your daughter. If he had been, I would have gone after him myself—and killed him with my bare hands. . . . But you have to admit, she *is* a glory when that hot temper of hers is roused. You should have been there!"

In spite of himself, Don Andrés felt his lips twitching. "I was there when she came home with that dreadful scraggly puppy . . . and poor René LeClerc in tow. The little thing was so scared it cringed if it caught sight of its own shadow—the dog, I mean, not LeClerc. Now it thinks it owns the stable, though it still comes running if it so much as hears her voice." He was surprised to feel something catch in his throat, and he got up, turning to the window himself, his back to his visitor. Usually he could make his face into a mask, not an emotion showing that he didn't choose. Today he was not so sure of himself.

"So," came the voice from behind, "you *are* having doubts."

"Not about you." He turned his head briefly, looking into the room again. At seventy, he was still a handsome man; the lines in his face added character, not age, and silver was more flattering to strong Spanish features than black hair had ever been. "I am sure about the decision we have made together. But I am wondering if, truly, this is the right way."

"You could always be modern and free-thinking and let her make the choice herself. It is unheard-of in New Orleans, of course, at least among the better Creole families. But there are whole parts of the country where women do select their own husbands nowadays."

"No . . ." Don Andrés turned back to the window, which faced onto the garden, quiet now, with the only motion a hint of wind rustling the leaves. He could almost see her there, Lili, a little girl again, *his* little girl, playing little-girl games all by herself. It was funny, that other, shadowy figure was only the faintest memory, but he could still see the child so clearly, still hear shrieks and giggles in ears that were no longer keen to the sounds of today. From the moment they had placed her in his arms, she had been his child, not another man's, not the baby of the wife he adored, but his, as surely as if that were his blood in her veins, and his love for her had never wavered.

"No, I could not take the chance. Lili is too impetuous—

she would follow her heart and not her head . . . and when has the heart of a nineteen-year-old ever been wise?"

"You are afraid she would pick someone like LeClerc, for instance? I hear he asked for her and was rejected."

Don Andrés shook his head. "I'm not the least bit worried about that. Lili would never look at him, poor wretch. Not that he isn't a scoundrel—I sent him packing, and good riddance!—but he's not the kind of scoundrel that would appeal to a willful young girl. No, I see a smoother, racier sort catching her eye, especially with that ridiculous curse the servants have been spoon-feeding her since she was a baby. Perhaps if I'd been able to keep her from hearing it until she was older . . . But never mind. She *did* hear, and for all that she protests sometimes, I think she half-believes it. She would be attracted to the wrong man just because he was wrong and the danger seemed romantic."

"Still, there are more conventional ways—"

Don Andrés raised his hand, breaking into the sentence, and the other man fell silent. "I think not in this case. I'm sure I am right. Though I must admit, it makes me nervous, the way you encourage her high spirits . . . and the way you look when you talk about her. It is not, you understand, quite the look a father wants to see when a man is speaking of his daughter."

The man smiled faintly as he sat down in the only other comfortable chair, on the opposite side of the desk. Helping himself to another glass of Amontillado, he swirled it thoughtfully in his fingers for a moment. "Tell me, *amigo*," he said, lapsing into the other man's native tongue, though in that Creole city with its mingling of two cultures, even the Spanish spoke flawless French, "what is it you want for your daughter? A comfortable marriage of convenience, with affection but no passion to confuse the issue? That is the standard in New Orleans, I know. Some would call it sensible. But I have seen too many marriages like that, and they do not satisfy the soul."

"No . . . that they do not." Don Andrés' face tightened, but he did not turn to the window again, as if he sensed, just for a second, he might catch a glimpse of the gentle shadow that had been gone these many years. He had loved his wife with every fiber of his being when he had brought her into his home; he had tried desperately

to make her love, or even *like* him in return. A smile
would have warmed his heart, a laugh brought the sunshine back into his life. But there were no smiles left in
her, even for her baby daughter, no capacity for laughter, and after a while, desire had turned to compassion,
and the terrible longing he once felt when he looked at
her had been gone long before she died. The pains of
middle age healed, if not as quickly, as thoroughly as
those of youth, and the scars had long since hardened,
numbing the memories in his heart. "No one knows
better than I that a marriage must be based on more than
convenience. My own, as I am sure you are aware, was
based solely on that, on one side at least. Such a marriage satisfies neither the soul nor the body."

"So, naturally . . . you took a mistress."

Don Andrés' jaw tightened, and a faint tic showed at
the corner of his mouth. "Yes . . . if that is any concern
of yours."

"I am sorry, my friend." The man spoke lightly, but
with emphasis. "I have met the beautiful Chartreuse, and
I have nothing but the greatest admiration for her. I did
not mean to judge, believe me. I think it is only reasonable
that a man seek companionship elsewhere when he finds
no pleasure at home. I would not hesitate to do so if
circumstances forced me into it. No man with blood in
his veins would. But I would infinitely prefer a wife who
stirs my senses . . . and I cannot think you want your
daughter living with someone who is indifferent to her."

"No, you are right." Don Andrés lifted his glass and
stared into the amber liquid, glowing fire-bright in the
rays from the window. "No, I do not want that."

"Well, then, it seems to me you have two choices. You
can take me on my terms, as I am . . . or you can look
elsewhere for an acceptable suitor for your daughter."

"I think, under the circumstances"—Don Andrés held
the glass up, half-surrender, half-salute—"I will take you."

"A wise decision."

Smiling, he raised his own glass, and the two men
drank.

4

The light left the parlor early. By two-thirty, while Lili and her cousin were still at lunch, the shadows had already begun to deepen, and M'mère's bulky figure in her plain gray dress barely showed against the deep rose draperies, nearly gray themselves in the dusklike haze. Outside, sunlight still shimmered, looking almost unreal on the tamped-earth thoroughfare, where only a moment before a magnificent carriage and a pair of perfectly matched black horses had stood.

"I hope he knows what he's doing," she muttered under her breath. There was no one to hear, but she had stopped worrying about things like that long ago. It was an old woman's prerogative, talking to herself.

Not that anyone was likely to notice.

She straightened an imaginary wrinkle in the draperies and turned back into the room. That was one of the advantages of growing old; one of the disadvantages too. Half the time, no one even remembered you were there.

The light looked suspiciously soft on a brilliantly polished mahogany side table, and she ran her finger across it, noting with satisfaction a faintly gritty feel, though there was no visible dust. She would be back later with a broom and feather mop to set things right. It was not her job, cleaning the house. Don Andrés, who did not believe in slavery, maintained a full staff of maids, upstairs and downstairs, kitchen and parlor, and because he paid the highest wages, they were more than usually efficient. But M'mère had worked all her life. There was, to her, something vaguely unnatural in hands that were not permanently attached to a pail and mop, and idleness made her uncomfortable.

Her eye lit on a portrait over the sculptured marble mantel, slightly crooked as usual—it never seemed to hang straight. She winced as she reached up and adjusted it. The arthritis that had stiffened her hands for years was beginning to move into her back. Or perhaps it was just age, no longer creeping up on her, but galloping like a team of horses hell-bent to win the race.

The portrait was of Lili, the only painting, indeed the only decoration, in the room. The family portraits, which had been saved from the fire by servants in the generous if somewhat mistaken notion that they were what Don Andrés valued most, were hanging in the hall downstairs. In point of fact, he had been appalled when he learned that lives had been risked to rescue them. He was a man to whom such things did not matter, a man utterly without sentiment . . . except where his daughter was concerned.

M'mère paused for a moment, her manner softening subtly as she studied the portrait. It was an excellent likeness, if not excellent in technique, for the artist was more intuitive than skilled. The brushstrokes were uneven, the lines almost childishly simple in execution, but the spirit was there—the intense youthfulness, the vibrancy, the look of fun in the eyes and at the corners of the lips. And the coloring was perfect, so exactly like Lili, a little too exotic to be conventionally pretty. But then, convention was hardly an air that would sit well on her.

He had captured the minx, all right! M'mère chuckled softly, feeling the pride she always allowed herself when Lili was not there to catch her at it. Like many a woman who had devoted her life to raising other women's children, she felt a bond with her young charge, as fiercely protective—and helplessly vulnerable—as if she had been a mother herself. And because vulnerability was another thing that made her uncomfortable, she went to great extremes to cover it up.

She had been just fifteen when she had left the small village of Touques in Normandy, heading for La Rochelle, where she had planned to sign on as an indentured servant in exchange for passage to French Canada. But Lorient had been closer, and there had been a contingent of kindly Ursuline nuns sailing to a place called Nouvelle Orléans . . . and they had just lost both their servants, one to illness, the other to cold feet.

She had thought, when she arrived in the New World and worked off her few short years of service, that she

would marry and settle down, for women were in great
shortage, and even the plainest could find a husband if
she was healthy and not afraid of hard work. But somehow, there had always seemed to be children who needed
her. Fleurette first, a fiery little creature, but so winsome
when she was small. And then, when she had proved too
much to handle and had run off with that scoundrel—
who had nothing to recommend him but a long dramatic
scar down one cheek and a rather coarse male body—
there had been the orphans in the school, for the Ursulines
educated not just the daughters of the rich, but free
blacks as well, and Indian waifs . . . so many who needed
an extra measure of guidance and encouragement.

She had almost married once. She remembered little
about him now except his name. Étienne it was, and he
had been a farmer, a simple, good-hearted man. But it
was then that Fleurette had been murdered, knifed in a
vicious barroom brawl, and she had gone to that horrible
hotel with the absurd name—the Sure Enuf—to hold her
in her arms while she lay dying, without even the last
rites, for no priest could be found who dared venture into
the infamous Swamp. After that, there had been Cybèle
to look after, dear gentle Cybèle . . . and then Lili. By
that time she had been too old to have children of her
own, and it had not mattered so much anymore.

The portrait held her gaze a moment longer; then she
looked away, feeling vaguely uneasy as she glanced back
at the street where the carriage had been standing a short
time before. The morning's events, though she had agreed
to them in advance and even participated in their execution, were beginning to worry her again, and she headed
toward the door. Don Andrés would be in his office. He
was troubled too—he had to be—and he was a man of
habit. Whenever he was troubled, he shut himself in
the office.

The large window at the far end of the hall faced south-
west, and a welcome burst of light spilled through rippled
panes, turning the oak parquet floor a deep, glowing
gold. Don Andrés was a man of simple tastes himself,
but he was wise enough to know that appearances were
important, especially to the old French families who were
the backbone of Creole society, and for his daughter's
sake, he cared. No cypress floors with wide, uneven
planking for him, no plain cherry or walnut furnishings.

His daughter was going to be raised with nothing but the best. Everyone who stepped across the threshold of his house would know instantly who she was and where she had come from.

The office door was ajar, and M'mère pushed it open, thinking Don Andrés would hear the faint creaking sound and look around to see her. He was there, as she had assumed, seated behind his desk, but he was turned away, staring through the window. Something in his manner, the way his shoulders almost seemed to sag, made her uncharacteristically hesitant.

Or perhaps it was the room rather than the man himself.

M'mère lingered briefly on the threshold, looking in. She had never liked Don Andrés' study. It was the one place in the house that did not fit. The windows were too high and narrow, the dark woodwork much too Spanish in feel. And the rugs that half-covered the terra-cotta tiles on the floor, with their bold, almost gaudy stripes, smacked somehow of heathenism, though they did say that the Spanish—in their flamboyant way—were as devoutly Catholic as the French.

"I hope you know what you're doing," she said abruptly, repeating her earlier thought, this time for the appropriate audience. The words brought a quick turn of his head and a sharp look from Don Andrés.

"I think I do," he said, then softened as he caught sight of her face. The woman had, after all, been a faithful servant for many years, and she was devoted to his daughter. "I understand you are worried . . . and I share your concern— it would be unnatural if I didn't. But you are fretting in vain. This is a good plan I have come up with."

"But not foolproof."

"No . . . not foolproof. What on this earth is? But here—will you not sit down? The floor is hard, and I know your legs have been troubling you of late." He suppressed a smile as he saw her choose the most uncomfortable chair in the office, shallow-seated, with a straight wooden back. Her spine had been stiff as a broom handle the first time she sat in his house; it had not grown more flexible with the passing years. "I cannot give any guarantees, of course, but I think all will go well. I've worked it out very carefully, leaving as little as possible to chance. At any rate, we'll know soon enough. It all depends on how she reacts today."

The old woman nodded. "Yes. Today is the critical time. But it could backfire. You know that."

"It could, but I'm betting it won't." He picked up the half-empty glass in front of him, twirling it thoughtfully in his fingers. "I don't suppose I could persuade you to take a little sherry with me. A celebration in anticipation, shall we say?"

He was not surprised when she refused. "Maybe later, at the wedding . . . if it comes off. Not now."

"Later, then." He set the glass down, sighing heavily as he rose and stepped over to a massive bookcase that filled nearly all of one side of the room. A bracelet was lying on one of the open shelves, as if it had been carelessly dropped—a heavy, ornate gold band set with large rubies so clear and shimmering that even a casual eye would know at once they weren't garnets. He had bought it for his wife soon after their marriage, thinking the extravagance and magnificent beauty would please her, but she had barely looked at it, and he had set it aside, almost forgetting it until today. It was shortly after the visitor left that he had remembered, and taking it out, had studied it for a while in the light before placing it on the shelf. Once he had thought he would give it to Lili on her wedding day. Now he was not sure. There was so much sadness associated with it.

"I loved her very much, you know."

There was no question who the "her" of that soft utterance was, and for all her broom-stiff back and gruff expression, M'mère unbent inside. They had so little in common, she and this Spaniard who was nearly her contemporary. Only the love they shared for a beautiful woman and her daughter, but that love had created a bond.

"I know you did," she said quietly. "I have always known that. I have never spoken of it, because I did not think you wanted me to, but I knew."

Don Andrés put the bracelet back on the shelf and turned. "I tried to make her happy. With God as my witness, I tried! I thought at first I was going to succeed. I didn't expect her to love me. I knew that was impossible —the age difference alone would have precluded it—but I thought I could bring peace into her life. And perhaps some small measure of joy."

"It was not your fault that you failed. Age had nothing

to do with it. No man could have made her happy after *he* had broken her heart. She loved too much, my *pauvre petite*. She was the kind of woman who could love only once . . . and that once too deeply. Without him, she did not want to survive."

"So I learned." He crossed back to the desk, looking darkly somber as he lifted the glass again and stared moodily into its depths. But when he looked up, there was the slightest hint of a smile on his lips. "You wanted her to run off with him, didn't you? I always suspected that you counseled her to sin rather than sacrifice—that you urged it on her, as a matter of fact. And that you were more than a little disappointed when she failed to take your advice and married me instead."

M'mère's back stiffened even more, if that was possible, and Don Andrés noticed that she did not look him in the eye. "Well . . . and what if I did?" she muttered. "It was cruelly unfair. Why should her life be ruined, and all because of some insane woman who screamed, they said, if she so much as heard his name? He was no comfort to her, and he meant the world to Cybèle. She was so young . . . and so pretty. I wanted her to be happy! What was wrong with that?"

"Nothing at all," he said gently. "I would respect you less if you had thought anything else. Only it wouldn't have worked . . . he would never have made her happy. Do you think I didn't have him thoroughly investigated before I decided what to tell her? It was more than circumstance that created their problems—it was character as well. There would have been no joy for her beyond that brief burst of ecstasy if she had dared to throw off conscience and faith and follow the yearnings of her heart."

"Perhaps not." M'mère met his eyes at last, her own gaze troubled. "I have often wondered if they would have been able to start again, as he promised, or if things would have turned out the same somewhere else."

"Exactly the same. I have no doubt of it. A man who does not love a woman enough to be honest with her—in the things that count—is not the man who will make her happy. He would have broken her heart anyway, later rather than sooner, and she would have died of grief in the end."

"Perhaps. Now we'll never know."

"No, we never shall."

He leaned back against the window, unconsciously taking the same pose the other man had before. Then, abruptly, without warning, he finished the sherry in one gulp and threw the glass at the fireplace, spraying shards of tinkling crystal across the hearth.

"But I promise you one thing—it's not going to be like that for Lili. No scoundrel preying on girlish innocence will get his hands on her. The man who wins my daughter is going to be honorable and trustworthy—and strong enough to be a match for her!"

"And, of course, he will be the man of your choice." M'mère stood up slowly, grasping the back of the chair with her hand to steady herself for a second before she started toward the door. "You think all you have to do is pick the right man and throw him in her path, and she will swoon at his feet." She reached the threshold and turned, shaking her head back and forth for emphasis. "You are a good man, Don Andrés, and a good father, but you have something to learn about young girls. They do not always swoon when you want them to."

"Yes, but they *do* swoon, and over very predictable things—and people. If the man I have chosen is right, then the desired effect will follow. Not instantly, perhaps. It may take a while, but I am sure it will come out as I have planned. I only have to arrange things, just so, and she will see reason in the end."

"You are so confident," the old woman said slowly. "You worry me. You do not even look at the possibility that this could blow up in our faces."

"I am not as confident as I appear, and, yes—I have looked at all the possibilities. Including what might happen if I choose another course. I am only doing what any father would, you understand. I am trying the best I can to find happiness for my daughter."

"Well, then, let us hope you are right." She started to leave, but his voice held her one last moment.

"Let us *pray* I am right."

5

Lili was in the garden, just finishing the coffee she had brought from the dining room, when she received the summons to her father's study. It hardly came as a surprise, for Don Andrés often called her in after lunch, but she did find herself wondering if the black carriage with its elegant upholstery and inconspicuous crest had something to do with the reason he wanted to see her. More likely, though, she thought as she made her way down the long sunlit hall, he was planning on asking which ball she had chosen for that evening. Although he no longer attended such functions himself, leaving it to M'mère to chaperone her, he always kept an eye on her plans.

She was smiling to herself as she threw open the door and burst with her usual impetuosity into the room. Unlike M'mère, she had always adored her father's office, preferring it to the more properly formal parlors and front salon. The very strangeness of the dark wood and bold colors appealed to her, and she liked the sense of being cherished and included that came with the special time she spent here.

"Papa . . ."

She hesitated unexpectedly, feeling the faintest hint of apprehension, though she could not for the life of her have said why. Perhaps it was the way he was scowling at the official-looking papers in his hand instead of looking up. Or perhaps it was just the coldness of the room. With its thick walls and narrow windows, the study could be wonderfully pleasant on a steamy day, but it needed a fire well into spring, and the hearth was empty now.

"Come in, daughter, and close the door behind you." Don Andrés set the papers aside and gestured with one hand toward the chair opposite his desk. "Be seated, if you please. I am glad you were so prompt. There's something I want to discuss with you."

"As you wish, Papa, but . . ." Lili got halfway to the chair, then stopped, the sense of foreboding growing stronger. Papa never said "please" to her in that proper tone of voice. And whenever he got all stiff and formal, it meant she was in trouble. But surely she hadn't done anything wrong . . . unless, if course, he had heard about that trip to the levee this morning and disapproved. "If you don't mind, I think I'd rather stand."

"But I do mind," he said evenly. "I have something of importance to tell you, and I would like eyes on a level while I do. It is very difficult at my age, craning my neck to look up."

Lili felt a lump in her throat as she sat, rather more obediently than usual, on the edge of the chair. She didn't like the look on his face, and she had a feeling she was going to like even less what he was about to say.

"You frighten me when you look like that, Papa. You're much too solemn—and you know I hate it when you're solemn! I want my old, darling Papa back. The one with the eyes that twinkle. And the lips that keep quivering at the corners—even when he's trying to be angry and stern."

She had worked her mouth into a passable imitation of his, and in spite of himself, Don Andrés felt a temptation to smile, which he had to work to control. It was lucky, he thought, that he had decided in advance exactly what he was going to do and had his mind firmly set. She had always been able to wheedle anything out of him, the little *coqueta*!

"There are some things best said without a twinkle in the eye, daughter. Or an inappropriate snicker, I might add . . . and this is one. You have reached an age when a little seriousness might be more becoming. Especially in a matter such as this."

"A matter such as *this*?" There was a paperweight on the desk, fashioned out of agate, and Lili picked it up absently, rubbing it in her hands as she stared at him.

"You have recently turned nineteen, as you are well aware from the number of expensive presents you coaxed out of me. At nineteen, you can no longer be considered a girl, but a woman. It is time you were married. I have put a great deal of thought into this of late, and I have come to a conclusion."

"You want me to get married?" Lili gaped at him, shocked, though she knew she had no right to be. Nineteen *was* quite an advanced age. Creole marriages were usually arranged long before that, and, of course, bridegrooms were always chosen by the girls' fathers. But everything was happening so abruptly. She had expected months of hints, little teasing comments thrown into the conversation to prepare her, perhaps even a judicious question or two about the young men she had danced with at various balls and which ones most suited her fancy. "You have been thinking about it, you say? And you have come to a conclusion. I . . . I'm not sure I know what you mean."

"I mean, of course, that I have chosen a husband for you. He is a good man, one whom I admire and respect. I am certain you will come to feel the same in time. And you can get that look of alarm off your face. You need not fear for your future with him. He will treat you well . . . and buy you all the little baubles your heart thrives on."

Lili rose from the chair, unaware that she was still clinging to the paperweight. He had already *chosen* her husband? Without even asking her opinion? She had not expected to pick the man herself, of course. In the New Orleans of 1808, where many a girl met her husband-to-be for the first time when they exchanged betrothal rings, that was out of the question. But an indulgent father took his daughter's feelings into consideration. And Don Andrés had always been the most indulgent of all.

"How can you say you have chosen the man when you didn't even discuss it with me?" she cried out, stunned. "Don't you care at all how I feel? What I want?" Her head was reeling so dizzily, it was hard to think. *He will treat you well*, Papa had said. Not: *He will love you* or *He will make your life lively and satisfying*. He would treat her well—and she would suffocate with boredom! "Do I even know him, this man you have already decided upon without so much as mentioning the fact to me?"

Don Andrés heard the sarcasm in her voice, and his breath came out in a tired sigh. It was no more than he had expected. She had always been a willful creature. That was his fault, no doubt; he had spoiled her outrage-

ously, and now he was paying the price. But somehow he
had hoped the matter wouldn't be quite so painful.

"No, you do not know him, nor do you need to. I have
chosen wisely and carefully, with your best interests at
heart. My mind is made up. The subject is closed. You
will marry the man I have selected for you, and that is
that."

Lili's heart sank as she heard the finality in his tone.
Never had Papa talked to her like that before, so coldly—
almost as if he knew in advance she was going to object
to his choice. Suddenly the image of the carriage came
back, parked mysteriously in front of the house, and she
struggled to recall Simone's words about the man who
must have come in it. Handsome? Yes, he was handsome, she had said, but different somehow, as if he might
be . . .

An American!

Her fingers tightened around the paperweight, knuck-
les turning stark white. Papa was always dealing with
Americans. It was their city now, he said. It was only
reasonable to come to terms with them. After all, the
future lay to the north, and most of the money in New
Orleans was already coming from there.

Only, those were *business* dealings, nothing personal.
At least that was what she had thought.

"You have picked an American for me?" The room
seemed to be spinning, and it was all she could do to hide
her faintness. There *was* a Fleurie curse—she knew that
now with a terrible cold certainty—and it was not romantic at all, but dreadfully, frighteningly ugly. If Papa persisted in his plans, if he forced her into this loveless
marriage, her heart was going to search for comfort where
it could . . . and all the old prophecies would come back
to haunt her! "You cannot make me marry one of those
. . . those barbarians! They are crude and disgusting,
every one of them. Why, they hardly speak French at
all—and they don't even dress well! I would die before
I'd marry one of them!"

Don Andrés sighed again and turned toward the window. His daughter was so predictable sometimes, he
knew exactly what she was thinking, but then all of a
sudden her mind came up with the most unexpected
twists. "You will marry whom I tell you, and there will
be no more talk of dying. I am your father. If I tell you

to marry an American, you will, or a Frenchman, or a Spaniard—or a Cajun from the swamps! I demand obedience only occasionally, but when I do, I expect my orders to be carried out without question."

"And if I refuse . . . ?" Lili tilted her head back, nostrils flaring as she met his gaze. The look on her face was so stubborn, he could have sworn for a second he saw his own features mirrored in hers.

"If you refuse, I will have no choice. Naturally, you will be sent to the convent."

"The convent?" Defiance flashed in her eyes. Don Andrés knew without having to be told what was running through her mind. This was the threat that fathers had hurled at recalcitrant daughters over the centuries . . . and rarely had the stomach to carry out. "You think I am afraid of the convent? The walls are not high enough to hold me. I'd climb over the top if they tried to lock me in. Besides, the Ursulines aren't like that. No matter what you paid them, they wouldn't keep me against my will."

"I was not thinking of the Ursulines," he replied quietly. "Or of the convent on Chartres Street. My sister, Carmela, as you will recall, is the mother superior of a small order just outside Madrid, which is known for its strictness. And its regard for parental authority. The walls there, I assure you, are very high."

Lili felt suddenly as if the air had been knocked out of her. For the first time, she realized he meant what he said. This was not an idle threat. She would do as he ordered, or he was going to send her to his sister in Spain . . . and she could not even imagine what her life would be like there! "You *are* going to force me, then? You would make me marry an American—even knowing how I despise them?"

"I did not say that." His shoulders hunched slightly, as if a weight had settled on them, and he was more than usually aware of his age. "That was your own idea— though heaven knows where you got it. I am well aware of how you feel about Americans, and while I do not share your opinion, I would never press you into such a union if there were other options. Fortunately, a more acceptable alternative has been presented to me."

"Then . . . you haven't settled on an American?" Relief flooded over her, and youthful optimism returning,

Lili started to think that perhaps, after all, the situation might not be so bad. Plainly, Papa was not as unrelenting as he seemed. While she was sure the man he had in mind was dreadfully stuffy—and a hundred years old at least!—there was still time to talk him out of it and settle on a more appropriate choice between them. What foolishness, letting herself get into a state over something that was months away at least. "You aren't going to force me to marry someone horrid and hateful?"

"Horrid and hateful! What a way you have with words. Of course I have not picked anyone 'horrid and hateful' for you . . . or socially unacceptable either. You have heard of the Cavarelle family?"

"Yes, of course." Lili brushed the subject away with a wave of her hand, wondering why he had picked such an inappropriate moment to bring it up. The Cavarelles were the most important family in New Orleans, but they kept to themselves and had not attended any of the fashionable soirees for years. To her knowledge, she had never even seen one, except the widow Marguerite, a silly woman with hair much too black for her age. "Everyone has heard of the Cavarelles, though no one knows them. And everyone is terribly curious. But what do they have to do with . . . ? Oh!"

She broke off suddenly. There could only be one reason why Papa wanted to talk about the Cavarelles now. Yet it seemed so incredible, so farfetched—she was sure she must have misunderstood.

"You mean one of the Cavarelles has asked for *me*? But . . . which one? I don't even know who they are. The old man died before I was born, and Marguerite is gone now too—that was the wife. But wasn't there a son? Or were there two?"

"There was one—and, in fact, there still is. And, yes, that is the man we are discussing now. His name is Jean-Baptiste, and he is the sole heir to the Cavarelle fortune, which I need not tell you is considerable. He will make an excellent husband. Your financial position will be secure with him."

And her social position too, Lili thought bitterly, though he had been tactful enough not to say it. Purity of lineage was important, especially to the old Creole families, who rarely married out of their own circle. Women having been in short supply in New Orleans, there had been a certain mingling of the races, and even some of the finest families were believed to be tainted. A son or daughter whose heritage could not be traced directly back to France, or at least Spain, was difficult to dispose of on the marriage market.

. And a girl with a background as indiscriminate—and undocumented—as Lili's faced almost insurmountable problems. She could attend all the parties and balls, but when it came time to marry, she would be expected to settle for a banker or businessman, or perhaps a wastrel younger son with a habit for cards and horses he couldn't support any other way. For all Don Andrés' wealth—and the large dowry that would come with her—there were doors that would remain closed.

"And he wants *me*? This Jean-Baptiste—with the entire Cavarelle fortune at his disposal?"

"So it seems. He has asked for your hand—he was here a while ago, as a matter of fact—and I have given it."

"But why me?" Lili struggled to collect her thoughts. She had never met the man, she was sure of that. He had never come to any of the soirees she had been at, unless, of course, it was a *bal masque* and he was in disguise. But even then, she was almost certain there had been no strangers unaccounted for. "Why on earth would he pick me out of all the girls in New Orleans?"

For your spirit, the old don was tempted to say, but she was already showing a bit more spirit than he was comfortable with. "He has seen you—more than once—and it seems he is quite taken by your charms. I gather he thinks you have the qualities he is looking for in a wife."

"What qualities?" Lili's eyes narrowed, turning almost brown, even though the light from the window was striking her full in the face. "He doesn't *know* me! He's never even talked to me! He hasn't the vaguest notion how I feel. What I think! What 'qualities' could he possibly detect, just seeing me—even more than once?"

"Possibly the same qualities you seem to be looking for in a man," Don Andrés remarked dryly. "Your French is excellent—I paid enough for the tutors who coached you after you left the convent day school. And of course you dress very well. But enough of this. The subject is closed. I have made an excellent match for you, as I am sure you are aware. I expect, when you have had time to think it over, you will be suitably grateful."

Grateful? Lili closed her eyes for an instant, feeling faint as the full impact closed in on her. Grateful for a forced marriage? To a man she didn't even know? And yet, of course, Don Andrés was right, from his point of view. It *was* an excellent match. In his wildest dreams, he could never have expected to do so well for his daughter. Whatever little hope she had had of somehow getting him to change his mind was rapidly ebbing away. She might have persuaded him to give up a lesser match, but a Cavarelle? Who could offer more? Money, position, security—it would all be hers with this man Papa had chosen.

Only she didn't want to marry him!

She opened her eyes, staring at the light that flooded through the window onto the red tile floor. Plainly, what she wanted—and didn't want—wasn't going to be an issue.

What is he like, she wondered, this man I am expected to marry? She racked her brains, but try as she would, she couldn't think of a thing she had heard about him. Was he old? No doubt, for his father had been quite elderly when he died, and that was a long time ago. And who but an old man, and a dotty one at that, would spy on a pretty girl in secret and decide he had to have her? A young man would arrange an introduction and at least have a word with her first.

"Please, Papa," she said softly, "please, don't make me marry him just because he's rich and all the best people fawn over him. *Please*, let me marry a man I've met and for whom I at least have a degree of affection."

Tears glistened on her lashes, and Don Andrés, seeing them, felt himself waver. She was still his little girl, his one true treasure, and it was hard to hurt her, even for her own good. But painful as it was, he knew he had to protect her. "I have told you before. My mind is made up. I have given the man my word, and I will not go back on it. As for meeting him and first developing an affection, you'll have an opportunity this afternoon. I have arranged for you to receive him in the parlor for tea . . . or sherry, if he prefers. Naturally, at that time he will give you a ring. To solemnize the engagement."

"This afternoon?" Lili stared at him helplessly. The

tears still shone on her lashes, turning the room into a hazy shimmer, but somehow she managed to hold them back. Naturally, it would be this afternoon, and naturally he would give her a ring—to seal the bargain she did not want. "Papa, I beg you one last time . . ."

"No. The matter is settled. He is a good man, and you are lucky to have him. And, daughter, see that you let him know that this afternoon when you meet."

Lili started to protest again, but something in his eyes warned her he would tolerate no further argument. Without another word, she turned and walked out of the room, only dimly aware that she was still holding the heavy paperweight.

It *was* real, after all. She leaned against the wall, clutching the weight to her breast. There was no use trying to pretend anymore that it wasn't—or trying to hold it back. The curse of the Fleurie women was not just a story made up by servants to amuse her. It was real . . . and she was not going to escape its pain.

6

"**I** won't marry him. I won't, I won't, I *won't*!" All the rebellion and frustration burst out in a torrent of words, and Lili hurled the paperweight as hard as she could against the garden wall. "He can't make me! I don't care if he threatens me with the convent—I don't even care if he really *sends* me there! I won't marry some dreadful old man just because he's rich!"

M'mère waited patiently until the pieces had settled, then stooped painfully and picked up what was left of the paperweight. It had been a pretty thing, dark red agate streaked with dusty rose. Now it was split almost exactly in two, with jagged edges and a glass-bright sheen along the broken surface.

"A pity," she said quietly. "Your papa always set great store by this. He liked the way it looked on his desk. Still, it's a clean break. I suppose it can be mended."

"Unlike my heart," Lili said glumly, though now that she was calmer, she was beginning to feel a little foolish. She had outgrown temper tantrums years ago, and the paperweight *had* looked nice on a cluttered expanse of white paper in Papa's otherwise tidy office. "It's only a piece of stone, after all. It isn't important. But my future is . . . and I'm not going to be pushed into a marriage I don't want!"

"How do you know you don't want it?" M'mère replied with maddening logic. "You haven't met the man. You've never even set your eyes on him."

"Maybe not . . ." Lili turned away, avoiding the penetrating look which even now must be fixed on her back. "But I don't need eyes to tell me I don't want him. He's got to be old, thirty or forty at least—probably more! And he certainly isn't handsome or charming."

"All this without eyes?" The table had been cleared, and M'mère set the pieces of agate on it, propping them together until they looked almost whole, except for a small gap still showing on one side. "What makes you so sure?"

"Rich men are never handsome or charming. Well . . . almost never. And a handsome man isn't the sort fathers welcome with open arms. Why, if this Jean-Baptiste looked like he might please me, Papa would probably be so suspicious he'd send him away—even if he is a Cavarelle!"

"And if he *were* handsome . . ." M'mère paused, the silence so questioning Lili was drawn around in spite of herself. "If he did look like he would please you, this man your papa has chosen, would that make a difference? Would you abide then by his choice?"

"Nooo . . ." Lili was a little surprised at the answer herself, but she knew it was true. "No, it's not just his age I mind, or the fact that he's not handsome—though I'm sure that's the case! I mind being forced into a marriage in which I have no say. Oh, M'mère, don't you see? The Fleurie women have always suffered . . . and their unhappiness came from not being able to have the men they wanted! If I marry someone of Papa's choosing, not mine, my life is going to be ruined too."

"*Eh bien*, there's no point worrying about it then, is there? What he looks like? Whether he's old and ugly?" She avoided Lili's eyes as she gathered the pieces together, having found the last little sliver which had escaped her before, and wrapped them in her apron to take to one of the black kitchen maids who was good at fixing things. "Still, you might as well have a look at him this afternoon anyway. Just out of curiosity. So you know what you're up against, eh?"

It was a good point, and an hour later, when she had had time to cool down somewhat, Lili had the sense to realize it. She had spent a good part of that hour considering the only option open to her, and wondering if she ought not to call Papa's bluff after all and let him send her to the convent. There was something strangely compelling in the image that came to mind, high gray stone walls and dank, silent corridors, suiting her morose mood, and she had lingered on it almost lovingly for a while.

But melancholy never held her long, and reason returning, she had reminded herself that even the *thought* of the convent was out of the question. She had not been born for piety and silence; it was not in her nature. She would wither and die there, like the roses that were already wilting in a French porcelain vase on the table in the formal front parlor.

Besides, she could not bear the thought of leaving home—or Papa. No matter how furious she got with him, she never for a moment doubted that he loved her. There was no meanness in what he was doing. No deliberate cruelty. If only he weren't so rigid about things!

She was tempted, briefly, to send for her cousin so she would have someone to talk to. But Simone was two years younger—still so wrapped up in adolescent dreams of marriage and romance, she'd never understand—and besides, the last thing Lili wanted now was to be reminded of who the girl was and how she had arrived in the Santana household. Her mother, Gabriel Dubois's youngest sister, had long since been disowned by the family, for she had married beneath her, a sin that might be forgiven a man, but never a woman. When she had died, a short time after her brother, there had been no one to take care of the orphaned daughter, and Don Andrés, with his intense sense of honor, had felt obligated to take her in—simply because she was related to Lili.

And that same sense of honor would never let him back down now that he had given his word to Jean-Baptiste Cavarelle!

Sighing, Lili got up, trying not to think about it as she headed toward the wardrobe to pick out a dress to wear. M'mère was right. She might as well meet this man, if only out of curiosity. After all, engagements lasted several months—at least. All sorts of things could happen in that time. Why, if the man was as old as she believed, he might even die before then!

The thought raised her spirits somewhat, and she paused as her eye lit on a shimmer of silver sprawled extravagantly across a quilted coverlet on the mahogany four-poster bed. Her costume for the *bal masque* that evening. It had been delivered while she was at lunch, and she had planned to come upstairs as soon as she finished her coffee to make sure all the last-minute alterations had been properly completed. But with everything that had happened, it had completely slipped her mind.

She had created the design herself, and she was rather smugly pleased with the way it had come out. Simone, who still attended children's parties, always liked to go as something real, a modest little shepherdess perhaps, in a sweet flowered dress and old-fashioned powdered wig. But Lili's ideas tended toward the more fanciful, like white silk taffeta, cut in petal patterns to make a lily for her name, or the brilliant plumage and crest of a tropical bird. This time she had decided to go as a waterfall!

Papa had been beside himself with laughter when he heard, but he was too indulgent to forbid her anything, and M'mère's snorts of derision had been abruptly stilled the afternoon before when Lili went for her final fitting. The dress had turned out perfectly, even more exquisite than she had dared to hope. The underskirt of pure silk was cut to flare around her ankles, and over it, hundreds of silver ribbons flowed lengthwise, frothing out like sprays of water as she twirled, enchanted, in front of the seamstress's mirror. Strands of gossamer-delicate lace would be threaded later through hair that had been darkened with bootblack, setting a dozen tiny diamonds to glitter like reflections in a midnight mountain pool. The final touch was a mask of raven's feathers, a dramatic jet-black contrast to that spilling cascade of silver.

A roguish impulse flashed into her mind, and just for an instant she was tempted to put it on. What would Monsieur Jean-Baptiste Cavarelle think, she wondered, if he looked up at the parlor door and saw a waterfall coming in at him?

But the costume was much too pretty, if somewhat unconventional . . . and much too flattering. She was not at all sure she wanted to look her best today.

She was a little surprised when she opened the wardrobe door to find only one neatly pressed garment hanging in the shadows, and she wondered vaguely if it was Papa himself, or M'mère, who had decided that that was what she should wear, and had sent everything else to the laundress.

It was not the dress she would have chosen, for it was new, and altogether the most daring of her gowns. In fact, she had been quite surprised when M'mère, who supervised the selection of her gowns and reported strictly

to Papa, had allowed her to order it. Pale sea green was
not her favorite color, but it was fashionable, and she
had to admit it suited her, bringing out the red highlights
in her hair and turning tawny eyes almost to jade. The
fabric was muslin, so sheer it was nearly diaphanous,
worn with the appropriate silk undergarments, to be sure,
but surprisingly prone to cling when she moved. A tight
bodice, ending Empire fashion just below the bosom, did
nothing to hide the fact that her figure had ripened nicely
into soft feminine curves, and the skirt, which barely
reached her ankles, fell in graceful folds like the drapery
of a classical statue. Even the neckline was impudently *à
la mode*, rising to little puffy sleeves on her shoulders,
then dipping in a deep curve, with just a hint of cleavage
peeking out from a dainty edging of Brussels lace.

Any other time, she would have been delighted with
the dress. Now, as she stood in front of the mirror and
stared at her reflection, she caught a glimpse of what
Jean-Baptise Cavarelle was going to see in a few minutes,
and suddenly she was frightened.

He had seen her before, Papa had said. This man had
seen—and he had desired. And she had the feeling he
was going to like what he saw now even more.

She went downstairs slowly, dragging her feet. Is the
same black carriage parked in front, she wondered, and
is Simone at an upstairs window with her nose pressed to
the glass? Unexpectedly, the memory of the levee came
flooding back, and she felt again, briefly, the same eerie
sensation of someone watching from the shadows. Had
that been her unwanted suitor? Was that where he had
seen her . . . "more than once"? But then she remembered the intensity of the feeling, and she knew instinctively that whoever belonged to those invisible eyes was
young and arrogantly sure of himself, not an elderly
gentleman of unpleasing countenance who rode around
in a dark, conservative coach and peered out at pretty
girls he did not have the courage to approach.

Shrugging off the thought, she forced herself down the
hall to the formal front parlor.

The man she had been expecting was not there. One
glance was enough to tell her that. The door was open,
and she found herself staring in at a slender figure positioned beside one of the windows, half-turned away from
her. Jean-Baptiste Cavarelle was not old at all, and from

where she stood, he certainly was not ugly. In fact, he was quite young, and tallish, with black hair waving back from a nicely shaped brow, and a nose that looked like it belonged in a sculptor's fantasy. Her cousin's mysterious stranger leapt to mind, and Lili had no doubt that this was he.

She could see why Simone had said there was something different about him. He did not look American—in fawn-colored breeches and a deep burgundy jacket with cambric frills showing at neck and cuffs, he was much too stylishly dressed—but he didn't look Creole either. There was something quietly tasteful about him, almost unassuming, as if despite his great wealth, he was a modest man. And modesty was not an image that suited the arrogant Creole male.

Was this the man with whom she was going to spend the rest of her life?

Helplessly Lili stared at him, wondering why the thought filled her with such dismay. He was younger than she had dared to dream, and considerably better-looking—she should have been beside herself with excitement. But all she could think was that this was Papa's choice, not hers, and more than anything in the world, she did not want to have to marry him!

She must have made a sound, for he turned and advanced toward her, his expression one of polite interest, with, she had to admit, none of the lechery she had expected. Now that he was nearer, she realized he was even more youthful than he had seemed. Indeed, if she hadn't known who he was, she would have guessed him at about the same age as she, though plainly appearances were deceptive. The elder Cavarelle had been dead well over twenty years. If Jean-Baptiste wasn't older than he looked, not only had he come into the world after his father died, he had been conceived posthumously as well!

For some reason, the thought struck her as funny, and to her horror, she started to giggle. She managed to choke it back, but apparently not soon enough, for a look of amusement came over his face.

"What a surprise, *mademoiselle* . . . and not an unpleasant one. I had expected this meeting to be awkward and self-conscious, and here you are, laughing already. Permit me to introduce myself. I am Jean-Baptiste—"

"I know who you are, *monsieur*," Lili broke in, trying

belatedly to compose her face in formal lines. Despite his surprising good looks, she found herself disliking him almost on sight, though she would have been hard-pressed to say why. Perhaps, again, simply because he was not her choice—or perhaps there was something in the aloof way he seemed to hold himself back from her. "My papa has naturally informed me who you are. And why you are calling this afternoon."

"And you are not, I assume, adverse to the idea . . . since you have agreed to meet me."

"I agreed because Papa requested it," she said primly. "How could I go against his wishes? That would hardly be proper." The expression on his face turned faintly mocking, and Lili blushed, recalling the distinct impropriety of her giggle a moment before. "I must apologize for my unseemly behavior, but you see . . . well, you're not at all what I imagined. I pictured an old man with gray hair—if he had any hair at all—and a dreadfully ugly face. And quite thick around the middle!"

The words brought a smile, but strangely, Lili sensed no warmth in it. If anything, the amusement had gone out of his eyes. "Dare I hope, *mademoiselle*, since you express surprise, that my face is not quite as dreadful as you feared?"

"No, not dreadful at all—and you're definitely not old." She went over to the table, which had been set for tea. Lamps had been lighted against the afternoon shadows, and a golden glow fell on imported white china so thin it was translucent, with hand-painted lily patterns in the center, and wide gilt rims. All the best has been laid out today, she thought, and for some reason the idea annoyed her. "Will you take tea, *monsieur*? Perhaps one of these little marzipan cakes? Our cook is quite famous for them. Or do you prefer sherry?"

"Tea will be fine," came the voice from behind, smooth, but not as deep as she liked. "It's a bit early in the day for alcohol. And no cake, thank you. With your warning ringing in my ears, I shall have to watch my middle."

"As you wish," Lili replied coolly. She rather liked tea herself, but it was a foreign custom, not at all fashionable among the Creoles. Nor did it seem particularly masculine. She would have respected him more if he'd accepted sherry in a cut-crystal glass, or better yet, demanded that she ring for the servants to bring a good stiff brandy, and a smelly cigar to boot! "Would you care for sugar? I don't think it will damage your middle too much. Or perhaps some milk?"

"Neither, thank you. That looks like quite an excellent tea. Indian, by the smell of it. I would hate to spoil the flavor."

Lili handed him the cup and proceeded to pour her own, pointedly dumping in two spoonfuls of sugar, though in truth her stomach had begun to tighten and just the smell was cloying. "I trust you will not object if I 'spoil' mine."

"Not at all . . . though I must admit I'm surprised. I would have thought you were sweet enough already."

"Indeed?" She raised the cup, barely touching it to her lips as she recognized the flirtatious banter that had become familiar over two seasons of balls and soirees. "Do I strike you as sweet, *monsieur*?"

"I think you can be. Very sweet . . . if you want to. I think you can also be tart, which is an interesting combination."

"Most gentlemen, I believe, are not attracted to tartness in a potential wife. You must be an unusual man."

"It has been said that Jean-Baptiste Cavarelle is *very* unusual." He carried his cup over to a velvet-upholstered settee, and without asking permission, or even waiting for her, casually sat down. "In ways, of course, that is true. But he is very usual in others. He is, for instance, a great, uh"—he paused, letting his eyes speak for him— "admirer of feminine charm."

"By charm, I gather you mean pleasing features. And you seem to be admiring mine. Should I be flattered?"

"You should be . . . but you aren't." He set the cup in its saucer on a marble-topped mahogany side table and leaned back. "You are very pretty, and you know it. I'm not the first man to have admired you, nor will I be the last. And heartless little creature that you are, you take us all for granted."

Lili looked down warily, staring into the pale, much-too-sugary liquid in her cup. He was flirting, quite easily, and it was clear that he was good at it. But his heart didn't seem to be in it. It was almost as if he were doing it because he thought he ought to—and because he enjoyed flirting—not because he wanted to flirt with *her*.

She raised her head again, eyes narrowing slightly. He was still watching her with that same composed expression, still slightly aloof, and she sensed more than ever that something was not right. He had to want her—he had come to Papa, and not the other way around—yet he didn't act as if he were really interested at all. Or was that just his way of trying to pique her interest?

"Why did you choose me?" she said abruptly. "Papa says you *saw* me someplace, but he didn't say where."

"Does it make a difference?"

"Nooo . . ." Just for an instant she thought again of the unseen watcher in the shadows that morning, and she half-wondered. But the intensity was still missing, the sheer power of whatever it was she had felt, and she knew, beyond any doubt, that if someone had indeed been there, it could not have been this tame, cultivated gentleman. "No, where and when isn't important. But *why* is. It all sounds like nonsense to me, especially now that I know you're not old and dotty. No sensible man sees a woman and falls madly in love at first sight."

"Not *madly* perhaps," he admitted. "But it is possible to conceive, shall we say, a certain fascination. You are an exceptionally attractive young lady."

"New Orleans is full of attractive young ladies, if that's what you're looking for. And you have a great fortune of your own, so it can't be my dowry that you want. Why, out of all those attractive ladies, did you set your sights on me?"

"Why not?" he said easily, "since it had to be someone? Surely you are at least as good a choice as the others."

"No . . . not in everyone's eyes." Lili took a deep breath, daring herself to go on, not even caring that Don Andrés was going to be livid when he found out. She might not be able to get Papa to call off this unwelcome match, but perhaps, if she was outrageous enough, Jean-Baptiste Cavarelle would decide he didn't want her after all! "You do know, of course, that my background is not considered quite . . . suitable. The women of my family have not always been married to the men who fathered their children. In fact, there is some question that they even knew, in all cases, who those fathers were. So you see, my bloodline is really quite, uh, common."

"Yes, I am well aware of that." If the boldness of her speech shocked him, it did not show as he raised his cup, emptying it of the cooling liquid. "Quite honestly, aside from your very apparent loveliness, that's one of the things that appealed to me. There has been, you see, a lack of 'variety' in my own background. Cousin married too often to cousin, that sort of thing—with the only outside influences coming from families as inbred as our own. It has weakened the line. It's time to introduce strong new blood."

Lili stared at him, genuinely stunned. Of all the things he might have said, that was the one she hadn't anticipated. "You make it sound like I'm some kind of . . . breeding cow!"

A touch of humor showed, just for a second, around the corners of his lips. "I wouldn't have put it quite that way. But breeding *is* important, in humans as in animals. I want strong, healthy children. Of course"—his eyelids drooped deliberately, the same flirtation again, but no more convincing than before—"I don't object to their being good-looking too. If I'm going to found a new family line, why not a handsome one?"

"And if you're going to find a mother for that family, why not one who's attractive?"

"Why not? It isn't essential, of course, but it does make things pleasanter."

Lili rose and walked over to the table, setting her cup, virtually untouched, on the immaculate white lace cloth. Pleasanter for him, perhaps, but not for her. She was not ignorant of what went on between a man and woman in their bedroom—and other, quite surprising places, as she had sometimes learned. All that time in the kitchen and back quarters had left her with at least a vague awareness, and while her grasp of the details was sketchy, she did know enough to realize that that was one thing she wanted to share only with a man for whom she had very special feelings.

"Let me be perfectly frank." She turned slowly to face him. "I am here only because my papa ordered it. The choice was not mine. I have absolutely no desire to marry you."

She watched closely, waiting for him to redden with anger. But he did not so much as turn a hair as he placed his own cup on the table beside him and studied her calmly.

"Let me be equally frank, since that seems to be what you desire. It does not matter what you choose—or don't choose. The decision rests with your father and me. It would make the affair more interesting, I confess, if you were a little more enthusiastic. But I'm confident you'll become reconciled in time. I am not an unkind man, and I do not intend to be ungenerous with you. If not, well . . . all I demand, *absolutely*, is tall, strong sons to carry on my name."

Was that all this was for him? Lili turned away, not wanting him to see the tears that shimmered on her lashes. Tall, *strong* sons? A scientific experiment in superior breeding? What if it didn't turn out the way he thought? What if having indiscretions in one's background did not result in stronger offspring after all? Or what if, true to family tradition, she produced nothing but daughters? How kind—and generous—would he be then?

Somehow she forced herself to turn back, and their conversation continued for some minutes, though Lili barely heard what he was saying, or gave any thought to her own automatic replies. Even when they exchanged rings, everything seemed to pass in a fog. Later, all she could remember about her gift to him was that it had appeared suddenly in a box on the tea tray. His to her was a large red stone, not the usual garnet, but a far more valuable ruby, set in gold and surrounded by diamonds. Much too overbearing, the ring had been designed for someone larger, and she was conscious of an oppressive sense of heaviness as she felt him slip it on her hand.

At least it would be several months before the ceremony took place. That was her only comfort as she looked up and saw him watching her, more intently than she had expected. He might be sure now he wanted to marry her, but perhaps in time—if she managed to irritate him enough—he would change his mind.

"I expect we'll be seeing a great deal of each other," she said dully. "I believe engagements are usually quite lengthy."

"They are—usually," he conceded. "But not this time. We are going to be married as soon as Lent is over. And I'm afraid I will be deprived of your charming company in the meantime. Your father has stipulated that we not see each other again until then."

"We're to be married . . . at the end of Lent? But

. . ." Lili gasped. "That's forty days and six Sundays—forty-six days from now!"

"Forty-seven actually. Naturally, we can't be wed on Easter Sunday, just as it would be unsuitable to be married during Lent. But we will meet at the altar of the Cathédrale de St. Louis the day after that. Monday."

Forty-seven days! And she would not have a chance to see him until then! Lili felt faint, and she took a deep breath to steady herself. That was why Papa had sounded so confident before, when he gave her his ultimatum. Not because he thought threats of the convent would make her obedient, but because he knew he had arranged things so cleverly she would never be able to worm her way out. This was not a conventional engagement he had planned for her. Or a conventional wedding.

"The Monday after Easter? You are sure?"

"Very sure. Forty-seven days from now, almost to the hour, you will be my bride."

7

Forty-seven days, and then her life would be over.

Lili stood in the center of a small second-floor parlor and stared gloomily at pink-clad shepherds and rosy shepherdesses frolicking across the old-fashioned wallpaper. Delicate mosaic tables and carved gilt furnishings gave the room a feminine look, but it had never had a mistress and was seldom used. She could not have said herself why she chose to come there—perhaps only because she rarely did. If anyone wanted to find her, this was the last place he would look, and she needed to be alone with her thoughts.

Her mind was still in a whirl, the way everything had happened, not at all as she had expected, though ultimately, when all was said and done, it came out the same. Jean-Baptiste Cavarelle was young, and quite definitely handsome—if she had seen him anyplace else, she would have been intrigued—but she was no happier than if he'd been as old and ugly as she had imagined. She was still committed to marrying a man she would never love.

Only now she knew that he would never love her either.

It doesn't matter what you want, he had said, or words to that effect. And, dear heaven, he had meant them! Marriage was a business arrangement for him, a chance to try out all those theories about genetics and bloodlines, and except for coming together once in a while to create the sons he craved—and perhaps meeting occasionally after that to discuss them—she had the feeling they would never even see each other. As far as he was concerned, her wants and needs didn't exist.

She stepped over to the window, which faced out on

the backyard, with a view of the garden gate at the side.
One of the footmen was hurrying toward the stables,
head hunched deep into his shoulders, for it was late and
the wind was getting crisp. The sound of barking came
briefly from somewhere far away; then everything was
still.

Or was she being unfair?

She sank down on the arm of a chair and continued to
stare at the empty yard through faintly rippled panes.
She had come into the formal parlor this afternoon determined to reject whomever she found there. She had been
so preoccupied with the heartbreak of the Fleurie women
and Papa's determination to marry her off to a man of *his*
choice, no one would have had a chance. Jean-Baptiste
Cavarelle could have been exciting and dynamic—he could
have been the most romantic man in the world!—and she
would have disliked him anyway, just on principle.

And he had said he didn't care about her feelings only
after she looked him right in the face and told him that
she didn't want him. What had she expected? That he
was going to sit there docilely sipping India tea and
continue to court her? He *had* done his best before that
to keep up a pleasant, if somewhat stilted conversation.
And there had been that one glimmer of humor, which
she had done nothing to encourage.

Maybe Papa was right after all. It was unfair, the way
he had decided everything without consulting her—and
plotted it so cleverly that she had no way to weasel
out—but he wasn't selling her into slavery on a plantation up the river! Maybe she ought to be sensible and try
to work things out. It *was* a brilliant match, she could not
deny that. Wealth and status and the security of the
Cavarelle name. The children of this stranger would be
her children as well, and they would never want for
anything. Why couldn't she be satisfied with that?

But, oh, it was hard to give up her dreams.

She leaned her head against the thick draperies, catching a scent of something faintly musty in her nostrils.
Like every pretty young girl, she had grown up dreaming
of love, and though she had seen her share of reality, she
had always thought that things would be different for
her, that dreams of romance would one day culminate in
a storybook-perfect marriage. Now, abruptly, she was
learning a bitter lesson. Creole marriages were arranged,

not in heaven, but by practical papas, and love had nothing to do with it.

Her cheeks felt warm, and she lifted both hands, laying them against her own soft skin the way she had imagined a man would someday do. She was still essentially ignorant of passion, despite her knowledge of the bare facts. Her fantasies were more naive than knowing, based on limpid eyes staring deeply into hers, and a generously curving male mouth that dared, ever so gently, to brush her quivering lips. But lately her body had begun to take on yearnings of its own, sweet aching feelings that came and went, as much in dreams as waking, and while she could not put a name to them, she knew instinctively that whatever she was searching for, she would not find it with the man she had seen in the parlor.

He could be as kind as he had said—and as generous— but there was no excitement in him, nothing that challenged. Nothing that called to new feelings trembling deep inside her, and promised to set them free. She had just turned nineteen! How could Papa expect her to trade in pretty pastels for a matron's somber hues and spend day after day in stifling rooms waiting for a man who bored her to tears . . . wondering where her dreams had gone?

Only that, of course, was exactly what he *did* expect, and she was just honest enough to admit, with a part of her mind at least, that every other time she had defied him, she had always been wrong. Perhaps, after all, she ought to give in. Perhaps she should swallow her pride and her fear and go to him and say: I was wrong, Papa. I am sorry, Papa. I do not want this marriage, but you are wiser than I, and I will do as you wish.

She had just started to leave when she became aware of a shadow in the yard below. Looking down, she was startled to see Simone, still wearing the same light wrap she had had on earlier. She must have come from the garden, though Lili had been so absorbed in her thoughts, she hadn't seen her at the gate. Now she watched curiously as the girl half-walked, half-skittered across the dusty rectangle toward the door.

Lili had never seen her cousin look like that before. Intrigued, she leaned forward. Simone's face was flushed, not with embarrassment, but a kind of heightened excitement, and her dark eyes glowed almost unnaturally, giv-

ing her a momentary illusion of beauty. The idea came as
a jolt, for Lili was used to thinking of Simone as plain,
and very definitely a child. But she did not look plain
now, or childlike. She looked like a woman on the way
back from an assignation with her lover.

Now, what has she been up to? Lili thought, forgetting
everything else as her cousin disappeared into the shadows at the rear of the house. It was hard to imagine what
she could have been doing, yet plainly she had been
doing something. That look on her face hadn't come
from nowhere.

Then, before she could speculate further, her eye caught
another flash of movement. Glancing back at the garden
gate, she was just in time to see the first fiery rays of
sunset catch in black-black hair.

Jean-Baptise Cavarelle. What on earth was he doing
there? She had left him more than an hour ago in the
formal parlor. He ought to have been gone long since.
Unless . . .

"Oh!"

The sound slipped out of her lips, and she was grateful
no one was there to hear. Jean-Baptiste had not been
gone all this time. He had been in the garden—with her
young cousin! Simone *had* had an assignation . . . and it
was with the man who had given *her* a betrothal ring not
an hour before!

Lili felt sick inside as she stood and looked down at
that slender, well-tailored figure until it too vanished
somewhere beyond the wall. She had thought before that
Jean-Baptiste was fond of flirting—and she hadn't been
wrong. Whether by chance or design, he had encountered Simone in the garden and practiced the art on her.

Only Simone was much too innocent to play the game
by his rules. Simone wouldn't even know it *was* a game.
She would take it seriously, and she would be hurt.

Dear heaven! The girl might be too naive to realize
what was going on, but Lili wasn't. All the color drained
out of her face as she thought of the intolerable situation
her fiancé was setting up. Poor-relation Simone could
never hope to catch a suitable husband. If she had had a
more fortunate sister, one pretty enough to wed without
a dowry, she would have gone to live with her, acting as
friend and confidante, and second mother to her children. But all she had was her cousin, and she would be

dragged along like so much excess baggage when Lili took up residence in her new household. Day after day she would be forced to remain under the same roof with this man who had already roused her passion. Life was going to be a living hell for her if he did not respond.

And it would be a constant shame and humiliation for Lili if he did.

She jumped up impulsively. Whatever conflicting thoughts had been whirling around in her brain, one thing was suddenly clear. She could not accept this insufferable situation. If her wayward suitor had kept his roving eye to himself and not brought it blatantly, tastelessly into her own home, she might have given up her objections and agreed to marry him. But this behavior she would not tolerate! If she couldn't get Papa to listen to reason—and every instinct warned her she couldn't—then she had to get away from there!

She raced up the stairs, already planning what she was going to wear and how she was going to slip out of the house. Thank heaven, it was Mardi Gras night, and her presence wouldn't be expected at the supper table. She didn't know where she was going once she got outside; she didn't have the vaguest notion what she wanted to do. She didn't even know if she was running away, or just staying out a few hours—a few days—in a desperate attempt to alarm Papa into reconsidering his decision. She only knew that she had to get out of there before the walls closed in and started screaming at her.

8

The street was dark. Heavy clouds were massing in the sky, and a smell of moisture hinted at rain before morning. A misty halo showed around the oil lamp at the corner, giving just enough light so Lili could make out where she was going. The wind was coming from the river, light but winter-cold, and she slipped into a shop doorway to adjust the long black cloak and voluminous hood that covered her from head to foot.

The evening's festivities had already begun. Here and there, light spilled out of open doors onto the wooden *banquettes*, and strains of music drifted eerily through the darkness. A procession of merrymakers passed, on foot, for Creoles rarely used carriages on the rutted streets after dark. Slaves came first, bearing lanterns; then maids with boxes containing black kid pumps and frilly petticoats and dainty satin slippers; then finally the family, the ladies bunched together, chatting and laughing, the gentlemen following in high leather boots, each with his own light making hazy circles in the darkness. They sounded so gay, Lili could not help feeling a pang of envy. If only Papa had waited one more day! At least she would have had this last enchanted Mardi Gras to remember.

The revelers were gone and the street empty again before she stepped out of the shadows. Surprisingly, she had had no trouble getting away from the house, or finding something suitable to wear. She had hated giving up the glamorous silver gown that had looked so pretty on her. But it was much too conspicuous for what she had in mind, and with only one brief backward glance, she had traded costumes with an astonished mulatto serv-

ing girl. Now, under the folds of her cloak she was clad in
deep wine red, almost as conspicuous in its own way, for
the old-fashioned garment followed every contour of her
body, down to the waist and beyond, fitting as snugly as
if it had been made to her measure. Her hair had been
darkened as planned, with some vague thought of disguise, and flame-colored feathers twined among jet-black
curls. All she had kept was the mask, though she had
taken it off the stick and sewn on black satin ribbons.

Or rather M'mère had sewn them on for her. To Lili's
amazement, the woman had neither bristled nor scolded
when she came in the room by accident and saw what her
young charge was doing. Nor had she threatened to go
running to Don Andrés with the tale. Her lips set in a
taut line, clearly disapproving, but not once protesting,
she had helped put the finishing touches on the costume,
and even gone downstairs first to make sure no one was
in the lower hallway when Lili slipped away.

Of all the things that could have happened, that was
the most unexpected . . . and the most ominous. If even
M'mère, who would have gotten off her deathbed to
chaperone Lili to a party—M'mère, who had cau-
tioned her not to get out of sight on the levee in broad
daylight!—was willing to let her go out alone, then this
marriage Papa had planned must be even worse than she
had imagined.

The night seemed to have grown darker, and she was
almost at the next corner when she realized she had
nearly overtaken another party of revelers. At first glance
they seemed much the same as the last; then she noticed
that except for slaves in front and behind with lanterns,
they were all women. Fascinated, she realized they must
be heading for the old ballroom on Condé Street, where
a quadroon ball had been advertised for that evening.

Lili quickened her pace, trying to catch up, but they
were moving faster too, and the rickety planks of the
banquette had a nasty way of catching her toes. The
quadroon balls had begun less than three years ago, but
they were already infamous. There wasn't a woman of
any age who didn't gossip about them when she was
alone with her friends. Gatherings had long been held for
the *gens de couleur libres*, of course—New Orleans was a
vibrant, festive city with a long tradition of music and
dancing—and no one had minded if the rakish son of a

well-to-do planter slipped in occasionally to join the fun.
But it was only in the fall of 1805 that one Auguste
Tessier had come up with the inspired idea of holding
dances to which only white gentlemen and free women of
color would be admitted.

Not that the balls were mere diversions. Lili knew, like
everyone else, that they were marketplaces where merchandise was displayed and purchased. There, young gentlemen went in search of the dusky beauties they installed
in little houses on the ramparts, and dissatisfied husbands
found an extra bit of spice for their lives. There, the most
attractive and fairest descendants of slaves were brought
by ambitious mothers for much the same reason Papa
had sent her into the formal salon this afternoon. Only
for the quadroons there could be no question of marriage
—or even lasting relationships. The most they could expect was small cottages that might or might not be theirs
to keep, financial settlements worked out meticulously in
advance, and the hope that their children would be educated at Montpelier in France.

Creole women were outraged, of course, not so much
because of the immorality as because the quadroon balls
were supposed to be livelier and more fun than their own.
Many a fashionable soiree was empty of men by midnight, as bachelors and husbands alike deserted for more
rousing affairs. Occasionally, if it was a *bal masque*, one
of the more daring wives was rumored to have put on a
mask herself and gone to Condé Street to see if her
husband was there. And more than once, she was rumored to have found him!

Lili crossed at the corner, lifting her skirt as she picked
her way through patches of mud, though fortunately the
street was relatively dry for that time of year. It was not
just white ladies who sneaked into quadroon balls; dark-
skinned women had been taking advantage of masquerades for years. Sometimes an especially bold mistress
ventured into a man's house with the wife right there.
And sometimes the man actually encouraged it! Hadn't
her own father done just that—with the beautiful Chartreuse?

Lili burned with humiliation as she recalled the occasion. It hadn't been quite the same thing. Her mother
had been dead for some time, and there had been no
wife in the house to shame, but she had hated it all the

same. She had been just a child at the time, peeking through an upstairs railing at the foyer below, but she had known instantly who the new arrival was. Kitchen gossip had long linked Don Andrés with a stunning quadroon beauty—and even masked, with long gloves hiding dark skin, it had been obvious that this was a woman sure of her beauty . . . and her welcome.

It still made Lili's stomach churn to think of it. It was not that she minded her father's seeking feminine companionship. She had understood even then that there had been something missing in his relationship with her mother, and it was not unnatural that he might turn to another woman. But she had minded terribly the look of pleasure and amusement on his face as he stepped across the entry hall to greet her. It had seemed somehow a desecration of the memory of that pale, sad figure in the garden, and Lili had cried herself sick for days. She had refused to talk about it, but Don Andrés must have guessed, or perhaps M'mère had told him, for that was the last time a formal gathering had ever been held in his home.

The lights of the old Condé Street Ballroom came into view, and Lili realized suddenly, without even knowing it, that she had been heading that way all the time. She had planned, when she left home, to seek hospitality at one of the plantations along the Mississippi. Now it occurred to her that that would be foolish, even dangerous. The nearest house was hours away, and it was too dark to wander alone along the riverbank. She was going to have to find someplace to go until she could come up with a new idea. And where better than this, with music drawing a lively crowd, and everyone masked and anonymous?

Besides, if Chartreuse could push her way into a ball at the Santana house, why shouldn't she do the same thing here?

She had nearly reached the entrance when she saw a man at the door. At first she thought he was there to make sure only women with at least an ivory tinge to their skin and gentlemen with white faces went in. Then she saw that he was collecting money, and her heart sank. She had never carried cash in her life! All the merchants knew Papa and marked down whatever she wanted to his account. It hadn't even occurred to her, in her haste to get away, that she might need money tonight.

Helplessly she cast her eyes about, looking for something that might tell her what to do. The party she had been following were already inside; only an echo of laughter remained as they shook off their mantles and headed toward the cloakroom. A coach had just pulled up, and a man was getting out, a tall fair-haired giant with wide shoulders and a rather clumsily cut greatcoat that came to his ankles. Lili did not particularly like his looks. There was something stupid, and rather mean, in the square jaw and close-set eyes. But the doorkeeper was beginning to look at her strangely, and she had to do something.

"Excuse me," she said, in French first, then switched to English when he did not respond. "You seem to be a kind person—and I am in need of kindness now."

"Well . . . little lady." The eyes that turned toward her were pale and insolent, running up and down her figure with an appraisal that would have been unspeakably rude if Lili hadn't remembered suddenly what he was doing there. And what he no doubt thought *she* was doing! "Never let it be said that Mordecai Braddock is not kind. Especially with a lady as lovely as this."

Lili blushed, as much from the realization of where she was as the lewd insinuation in his tone. "I'm afraid I rushed off without the money for my entrance," she said hastily. "I know it was careless, but it's such a long way back . . . and so cold tonight. I hoped you might be good enough to lend it to me. If you give me your address, I'll see that you get it back."

"Well, now, maybe that won't be necessary." He caught hold of her arm, trying to turn her around toward the light. "Let's just have a look at you, missy. Maybe neither one of us will have to go inside. We might just settle things right here."

Lili twisted away, laughing for the benefit of the doorman, who had sidled closer, no doubt to hear what they were saying, if he understood English. "But that would be spoiling the fun, sir." Pulling the mask out from under her cloak, she held it up to her face. "Have you forgotten? This is Mardi Gras night. You can't see my face until the stroke of midnight. It would be bad luck."

"Bad luck? I've never heard anything like that." The man's voice was fuzzy, as if he had already had a considerable amount to drink, and the American twang in it set

Lili's teeth on edge. She had just made up the superstition that very minute, but she sensed he was too ignorant to realize it.

"Well, it's true. My grandmother told me herself. You may have heard of her? Vévé Valcouré—the great voodoo queen? She calls zombies out of her caldron in deserted clearings at midnight, and knows all about what happens if you break a superstition." It was the kind of nonsense Americans usually lapped up, but if this man was impressed, it did not show. Indeed, he was beginning to look bored. Lili, realizing that her fate that evening might well depend on him, hastened to change her tactics. "You needn't fear I'm going to elude you once we get inside, sir. When the time is right, I promise . . . we will be together. And I will reveal my face only to you."

He seemed to hesitate, but there was just enough intimacy in her manner to persuade him to dip his hand into his pocket. "I take that as a promise, missy," he said, holding up two fingers to the doorman, who apparently could not speak English after all. "And I always expect people to keep their promises."

"Oh, I intend to, Mr. . . . uh, Braddock," replied Lili, who intended no such thing at all. Any more than she anticipated repaying the paltry fifty cents he had just paid for her admission, though it hardly seemed politic to mention that now. "You'll have to write your address out for me. So I'll know where to send the money."

"I'm not worried about that." Braddock took her elbow, pinching it as he guided her past the doorkeeper and into the entry hall. Fortunately, it was not well lit, for the mask kept slipping, and he was still trying to peer at her features. "I never lend cash. And I never pay for anything in advance. I intend to get my money's worth—tonight!"

And he meant it, too, Lili thought with a rush of disgust. Of course, he had every reason to believe she had come for precisely what he was offering. But there was no need to be crude about it. "Then I'll have to make sure I don't disappoint you, won't I? But I'm afraid you're going to have to let me go . . . just for a moment. I want to leave my cloak and—"

"Hold it right there, little lady." The words were sharp enough to bring Lili to a stop. "I didn't pay your admission to have you run away when we got inside. Get one of the maids to take care of your cloak. That's what the black biddies are here for."

"And go into the ballroom with my hair mussed?" Lili retorted, ignoring the deliberate cruelty of that last comment, when he had to think she was at least partly black herself. "I have to scrape the mud from my shoes, sir, and repair the damage the wind has done. Surely you wouldn't deny me that? No lady would show herself in public in such a state of disarray. Besides, a short time alone with a mirror, and I think you'll be pleased with the result."

She put a hint of seduction in her tone, the kind she used when she wanted to flirt with a man. She was relieved to feel the pressure ease on her arm.

"Very well, but I'll be waiting when you come out. Right here by the door. I won't be going anywhere."

Lili brushed aside the unpleasant implication in those words as she stepped gratefully into the cluttered rectangular cloakroom. She didn't even wonder how she was going to slip past him later; it was enough just to get away for a few minutes. If she had deliberately planned it, she couldn't have chosen a worse protector, though she still didn't see what else she could have done. With the doorman eyeing her like that, she'd had to come up with something, and quickly!

The dance had been going on for some time. Everyone seemed to have arrived, for the cloakroom was nearly empty, smelling of powder and cheap perfume and muddy woolen outer garments that looked as if they had never been cleaned. There were only three women besides the elderly black attendant, who was busying herself in one corner. As Lili entered, two of them brushed past her on the way out. Going over to the far wall, she turned her back while she juggled awkwardly with the hooded mantle, which she finally managed to get off without dropping her mask. When she tried to tie the raven feathers in place, however, she was less successful, for the satin ribbons were slippery, and the ends had been trimmed too short.

She was still struggling with them when she heard a voice from behind.

"Here, let me help you, honey."

"Oh . . . yes, thank you." Lili was happy to relinquish the task, and in no time at all the top part of her face was securely hidden. Only a teasing glimpse of full red lips showed beneath.

"There you go. Say . . ." The girl's voice was admiring as Lili turned around. "Ain't that fancy? Real bird feathers, and all done up nice'n elegant. You must be doin' good, you can afford somethin' like that."

"It was . . . a present," Lili murmured, smiling in spite of herself. The girl had not put on her own mask, and her youthful features crinkled with good-natured humor. She was light-complexioned, though not at all pretty, almost homely in fact, with coarse features and a distinct gap showing between her teeth.

"Well, if you've got someone to give you presents like that, I guess I know what brought *you* here. The music—and the dancin'."

"And the need to escape," Lili said impulsively, the words slipping out before she realized what she was saying. To her dismay, the girl commented on it at once.

"You came to escape?"

"Uh, yes . . . for the moment." Luckily it was a gaffe that could be mended. "There's a perfectly dreadful man out there. In the hallway. Just on the other side of the door. He attached himself to me when I came in, and he swears he's going to wait until I show up again! I don't suppose there's another way out of here."

"Why, sure, honey." The girl's laughter, like her voice, was warm and husky. "You ain't the first to have problems with a pesky male. See that alcove over there? With the little door that looks like a closet? Well, it is—that's where the maids keep their mops'n such—but there's another door on the other side, leadin' to the back hall. Jest follow it to the end, it'll take you right to the ballroom."

"Thanks . . ." Lili hesitated, tempted for a second to spill out all the fear and doubt in her heart and beg this kind, friendly girl for help. Without a penny in her pocket and nowhere to go when the dance ended, she was going to have to trust someone, and it certainly wasn't going to be that boor in the hall! But just as she wavered, the door opened and a flurry of red and gold appeared, a dancer whose hem had been torn and was in urgent need of repair. The attendant had disappeared somewhere, and Lili's newfound friend went over to see if she could help.

And just as well! Lili thought as she made her way through the closet and down the dim corridor in back. Another minute, and heaven knows what she might have done! Maybe the girl was as trustworthy as she seemed, maybe not—it was hard to know for sure. Anyway, she had the whole evening to sort through other plans and make up her mind. If she couldn't think of something better before the ball was over, then perhaps she *would* decide to take a chance. But she had plenty of time until then.

The lights of the ballroom were almost uncomfortably bright after the dingy hallway, and Lili stood for a moment at the edge of the dance floor, slightly bewildered by the dizzying swirl of color and movement. The music was much louder here, a boisterous blare that made soirees in elegant town homes tame by comparison, and the sound of laughter and conversation ebbed and swelled until it seemed to fill the hall.

She had never been inside the Condé Street Ballroom before, though she had always been curious about it. Now, as she looked around, she was aware of a vague sense of disappointment. The building had been erected sixteen years ago, the first in New Orleans to be devoted exclusively to dancing, and those of her friends who attended the subscription balls—which had almost always been held here until the more fashionable St. Philip opened last month—swore it was *the* most magnificent hall in the world. Plainly, they were either taking advantage of her ignorance, or they had gone to wild lengths to convince themselves. Most likely the latter, Lili thought, amused. There was something about Creole pride that had a way of glossing over such trivialities as the truth.

Certainly the building itself was not prepossessing. It was a plain wooden structure, somewhat worse for the wear, perhaps sixty or seventy feet long, though she had never been good at judging distances. Along the sides, arranged in gradually ascending tiers, were the benches where M'mère would no doubt have taken her place among the mothers and chaperones, and from which her eyes would have followed Lili every second of the time to make sure no improprieties took place. That the dark-skinned mamas seated there now were every bit as particular was quickly apparent, for while they took the opportunity to joke and gossip with each other, their attention

never left the floor, and Lili could almost hear their
tongues clicking disapprovingly against the roofs of their
mouths.

The young ladies for whom the ball had been arranged
rested between gallopades and cotillions in rows of chairs
that ran along the edge of the dance floor. In the narrow
space behind them, gentlemen formed a line, chatting
with each other while they eyed potential partners or
waited their turn in the sets. Some were in costume,
showing wonderfully bizarre flights of imagination; others, though masked, had chosen formal garb, with fancy-
stitched boots and superbly cut coats of the finest French
silk. But costumed or not, nearly every one carried a
colchemarde, or sword cane, tapering from a wide hilt to
a rapier-fine tip, for dueling was a favorite pastime, indulged in by young and old alike, and it was a rare ball
that did not end with at least one hot-tempered confrontation in the moonlit garden of St. Antoine's.

The room itself might be plain, but the dancers made
up for it in spirit, and the music had a vitality Lili had
never encountered before. The musicians were black, as
they would have been at a society function, and they
played much the same tunes, but she had never looked
over at them there and seen sweat glistening on their
faces or soaking the open collars of their shirts. She
couldn't help remembering all those whispered rumors—
how the quadroon balls were supposed to be so much
more exciting than their own—and in spite of herself, she
had to agree. If she were a man, with any degree of
choice, she would leave those stuffy *haut monde* salons
too, and come to a place like this!

The music stopped, and the dance floor emptied, colors whirling and blending as everyone headed for the
sidelines. The men, in their burgundies and plums, bottle-
greens and blues, formed a rich backdrop for the more
vivid hues of the ladies. No white for these quadroon
beauties, or the pastels of a proper Creole *demoiselle*.
Their dresses were a tropical rainbow, hot and intense,
strong yellow against orange flame, heliotrope and vermilion and violet setting off hair that was sometimes
fairer than Lili's, with even more auburn in its depths,
sometimes as deep and luxuriant as the raven-black she
had affected tonight. She had been afraid, when she
looked in her mirror, that she was going to feel out of

place, for while the red in her dress was relatively dark, the fabric had a shimmery way of catching and reflecting the light. Now she knew she *would* stand out . . . but because her outfit was more subtle than the others.

There was only a brief pause between dances. The musicians no sooner put down their instruments than they picked them up again, and Lili found herself claimed by a dark-haired man in an odd costume with a rather fiendish mask, though whether he was supposed to be a beast or a satyr, she had no idea. She had intended to sit out the first few dances in the section reserved for the chaperones, but the music had such an infectious beat, her toes were already tapping and it was impossible to resist.

Besides, she thought with a glance at the door, Mr. Braddock with the odd first name—probably from the Bible, Americans had a silly propensity for things like that—was apparently still waiting, but she had the feeling his patience would not hold out much longer. He was perfectly capable of barging into the cloakroom with no regard for the fact that ladies might be swooning from faintness or making adjustments in their petticoats. And when he did, and discovered she was gone, she would just as soon be out in the middle of the floor.

A *contre-danse* was forming, seven sets that filled up most of the room, and as Lili focused on the first strains of music, she was relieved to hear that it was French. Papa, with his peculiar bias, had insisted that she learn the English dances too, but they were never performed at the parties she went to, and she was not as sure of them as she would have liked. When the Americans had taken over the territory, they had been mildly astonished to find that one of the major points of contention was not politics at all, but dancing—though Lili, with Creole blood flowing through her veins, had understood perfectly, and had only contempt for them because they did not. Music was a part of the Louisiana soul. Being forced to do clumsy jigs and laughable reels was as much an affront as having a foreign language shoved down throats that were used to the more liquid sound of French, and Creole gentlemen had been quick to defend Creole honor with riots that started in the ballrooms but ended under the dueling oaks outside.

And the Americans, with their stuffy ethics and emphasis on "good sense" and "hard work," had found it frivolous to the extreme, though Lili noticed they were ready enough to join in the fight once it got started.

The music rose, throbbing and echoing through the wood-walled room, and Lili felt as if her feet were moving of their own accord as she lost herself in the rhythm of the dance. She was glad once again that it was a *contre-danse française*, for the tempo was much faster than she was used to, and she would have had trouble if she had had to stop and think. Time seemed to float by, like the wisps of silk and velvet that caught her eye as gentlemen and ladies executed their steps opposite each other, and it was almost a shock when everything stopped and the soles of her slippers came to earth again.

She was laughing as she swept a low curtsy to her partner, who bowed deeply in return, lingering for a moment as if he wanted to stay but was too much of a gentleman to force himself on her. Hadn't she thought, when she came inside, that all she wanted was to forget her troubles for a while? What was there about music that drew one out of oneself . . . and took everything else in the world away?

She had nearly reached the edge of the dance floor when she became aware suddenly that someone was watching her. A strangely familiar sensation prickled down her spine, almost like this morning on the levee, when she had let her imagination run away with her. Only this time she knew she was not making it up. This time, when she turned around, she knew she would see someone there.

She was not wrong.

He was standing on the other side of the room in a crowd of people, but the minute her eye picked him out, everything else faded away, like the background in a half-finished painting. She had never seen anyone like him, and almost in spite of herself, she found it impossible to tear her gaze from that compelling figure. He was taller than average, but it was not height alone that drew her to him, or the breadth of strong male shoulders straining the taut fabric of his jacket, or even his hair, which was a light brown with sun-bleached streaks that caught the lamplight like fluid gold. It was his manner, his supreme confidence, the almost arrogant way he held himself a little apart from the others.

There were men around him, so close they nearly brushed

his sleeve, but somehow he seemed apart from them, as if an infinity separated his body from theirs. As if they could stretch out both hands and still not touch him.

Lili's lips parted and she let out a little gasp, not even aware she had made the sound. There was something about him that was vaguely menacing, though not altogether in an unpleasant way. He was dressed simply but starkly, with a better instinct for drama than all those costumed revelers. Fine black kerseymere had been cut to follow the lines of legs that were long and slim but firmly muscled, and she couldn't help noticing, with a certain tantalizing immodesty, that his thighs and hips looked attractively lean too. He was not wearing a waistcoat, and the white silk shirt that showed beneath a severe black jacket was sleek and flowingly elegant.

Black and white, she thought, fascinated. Utter simplicity against a backdrop of gaudy color. She was watching him much too openly, even from the concealment of artfully arranged raven feathers—she knew she ought to tear her eyes away—but everything in her longed to hold on. This was the kind of man who had never come into her life before, a man whose very presence was somehow intriguing and dangerous, and her heart ached suddenly to think she was never going to see him again.

Security, that was what she would have if Papa got his way. A nice cozy future with a comfortable, steady, dull, dull man . . . and she would never come to a place like this again. And never look at a man who gave off vibrations of danger, just standing across the room.

He must have sensed what she was thinking, for he smiled, or half-smiled, a mocking, challenging look. Against her will, Lili felt her eyes drawn to his face. He was masked, like everyone else, but his was a small black domino, concealing little, and she was conscious of a generously curving, sensual mouth and rugged masculine jaw bronzed by the sun. Even in shadow, she could feel the intensity of his eyes—they looked so dark from a distance—as he let them play frankly up and down every softly defined curve of her body.

Warm, tingling sensations ran through every place those bold eyes touched, and she was dimly aware of something deep inside, some unnamed yearning she had sensed only in dreams and was still too inexperienced to recognize. Just for a second, everything else vanished, and she let herself stand there and dare to look at him . . . and imagine all the things that might be hers if only she had the courage to reach out and grasp them. Then his expression changed, growing even bolder, amused, and a rush of horror flooded over her as she realized what she was doing.

She had thought before that this man was dangerous. Now she was sure of it. And she was standing in the middle of a quadroon ball, dressed like a quadroon herself, meeting his eyes with her own. And issuing what he no doubt considered an invitation.

Color rose to her cheeks. She was grateful for the mask that hid them as she hastily averted her gaze, trying to pretend she had only been glancing his way out of idle curiosity and was not the least bit interested.

Too late, she realized it was not going to work. The last thing she was conscious of as she stared down at the rounded toes of burgundy kid slippers was a tall male figure starting across the empty dance floor.

And he was heading straight for her.

9

Lili kept her eyes primly averted, but her heart beat wildly as she felt him drawing nearer. The last thing she needed now was another complication in her life. Every instinct in her body told her she ought to whirl around, while she still could, and seek refuge in the cloakroom. But it was hard when he was so exciting it sent shivers through her just thinking about those dark, mocking eyes and the way they had been watching her.

Then he was there, and it was too late.

"I believe you have reserved this dance for me, *mademoiselle*."

His voice was low and resonant, with sensual undertones that went beyond the harmless courtesy of his words. Lili felt herself responding, as she knew he had intended.

"I think, *monsieur*, you must be mistaken." She dared to look up at last. His eyes seemed even darker now, half-hidden in the shadows of his mask. An intense blue-violet filled with glimmers of laughter he made no effort to conceal. "I do not recall reserving anything for you. Or even speaking to you, for that matter."

"Ah, but you did. From across the room. You spoke with those fascinating golden eyes . . . and I answered. And we were both aware of it."

"Were we, *monsieur*?" In spite of herself, Lili couldn't help being intrigued. The man *was* dangerous. She knew more than ever that she ought to turn and run away, but she had never met anyone like him before. Or felt the way he was making her feel, all quivery inside. "I spoke to you indeed? And what did I say, pray tell?"

He paused a fraction of a second, and she flushed

again as she sensed the racy thoughts that must be running through his mind. But his answer, when it came, was almost deliberately casual.

"You said, 'I would like to dance with you, *monsieur*.' And I said, 'It would be my pleasure' . . . and here I am." He was reaching out as he spoke, his hand on her arm, a light pressure that sent rushes of heat flooding through her, making her self-conscious, but somehow not as cautious as she ought to have felt. She was not even aware that the music had started up again, yet there it was, slow this time, and melodic, with a strangely haunting sweetness, and he was drawing her into his arms.

It was a second before she realized what the band was playing. Not the impersonal rhythm of a quadrille or *contre-danse*, which she could with some decency have danced with a stranger, but the distinctly personal three-quarters beat of a waltz.

"I . . . I'm sorry," she murmured awkwardly, pulling back as far as he would let her. "I couldn't possibly dance a waltz with you. It . . . it wouldn't be proper!"

"Proper?"

His rugged features contorted with amusement, and Lili, reminded abruptly of where she was, felt an unpleasant warmth seeping out from under her mask. She hated blushing! She almost never blushed, but this man had turned her crimson three times in as many minutes. And she knew he had not failed to notice.

"There is propriety, even here," she ventured, covering her confusion with what she hoped sounded like indignation. It was true that women came to Condé Street looking for illicit liaisons, but they were hardly ladies of the evening. All those mamas and sharp-eyed chaperones wouldn't be here if they were. "Poverty and need don't preclude a sense of decency . . . though that might be hard for a 'gentleman' like you to understand. Or do you think a girl cannot be decent because she has a dusky tone to her skin?"

"What I think—actually, what I *see*—is that there is just the slightest hint of amber beneath that provocative pink in your neck. Many Creole women are far 'duskier.' And I think you want to dance with me as much as I want to dance with you. Propriety has nothing to do with it."

Strong arms urged her close, and Lili felt her resistance

ebbing away. He was right. She did want to dance—she had never wanted anything so much in her life. And after all, what harm would it do? They were in the middle of a crowded hall; there were people all around. Even if he did get the wrong idea, he could hardly do anything about it. But . . .

"I . . . I'm afraid I don't know how! I've never learned to waltz."

"I see." He was almost laughing now. She could sense it in that tightly controlled mouth, the highlights in his deep violet eyes. "It's easy to learn. Much easier than the *contre-danse,* which you executed to perfection. Come, let me teach you."

"I don't know . . ." Lili held back one last second. Then the music seemed to flow through her, beckoning with subtle sweetness, and there was the tempting warmth of his body, closer than she had ever been to any man except Papa in her life. Colors swirled past, other women in the arms of other handsome men, and she let go of the last of her hesitance, allowing him to move her out into the center of the floor.

"You see, I told you it was easy," he said, steering her with such deftness it would have been impossible to make a misstep. "It's a simple rhythm, one-two-three, one-two-three, one-two-three . . . just like that. Around and around . . . and around again. But I don't think I have to teach you at all, *mademoiselle.* You're doing wonderfully well."

It was not, in fact, she who was doing anything at all, but he who was so smooth and skillful that even the clumsiest dancer would have been able to follow. It *was* a simple rhythm. All she had to do was count the same one-two-three herself—taking care not to move her lips, so he wouldn't see the effort—and everything else came by itself. There was something so natural, being in his arms like that, something that felt so right, she almost forgot how dangerous he had seemed before, and how afraid she had been to let him come close.

"I think you have it, *mademoiselle.*" His voice broke into the music, startling her out of her complacency. "Here . . . one-two-three, one-two-three . . . that's it. But I can't keep on calling you *mademoiselle.* It's too formal. Surely you have a name."

"I do," she admitted, looking pointedly at his left

shoulder, which, now that she noticed, was even more powerful than it had seemed from a distance.

"Do you suppose I could persuade you to tell me what it is?"

"Oh . . . I think not." Lili smiled to herself. Though it made her nervous, she couldn't help enjoying the way the conversation was going. Like all the daring flirtations she had imagined so many times, but never had a chance to experience. "But you are right. '*Mademoiselle*' is much too formal. And dreadfully boring. Why don't you call me . . . Fleur-de-Lys?"

She could not have said herself where it came from. Maybe she just liked the romantic sound, or maybe her boldness was reminding her of the scandalous boldness that had ruined every woman of the family, from Lili-Ange on down. Whatever it was, it seemed to amuse him.

"A pretty image, but it doesn't suit you. Fleur-de-Lys . . . the flower of the lily. No, I do not see you as a lily flower at all."

"No?"

"Lilies are slender and graceful, I admit. And you *are* delightfully slim—and quite exceptionally graceful when you dance. But they're pallid things. Not interesting at all. And the bearded irises that are sometimes called by that name are much too cool with their deep blues and purples. I should have thought you'd take the rose as your symbol. A wild rose perhaps, spilling over open meadows, vivid red, like the red dress you're wearing . . . and the red highlights beneath whatever that is you've done to your hair."

"A rose?" She felt herself falter, and she had to count again to pick up the steps. Could he possibly have sensed the way she felt about roses? Were they so in tune, she and this stranger, that he guessed the secrets of her heart? Or was it just a coincidence? "Why did you pick that, of all flowers? The rose?"

"I told you," he said gently, "because it suits you. Much more so then the coolly aloof *fleur-de-lys*."

Something in his voice seemed to draw her, against her will, and Lili could not keep from looking up again, though she had promised herself she would not. His face was as she had remembered, intensely, almost overpoweringly masculine, with a virility that matched the lean, muscular power of his body. Strong, straight lines accented his nose and squared his jaw, framing a mouth that held both hardness and softness, as if it had been made to curse and kiss and tease . . . as he was teasing now. He whirled her around again, faster this time, and for a brief, tantalizing second, light flashed on eyes that were not violet at all, but a deep, pure blue.

Blue eyes, and a black half-mask . . . and a country lane somewhere in France where a highwayman had stolen more than gold on a cold afternoon nearly a century before. The Fleurie curse . . . Lili felt herself shiver, and she tried to pull away, but his arms were too tight. Just when she had forgotten about it, if only for a moment, the curse had come back to torment one last Fleurie woman. There was absolutely no doubt in her mind that that was what was happening now. That this was her Roger de Courbet Montaigne, the man she was destined to see and love . . . and she would be as deeply hurt as Lili-Ange, all those many years ago.

Tears blurred her eyes, shimmering like a halo around his head as she continued to stare up at him. She would love this man forever, she thought sadly. Or perhaps "love" was too strong a word. She would be fascinated forever by the excitement and sheer physical magnetism she had barely had a chance to glimpse. She would go home again; she realized that now. It had been only an impetuous gesture, running away when there was no place to run. She would go home and marry the suitor Papa had chosen for her, and sit across the dinner table from him—and lie beside him in his bed—and dream of a man she had met only once, who had changed her heart forever.

And she didn't even know what he looked like.

She continued to scan his face, memorizing every visible detail, not caring anymore if he noticed, or what he thought. He had a strong, forceful chin—only, other men had forceful chins too—and a wide, curving mouth. And blue eyes she would know anywhere. But he could pass her on the street, steering his horse around a puddle, and if those eyes were averted, she might not even recognize him.

"You asked my name," she said softly. "But you never mentioned yours. Don't you think that's unfair?"

"No more unfair than you, pretty Fleur-de-Lys. I did ask, as I recall, and you refused to tell me."

"So you're not going to answer me?"

"It's only a name, after all. One-two-three, one-two-three—you are forgetting the dance. Names are merely a convenience. I could have one name one day and another the next, and I'd be the same person underneath. Here, I'll tell you what. Why don't you choose a name for me yourself? What would you like?"

"I think . . ." Lili smiled up at him, enjoying the moment suddenly, not quite knowing why. "I think I shall call you Roger."

He stiffened slightly, as if for some reason it had caught him off guard. "No, I've never cared for 'Roger.' It's much too pedestrian. Surely you can come up with something a little more . . . distinctive."

"Like 'Hercule,' you mean, or 'Claude-Honoré'—or 'Jean-Baptiste.' " Her feet lost the beat for a second as that unexpected name slipped out, no doubt because it had been on her mind so much these past several hours. But Jean-Baptiste Cavarelle and the unwelcome engagement that had been thrust upon her were the last things she wanted to think about now. "Or 'Algernon.' You have to admit, there's nothing common about 'Algernon.' "

"Nothing very dashing either," he replied dryly. "I am crushed, *mademoiselle*, to discover that you think of me in such unglamorous terms. I had hoped for something adventurous and daring, with a touch of the sinister perhaps—to show I was a man of the world. 'El Diablo,' now. That has a virile ring. Or 'the Buccaneer.' "

" 'The Buccaneer'?" Lili tossed her head coyly, relishing the freedom she had never felt before and sensed she would never be allowed again. "That's right up there with 'the Blaze'—as ridiculous a name as I've ever heard, for all that the man seems to have taken New Orleans by storm. No doubt he thought it up himself, too . . . or had some lady choose it for him at a ball. I can't imagine anything sillier . . . unless it's 'the Buccaneer.' "

"Can't you indeed?" The man's mouth twisted with amusement as he watched her from behind his mask. Her pose was more obvious than she realized, making her look not sophisticated, but charmingly vulnerable, and he drew her a little closer, taking care not to let her catch him at it. "And what, my enchanting Fleur-de-Lys, is wrong with 'the Buccaneer'?"

"For one thing, it doesn't go with a black broadcloth coat cut by an expensive tailor. And besides, it isn't even French."

"Neither is 'Algernon'," he reminded her, counting pointedly under his breath, which wasn't fair, since she had been doing quite well except for that one stumble a moment ago. "Anyone can wear a black coat, even a well-tailored one. Surely a successful pirate—or a buccaneer—could afford the best. And why does the name have to be French?"

Why, indeed? The subtle nearness of his body was a distinct distraction, and Lili found it hard to concentrate. They had been speaking French, and his accent was flawless, without so much as a hint of Creole, but many people spoke flawless French. Why, he could even be an American, educated in Europe, though that hardly seemed likely. Despite his rather forward behavior—which, heaven knew, might be natural in a place like this—his manners were impeccable.

"French just . . . sounds better. And in French it would have to be *boucanier,* which is much too much like *boucanière,*—a place where you smoke fish. No, I think I *will* call you Roger. Despite the fact that you don't like it."

"Or perhaps *because* I don't?"

He spun her around, weaving a nimble course between the other dancers, out into the center of the floor, which they had to themselves for the moment. His movements were so easy, so sure, they took her breath away, though she was not too light-headed to notice that he had pointedly avoided giving his name. Of course, she had done the same thing—but that was because she hadn't wanted him to know she was Lili Santana, a rich man's daughter playing at being an octoroon. Did he, too, have something to hide?

"I think, after all, you might be a buccaneer. You're right. Anyone with enough money or credit can find a good tailor. And anyone who goes to such lengths to make himself sound mysterious must definitely be a privateer. Or a smuggler."

"Like the Blaze?"

There was a faint edge to his voice, and just for a

second Lili felt her mouth go dry, though she knew she was being foolish. "Surely you don't expect me to believe *you* are the Blaze? The man who has single-handedly taken over sidewalk gossip for the last several weeks? Is that your vanity talking, Monsieur le Boucanier? Or do you feel safe deluding young ladies as long as you have a mask to hide behind?"

"Perhaps it's you who feel safe . . . or want to. Tell me, is it really so impossible? You said it yourself just now. I *am* masked. You don't know the first thing about me, a stranger you have never seen before, just as I don't know the first thing about you. I could be anyone."

"Even the infamous Blaze?"

"*Especially* the infamous Blaze." He grinned rakishly, enjoying her reaction. She was trying so hard to be worldly. Sometimes she almost succeeded; other times, she looked like what she plainly was, a young girl out unchaperoned for the first time, longing to be womanly but not quite sure she dared. "Tell me," he said, deliberately lowering his voice, "do you find it difficult, picturing me as a man who exists on the razor edge of danger? A man who lives by his wits and has a certain—how shall I put it?—disregard for the law? A man who sees what he wants . . . and dares to take it?"

And a man who kills when he has to?

Lili shivered slightly as she recalled the stories that had been going around about acts the Blaze had committed while robbing wayfarers on the Natchez Trace. She looked up, scanning his mouth, his firm, hard jaw . . . the glint of his eyes through the narrow slits in the mask. Yes, she could picture him as a man who was capable of anything, including murder, if he was driven to it.

Strangely, the thought did not frighten her. If anything, it added to his forbidden appeal. Perhaps because she did not truly believe he was an outlaw—perhaps because it was all fantasy anyhow, with the masks and the music and the sense of unreality that seemed to be everywhere.

Or perhaps it was simply that she knew the dance was going to come to an end and she would leave his arms, never see him again.

The music seemed to change, slowing subtly, and he grew bolder, tightening his hold until she could almost

feel her bosom against the strong expanse of his chest.
Too close. She knew they were dancing much too close.
All the old women on the sidelines would have their
heads together, their eyes on her as they whispered,
shocked, to each other, but she did not care. All she had
were these few last minutes, these few *sweet* minutes, and
the dream would be over forever.

If only Papa had chosen a man like this for her!

Her hand closed around his, unconsciously holding on.
If only she could have walked into the formal front parlor
and seen a tall, strong, mysterious stranger with mocking
eyes and lips that hinted at things she could only guess.
But Papa, of course, would never have chosen anyone of
the sort. She had known that even before she crossed the
threshold and stepped into the room. She could indeed
picture this man as an adventurer or a privateer—even a
notorious smuggler like the Blaze. What she couldn't
picture was a banker or a prosperous merchant or the
elder son of some fine old Creole family. And a banker
or an outstanding member of the Creole community was
all Papa would ever have considered.

She let herself sway closer, not even thinking anymore
how scandalous it must look as she felt their bodies move
in rhythm with each other. The music took over, and she
let it, following the bittersweet mood of the first sensuous
waltz she had ever danced in her life—and the last.
Waltzes were not done in her circle. Papa was conservative, and she sensed that Jean-Baptiste Cavarelle was conservative, and she would never feel the blood flowing in
quite the same way through her veins again.

Heaven help her, she was just nineteen, and unless she
counted these few stolen moments in a stranger's arms,
she had never been in love, and never would be. She
would lead a comfortable, sheltered, safe, safe life, and
all the excitement and passion would be centered in one
brief memory.

She was not even aware of the moment they stopped.
She knew only that suddenly she was at the side of the
room—how had he maneuvered her there without her
knowing?—and they were standing a little apart from the
others. And he was staring deeply into her eyes with an
expression her body seemed to understand but her mind
could not grasp.

"What . . . what are we doing here?" She heard a quaver in her voice, and she had the sudden idiotic feeling she sounded like a little girl. "Why did you stop?"

"It is customary to stop, I believe, when the music ends. Even with a waltz."

"Oh." Lili stared at him, too stunned for a moment to take in what he was saying. "I must have been concentrating . . . I mean, counting. So I wouldn't make a mistake. I wasn't paying attention to—"

"You weren't pay attention to anything," he cut in with a pointedly wicked look. "And you aren't counting. You were thinking about the way our hands were touching . . . and how well our bodies moved together. Just as I was thinking about that provocative little shiver you give every time I look down at you."

"No!" Lili drew back, trying but unable to tear her eyes away. It was almost as if he had her under a spell. "You are too bold, *monsieur*—even for a flirtation. I must excuse myself now."

"I think not." He reached out and caught her by the wrist, sensing the contradictions in her feelings, and holding her back. The confusion that was written all over her face was touching. She looked so young at that moment, his heart ached for her. But there was longing in her gaze too, and longing was a temptation a man of strength and passion was not likely to run from. "You're not going to get away so easily. Surely you didn't think, my sweet enchantress, that I would be satisfied with one dance and a quick good-bye."

"I . . . I don't know what you mean. It's very hot in here, and I feel faint. I would like to go to the cloakroom and lie down for a few minutes."

"Would you?" She looked even more confused now, bewitching his senses, and he wondered suddenly what would happen if he drew her closer, daring her to respond. But there was panic in her eyes, and he realized he had frightened her. "All right, go if you must . . . for now. But we have just begun with each other, Fleur-de-Lys. This dance was an overture, not a finale. I think you know that as well as I."

He let go of her arm, but to his surprise, she did not move. Once again he was aware of an almost irresistible urge to reach out and take hold of her. To do something shocking, scandalous, just to see how she would react.

But then she was gone, her skirt in her hands, and he could only watch as she hurried, not toward the main entryway, but somewhere at the back of the hall. She had nearly reached what appeared to be a rear corridor when he saw her hesitate. Just for a second he thought she was going to turn back—he *hoped* she would turn, and he could will her to stay with his eyes—but she only paused briefly and vanished into the shadows.

She had been even more captivating than he had expected. He leaned against the back of an unoccupied chair, his eyes still riveted on the spot where he had last seen her. All fire and boldness one minute, timid the next, like a frightened fawn scampering out of sight. He could have sworn, he had been so sure—until the moment he laid eyes on her—that this was the exact opposite of everything he wanted. Child-women had never appealed to him. The innocence and virginity that swelled other men's egos had always seemed a bore, and he had chosen feminine companions with an eye toward maturity. Ladies who were experienced enough to know what they were doing, and sophisticated enough not to weep when it was over.

Now, for the first time it occurred to him that awakening innocence might have an enchantment all its own . . . and a patient teacher might be rewarded with undreamed-of delights.

God, she was a beauty. He was surprised at the throbbing in his groin as he continued to stare at the darkened opening in the rear of the hall. When he had asked her to dance, he had thought he knew exactly what he was doing. A mild flirtation to turn her head, that was all—his would still be clear as he escorted her back to the sidelines. Now he found himself going over every detail of that brief encounter in his mind. The way her mouth parted when she laughed. The curve of her lower lip, jutting out slightly, a little-girl pout, but smoldering somehow, a year or a month—or a day—from being worldly. The creamy texture of her neck as it disappeared into the elusive modesty of high-cut silk.

And that dress . . .

He caught himself stepping forward, and he realized he

had been about to go after her. The dress had been perfectly chosen, dark enough not to be flashy, but a far cry from the bland pastels of Creole balls. And it fit superbly. Her face might hold reminders of childhood, but her body was the body of a woman. It was the kind of body that had always appealed to him, full-breasted but not top-heavy, slim waist melting into slim hips and long, long legs . . . the kind of body a man could enjoy. The aching in his loins intensified as he thought again of the lessons she had to learn of love, and what it would be like to teach her.

He might have followed through on the impulse and gone after her—and the devil take the consternation in the cloakroom!—had not an acquaintance come over to him at just that moment. She was a tall woman, almost languidly elegant, in expensive blue-green silk with a lace-edged half-mask that gave her an air of ageless mystery.

"Well, Chartreuse, you're looking lovely tonight."

Lili could not have said herself what prompted her to return to the cloakroom the way she had come instead of going by the proper entrance. Perhaps just because her feet had followed that path before, or perhaps because it was a few steps closer, and she had to get away from the eyes that were boring into her back.

What could she have been thinking of? Behaving that way with a perfect stranger. A stranger who had to think she was something she wasn't.

She leaned against the wall, so giddy for a second she couldn't go on. She had almost stopped, just as she reached the hallway. It had taken all her strength to keep from turning and meeting the challenge in those startlingly blue eyes. And if she had, she couldn't even imagine what might have happened.

She started to move again, her legs so shaky it was hard to walk. The hall was dim after the bright lights of the ballroom, and shadows seemed to brood, looming up frighteningly, though she knew they were only mops and old rags heaped against the wall. It was the hardest thing she had ever done, fetching her cloak and slipping away without so much as a last glance at the man who, in a few short minutes, had already become part of her life. But lingering would only give him an excuse to wait for her outside. It was one thing to flirt with a stranger in a crowded dance hall, however outrageously—to let her body cling so tantalizingly it was almost touching his—but to allow him to waylay her someplace where there were no lights and no people would be sheer insanity.

And yet, if she dared . . .

She reached the end of the hall and slipped through the door, leaving it half-open so she could see where she was going. If only she dared to turn around and go back—to seek the one man who had the power to quicken her pulse—and take the romance and excitement he offered without calculating the consequences. But she was not Lili-Ange after all, or La Fleur, or gentle, trusting Cybèle. She was cautious and sensible and would do what was expected . . . even if it broke her heart. The Fleurie curse, it seemed, would not claim its last victim.

And she had the terrible feeling she was going to spend every last day of her life regretting it.

The door at the far end of the small storage room seemed to be jammed. Lili shook it impatiently, trying to shove it open. It wasn't locked, for the knob turned easily, but she could move it only a scant inch or so and then it stopped. It's almost as if someone has put something in front of it, she thought, surprised. A heavy couch or a bureau. Only she hadn't seen any bureaus in the alcove. And the only couch was on the other wall.

She pounded several times, but she was not surprised when no one responded. A gallopade had started in the main hall, the music so rousing she could barely hear the loud rapping herself. Besides, the attendant hardly seemed the conscientious type, and there was probably no one around. All she could do was go back down the long passage and out through the ballroom . . . and hope that the man in the black domino had forgotten all about her and was dancing with someone else.

And probably he was, she thought ruefully. He didn't seem the sort to brood over any woman for long.

She had just stepped back into hall when she caught a flicker of motion in the shadows. A silhouette appeared suddenly against the light that flooded in from the end of the corridor. A tall man with broad shoulders and something bright, like gold, in his hair.

Her masked stranger?

Lili's heart stopped beating for an instant, though

whether from fear or anticipation, she did not know. Then he moved, and a ray of light picked out the last features in the world she wanted to see.

Mordecai Braddock. She had completely forgotten about him. But plainly he had not forgotten her.

And the look on his face warned her he was not pleased with the trick she had played on him.

10

"Why, Mr. Braddock, what a surprise." Lili tried to sound cool as she stepped away from the door, but she couldn't help thinking how isolated the hall was, and how completely the sound of the band drowned out everything else. "You're the last person in the world I'd expect to find in a dingy back corridor. With a bunch of brooms and old scrub pails!"

"I might have said the same about you, missy." He had turned, drenching his face in shadow, but his voice was menacing enough to make Lili wish she had gone the long way round to the cloakroom. "I didn't think little ladies in ball gowns sought out places like this."

"Didn't you, indeed? But this *is* a passage leading to the room where ladies leave their wraps and occasionally go to rest between dances."

"A *back* passage," Braddock reminded her gruffly, "which you seem to use with surprising frequency. If I didn't know better, I'd say you were avoiding somebody. And here I thought we had an arrangement."

"The only arrangement I can recall," Lili replied much more calmly than she felt, "was to meet again sometime during the evening." He had moved forward just slightly, and she was unpleasantly conscious of the gaping door behind her. Her fingers itched to reach out and pull it shut, but she didn't want to call attention to it. "As we could have done, no doubt . . . and still will if you don't persist in behaving boorishly."

"Boorishly?" His voice was surprisingly high as he let out a short staccato laugh. "That wasn't what you said before, when you wanted something from me. How was it you referred to me then? Oh, yes—a kind man. Or don't you recall?"

"I do recall, very clearly. And I'm wondering now if I wasn't mistaken. Perhaps it was wrong to trust you."

"Trust has nothing to do with it," he said in that same nasal tone that had annoyed her before. "It was convenience. You wanted money, and I gave it to you. As a favor. It's time you learned: favors have a price."

"A *price*?" Lili gaped at him, too disgusted for a moment even to be cautious. "How very typical, Mr. Braddock. But then, what should I expect? You Americans are all alike. Money is the only thing that matters. Everything has a price—even a 'favor' of fifty cents. And courtesy, of course, and good breeding don't exist."

"I suppose you think you're better? Well, let me tell you, missy, you're not. You tease a man for fifty cents— and God knows what else—and it amuses you not to pay him back. I've been in this city over a year, and there isn't a Creole 'lady,' for all her courtesy and soft-spoken manners, who'll so much as nod to me on the street, much less invite me into her house. They act as if I were dirt under their feet. But you're not even Creole, are you? You're a little black bitch with the same airs as her betters."

Lili could almost feel the anger emanating from him, wounded pride fed by months of snubs, and she realized with a rush of horror that he was aching to take it out on someone. She had to find a way to get past the spot where his bulky form was blocking the end of the hall. She didn't dare even think about what might happen if he guessed she couldn't go back.

"That is quite enough, sir. There may be color in my skin, but I am a human being, and what you call 'airs,' we call self-respect and dignity. Now, step aside and let me pass. Or—"

"Or what, missy? Do you really think you can push past me if I don't want you to?"

"Maybe not." It was all she could do not to let him see that she had begun to tremble. It was going to be dangerous, trying to bluff him down, but that was the only thing that might work. "I can always turn around and go the other way. I may not be as big as you, but I'm fast. I could be through the closet back there and into the cloakroom before you were halfway—"

"No you couldn't," he cut in quietly. "The door to the cloakroom is jammed shut, as I'm sure you already know. There's a heavy couch in front of it."

"There's a . . . what?" Lili stared, stunned, as she realized suddenly what must have happened. Hadn't she thought before that there was only one couch in the alcove . . . on the other wall! She could almost see him, red-faced and blustering as he stormed into the cloakroom to find no one there. Not even the lax attendant who was off somewhere doing heaven knows what on her own. "You mean you planned this? You pushed the couch across the door just so this would happen? But how did you know I'd come back the same way?"

"I didn't. It was only a possibility, but it seems to have been a good one."

The blare of the band had stopped, and the silence in the corridor was almost ominous. His face was enveloped in shadow, but hints of light caught his eyes, and his teeth gleamed almost unnaturally white, giving him a feral look.

Scream, a little voice in the back of her mind urged. Scream for help while it's quiet and someone will hear! This is a man who can be ruthless and brutal. It would be madness to stand here and match wits with him!

But screaming meant the embarrassment of everyone gathering around, fussing over her. Her mask would be sure to come off, and what if some sharp-eyed male recognized her as the daughter of an old family friend? Dear heaven! She couldn't bear the thought of all the gossip that would be going around for months after that. Especially when Braddock claimed—as he was certain to—that she had lured him there with teasing promises and done all sorts of unspeakable things before turning capricious and calling for help.

She had wanted something that would make Jean-Baptiste Cavarelle change his mind about marrying her. But she hadn't wanted to ruin her reputation forever!

"I'll scream if I have to," she said, startled at how harsh her voice sounded in the stillness. "If you don't let me go, I swear I will! And when people come, I . . . I'll tell them you tried to rape me!"

"Oh, I don't think you'll do that." Braddock started forward, but slowly, as if he were afraid she'd bolt, though he had to know she couldn't. "If you wanted to scream, you'd have done it already. And anyhow, it's too late."

As if to emphasize his words, the music began again, even louder, more rollicking than before, and Lili's heart sank as she realized he was right. It *was* too late. She could scream her lungs out, and in all that noise, no one would notice.

"What . . . what are you going to do?"

Fear was sharp in her voice now. She knew he could hear it. He was even closer, and she could almost feel the moist heat of his body. His breath reeked of whiskey. "I'm going to do just what you think, so when you claim later, if you dare, that I raped you, you'll be telling the truth. Only I don't think you *will* dare. Who'd believe a trollop like you?"

The sound of his laughter was ugly and brittle. Terrified, Lili made a rush to get past him. But he had anticipated the move and was ready for her. Rough hands grasped her shoulders, jerking her back, pinning her painfully against the wall.

"Please," she whispered helplessly. It was the wrong move, she knew it was—he would never respond to tears and entreaties—but she had to try, somehow, to get him to relent. "Please . . . I'm sorry if I seemed to be playing games before. It's all part of Mardi Gras night . . . I didn't mean any harm. Please don't hurt me."

"*Please—?*" The laughter was gone from his voice. Something hard and infinitely more frightening had taken its place. "How prettily you beg . . . when you want something. You pulled that fluttery feminine routine on me once already—remember? I told you then I was going to get my money's worth. And I am."

"Oh, *mon Dieu* . . . " Lili squirmed frantically, twisting this way and that in a futile attempt to get out of his viselike grasp. But the hands on her shoulders were much too strong. She heard something tear—her bodice, she realized with sickening dismay. Then his chest was against hers, and he had one knee jammed between her legs, pressing her, hard, to the wall.

"All right, bitch, time to keep your promise." Braddock reached up, ripping off the mask rudely, leaving her cheeks exposed to the hot blast of his breath. "Let's get a look at your face."

The hall was dim, but his eyes must have adjusted, for she heard a startled grunt.

"So, you're not as dark as you seemed, hey, blackie? You've got a white daddy somewhere, that's for sure. You could pass for white yourself. Hell, I'll bet you *have* passed for white. Or maybe . . ." He gave her a long slow look. One hand slid up to her chin, forcing her head back while the other fanned out on her chest, fingers touching but not responding to the soft curves of her cleavage. "Maybe you're a little white girl after all. Now, wouldn't that be something? A curious Creole virgin, out to see a piece of the world . . . and getting more than she bargained for."

"Well, and what if I am?" Lili said boldly, grasping at the truth and wishing desperately she had had the sense to scream before. "If I really am one of those Creole ladies you hate so much, then I've got a father who'd die to defend my honor—and a half-dozen hot-blooded brothers! You're going to be in a lot of trouble if you hurt me."

"Only if you decide to mention what happened. And if you really are one of those *ladies*"—he drawled out the word with deliberate emphasis—"then all the more reason to hold your tongue. Pretty Creoles who've lost their virtue don't catch husbands, now, do they? And scandal is the kiss of death for a fine old Creole family."

"You bastard!" Lili wrenched herself out of his grip, managing to work free for a split second. But even though she was no longer against the wall, she still couldn't move, much less get away. She had one last glimpse of his face, bloated, not with lust but anger, as he caught her up again, pushing her back into the storage closet, kicking the door savagely shut behind them.

The darkness was sudden and terrifying. Lili had thought, an instant before, that nothing in the world could be as intimidating as the leering rage on his face. Now she realized with an awful, sick feeling that it was even worse not being able to see him. Not having a clue what he was going to do next in that terrible black vacuum.

His hands had already begun to move, ravishing her everywhere at once, not seductively, but cruelly, as if he wanted to leave bruises, and she could feel him trying to force her down on the floor. She was fighting irrationally now, fighting with every last ounce of her strength, and she knew she was going to lose.

"No!" she cried out suddenly, summoning all her strength for one last bid for help. She should have screamed before, and she hadn't. But she was going to scream now, and keep on screaming as long as there was a breath left in her body. Maybe there *was* someone in the cloakroom alcove—the odds were against it, but maybe there was—and maybe that someone was lying on the very couch he had pushed against the door.

Braddock must have sensed what she was thinking, or perhaps he heard the feeble beginning of a cry, for suddenly his hand was over her mouth, choking off the air. Lili clawed frantically, but she could not get him to budge. His skin was so smooth, it felt slimy—she could almost taste it against her lips—and the stench of liquor was nauseating. She continued to resist, kicking as hard as she could, scratching, trying to bite his hand, but nothing did any good. And the only sounds she could manage were a few muffled moans in the back of her throat.

It was all over. She knew that as she felt him shove her roughly down. The bitterness of defeat mingled with anger and fear until she thought she was going to drown in it. It was all over, except for the last token struggle they both knew would not make any difference, and she was overwhelmed with a sense of shame and horror.

Before, she had fought to get away; then she had fought because his hand was tight on her mouth and she was afraid she would suffocate. Now she half-hoped he *would* kill her. Anything to spare her that last brutal humiliation.

She was so caught up in her own despair, she barely heard the harsh scraping sound that came from somewhere nearby. Only when her ears picked up a sharp "hunhh!" bursting out of his lips did she realize something had happened. A second later, the repulsive pressure of his body was gone.

Her eyes must have been closed, without her even realizing, for when she looked up, light was streaming into the small closet from the open cloakroom door. A darkly powerful masculine figure was bent over Braddock, jerking him up by the back of his jacket, pulling him roughly away from her.

The man she had danced with in the hall.

Lili could have wept with relief as she stumbled awkwardly to her feet and stared into the candlelit cloakroom. Plainly, her rescuer was wasting no time. Although Braddock had half a head on him and was easily twenty pounds heavier, she had no fears about the outcome of the fight. He had already downed his sniveling opponent once, and barely waited until the man rose groggily from his knees before slamming an angry fist into his face again, sending him sprawling back on the ground.

A blind, instinctive rage seemed to have hold of him—Lili could sense it in every rippling muscle in that strong, tense body—and she had the feeling he would have killed the man had he not turned at just that moment and seen her cowering in the doorway. He hesitated briefly, studying her with eyes that were unreadable behind the mask he was still wearing. But the worst of his anger seemed to have abated, for when he glanced back, he only watched contemptuously while Braddock half-crawled, half-staggered into the front hallway.

Lili swayed weakly against the doorframe. She did not know whether she was relieved or disappointed that the swine had escaped with only that one short beating, though she sensed that both his eyes had been thoroughly blacked and his jaw would be sore for days. She had never hated anyone as much as she hated him during those long minutes he had terrorized her, and she would have loved nothing as much as seeing him get exactly what he deserved. But to have a man killed right in front of her was a horrifying thought, no matter how vile he was.

It was a moment before she collected herself enough to look at the man who had so gallantly come to her aid. When she did, she saw that he was standing in the center of the alcove. Light from candles in the wall sconces reflected off eyes that were every bit as blue as she had remembered. The rage was almost gone from them now, and the concern as well, for he had taken in her condition with one brief glance, which had told him she was frightened but unharmed.

In their place was an expression she could not understand . . . until she recalled suddenly that her dress had been badly torn and she was standing in front of him half-naked.

"Oh!"

She reached up clumsily, clutching ripped fragments of fabric and trying futilely to close them across her breast. The gesture accomplished little, for while she did manage to protect her cleavage, soft, rounded shoulders were still exposed to his gaze. She was keenly aware of how pale they must look as silken hair cascaded over them, red streaks showing underneath, where the black coloring had not reached.

His eyes went from surprise to amusement to something she was not sure she wanted to understand as he took it all in, boldly, leisurely, making no attempt to conceal his impudence.

If he had come out with a lewd comment to match the plainly interested look in his eye, Lili would not have been surprised, nor could she have truly blamed him, considering where she was—and the odd circumstances in which she had been found in a back closet with a man whose intentions were clearly not honorable. But her embarrassment must have moved him, or perhaps, despite that deliberate boldness, he was inherently a gentleman, for suddenly he had covered the distance between them and a velvet-lined cloak was around her shoulders, comforting and warm, for while the room was close, her dress was saturated with perspiration and she had begun to shiver.

It was only after the closet door had been securely closed and the couch was safely back on the side wall, where it belonged, that he turned to her again.

The expression on his face had eased, and even with the shadows of the mask, Lili could see that his eyes were laughing.

"You have a rather unconventional way of entering and leaving the cloakroom, I must say. Are you always so contrary?"

To her surprise, Lili found herself fighting the impulse to giggle—and losing. It was, in fact, the most conventional thing in the world, if one was trying to avoid an unwanted suitor. But there hardly seemed any point, going into that now.

"Not always—only when it serves my purpose. But how on earth did you know I was in trouble? Did you see that dreadful man come into the corridor after me?"

"No. I was conversing with someone else at the time.

Fortunately, she did—and was suspicious enough to mention it to me. Naturally, I sent her into the cloakroom to make sure you were all right. When she came back and told me you weren't there, I decided to check on you. And a damned good thing, too." He stepped forward, half-covering the space between them. Lili was conscious suddenly of the emptiness of the room, and the subdued strains of a waltz which seemed to come from far away. "Whatever possessed you to go through that back hall by yourself? If I hadn't heard a faint sound from behind the closet door, I might never have thought to look in there. Didn't it occur to you you could be putting yourself in danger?"

Lili looked away, avoided those vivid, penetrating eyes. He had been conversing with someone, he said—a woman. Just seconds after she had left him! She hated herself for the little pang that caught at her heart, but she couldn't help it. Just seconds after the dance that meant the world to her, he had forgotten she existed. He wouldn't even have come to her rescue if that other woman hadn't noticed she was in trouble.

She was only a diversion for him. One of any number of pleasant diversions he would no doubt experience that evening.

"Of course it didn't," she said rather snappily. "If I had thought it was going to be dangerous, I wouldn't have gone that way."

"But what made you do it?" he persisted. "Were you so anxious to get away from me?"

"Perhaps," Lili admitted, a little startled at her own honesty. But then, it was easier being honest with someone she was never going to see again. "You are very unsettling, you know."

"Why, pretty Fleur-de-Lys? Because I insist on telling the truth? Because I won't pretend that this is a nice little social occasion and all I have for you are nice little 'social' feelings? Do you find the truth unsettling?"

"No," she murmured, confused, though she was not quite sure why. "Not if it *is* the truth."

"Ah? You think I have been lying?" There was a wry edge to his voice, and she had the feeling he was smiling. But when she looked up, his lips had not moved. "Well, perhaps you're right. Perhaps I have . . . evaded the truth. Just a bit."

"Just a bit?"

"Did I tell you," he said softly, "that when you looked across the room, your eyes were saying, '*Monsieur*, I would like you to dance with me?' That was a lie. What they were really saying was, '*Monsieur*, I would like you to do this.'"

He was so close, his face could have been no more than an inch or two from hers. Lili thought for an instant he was going to take her in his arms, and her heart nearly stopped beating. But he only reached up with both hands and laid his thumbs on her eyelids, gently easing them shut.

His lips were so light she could barely feel them as he touched first one closed lid, then the other.

"'I would like you to do this, *monsieur*,'" he repeated huskily, "'and *this* . . .'"

And then he was kissing her, so softly at first she half-thought she was imagining it, and her body swelled with longings she had barely sensed in dreams before. So perfect, was all she had time to think—so wonderfully, sweetly perfect—and then his mouth was changing, growing harder, hungrier, insolently demanding responses it would be unthinkable to give.

Lili felt a surge of betrayal. He had tricked her! He had made her think he was going to woo her tenderly, romantically, offering all the pretty illusions her heart craved. And all the time he had only been concerned with his own coarse male desires! She raised her arms to push him back, to show him just what she thought of his disgusting behavior. But somehow they were around his neck instead, twining, not rejecting, and she was holding onto him, clinging, while the warmth of his mouth spread through her body, all the way down to her toes.

She felt his hands move, felt the cloak slip from her shoulders. His fingers were on her breast, easing back the tattered shreds of her torn gown. She knew she ought to do something—she had to push him back!—but his mouth was still on hers, so hard she couldn't breathe, and his arms were iron-strong. And her own arms would not obey her commands, but persisted in coiling around him, as if they were separate entities, with wills of their own.

She had been so frightened before . . . and so relieved when he saved her from that monster. Her emotions had run the gamut, and she was too drained to fight anymore, or even to think. He had caught her off guard in that one sweet moment of tenderness, and the dormant passions he had awakened would never be stilled again.

Her body arched toward him instinctively, pressing against him until their two forms seemed to merge into one. She felt him respond, felt male hardness thrusting into her belly, and she knew what it meant, but she could not bring herself to draw back. At last she realized what she had been too naive to understand when she saw him watching her across the room. She wanted this man— wanted him more than she had ever wanted anything in her life, more than she would ever want anything again— and she had no will to resist.

Her acquiescence seemed to embolden him, for his hands took new liberties. Her cloak was on the floor now, the last protection of her bodice gone, and he had claimed her breast, caressing it roughly, urgently, all the while his mouth still toyed with hers. Lili's lips parted. She was not even aware of it until his tongue was darting into her, arrogantly, possessively, not asking first if she wanted or was ready for him, and she felt the complete-ness of his mastery. No matter what happened, no matter whom she was forced to marry, or lie beside in bed, she would belong to this man and this man only as long as she lived.

She was never to know—later she could not even guess— where that seething passion might have carried them had not the sound of voices broken rudely into their con-sciousness.

He heard them first. His arms had already released her before she was even aware of them, and suddenly the cloak was off the ground and around her shoulders again. Giggles and fragments of conversations were already au-dible; someone might slip around the corner and into the alcove at any moment, but still he lingered, as if tempting fate.

"You can't stay," Lili whispered, terrified for one sec-ond that he was going to draw her into his arms again . . . and that she would let him.

"Can't I? Because it would be scandalous if we were caught? But I am not the least afraid of scandal, *petite*— are you?" Then, seeing the look on her face, he laughed again and headed for the door to the storage closet.

"Very well, I will leave—if you insist. But do not think you've seen the last of me. I told you before. This is only the beginning for us . . . the sweet opening prologue. The final act has yet to be written."

He blew her a kiss from the doorway, half-teasing, half-daring, and disappeared into the shadowy clutter of pails and brooms behind him.

Dazed, Lili could only stand there and stare at the blank, empty wall, even after he had gone. Now that the door was closed, everything looked exactly as it had before. As if nothing had happened. If it weren't for red marks where his hands had held her so tightly—and the fact that her skin was tingling—she might almost have believed he had never been there at all.

But her skin *was* tingling, and he had been there . . . and nothing in her life would ever be the same again. Lili sank down on the couch, feeling suddenly so weak she was afraid she'd collapse. The women who had come in seemed to be occupying themselves in the main part of the cloakroom, at least for the time being, but even though she couldn't see them, she was intensely aware of the lack of privacy. Wrapping the mantle tightly around her to cover her badly ripped garment, she laid her head on the back of the couch so it would look like she was resting if anyone glanced around the corner.

The smoothness of velvet surprised her bare shoulders, and she looked down to see that by some strange coincidence the cloak her rescuer had brought her was her own. It's almost, she thought, pinching her brows together, as if he knew it was mine.

But then, it was undoubtedly the most expensive cloak in the chamber. And he seemed the sort of man who would be drawn to the finer things in life . . . regardless of whom they belonged to.

She had come so close to letting him do whatever he wanted with her. Lili shivered, not altogether with horror, as she recalled the feel of his arms, strong and virile around her. The ravishing heat of his mouth, pressing relentlessly down on hers. One minute more—if those giggling, chattering women had burst into the room just one minute later—heaven knew what might have happened.

She closed her eyes, careful to keep her head turned to the wall as she savored one more time the bittersweet taste of those rugged masculine lips. She half-wished now that she had not been so sensible before. That she had stayed in the ballroom and danced every dance with him, and not given a thought to the consequences. Or gone back to the cloakroom by the proper way, and tarried just long enough to let him get outside before she did. If the first kiss had come there, catching her unaware, too naive to understand what was happening . . . or to resist . . .

Now that would never happen. Now she knew what it was like, knew how treacherously her body responded to his every urging. Now, even if she did see him again, she would be on her guard.

She had had one chance at passion. One time when her cautious heart might have let her reach out and grasp the sweet, forbidden temptation that would never be hers again.

The voices from the adjacent room grew louder, punctuated with bursts of laughter. Lili recognized one of them as the girl she had met earlier while she was struggling with her mask. How long ago that seemed now. Another lifetime, when she had been tempted to trust and ask for help. Another lifetime, filled with youth and a spirit of adventure, and she had thought all she had to do was dare and she would succeed.

But that was before she had discovered how dangerous the world could be. How easily a woman alone could be hurt by a beastly giant of a man who only wanted to use and degrade her.

Or a handsome masked stranger who wanted to use and love her.

The voices were silent now. Lili forced herself to get up, surprised to find that her muscles were stiff and aching. From the struggle with Braddock, she supposed. Or just the tension. There was no one in the other part of the room, and she took a minute in front of the mirror, adjusting the hood so it hung low over her forehead. Her mask must still be somewhere in that hideous closet where her attacker had thrown it, or in the service hall beyond. Nothing could have induced her to go back and look for it.

Petite. He had called her that just before he left her. Lili stared at her own parted lips, all that showed of her shaded face in the glass. Like Roger with Lili-Ange in the stories that had tantalized her childhood. It was just a coincidence—the nickname was a common one—but it reminded her of the Fleurie curse, and she felt cheated somehow to realize she had been wrong after all. The curse did *not* exist, at least not for her. There would not be one doomed, illicit love to punctuate the passage of her youth.

Her precautions with the hood proved unnecessary, for the front hall was empty when she reached it. Candlelight flickered, half-golden, half-shadow, in the draft from the open outer door. It would have been agonizing, loving a man, belonging to him so completely, only to be torn away. But it was even more agonizing facing the long emptiness of her life with not one dazzling passion to remember.

This is only the beginning for us, he had said. But he was wrong. The final act *had* been written . . . and played out. The curtain was down on the achingly sweet interlude that was all she would ever know of love. One brief evening, and it was over forever.

11

The rain that had threatened earlier would come down any minute. Lili could feel it in the air as she stepped through the open door and out onto the *banquette*. The man who had been collecting money was gone, and the street was dark and empty.

The wind howled. Lili put her hand up to shield her face. Even muted, the music had a haunting lilt, a waltz again, and she couldn't help wondering if her mysterious stranger had forgotten her and was dancing with someone else.

It shouldn't hurt so much, she thought—she hated herself for letting it hurt—but, oh, somehow it did!

Lowering her head against the wind, she started down the street. The darkness seemed to intensify, wrapping itself around her like a thick, invisible blanket, and she had to move slowly, for the only light came from streetlamps that were barely misty orbs in the distance.

Whatever had possessed her to think she could come out all by herself and find a solution to her problems? If she had stopped to think, even for a minute, she would have realized she had no money, no one to turn to, no place she could go. Only she *hadn't* stopped to think. She had acted impulsively, trusting blind luck to see her through.

A burst of laughter came from the dance hall, and she turned to see a party emerging. It had just begun to drizzle, and the ladies squealed and bunched together, trying to shield their hair. Lili pressed against the wall, groping for a doorway so they wouldn't see her as they passed. But they turned the other way, and she stood and watched as their lanterns swung back and forth, flickering fainter and fainter into the darkness.

It was a moment before she realized that a carriage had drawn up and was moving alongside her. Even then, she couldn't see it. She could only hear the plodding of hooves and a faint creaking of well-oiled wheels.

A *carriage*?

Her heart shot into her throat. It was a rare Creole who took anything on wheels out at night. Native New Orleanians knew their rutted streets and were loath to trust horses on them after dark.

But Mordecai Braddock, being an American, had had no compunction about pulling up in a carriage!

Lili stared into the darkness, trying to pierce it with her eyes. It took several seconds, but slowly a shape emerged, bulkier than she had expected, and squarer. Not Braddock's vehicle, then. His had been a sporty little cabriolet, tastelessly overtrimmed with too much polished metal. This was equally small, but more solid, and unrelievedly black as near as she could tell.

Then who—

She didn't have time to finish the thought. The door opened abruptly and hands came out, grasping her firmly, pulling her inside. She tried to cry out, but it happened so fast, all she could manage was a startled little "Oh!" Then she was in the closed carriage, and those same hands were slamming the door, shutting out the rest of the world. Helplessly, Lili realized that any sound she made now would be muffled by the walls and the steady *clop-clop, clop-clop* of the horses' hooves.

She turned, alarmed, wanting to face her abductor. But in the darkness she couldn't even be sure where he was. Then she heard a disconcerting murmur of laughter.

"I told you, pretty Fleur-de-Lys, this was only the beginning for us. Why do I get the feeling you didn't believe me?"

Her masked stranger! Outside, as she had imagined, and all alone—and this time there *would* be no interruptions! A cold fear rushed through Lili as she realized what she had done. It had seemed so safe, flirting with him on the dance floor, responding to his kiss in a place where nothing could happen. Safe and romantic, as long as it was fantasy and she had known that soon she would be tucked in her own bed at home.

But this wasn't fantasy. This was real. And she was at his mercy!

"What makes you think I wanted to believe you?" she said, trying to sound bolder than she felt.

He laughed again, a soft sound, directly in her ear. He must have moved closer, but still she sensed rather than saw him. "Oh, you wanted to believe, all right, my little Fleur-de-Lys . . . and I wanted you to."

"No . . ." Lili was intensely aware of her vulnerability. His hands brushed the side of her face, pushing back the hood, touching her cheek, but gently, so gently, like the first kiss that had beguiled away her inhibitions. "No, I *didn't* want to believe you! And you have no right to accost me on the street. I . . . I wasn't looking for anything like this! I just wanted . . . I wanted . . ."

"What did you want, *petite*?" He eased back a curl the rain had plastered to her forehead.

"I wanted a flirtation! That's all. Surely you can understand that? I just wanted a dance and . . . and a few flirting words!"

"Just . . . words?" Sensing her confusion, he made his voice low, suggestive. The flood of warmth that met his fingers told him she had not missed his meaning.

"All right, I wanted the kiss too. I admit it! I shouldn't have, but I did . . . and I'd be a fool to deny it. You already knew anyway—before it even happened. When I first looked across the room, remember? You told me that was what I was asking for with my eyes."

"Is *that* what I told you?" He ran his fingertips along a dainty shell-shaped ear, surprised at the hunger in his lips to follow. He had not realized he would be so conscious of quivering body warmth next to him in the darkness, of the scent of her perfume, rising heady and seductive, inflaming strong masculine senses. When he had drawn her into the carriage, he had been so sure he had everything planned out. Now . . . "Shame, shame on me. That was twice I lied to you. What you were really saying you wanted was this."

He pulled her against him forcefully, without warning, his mouth sinking onto her neck with what sounded like a groan. Lili could feel him pushing the cloak away from her shoulders, finding what was left of her bodice, ripping it impatiently aside. His hands were hard on her breasts, not gentle, but rough, bruising, calling to the same deep sensations he had aroused before. Her body surged toward him—no amount of will could hold it back—and she knew that, more than anything, she longed to let go, to surrender to the power of those arms, that mouth, that potent male body.

Desperately she tried to wrench out of his grasp, tried to move away, but in that cramped interior, there was nowhere to go.

"Oh, please . . ." she cried, half-whispering in her fear. "Please, please . . ."

"Hush, sweet," came the hoarse murmur in response. He had spread his hands out on her back. Lili was keenly conscious of the places where every finger gouged into her flesh. "Why are you fighting so hard? Foolish little girl. You know you want this as much as I."

I don't! she longed to cry out. I don't! But even as the thought flashed through her mind, she knew it was false. She *did* want the passion he was offering. Dear heaven, she wanted it with every instinct in her being!

"You're mistaken," she demurred weakly. "You're wrong."

"I am not wrong. And you're not the sweet little innocent you pretend." His hands slid up to her shoulders. He was holding her against him, so tight Lili could feel every rippling muscle in his chest. Only a thin silk shirt separated him from her naked bosom. "I sensed it before, when you enjoyed my caresses so delightfully in the cloakroom. I was sure of it a moment ago, the way your body responded. Your desires are as strong as mine, Fleur-de-Lys . . . and they are going to be satisfied. Here . . . tonight."

"No . . ." Lili gasped. She meant to say more, meant to protest, but his mouth was closing over hers, a demanding kiss that left her reeling.

There was no tenderness in him now, none of the softness that had wooed her before. Terrified, Lili realized that her struggles had angered him . . . or perhaps they excited him in some male way she didn't understand. This time, his lips were hard, arrogant, unrelenting—confident that her own lips were going to part under that savage assault. And somehow they did, instinctively, traitorously opening to him. His tongue was inside her, ravaging her thoroughly, frighteningly, yet provocatively too, and her body was swaying toward him.

With a last frantic effort she tried to summon her strength, to push him away. But he was holding her unyieldingly against him, the man-hardness of his body touching her everywhere at once, and the fire that had started in her mouth, her breast, moved downward, tinging every nerve. As though in a daze, she felt herself go limp. There was no more struggle left in her, nothing but an overwhelming sense of the powerful new emotions he had stirred, an aching sensation of something terrible and sweet that had to be assuaged.

It's going to happen, she thought helplessly. It's going to happen, and there's nothing I can do to stop it. There's nothing I *want* to do to stop it!

He felt her sudden acquiescence, and his hands left her, tearing at the front of his clothes, loosening shirt and trousers. In that brief second, a flicker of reason returned, helped along by a pothole that jolted the carriage and sent Lili sprawling against the wall.

There was just enough light for her to make out his chest, bare now, brown hair matted and glistening with sweat. His pants were opening, and something she had never seen before was coming out.

"No," she cried, suddenly horrified. "I . . . I can't let you do this!" She did want the love her body was screaming for. She wanted it with the most compelling urgency she had ever known. But not here! Not in a carriage in the street, with a man who thought she was little better than a harlot! "Don't you see? Don't you understand . . . I can't!"

"You can't, or is the word 'won't'?"

"What difference does it make? Can't or won't, I'm still going to fight as long as there's a breath in my body! What kind of man are you, forcing yourself on a woman who doesn't want you? You're . . . you're as bad as that animal who attacked me before!"

He stiffened. Lili could feel controlled rage radiating in waves from his rigid body. For an instant she was afraid she had gone too far. But instead of lashing out, he drew back, leaving her alone, as she had thought she wanted.

"So," he said slowly, letting the word slide through his lips, "you like to play games. Is this a part of the game too? To whet my appetite and spur me on?"

"Oh, no!" Lili burst out, stunned. "Truly! I never

thought . . . I didn't mean anything like *that*! It's just I . . . I've never . . ."

She stopped. How could she tell him she had never even *kissed* a man before? It would be too horribly embarrassing. Besides, he'd never believe her after the way she had behaved tonight.

". . . you've never been called to account for your actions?" His voice was harsh, mocking. The storm that had been building burst suddenly, and rain vibrated on the carriage roof, rattling the windows with fierce intensity. Strangely, it seemed to have grown lighter. Lili could almost make out his features as he stared at her with an expression she could not fathom. "You're the little virgin, is that it? Satisfying your curiosity behind a mask? Or does it amuse you, teasing a man, leading him on, watching him squirm when you pull away?"

"No . . ." she started to protest, then caught herself. The only thing that could save her now was honesty. "Well, yes . . . maybe I *was* teasing. In a way. But I never meant to hurt anyone. I just wanted . . . I wanted some fun for one night in my life!"

To her chagrin, she started to cry. Not noisily, but a stream of tears she knew had to be visible on her cheeks. All of a sudden, everything came spilling out. The unwanted marriage Papa was forcing on her. The legendary Fleurie curse, which had seemed so romantic before. The awful way she felt when she met her fiancé and realized she would never be able to love him. Even how she had traded dresses with one of the serving maids and slipped out, coming to the quadroon ball because she knew it was the liveliest party in town.

He listened quietly, not interrupting until she had finished. Then he leaned back against the far side of the carriage.

"I see," he said. "I could reproach you, but I daresay you've done that already. Here, stop making those little sniffling noises. If you really *don't* want me, you've nothing to fear. I'm not the animal you accused me of being before. I've never forced myself on a woman in my life, and I never will."

He half-turned away, leaving only his profile showing against light that flickered on the rain-spattered glass from somewhere outside. Lili sensed he was still angry, but it was an anger that seemed to be directed inward, more at himself than at her. As if he were angry, not because she had rejected him, but because he let himself want her . . . as if he knew he had been too harsh and was beginning to regret it.

Lili huddled miserably in the corner of the carriage, unable to take her eyes off him, though he didn't look her way again. She saw now why it had seemed lighter before. Lanterns dangled from either side of the carriage, illuminating, at least to some extent, the narrow lane through which they were passing.

Funny, she hadn't felt the coach stop, or even slow down, though clearly the driver had lighted them after she got in. But then, she had been much too involved to notice anything.

The carriage lurched around a corner, and a beam of light flashed through the window, giving Lili a glimpse of the man seated beside her. In spite of herself, she couldn't help being intrigued. He had called himself a "buccaneer," and certainly there was an aura of recklessness about him, which would sit well on an adventurer or soldier of fortune. But there was something else too, something she couldn't quite put her finger on, and she sensed there were facets to this man that she, in her sheltered life, would never be exposed to again.

Even seated, he looked tall, with a leanness that lent grace to his muscular body. His face, unmasked now, was rugged and intensely masculine, but there was nothing coarse about him. No rough edges Lili could detect, no bullying male ego, not even the innate arrogance she might have expected after the way he had behaved with her in the ballroom—and later. Everything about him exuded confidence, but it was the kind of confidence she had always associated with money and breeding, and she let herself imagine for a moment that he was a European prince amusing himself by exploring the city incognito in a black domino mask.

Certainly he looked like a prince. Lili studied his profile, indistinct now that the light had retreated through the window again. His features were almost classically strong, his brow high and aristocratic, his nose slightly aquiline, his jaw forceful enough to accent dramatically chiseled cheekbones and full, sensuous lips, tautly drawn now in an expression that looked as if it might turn without warning either mocking or cruel. His hair fascinated her, dark blond or light brown, it was hard to tell which, with shimmers of gold where the light touched it, curling almost boyishly on his neck.

And how could she forget the dazzling blue of his eyes as they gazed into hers in the ballroom?

Sighing, she turned to the window, hating herself for the way she was staring at him. Doubly hating herself for the warmth that ran through her veins as she did. He only wanted a brief dalliance with her, and that not very badly, if his present indifference was any indication. She was a fool even to *think* about wanting him.

And she would be twice the fool if she let him see it.

The storm seemed to have intensified. Outside, the rain was so heavy the lanterns barely gave off a feeble glow. Light filtered downward, catching globules of mud as they spattered up from the wheels, but beneath, the ground could not even be seen. The walls and roofs of passing buildings were invisible behind a curtain of water.

It was some minutes before it even occurred to Lili that she had no idea where they were. The carriage had turned and pitched and careened many times, but she had been so caught up in other things, she hadn't stopped to think that she was going to have to get out soon and find her way home.

She glanced around nervously. Her half-styled Buccaneer was still turned away, seemingly oblivious of her as he stared into the rain-drenched night. She could hardly blurt out her name and address and ask if he would see her home. He was annoyed enough as it was. But the farther they went, the more difficult it was going to be to make her way back.

"I think," she said awkwardly, "you'd better pull over and let me out."

Her voice seemed to startle him. He turned abruptly, as if he had forgotten she was there, which indeed he must have, or he would long since have signaled the driver to stop.

To her surprise, he smiled faintly.

"That wouldn't be gentlemanly, now, would it? Letting a pretty lady out by herself in the middle of a stormy night."

"Are you saying you're going to take me home?"

"Not exactly. Not the way you mean it. I am planning

on taking you home, but not *your* home. I have other
things in mind for you . . . Miss Lili Santana."

Lili gasped. "You know who I am?"

"Certainly. Your father is a prominent man. Do you
think you haven't been noticed riding in his carriage
through the streets of town? You're very distinctive-
looking. I can't believe I'd have trouble picking you out
anywhere—even hiding behind a mask of raven feathers."

"You knew all along!" Indignation rose, making Lili
forget everything else. "You knew I was pretending, and
still you treated me like . . . like a quadroon! Not gentlemanly, indeed? You were hardly a gentleman, sir, when
you took advantage of my disguise to insult me."

"To *insult* you?" He laughed. "My, my, how quick we
are to throw the blame on someone else for little tricks
we play ourselves. How could I insult you, *mademoiselle*,
when I simply took you at your word?"

Lili looked down, confused. He was right, of course. She
had pretended to be a quadroon, and he had just gone
along with it. But that hardly made it more palatable.

"You said you had . . . other things in mind for me.
What did you mean by that?"

He paused a fraction of a second.

"What do you think I meant?"

She looked up to find him staring at her. His eyes, in
the shadows, had turned almost violet again. She still
caught hints of mockery in that generous curved mouth,
and the passion that had been there before. But there
was amusement too, as if he were laughing at her. Or
wanted to laugh but had suddenly turned too kind.

"I haven't the vaguest idea," she said, trying to sound
haughty so he wouldn't see how helpless she felt. "And
after everything that has transpired tonight, I'm in no
mood for guessing! Why don't you just tell me?"

"And spoil all the fun? Very well, as you wish." His
voice turned cool, noncommittal. "As it happens, I didn't
just stumble across you at the quadroon ball. I was waiting on the street in front of your father's house when you
came out. I followed—on foot, so you wouldn't become
suspicious. The carriage was sent for later, after I found
out where you were going. Which, I might add, came as
a surprise, though not an unwelcome one. Dancing with
you was a delight."

"You *followed* me? But why?"

"I should think that would be easy enough to figure out, if you set your mind to it. Your father is an extremely wealthy man. One of the wealthiest in New Orleans. Hasn't it occurred to you that there might be a simple way to . . . persuade him to part with some of his money?"

"You mean"—Lili gaped at him in horror—"you're kidnapping me?"

"I wouldn't have put it quite that way, but yes, that's precisely what I mean." He leaned back, letting the light catch his eyes—deliberately, she sensed. "In a very short time, if everything goes the way I think it will, your papa is going to have a little less money. And I am going to have a little more."

12

Kidnapped.

Lili took a deep breath, trying desperately to fight the fear that rose up from her stomach. The wind had begun to howl, and periodic gusts sent sheets of water splaying violently against the window. She had been kidnapped, and there was nothing she could do about it. What had started as a lark had turned into the worst kind of nightmare she could imagine.

Bitterly she recalled the signs she should have noticed before. The woman he had mentioned talking with in the ballroom—she had been so jealous, but it was probably only a confederate. Maybe that was how he had arranged to send for the carriage. And the carriage itself. Hadn't she noticed, when it pulled up, that it was dark, without a single lighted lantern? Why hadn't she been suspicious?

If only she had turned and run the instant she saw it!

And yet, where could she have gone? She tried not to sigh audibly as she ran over those last telltale seconds in her mind. It had been so dark, she couldn't have made any progress—and whom could she have turned to for help? The money man was no longer at the door. And the only party to come out had gone the other way.

She sank miserably into the cushions, surprised to feel that they were thick and soft. Everything was so quiet, she might almost have been alone. Not a sound came from the interior of the carriage. From outside, she could hear the wild pelting of the rain and the slow, steady plodding of the horses' hooves. But inside, the stillness was so heavy it was oppressive.

Finally she could bear it no longer.

"What are you planning to do with me?" she asked abruptly.

She hadn't expected an answer, and she didn't get one.

"Are you sure you want to know?" he parried with something frighteningly like amusement in his tone.

"No," she said softly. "No, I'm not sure, but—"

"Then I'd suggest you not ask questions. You're going to find out soon enough anyway."

As no doubt she would. Lili turned her head grimly and stared at the glass, faintly frosted now with the warmth of their breath. He had called himself a buccaneer before, and she had laughed, thinking he meant it only to tease. Why hadn't it occurred to her that he might be telling the truth? That he might indeed be a scoundrel and a criminal? If she had had the good sense then to realize he *was* dangerous, she wouldn't be sitting here now in a closed coach with a kidnapper who might well be somewhat less than amused if Papa did not come up with the money as quickly as he wanted.

Papa . . .

Lili squirmed uneasily. Papa was indeed a wealthy man—she had always known that—but it had never occurred to her to wonder just how much money he had. Would it be a hardship for him, trying to raise whatever the Buccaneer was demanding for her return? Would he, perhaps, have to go into debt to do it? He was not young anymore. It would not be easy to recover from financial disaster at his age.

"Can he afford it?" she whispered, as much to herself as to the man in the carriage. "Will it ruin him to pay?"

She thought she sensed surprise next to her in the darkness. Then she heard an unexpectedly hearty laugh.

"You have spirit. I like that! Any other woman would be crying and pleading now, but all you're worried about is whether this is going to hurt your precious papa! Well, rest assured, I am not quite as greedy as you seem to think. Don Andrés is going to have to share his fortune with me, but I don't intend to leave him destitute."

"And after he pays you?" Lili pressed. "What then?"

She did not turn, but she had the feeling he was looking at her.

"Why do you persist in asking questions, when you have already admitted you don't want the answers?"

Why, indeed? Lili did not try to speak again as she

listened to the rain drumming on the roof and the slushy sounds the wheels made sliding through the mud. She sensed that he had not been lying. Whatever he was asking, Papa *did* have enough money to cover it and still continue to live in style. It would come out of her inheritance in the end, of course—but that would serve her right for the foolish way she had behaved. At least Papa would not have to pay with the security he had taken a lifetime to build.

Only, he would be worried. Desperately worried. If it affected his health—if anything happened to him—how could she ever forgive herself?

The carriage continued to move through the darkness, but by this time Lili had lost all sense of direction. She had no idea how long they had been riding or how far they had come, or even how fast they were going. The rain ebbed and quickened, so dense sometimes it seemed like a waterfall cascading down the window, then easing so much she almost fancied she could see out. She had a sense of something solid on one side, the levee perhaps, which would indicate they were going along the river, but it was hard to be sure.

Her eyelids were growing so heavy they kept drifting shut. She had not realized she was so tired. Her head dropped occasionally against the side of the carriage, and despite the jolting discomfort, she fell asleep. But every time she did, she dreamed of a man on a lonely country highway in a black mask with a full flowing black cloak and dazzling blue eyes. And just as she started to look up, her heart swelling with hope and love, he drew his sword and touched the tip to her throat.

She had just dozed off again when she became vaguely aware that the carriage had slowed and was turning onto a different kind of surface. A drive? Opening her eyes, she saw that the storm had nearly let up and golden lantern light was playing on a moody world of deep velvet shadows and rain-sparkling vegetation.

They had indeed pulled into a drive, a long wide drive with trees arching over from either side, and Lili sensed they were on the grounds of one of the great plantations. Or what had once been a great plantation, for the massive oaks looked as if they had not been pruned in years, and tall grasses spread between them, flattening under the wheels as they passed. Only the lightest rain was still falling, but moisture had accumulated in the thick, shad-owy branches, and she could hear it pattering in a steady plop, plop on the ground. Then, in the distance, some-thing white loomed up. A house, she guessed, though even in the darkness it had a desolate air, as if it had been abandoned years before.

The rain picked up again as they drew to a stop in front of the broad pillared veranda. Lili could hear it beating on the muddy earth as the coachman flung open the door and it became clear she was expected to get out. She was just thinking that her slippers were going to be ruined when the Buccaneer, with a surprising burst of chivalry, leapt down and caught her up in his arms, carrying her the short distance to the house,

It took no more than a few seconds, but her cloak was drenched by the time he deposited her with an easy laugh on the veranda. The front door was already open. Some-one must have heard them coming—but then, of course, they were obviously expected. Lili had the barest impres-sion of muted colors and a long, dimly lit hallway; then her abductor was ushering her inside.

The hall seemed even dimmer as she stood just across the threshold and tried with little success to shake the water off her cloak. A pair of candles hissed and sput-tered in stands on either side; beyond, the hall disap-peared into shadows somewhere at the rear of the house. The only other light came from a door that was standing open on the wall to the left. An odor of mildew perme-ated the air, blending with the wet smell of rain, and Lili sensed she had been right before. It had been a long time since anyone had lived in this house and opened the shutters to let in the sun and the air.

"Well, Stevie, what do you think? Is it going to rain all night?"

The Buccaneer laughed as he took off his cape and tossed it to a man who had been standing, unnoticed by Lili, behind the door. He was middle-aged and stockily built, with a swarthy complexion and a mean-looking scar that ran down from one ear.

"Better it rain forty day, forty night dan you risk you' fool neck in somet'ing like dis ag'in," the man called Stevie grumbled. For some reason they were speaking English, though there was more than a touch of Cajun French in his accent. "I been waitin' at dat window

mebbe two, t'ree hour now. Didn't know, we was ever
gonna see you ag'in, I 'ope to tole you."

"What, so little faith—and with Tin-Tin at the reins!
I'm surprised at you, my friend."

"Ooo-eeee." The man chuckled. "Dat boy, he drive
more lak de devil dan de devil hisse'f. Ain't but one man
can shame him, and dat's his paw."

He tossed the saturated cape to another man, who had
stepped out of the gloom at the end of the hall. Looking
around, Lili saw that there were several others, all standing at a respectable distance, half-hidden in shadow, but
making no effort to conceal the fact that they were staring at her in frank curiosity. Like Stevie, they were
dressed in dark, loosely fitting pantaloons, with cords for
belts and shirts that looked as if they had seen better
days, though she had to admit they were clean and
mended. There was an earthy roughness about them, the
look of men who had lived their lives in the bayous—
leanly perhaps, though judging by their bellies, none of
them had actually gone hungry.

And there was not a woman in the lot!

Lili's heart sank, though she knew she was being idiotic. What on earth had she expected? These were desperadoes, who had just kidnapped a woman for ransom.
They would hardly bring their wives along to cook and
keep house for them.

The two men continued to chat, but Lili barely heard
what they were saying. The lighted doorway on the left
seemed to draw her, almost compulsively, as if there
were something inside she had to see. Half in curiosity,
half with a trepidation that seemed totally irrational, she
found herself going toward it. No one noticed what she
was doing—at least no one tried to stop her—and she
stepped into the room.

The sense of apprehension, of something unpleasant,
was even more noticeable here. Not that there was any
reason for it. The room was large and gracefully proportioned, with a kind of faded elegance that made her think
of late-afternoon parties and small informal dances shimmering in candlelight. Gilt-legged chairs were lined up
self-consciously along the walls, and little ornate tables
under the windows looked as if they had belonged to
another generation, even when they had been placed
there.

The only candles now were at one end of the room beside a blazing open fire that crackled welcomingly as it cast warm ripples of light on the freshly polished wooden floor. But it was not to that cozy scene she was drawn. It was to the other, unlighted end of the room, and while she could not for the life of her have said why, she felt as if she were being pulled over to it. Just for an instant, an image flicked across her mind, a vivid picture, clear in every detail, and she almost grasped what it was. Then a cold draft blew in from the shuttered windows, and she shivered.

Why did it seem so familiar, this room? Why did she have the feeling she had seen it before?

She looked around slowly. Nothing seemed even slightly unusual. The old-fashioned chairs were upholstered in deep-green velvet, no longer as bright as they must once have been, but free from dust, as if the covers had been thrown off only hours before. They were ordinary chairs, not distinctive at all, and she could have sworn she had never seen them before. Or the tables with their bare tops that looked as if no one had rested a candle or ornament or book on them for years. The whole place had a musty, stale smell. It must have been closed up since she was a little girl. Why, then, did she have the eerie feeling that she had been there before . . . that she had stood almost in the exact same spot, feeling just as strange as she felt now?

"You recognize the room?"

She whirled, startled, to find the man who had abducted her standing in the doorway. He had removed his jacket and looked deceptively casual in a white silk shirt with open neck and long, flowing sleeves.

"No," she said warily. "Should I?"

He shrugged. "I was just curious. You were looking at everything so intently. It is a closed world, you know— the landed gentry of New Orleans and its environs. It would hardly be surprising if you'd been here before."

"Well, I haven't," Lili snapped impatiently as she went over to the fire and held out her hands. He might have the power to hold her there against her will, but he couldn't force her to stand around and exchange idle chitchat! Besides, for some strange reason, it made her uncomfortable, talking about the room.

"You should thaw out nicely in front of the fire," he

said, pointedly ignoring her sharpness. "You'd do better
to take off that wet cloak, though . . . Ah, but I forget.
You can't do that, now, can you? Considering the state
of your garments beneath."

She half-expected him to follow through with a bawdy
reminder of how her garments had gotten into such a
state. But he didn't even give her a suggestive look as he
slipped out into the hallway, speaking with someone apparently, for a low murmur of conversation reached her
ears. A minute later the man who had been at the door,
the one they called Stevie, appeared with a familiar white
shirt in his hands. Not only was the Buccaneer proving
unexpectedly chivalrous, he must be positively blue with
cold!

Stevie indicated a small screen in the corner, and Lili,
who was beginning to feel miserable in the wet velvet-
lined mantle, slipped gratefully behind it.

The shirt fit surprisingly well, or if not well, at least
comfortably. The shoulders were much too wide, and she
had to roll the sleeves up several times, but the supple
fabric felt good against her skin, though it did have a way
of caressing every curve that was more provocative than
she would have chosen under the circumstances. Fortunately the waistband of her skirt was sturdy enough to
stand on its own, and all she had to do was tear off her
bodice, tossing it in a corner with the remnants of her
chemise. When she had finished, she had a rather bizarre
but not altogether unflattering two-piece outfit.

She had expected Stevie to be waiting when she emerged
from behind the screen, but the room was empty, and
she found herself alone again. Avoiding the darkened
area, which had made her so uncomfortable before, she
went back to the warmth of the hearth. At least here that
eerie sense of *déjà vu*—of having seen this room,
experienced it before—was not so strong.

Stevie reappeared a short time later. A sharp rap on
the wall outside announced his presence; then a minute
later he bustled in, bearing a black iron caldron. An
enticing aroma of onions, seafood, and pungent red pepper followed as he carried it over to the fire.

He made a point of not looking at Lili too obviously,
though the corner of his eye did not fail to notice that the
shirt, which had seemed so masculine on its previous
wearer, was having an altogether different effect now.

Cajuns were a hot-blooded race, as spicy as the food they fancied, and as far as Stevie was concerned, no Cajun worth his salt would be oblivious of the distinctly female form that showed beneath that sensuous sheen of silk. *Mon Dieu*—who would ever have thought there were so many rounded placed on a slim *fillette* like that?

Sighing, he fastened the pot on a hook over the fire and tested to make sure it was secure. Dédé would cut his heart out and throw it to the hounds if she knew what he was thinking! And the man who brought him here had made it clear that this little one was off limits.

"*Bon appétit*," he said, grinning as he straightened up. Several missing teeth showed at the back of his mouth.

"Thank you." Lili was surprised to find herself rather liking the man. He hardly seemed the sort to be an accomplice to a kidnapper. But then, she had no idea what a kidnapper's accomplice ought to be like! "Why do they call you Stevie?" she asked impulsively.

"Well, now . . . dat's a question." He scratched his head thoughtfully with the fingers of one hand. "Mebbe 'cause it's my name?"

Lili caught the twinkle in his eye and laughed. "Fair enough. What I meant was, where did you get a name like Stevie? You sound Louisiana French, not American. It ought to be Étienne."

"American?" He guffawed loudly at the idea. "Not dat I got a t'ing ag'in 'em, mind you," he added more generously than Lili would have. "And, tell you de trut', it *is* Étienne. But my paw, he's Étienne too, and my older brot'er, 'fore he gone and die on us. Maw, she so tire callin' Étienne all de time, her, she shorten it down to Tin-Tin."

"Tin-Tin?" Lili wrinkled her nose speculatively.

He grinned again. "Good enuf fo' a boy, dey say—an' I'm too old fo' dat. Me, I don't believe it. But I got a boy o' my own, an' he's Tin-Tin now, so all dey is left fo' me is Stevie. You sop up dat gumbo wit' some o' Mama's good bread, you hear? I be back fo' de kettle later."

Lili half-wished he would stay, but she couldn't think of a way to ask as she watched him lumber across the room and out into the hall. As it turned out, she was not to be left alone for long, however. His footsteps were still echoing when she heard a faint sound at the door and looked up to see that the Buccaneer had returned.

He had changed into more rugged attire, and for all her very real fears, Lili could not quite control the quickening of her pulse as she sat in her chair by the fire and tried not to let him see how intently she was staring. The garb of the bayou suited him, though in his case it had been cut to fit with considerably more elegance. His pants were not brown, as they had seemed at first, but a deep burgundy that stretched taut across strong, lean thighs and slim masculine hips. His shirt was the color of homespun, but of a much richer fabric, as loose and flowing as the one he had been wearing before. A deep slit down the front displayed a tangle of dark curls that contrasted intriguingly with the golden streaks in his hair.

It was a casual outfit, but there was nothing simple about it, and Lili couldn't help noticing that it was much more expensive than one would expect from a common criminal. And it had been tailored to show off the hard lines and rippling muscles of a powerful male physique to perfection.

"You must be hungry," he said as he came over to join her at the fire. "I see Stevie brought in the gumbo. It was prepared by his wife, Dédé. I think you'll find her an excellent cook. Here, allow me to help you."

He leaned over, picking up a sturdy brown bowl from a pile Lili had not noticed on the hearth. So casual, she thought—as if nothing had happened! As if he weren't a kidnapper at all. And she his helpless victim!

"No, thank you," she replied without thinking what she was saying. "I'm not the least bit hungry. I don't want anything to eat."

"No?" He gave her a mildly questioning look, but set the bowl back on the hearth beside a cloth-covered wicker basket that was giving off a faint aroma of freshly baked bread. "You really ought to take something. It was a long, cold ride, and you must have been soaked to the skin on the way in. Perhaps a cup of tea?"

"All right, tea then . . . yes, tea would be fine."

She watched with what she hoped was a disinterested air as he went out into the hall again. The smells coming from the caldron were even more enticing now, and she could hear her stomach rumbling. She would have given almost anything for a big earthenware bowl filled to the brim with gumbo, and a crusty chunk of French bread to dip into the sauce. Anything except admitting to him that she wanted it!

He was back a minute later, so the tea must have been prepared and waiting. He poured a cup and handed it to her, placing the pot on the hearth to keep it warm as he sat down again. Lili noticed that he didn't take a cup himself, but at least he hadn't brought a bottle of whiskey, which she supposed was a good sign. She had heard that men sometimes lost all sense of reason when they drank, though she had been too sheltered to see it herself. And the last thing she needed now was to have to deal with that.

She wrapped her fingers around the cup, enjoying the warmth as she took a sip of the sweetened liquid. It was warming on the inside too, and she felt a little better as she leaned back and looked at him in the firelight.

"You did warn me," she said softly. "I should have listened."

His face eased in the flickering rays. Little lines of laughter crinkled at the corners of his eyes. "Warned you what, *petite?*"

"That you lived on the razor edge of danger, with a certain 'disregard' for the law. Remember? You said I ought to call you the Buccaneer."

"And *you* said it was a foolish name. As bad as the Blaze, which, as I recall, you considered just this side of preposterous."

"Not this side at all," Lili bantered, forgetting for a second who he was and where they were. "It *is* preposterous. I suppose the man thought he could combine 'The Blade,' which is a popular term for 'highwayman,' with the intensity of a fire. That's the only reason I can think of for coming up with anything so silly."

He shrugged nonchalantly. "Unless it's simply his name."

"Oh, of course! No doubt his mother leaned over the cradle and looked into that little wrinkly red face and said: 'Obviously this lad is going to be an infamous outlaw. I shall give him a suitable name. 'Blaze Jones,' that's probably it. Or maybe 'The Blaze Jones'—first, middle, and last, all lined up to give him a good start in a life of crime."

"I didn't mean it quite that way," he said, laughing as he settled back in the chair. Spots of color had begun to show in her cheeks, which had been much too pale be-

fore, and he found himself enjoying the unexpected burst
of spirit. "Though your idea is much better than my
mundane suggestion that 'Blaze' might be his last name,
or perhaps a family name used in the middle. 'The Blaze
Jones'—that has rather a dashing air. And I like the
touch of the doting mama bending over the cradle and
seeing a little highwayman in his baby bonnet."

"And what did *your* mama see," Lili said suddenly,
"when she bent over the cradle and looked at you? Did
she see the kind of man who would kidnap an innocent
girl and scare her half to death by holding her against her
will?"

The words were a jesting challenge, he could see
that—an attempt to keep up her bravado. But the fear
that was just beneath the surface showed through, and
his face turned serious as he leaned forward.

"You needn't be alarmed, Lili," he said gently. "I
mean you no harm. No man in this house does. We have
a purpose, but that purpose does not include deliberately
frightening innocent young girls, or hurting them in any
way. You will go home again safely, I give you my word.
And one day you will look back on all this and laugh at
how frightened you were."

For some insane reason, Lili was tempted to believe
him, though every instinct warned her she would be a
fool. She got up and walked over to the other side of the
room, the cup of tea cooling in her hands as she stared
unseeing into the shadows. He had kidnapped her. He
had pulled her into his carriage on a deserted street at
night, and had come heaven knew how close to stealing
her virtue as well. A man who was capable of that could
not be trusted, no matter how sweet his words.

Or how sweet his lips had felt on hers.

The darkness seemed to have grown heavier; it was
thick and brooding. Lili could feel the draft again, cold
through the thin fabric of her shirt. More than anything,
she longed to go back to the fire, but she was afraid to
look at him—or to let him see the expression in her eyes.
The sense of the room was even more uncanny now,
more encompassing, and she felt as if she were straining
for something just beyond her grasp. Elusive images kept
flashing into her mind, as they had been before—only
urgent now, frightening—and she knew suddenly that she
did not want to remember.

Whatever it was, whatever dark secret that room was calling from the depths of her subconscious, she did not want to know it.

But just as she started to turn, the picture flashed back again, sharper this time, more intense. For an instant she almost felt it was real. She could see it all so clearly. Tall white tapers shimmering in silver candelabra on the empty tables . . . it was raining then, too, but the windows were open and there was something sweet in the air. And she was standing, just standing, like now . . . only everything was bigger, and she was looking around with wide and wondering eyes.

Then she saw the man who was lying on a table in the center of the room, his face so pale and still he looked as if he had been carved from wax.

"Oh, dear heaven. . . . This is my father's house. My *natural* father."

"I wondered if you would remember." He had come up and was standing directly behind her. "I thought you might. I understand you were here once, as a small child."

Lili could feel him in the shadows beside her. His voice was so close, it had to be right in her ear, but she did not turn and face him. She *had* been here, in this house, in this room, the night her father died.

"But *why*?" she whispered hoarsely. "Why would you bring me here? Of all places?"

"Why not? We needed something safe and out-of-the-way. What better choice than a house that's been abandoned for over a decade? And it isn't your father's anymore, incidentally. It's yours. Along with the rest of the plantation. Bellefleur was passed to you by the terms of his will. That's why nothing's been done with it. It's being kept intact until you marry and your husband can decide what to do with it."

Her house? Her plantation? Bellefleur belonged to *her*? Lili's brain whirled as she tried to take in everything at once. Why hadn't Don Andrés mentioned it to her? But then, it always made him uncomfortable talking about things that concerned her mother and the man she had once loved.

"So you find it amusing, bringing your captive to her own home."

"You might say that," he admitted. "But it has its

practical side as well. Think it over, *petite*. What is the last place you would look if you were searching for a kidnapped heiress?"

"Her own house," Lili replied dully.

"Exactly."

She felt something knot up in her stomach, and she went back to the fire, but there was no warmth in it anymore. This was no random act, inspired by the wild flight of a foolish girl into the darkness. It was carefully, meticulously planned, right down to the last detail. This man knew exactly what he wanted, and he had gone to great lengths to get it!

I mean you no harm, he had said, and unless he was acting—and why should he?—he had meant it. But what if everything did not go according to his plan? What if some unexpected snag came up? Something that made her an inconvenient liability? What would come of his promises then?

"You do live on the razor edge of danger," she said, staring into the flames, trying not to think of where that "certain disregard for the law" might lead him. And what it might mean to her.

"Like the Blaze?"

There was teasing in his voice, but Lili did not hear it.

"Yes, the Blaze . . . or his kind." She had been so smugly sure, when they danced together in the ballroom, that she was safe because he couldn't possibly be the Blaze. After all, the Blaze was basically crude, a sinister-looking man who committed the most despicable acts without a pang of conscience. Why hadn't it occurred to her that there were other outlaws too, with considerably fairer countenances? "But you're proud of that, aren't you? You like the image you've created for yourself."

"Perhaps." He strolled over to the fire and prodded it with a poker, waiting until it flared up again before he turned back. "But you're tired now. I will leave you. A room has been prepared for you at the head of the stairs. You'll find Dédé—Stevie's wife—waiting in the hall with a candle to show you up."

He headed toward the door, leaving Lili by herself in front of the fire. *A room has been prepared for you*—as if this were just a pleasant social visit. Only she couldn't forget how he had behaved when they were alone in the carriage. What was going to happen when she was upstairs and in that room—and Dédé and her candle had gone?

He seemed to sense what she was thinking, for he looked back, half-smiling.

"There is a good sturdy bolt on the door. You may feel safer if you use it, although there is no need. Dédé will be sleeping on a cot outside. If you need anything, just wake her. Oh, by the way . . ."

He paused in the doorway with a grin.

"Allow me to introduce myself. My name is Jeremy Blaze."

13

Bright rays of gold were streaming through the window
when Lili woke the next morning. Blinking in the
sunlight, she tried groggily to figure out where she was.
Someone's guest room apparently . . . simple but homey,
with wide pine flooring and a gaily patterned rose-and-
green bedcover and crisply fresh lace curtains . . .

Then suddenly she remembered. This was not a guest
room, and she was not a guest. She had been abducted
by a man called Jeremy Blaze.

She jumped up abruptly. Pulling the mannish white
silk shirt tighter around her, she went over to the window
and peered up at the sky. The storm that had buffeted
the carriage so wildly the night before seemed to have let
up, but only temporarily, for slender blue slivers were
wedged between huge rolling billows of gray.

Everything came rushing back in a jumble. The darkened carriage that had pulled up beside her on the drizzle-
dampened street, impudent hands reaching out and forcing
her inside, what had happened immediately afterward—
sweet heaven, it made her blush even to think of *that*.
Then he had brought her here, to Bellefleur, the plantation she had not even known was hers. The place where
her father had spent his last lonely years.

She opened the window and leaned out, shivering in
the cold as she surveyed the land that had once belonged
to him. The grounds that stretched out from the side of
the house must have been intended as formal gardens,
but even accounting for the ravages of time, there was a
strangely unfinished look about them. Paths were laid
out, with stones lined up along the edges, and spaces
where bordering flowerbeds might have been, but they
ended abruptly, for no reason at all. And lemons and
pecans had been plopped in the oddest places, like the

beginnings of groves left to fend for themselves. At one end, on a gentle rise, Lili noticed a small summerhouse, or belvedere, with bits of white paint clinging to weathered gray boards.

Was this for my mother? she wondered curiously. Had Gabriel Dubois started these elaborate gardens for the beautiful Cybèle? And given them up when he had lost her?

Sighing, she turned from the window. Probably, but she would never know. And there was no point dwelling on the past. Not when the present contained more urgent things to ponder. Like who *he* was, this man who had carried her off. And what she could expect at his hands.

Jeremy Blaze. . . . She sat on the coverlet, which was barely mussed, for she had slept surprisingly soundly. The infamous Blaze, who had taken local gossip by storm and set half the female hearts fluttering at the mere mention of his name. She racked her brains trying to remember the rumors that had been flying around. How contemptuous she had been when everyone carried on about his swashbuckling charm and the wonderful, romantic good looks that were already becoming legend. An evil man ought to have ugly traces of evil showing in his face! But she had been only too ready to believe tales of coarseness and blatant brutality.

Clearly she had gotten it backward. She got up and peered at her image in the mirror above a small dressing table. She looked a little disheveled, but otherwise no worse for the wear. Jeremy Blaze *was* good-looking, with all the dashing, mysterious charm the gossips had intimated. But the man who had sat across from her in the firelight last night, courteously pouring tea, was hardly the sort to indulge in gratuitous acts of brutality.

The sky darkened for a moment; then welcome sunlight flooded the room again. More out of restlessness than anything else, Lili wandered over to a massive pine *armoire*.

To her surprise, the interior was crammed with garments in bright shades of scarlet and emerald and gold. Forgetting everything else, she pulled out gown after gown and tossed them in a heap on the bed, together with a fur-lined redingote, a sage-green cashmere mantle, and several lace-trimmed nightdresses, which would have been much more comfortable to sleep in had she but

known they were there. They all appeared to be new—
not a one looked as if it had even been worn—and they
were exactly her size.

He had had them made for her, then . . . Lili stared at
the rainbow of color splashed across the bed and tried to
make her mind focus. He had planned everything carefully, even more carefully than she had thought. And he
must be intending to keep her for some time, judging
from the number of outfits he had provided.

She started to sort through them, intrigued in spite of
herself. She ought to be alarmed—she knew she should—
but it was hard when there were all these pretty frocks to
consider. And after all, if he'd gone to such lengths to
keep her happy, then he really *mustn't* mean her any
harm.

She carried the dresses over to the mirror one by one
and held them up in front of her. It was amazing how
perfectly they complemented her coloring and figure. A
simple cotton chemise, gathered with drawstrings to a
high waist and trimmed in red and gold chenille threads,
had looked almost plain on the bed. Now rich vermilion
warmed her cheeks and brought out the auburn highlights
in hair that was its own color again after having been
rinsed by the rain. Almost as stunning was a jaconet muslin
morning dress, snug-fitting in front, with cottage sleeves,
fashioned not in the usual white, but a wonderfully daring
cerise. As for that little jade-green China crepe—well, she
could just imagine how the low neckline was going to look,
without so much as a row of ruching to hide the fact that
her breasts were considerably plumper than the rest of her.

She blushed as she hung the garments back in the
closet. Plainly, Jeremy Blaze had planned not only for
her comfort, but also for his taste. And he was obviously
a man who wasn't overconcerned with modesty.

She decided on the chemise, not because it was the
prettiest, but because it seemed the least revealing, though
she wasn't so sure after she knotted the strings below her
bosom, creating a ruffling effect that gave her a distinctly
womanly look. Her hair took longer, for she had never
done it herself, except in fun. It was some time before
she finished arranging it in a fashionable upsweep—with
little curls she hoped looked like studied confusion on
her brow and nape—and was ready to open the door and
see what awaited her outside.

To her surprise, the hall was empty. Even the woman, Dédé, was gone, her cot neatly made up and pushed against the wall.

Why, it's almost as if I were alone in the house, Lili thought, feeling a little strange as she headed toward the stairway. As if I could go down the steps and out the front door—and no one would stop me!

The downstairs hall, too, was deserted. The door to the room that had brought such eerie memories the night before was closed, but another had been opened, giving glimpses of a cozy parlor with a fire burning on a marble hearth. The same green-upholstered chairs were there, as if they had been carried across the hall, and a small round table was charmingly, if somewhat oddly, covered with calico. The musty odor Lili had noticed earlier was overpowered by the fragrance of roses from a freshly cut bouquet.

Curious, she thought—roses again. A noise came from the rear of the house, and remembering suddenly that she'd had nothing to eat since the afternoon before, she decided to investigate. Surely any kidnapper who went to such lengths to make sure she was properly clothed would have made arrangements for her hunger as well.

A minute later she found herself in, not the dining room, but the kitchen, which was attached to the main house by a butler's pantry. Not a very sensible arrangement, in case of fire, but distinctly welcome this morning, for the smells were already beginning to make her stomach rumble.

Dédé was at a long table in front of the stove, arms plunged halfway up to the elbows in a bowl of something that looked like bread dough. Her broad face brightened when she saw Lili.

"Ah, here you are, poor little t'ing. You mus' be starvin', *eh bien?* I t'ink you gonna sleep till night, de way you goin. Well, never mine. Old Dédé, she gonna fix you up. Jus' you set you'se'f dere, an' I get somet'ing nice fo' dat empty tummy. De tea, it's ready." She indicated a long stone counter against one wall. "I make it good an' hot."

She was wiping her hands on her apron as she spoke, but Lili went over for the tea herself. The setting was so comfortable, the woman so friendly and open, it was hard to make herself believe she had been kidnapped and wasn't a guest in the house.

"Tea is all I need, thank you—and some bread, with jam if you have it."

"Bread an' jam—an' not'ing else? In Dédé Matouse's kitchen?" The woman looked scandalized as she set about clearing a space in front of Lili. She was a big, warmhearted Cajun, with half a dozen daughters of her own—the middle girl just about the size of this one, but healthier around the middle!—and she couldn't bear to think of anyone going hungry. Especially a little mite that had been spirited away in the middle of the night and must be quivering with fear. "You jus' set w'ere you are. Better put some meat on dem bone—or de firs' puff o' wind, it gonna blow you away. Dose egg, dey all w'ipped up fo' a nice *pain perdu*. And de sausage, it's spittin' and cussin' on de fire."

The sausage was indeed "spittin' and cussin'," with a heavenly aroma of pork fat and spices, and Lili had always loved *pain perdu*, which was the French way of describing stale bread that would have been "lost" if it hadn't been dipped in sweetened egg batter and fried to a golden crust.

"Well," she conceded, "maybe just a little."

"How you t'ink you gonna manage wit' jus' a little? Ain't no less'n two heppin' gonna fill you' back teet'." Dédé picked up a cleaver and whacked at a loaf of French bread. Being a good Cajun wife, she was used to taking orders from her menfolk, but that didn't keep her from questioning their judgment at times. And what they were thinking of now, she couldn't imagine—terrorizing a sweet child like that! Though she had to admit, stealing a sidelong glance, the girl didn't look terrorized. Fact is, Dédé thought, she looks right t' home.

Lili was feeling "right t' home" as she finished her tea and poured another cup. There was something warm and pleasant about being in the kitchen, and she didn't even object as the woman heaped sausage after sausage onto a plate next to several slices of *pain perdu* in a puddle of sweet cane syrup. She'd have meat on her bones, all right, if she ate like that! But she didn't want to hurt Dédé's feelings, and besides, she was even hungrier than she had thought.

Two helpings later, her back teeth were indeed satisfied, to say nothing of her stomach, and she was beginning to feel more optimistic as she headed back to the main hall and the cozy sitting room she had noticed before. Whatever else happened, at least Jeremy Blaze was seeing to it that she was fed and clothed. And as long as he kept her here, she didn't have to worry about Jean-Baptiste Cavarelle and the unwanted marriage Papa was forcing on her.

The fire was burning down when she reached the parlor. There was a pile of logs next to the hearth, and she had just picked one up and was trying to figure out what to do with it when she heard laughter in the doorway. Turning, she saw Jeremy Blaze looking in at her. He seemed to have brought an extensive wardrobe for himself too, for he was wearing freshly pressed moleskin pants and a shirt of king's blue that made her intensely aware of his eyes.

"Here, you'd better let me do that. You're holding that chunk of oak as if you thought it was going to rear up and take a nip out of you." He covered the ground between them in a pair of long strides and, taking the log from her, tossed it deftly on the fire. "Poor little princess. What a trial it must be, existing without servants. You had to do your own hair, I see. And I daresay you've never fed a fire in your life."

"Of course I have," snapped Lili, who had never so much as touched a log before. She refrained from reaching up with her hand to see how many telltale curls had straggled out of her coiffure. She *was* every bit as spoiled as he implied, but it wasn't fair, the way he made it sound! "It's just that . . . I didn't want to soil my dress."

He gave the log a kick to set it in place and turned with an appreciative grin.

"And a very pretty dress it is, too. I had a feeling that was the outfit you were going to choose this morning . . . and that I'd like the way it looked on you. Though I must say, I enjoyed the unexpected pleasure of seeing you in my shirt last night. It did have a way of, uh . . . emphasizing your charms."

Lili felt his gaze running up and down her body, slowly, lingering on everything he liked, with a candor that was not altogether displeasing. She shivered a little, trying not to remember how she had felt last night when he touched her with more than his eyes.

"I'm glad you approve of the dress," she said coolly. "Since I suspect you're the one who chose it. And the others in the *armoire* in my room. I must admit, you have good taste."

"Oh, I do," he drawled pointedly. "In clothes, that is."

Lili colored as she turned away, strolling with affected nonchalance to the window. Jeremy, standing at the hearth, followed with his eyes, enchanted by the alternate bursts of boldness and timidity that were so predictable, yet so unexpectedly charming. He had always found predictability boring, especially in a woman . . . and young women were too naive to be anything else. But now he was finding that youth could have its own appeal, particularly when the lady in question looked so fetching in red.

"Am I offending your innocence?" he asked, slipping up behind her. Without a petticoat—which he had made a point of not providing—the dress was clinging suggestively, forming a faint valley at the cleavage of her buttocks. What would she do, he wondered, if he laid his hand there lightly, cupping it around her? Would she respond . . . or would she pull away? And could he afford to take the chance? "I'm sorry if I did. That was not my intention."

"Wasn't it?" She turned slowly, eyes darkening almost to brown in the uncertain light. "But I think it was. I think you intended to make me uncomfortable . . . and you have."

She did indeed look uncomfortable. Jeremy squirmed slightly in the unblinking force of that sweetly helpless gaze. He wasn't used to women who expressed their feelings so openly, or left themselves so vulnerable. But then, he'd never been with a woman who was too inexperienced to know the rules . . . and how to play the game his way. Just for an instant he was tempted to take her in his arms and tell her how adorable she was, and reassure her that everything would be all right.

But that was hardly what he had in mind for her these next few days.

"Now you're playing the little virgin again," he said softly. "And doing it very convincingly."

"And you don't believe me?"

"Ah, but I do. Last night, when we, uh, kissed in the carriage—you have very hot, kissable lips, did you know that, *petite?*—I could have sworn you were a knowing wench." He lowered his voice sensuously, unable to resist the teasing that brought new floods of pink to her

cheeks. How delightfully obvious she was, still bewildered
about her own feelings, though he had already figured
them out. "But this morning, despite the way that gown
fits you, you're the picture of little-girl innocence."

"Then . . ." Lili studied him through faintly quivering
lashes, trying to make something of the expression on his
face. "You know you were wrong before?"

"Hardly. I was wrong one time or the other. Last night
or this morning. But which? That is the question. Ah,
well . . ." He paused, white teeth flashing against sun-
dark skin. "That remains to be seen, doesn't it?"

He was laughing disconcertingly as he went out of the
room, leaving Lili to stare at the empty doorway with a
breastful of hopelessly conflicting emotions. Really, the
man was impossible! He could be so considerate, she
almost believed he truly did care for her feelings. And
she was almost tempted to like him! Then he turned
horrid and rakish again, and she couldn't help remembering how close he had come to taking advantage of her
innocence.

Yes—and how likely it was that he'd try again if she
didn't keep up her guard.

Jeremy Blaze, indeed! Lili flounced over to the table
and plopped down on one of the chairs, a pointless
gesture, for there was no one to see, but she didn't care.
Even his name was impossible! It might not be as preposterous as "The Blaze Jones" maybe, but it wasn't a great
deal more real . . . and now that she thought about it, it
didn't suit him.

She frowned as she glanced at the window, misted
again with rain. Like his French, Jeremy's English was
flawless—much better than her own—but she thought
she detected something faintly Gallic, not so much an
accent as a softness of intonation. No doubt his name was
really Jérème Blaise. Or maybe Jérôme.

Yes, that was it! Jérôme. She had always disliked the
name Jérôme. Intensely. The only Jérôme she had ever
known was a pompous, affected ass. It would serve him
right, being stuck with something like that!

If that's his name at all, she thought, irritated. If he
didn't make the whole thing up to hide his true identity!

It was not until considerably later, when she had cooled
down somewhat, that Lili realized she hadn't even had
the presence of mind to ask what this Jeremy Blaze was

planning, or how long she could expect to be his "guest."
Last night he had parried her questions, and she had
been too frightened to push. But if he thought she was
some spineless little ninny who'd do what she was told
and not make waves, he was in for a big surprise.

She had ample opportunity to question him in the days
to come, for the rain let up periodically, and Jeremy,
astonishingly, tossed her a pair of someone's old galoshes
and insisted that she accompany him while he trudged
around the grounds. In spite of herself, Lili couldn't help
being intrigued. He seemed to know everything about
the plantation, from the high, flat-topped levee—the only
thing that remained in good repair—to the fields, to the
little wooden slave cottages in a row behind the main
house. She was surprised to find that the land was devoted to sugarcane. Somehow she had assumed it would
be indigo or cotton. But then, she'd never asked. And no
one had ever volunteered the information.

When it came to *her,* however—Jeremy's plans for her,
what was going to happen to her—his knowledge became
distinctly vague.

"I don't *have* any plans," he told her evasively one
afternoon as they sloshed ankle-deep through the red-
brown mud of what looked like wagon ruts. "How can I?
The next move is Don Andrés'. A man doesn't keep all
his assets in cash. It takes time to liquidate his holdings."

"But surely you have an idea how long it will be," Lili
pressed, gasping for breath as she struggled to keep up.
The boots, even with three pairs of woolen socks, were
much too big and had a way of staying on the ground as
her feet came up. "You said you weren't asking for more
than he could pay."

"And so I'm not, but I'm not valuing you cheaply
either. Surely you'd be insulted, *petite,* if I set too low a
price on your head."

And that was that. No amount of wheedling could coax
anything more out of him. In truth, Lili could not bring
herself to be disappointed. The fact that she'd been kidnapped was much more tolerable when she didn't have to
think about it. And it really was fascinating, learning
about the land that was hers, even if she knew she would
never live on it. All she had to do was picture the man
she had met over tea, with his perfectly cultivated
manners—and perfectly manicured hands—to know that

Jean-Baptiste Cavarelle would not be the least bit interested in tilling the soil.

Sometimes, when they went out, one of the men came along, usually Stevie's son, Tin-Tin, whose hair was as black as his father's must once have been, and his grin every bit as good-natured, though with all the teeth intact. Once he even brought his sister, Valérianne—or Vava, as she was called, with the Cajun love of diminutives —whose youthful chatter and lively, mischievous eyes reminded Lili how much she had gotten used to feminine companionship since Simone had come to live with them.

Occasionally, one of the others joined them, and Lili understood now why Jeremy had switched to English that first night. The men might dress like swamp dwellers, but they were not all Cajuns by any means. Some barely knew a few words of French, and several spoke with the twang of the hated "Kaintucks," who came down the river on flatboats loaded with ham and corn and huge barrels of whiskey, and raised hell in New Orleans until they ran out of money and had to take their bruised fists and bloodshot eyes back home.

Not that there was anything rude about these men. Lili had the feeling Jeremy Blaze was not one to countenance out-and-out vulgarity in his subordinates. They might be rough around the edges, but they all behaved like perfect gentlemen, at least in front of her.

All except one.

Lili saw the man only once, briefly, from a distance, but even then he gave her goose bumps. She didn't know anything about him. She didn't even know his name, but she knew she would never like—or trust—him. It was late afternoon, the last of the bright sun, and he was standing next to one of the storage sheds when she spotted him, speaking with Jeremy.

Then slowly he angled his head around, and the light caught on pale eyes, turning them nearly to mirrors.

It was those eyes that sent shivers down her spine, even later, just thinking about them. He was a mulatto, of average height and slightly built, but there was nothing of the slave in his rather gawdy clothes and oddly simpering manner. He might have seemed a dandy, had his jacket been finer, his skin lighter—but a cruel one, with a small scar that twisted one corner of his mouth and gave his face an evil look. His eyes were yellow, like hers sometimes, catlike . . . and he made no effort to conceal the fact that he was watching her.

Lili stared back, too horrified to look away. Who is this impudent man? she wondered, shivering. And what is he doing with Jeremy? She didn't for a minute believe that the bold highwayman who had kidnapped her would willingly choose such a sleazy companion—but there had to be some reason for his presence.

Did he have something Jeremy wanted? Some hold over him perhaps?

The man left a few minutes later, without looking at her again, but Lili was haunted by him for days, unable to forget the self-indulgence she had sensed behind the emptiness in those yellow-mirror eyes. He was, she was sure, a dangerous man, and she hoped she would never have to see him again.

Most of the time, fortunately, was passed more pleasantly. Jeremy was proving great fun to be with, though he did have peculiar notions, like dressing her in men's pantaloons when it was especially muddy, or encouraging her to go without a hat, which was already turning her skin unfashionably dark. He seemed to have decided on the part of the gallant *chevalier*, for he took to treating her like an old family friend in whom he had a vaguely avuncular interest.

As if nothing had happened between them! she thought, vaguely annoyed. As if he had not ripped off nearly all her clothes in the carriage—and touched her in the most intimate ways! She knew she ought to be thankful. She *was* thankful, not having to dread another scene like that first morning in the parlor, but it was hardly flattering, thinking he could dismiss her so easily.

Still, she couldn't deny he was being the perfect host. And if nothing else, she was finding out all sorts of things about Bellefleur.

"Did you know that your father—your natural father— was one of the first to grow sugar in quantity? If he'd stuck with it, he'd have been the first to show a profit, too. As it is, the credit for that goes to a chap named de Bore. He was the one who introduced ditches with locks for controlled irrigation, and made the crop attractive by figuring out how to crystallize the juice of the cane. It's going to be the coming thing. Bigger than tobacco or cotton."

His enthusiasm was contagious, and Lili listened, rapt, as he described the way the plantation would look if it were still active. Even now, blacks would be swarming across the muddy earth, planting a new strain of Tahitian cane, which matured—miraculously, according to Jeremy —in eight or ten months instead of the usual twenty. Tender shoots would be popping through the soil any day now. They would grow slowly at first, lying dormant through the dry months of May and June. Then, in summer, when the neighboring cotton fields were a froth of white blossoms, they would expand and thicken until they were taller than the tallest man.

Where had it come from? she wondered. This love for the land and its abundant fertility? Not from Gabriel Dubois, for the plantation had fallen into disrepair long before his death. But then, hadn't Lili-Ange's people been farmers in Normandy all those years ago? It was the kind of thing that got in your blood and stayed there.

"Hold up," she called out, for Jeremy had gotten ahead of her and was starting up a gentle slope that led to the plantation refinery. "Do you think everyone has legs as long as yours?"

He grinned as he turned, the wind blowing dark blond curls onto his forehead. His eyes were so blue they took her breath away. "You have the legs of a filly. You can keep up," he teased. But she noticed he stopped anyhow, and they walked the rest of the way together.

The refinery was a squat brick building, functional and ugly, looking exactly as it should on the outside, with a low, dark roof and several clumsy chimneys. But inside, layers of dust and spiderwebs settled on iron caldrons and outdated pieces of equipment that looked as if they had never been used.

"All ordered before your father lost interest," Jeremy explained. "The slaves, who were intensely loyal—I'll give the man that—uncrated everything and put it in place as best they knew how. But he never cared about anything after, uh . . . during the last years of his life."

Lili looked around, trying to imagine that silent room in a busy harvest season. Fires would be belching great puffs of black smoke up the chimneys, ablaze sometimes as they threw sparks on the roof and showered nearby fields with ash. The heat would be intense, the air so hazy her eyes and nostrils would be stinging. But the red

glow would be distinct enough to pick out slaves in coarse
trousers coming through the door, their backs laden with
huge bundles of *bagasse*—the stalks of the preceding
cane, crushed and drained of juices—to feed the flames.
Other black faces would be leaning over the caldrons,
bare black chests gleaming with sweat as muscular arms
stirred the boiling liquid.

If she closed her eyes, she could almost smell the
sweet, pungent aroma of sugar and burning cane. And
hear the crackling of the fire, and the bubbling kettles,
and the slow, wailing rhythm of African chants that somehow seemed to ease the backbreaking labor.

Lili was no stranger to sugar processing. Papa had
taken her on visits to refineries, and always made sure
someone was there to explain. The cane, she knew, would
be "ground" before it came in—or crushed to extract the
juices—by means of a crude mill wheel turned by mules.
Here, in the refinery, it would be treated in four kettles,
all with different names. First came the *grande*, where
the freshly extracted juice received its initial boiling.
Next, the *flambeau*, which was watched constantly for
the first signs of purification and thickening, and the
syrop, where the juice was supposed to attain the consis-
tency of syrup, though as near as Lili could make out, it
never did. And finally, the *batterie*, in which the last
cooking, the *cuite*, bubbled and churned while slaves
picked off the foam with great skimming ladles.

She had wondered sometimes, as she grew older, why
Papa went out of his way to make sure she learned so
much about cane. He owned several refineries, of course,
but he owned other businesses too, and he never took
her to any of them. Now, for the first time, it occurred to
her that he had been teaching her about her heritage and
the plantation that would one day belong to her.

Darling Papa. He had done his work too well. He had
given her an appreciation of the land and the sugar and
everything that went with it. And then he had betrothed her
to a man who couldn't possibly be interested in the grueling
physical labor it entailed! Perhaps if she were marrying someone different, someone more like the man beside her . . .

"Are you sure you aren't planning to ruin my papa?"
she said abruptly, stepping back through the doorway
into the light. "It's taking an awfully long time to 'liquidate his holdings,' as you put it."

"It's been nine days, *petite*. Nine days is not a long time in the world of business." He tugged at the door, creaking it shut behind him. A trailing ribbon of cloud drifted across the sun, shadowing the earth for a moment. "I told you before that I didn't intend to ruin your father. I meant it."

"But there's more than one way to ruin a man. He must be dreadfully worried."

"Nor have I any intention of alarming him unnecessarily," he said, taking her elbow firmly and guiding her down the hill. "I want something he has—very much—and I intend to get it. But I've no desire to hurt him in the process. He has had word, from someone he knows he can believe, that you are all right."

Lili pulled away, pausing to look at him. "You're sure?"

"I have promised," he said, smiling easily. The sun burst from behind its wispy veil, and suddenly the world seemed to be bathed in gold. "And I always keep my promises. Why can't you learn to trust me, *petite*?"

Why, indeed? she thought later as she lay in bed listening to the silence that was almost palpable after all those nights of rain dripping from the eaves. It was so easy to trust him, outside in the daylight, with his clothes all spattered with mud, and hair tumbling down on his brow. But it was harder when she was alone in the dark and she remembered who he was and what he had done. He was handsome enough to take her breath away, and deceptively charming, but a handsome face and charming manners did not always mask the purest of hearts.

Hadn't Lili-Ange trusted handsome, charming Roger de Courbet Montaigne that fateful night in a garret in France? And look where it had gotten her!

Lili fell asleep reminding herself how treacherous Jeremy Blaze could be and worrying about what was going to happen next. But her dreams must have changed sometime in the night, for when she woke, all she could think was how blue his eyes had looked that moment he turned to wait for her on the hill. And how even the sun had responded to his smile.

14

Take care, Lili warned herself the next morning as she sat alone on a narrow wooden bench in the open summerhouse she had glimpsed from her window. Take care, or you are going to forget yourself . . . and heaven help you if he knows you have let down your guard.

But her heart was finding it hard to be cautious, and the day was so glorious, with only a few wisps of white lazing across a crystalline sky, even her wary mind was inclined to agree. After all, she was safe enough. For the time being at least. Jeremy Blaze, for all his criminal intentions, was going out of his way to keep her well-fed and amused. And except for a few lapses, and those right in the beginning, he had treated her with unfailing courtesy.

Almost too *much* courtesy.

Lili frowned as she curled her feet up under her, leaving her skirt to blow in the gentle breeze that wafted up from the river. The sun was almost spring warm, and the light pelisse she had brought from the house was draped loosely over her shoulders. Beneath, she was wearing the most flattering of the gowns in her closet, if not the most modest—a figured cotton gauze in shades of gold and quince, with a deep heart-shaped neck that left very little to the imagination.

It was not that she wanted him to draw her into his arms again and force on her the dizzying passion of hard kisses that made her quiver all the way down to her toes. Just the thought left her giddy, though her nervousness, she had to admit, contained a certain forbidden appeal, now that he was not with her and she could give her fantasies free rein. But it *would* be nice if he looked at

164

her, just sometimes, as if he remembered she was a woman . . . and found her the least bit desirable.

She knew he enjoyed her company—he must, or he wouldn't have sought her out so often—but whatever bawdy ideas had been running through his mind that first night in the ballroom showed now only in an occasional glint in his eye. If that!

And just as well, she thought, composing her face in a neutral expression as she caught sight of him strolling up the path from the house. All she needed now was to have him come across her in that lonely little belvedere and guess what she had been thinking. Little girls who were way over their heads with obviously experienced men couldn't afford to play games.

She must not have concealed her feelings as well as she thought, for he was grinning suggestively as he drew near.

"What a wistful look," he called out. "Have I caught you daydreaming? Thinking of some secret love perhaps? Is there a handsome young man at home you're pining to return to?"

"There's only one man in my life right now," Lili replied, waiting until he had reached her and was leaning with studied indolence against one of the weathered posts. "And he's one man I would be delighted never to have to think about again."

"Ah, the absent fiancé." Little flecks of light danced in his deep azure eyes. "The heart does *not* grow fonder, it seems. You aren't missing him, then? Regretting these few precious days in which you might have gotten to know him better, so you wouldn't have to march down the aisle with a stranger."

"I wouldn't have gotten to know him anyway," Lili reminded him rather testily. Surely she had told him all this when she spilled out the truth in the carriage? How could he have forgotten? "Papa gave strict orders that we weren't to lay eyes on each other until we met in front of the altar at the Cathédrale de St. Louis. And he did it on purpose, too! He knew if I had a chance to see this Jean-Baptiste Cavarelle again—if I could spend some time with him—I'd be so nasty he'd decide he didn't want me after all!"

"I believe you'd do it, too!" He laughed openly as he sat beside her on the bench. "What a horrid little thing you are! All he's done, poor man, is offer an honorable proposal of marriage. And here you are, ready to tear his heart to shreds."

"I don't think he has a heart," Lili replied glumly. "And anyhow, I didn't want his 'honorable proposal.' It's so unfair, being a woman and having to do what everyone says. *He* didn't have all that pressure from some bullying papa, ordering him to come and propose!"

"Maybe he did," Jeremy suggested.

"He doesn't *have* a papa."

"What, no heart and no papa? What a singularly slighted creature. There are other pressures, you know, that propel a man into marriage. Perhaps the bully was your own papa. Have you thought of that? Maybe he has some hold over this man."

"No one has any hold over a Cavarelle. And anyhow, it's different for him. He's a man! Pressure or no, at least he has *some* rights in the matter! He doesn't have to sit there and say, 'Yes, Papa,' and, 'No, Papa,' and meekly do what he's told."

She tossed her head defiantly, shaking out long tresses, which had been pulled back with a comb but otherwise left free. Jeremy, watching, tried not to smile. Somehow he couldn't imagine her doing anything meekly.

God, she was a little beauty. He let his gaze linger on her, not obviously, as he had before, but discreetly. Did she have any idea how bewitching she looked at that moment? Probably not, or she wouldn't be sitting there so naturally, without striking a pose. All that absurd black was out of her hair now, and fire smoldered in its depths, an intriguing complement to high cheekbones and glowing ivory skin. If it weren't for her youth—and the delightfully elusive way she had of looking totally innocent sometimes—she might almost have been a courtesan from some exotic Eastern clime.

Dark lashes caressed her cheeks just for a second, teasing and childlike, and Jeremy felt his body respond, almost against his will. Then she looked up, and those same lashes were an inky frame for eyes that turned tawny in the sun and seemed to be full of questions.

But her mouth already knew the answers. It was an exquisite mouth, full and red, with just a hint of Cupid's bow, and much too much roundness in the lower lip. As if she had been playing with makeup, though he knew

she hadn't, for he had seen to all the contents of her
room himself.

"I think," he said quietly, "that you would do better to
listen to your papa. He does love you—very much."

"I know that." Lili got up restlessly, wandering over to
the edge of the belvedere, where there was an unre-
stricted view of green-mantled hills in the distance. "I
know he cares, and he only wants what's best for me. But
that doesn't mean he's always right."

"No," Jeremy said, smiling to himself. "It doesn't mean
he's right."

Lili turned slowly, missing both his look and the inflec-
tion in his voice, for a new thought was just starting to
take hold in her mind.

"How long are you going to keep me here?"

The question caught him unawares. She was standing
in the light, her back to the sun, and he had to squint to
make out her features. "I told you before—" he began
cautiously, but she cut him off.

"You told me before that you didn't know, but that's
not true. You *do* know, at least vaguely. Maybe you
can't put a specific time on it, but you've got a good
general idea. And I'd appreciate it if you let me in on the
secret."

"Why are you so eager to find out?"

"Because I am, that's all. Does that surprise you so
much? It's not an unnatural question."

"No, I suppose it isn't. Very well, then, since you
insist. I'm planning on keeping you a short time longer.
Several days at least. Is that general enough for you?"

Lili studied him intently, trying to see something in
those deep, mysterious eyes. Something that would tell
her if he had just made a concession, or was only being
evasive again.

"As long as thirty-six days?"

"Thirty-*six* days. Not thirty-five or thirty-seven? And
you said you didn't need anything specific. What is in
thirty-six days, *petite?*"

"Why," she said primly, "the Monday after Easter."

He leaned back, watching her through slightly narrowed eyes. "I see," he said quietly. Though whether he
really did or not, Lili couldn't be sure. She didn't recall
having mentioned the date of her wedding. "I don't

know if I can promise you thirty-six days. I'm rather inclined to doubt it. But one never knows, does one?"

No, one never does, Lili thought, surprised at the little surge of elation that coursed through her. He *might* keep her that long—he hadn't absolutely said he wouldn't. And even if he got her back before the scheduled date, she would still have spent the intervening days—or weeks—in the company of an infamous outlaw. A man who, in only a short time in New Orleans, had already become known as a lady-killer. Reputations had been ruined in considerably less time and with considerably less notorious men.

And would Jean-Baptiste, of the fine old family of Cavarelle, actually marry a woman of sullied reputation?

"But you are going to keep me several days?" she said, lowering her voice coyly as she sat beside him again.

"Oh, I wouldn't dream of letting you go before then."

"You're sure?" She felt almost scandalous as she peeked up through a dusky veil of lashes. She really *shouldn't* be so bold, but all of a sudden, everything seemed to be falling into place. "You *can* promise me that?"

"I could promise you a great deal more if I thought you were interested."

Lili heard the teasing in his voice, and she tried to be wary. What was there about the way he was looking at her that brought back the feelings she had had before . . . when he kissed her? But it was such a lovely day and this was such a welcome change from his previous coolness that she couldn't resist flirting, just a little.

"Are you trying to intrigue me, *monsieur?*"

Jeremy laughed softly. He hadn't missed the way her lips parted almost unconsciously. And her face was tilting up, for all the world as if she expected him to take advantage of her. "Am I succeeding? But I must be, if you're so eager to spend a few more days with me."

"Actually," Lili said, catching herself enough to pull back a little, "it hadn't even occurred to me I'd be spending the time with you. I was, of course, thinking about Bellefleur. It is interesting, learning all about the plantation, even though I never knew it was mine. It will be pleasant, having a few more days to explore the grounds."

"Aren't you jumping to conclusions?" Jeremy looked

vaguely amused. "Who said anything about staying here at Bellefleur?"

"But I thought . . ." Lili faltered, confused. "I just assumed . . . Well, you *did* bring me here, after all—and hardly by chance! The kitchen was stocked, and even the *armoire* in my room had been filled. Everything was very well prepared."

"Only an imbecile or a madman would kidnap an heiress without preparation, and I am neither. I *did* bring you here by plan, of course. But I never intended to stay. It's much too dangerous—don't you think?—remaining in one place for more than three or four days. Especially so close to the city, where comings and goings might be observed on a plantation that's supposed to be deserted. If it hadn't been for the rain, we'd have left some time ago."

Lili stared at him with wide eyes, trying to quell the sudden thumping of her heart. Here, at Bellefleur, strolling around the grounds with him, sitting in front of the fire in the cozy little sitting room, everything had seemed so civilized. She had felt safe here.

"But . . . where are you taking me?"

He was silent for a moment. When at last he spoke, his voice was low and noncommittal.

"I think right now I'll leave that for you to guess."

"I hate guessing games. I think they're silly. I'd much rather—"

"Ah, but I'm afraid it's guess or nothing, for the next few hours at any rate. We'll be leaving early in the evening. Then you'll see for yourself. And, Lili . . ."

He must have caught the panic in her voice, for he leaned forward, touching her gently on the arm.

"You don't have to be afraid. I promised no harm would come to you here, and it hasn't—has it? No more harm will come where I am taking you now. I would never, *never* hurt you. Surely you've learned to trust me—at least the tiniest bit—by now."

Trust? The same thing he had said before. The same thing he had asked for. Only, didn't he know how impossible it was? "How can I trust you," she cried helplessly, "when I don't know what's going on in your head? Or what you're going to come up with next. Sweet heaven, I don't even know who you are! You call yourself Jeremy

Blaze, but is that really your name? Or just some alias you made up?"

"It could be either, couldn't it? And unless you want to indulge in those guessing games you disdained before, you're going to have to leave it at that. Come, *petite*, is it truly so important? A name is just what you call someone. A superficial label that can be changed at will. It doesn't tell you anything about the essence of a man."

"And what is *your* essence?" she said softly. "Who are you, really? Deep down inside." His hand was still on her arm, and she was intensely conscious of that light, subtle, disturbingly warm touch. "What kind of man are you? And how am I supposed to *know*?"

"Listen to your heart, pretty Fleur-de-Lys. You've been trying to figure things out with your head, and that's all wrong. Follow your instincts. Let your heart tell you what to think. And how to feel."

He bent down slowly, deliberately, teasing her with his lips, only inches from her own. Lili felt her pulse race, and she tried desperately to think, but everything was all a jumble in her mind.

She knew she ought to pull away—she *meant* to pull away—but he was so close she could feel the whisper of his breath on her mouth. Then he was moving, and she was moving too, and she knew suddenly that there was no escape from what she had wanted all along.

It was a sweet, soft, gentle kiss, not at all what she had imagined. A thousand times more compelling than the rougher, wilder passion she had expected. He was barely touching her, and only with his lips—even his hand was gone now from her arm—but she had never felt anything so acutely in her life. So consumingly. Without thinking, without even knowing what she was doing, she leaned into him, longing to get closer, to drain the last dregs of honey from that warm, tender, surprising mouth.

Then, abruptly, his lips were gone, and she heard the distinctly annoying sound of laughter.

"I think, after all, *petite*, you do trust me a little."

"Oh!"

Lili could only gape at him. Anger and confusion flooded over her. He hadn't wanted her. He hadn't been the least bit interested in kissing her. If he had, he would never have been so restrained. All he had wanted was to massage

that arrogant male ego by proving she was still suscepti-
ble to his rugged charm.

"And now I suppose you're going to doubt my virginity again. Just because you think I responded to one silly
little kiss."

"I don't *think* you responded at all," he replied wickedly.
"And no, I am not going to question your precious
virginity. If anything, you just proved your innocence. I
am thoroughly convinced."

"You are?" Lili was not sure whether that was comforting or not. "But why?"

"Only a foolish little virgin would kiss a man like that . . .
if she wasn't ready to accept the consequences."

He was still laughing as he sauntered back down the
hill. Lili sat there seething with repressed fury as she
listened to the mocking echoes die away. It didn't help in
the least to realize she had asked for it. She had let him
kiss her without so much as a murmur of protest. She had
wanted him to kiss her, and just the way he had. But he
was right about one thing. She wasn't ready for the
consequences.

She got up abruptly, pacing back and forth across the
small structure. She was not at all sure which was more
insulting, having her innocence doubted, as he had done
before, or being called a foolish little virgin.

She turned to leave, then hesitated. There was only
one path down from the belvedere, and she could just
imagine him standing at the end waiting for her. Still
laughing while he prepared to show her just what the
consequences of that impulsive kiss might be.

It would have been better if he had told her he was
sending her home tonight! She didn't want to go back,
heaven knew. She dreaded facing a marriage that was
growing more repugnant with each passing hour. She
dreaded it with all her heart. But she wasn't sure she
wanted to face what might happen here either. At least
at home she would be safe and protected. And Papa
would not have to worry anymore.

And he *would* be worried, no matter what Jeremy had
said to reassure her. Lili glanced in the direction of the
river, but the levee was so tall she could only imagine
sunlight glinting on dark water. He would be terribly
worried. She could almost see him now, in his office,
sitting at the carved wood desk where he always sat when

he was fretting about something, staring into ashes that had grown cold on the hearth. He looked so old . . . and so tired. Why hadn't she noticed before that he was getting old? That he was not as strong as he used to be? His face was drawn and white, and pain was etched in little lines around his mouth.

"Oh, Papa," she whispered. "Don't worry so. I'll be home in a few days. Truly I will. And I promise . . . I'll never do anything to worry you again."

15

Don Andrés was, in fact, in his office, sitting in the chair behind his desk, as Lili had imagined. He was, at age seventy, too rigid of habit to be anyplace else. But the red-tiled hearth was not cold. A blazing fire had been lighted, and sunlight flooded in long shafts through the tall windows that faced on the street.

If a casual acquaintance had peered through the doorway, he would have assumed that everything in the room was normal and the man at the desk behind a clutter of notes and account books had not a care in the world. But those who knew the old Don well would have detected faint creases on his brow and the tension that tugged at the sides of flaring aristocratic nostrils. And for that reason, those who knew him had been denied access to the study. Anyone who showed up without an appointment would be turned away, politely but firmly, by the footman.

Don Andrés Santana de la Vega had always been known for playing a lone hand. That was exactly how he was going to play it now, when the stakes were his little girl's welfare.

A paper crackled in his fingers, and he glanced down, surprised to find that he was still holding the note that had been delivered an hour earlier. Impatiently he crumpled it and tossed it aside. It told him exactly what he had hoped to hear, that Lili was being well-cared-for, that she was not unhappy—and it came from the one person whose words he knew he could believe—yet somehow it brought no comfort. She was not unhappy now, but how long would that continue? Was he making a mistake, handling it this way?

And yet, given the situation, what else could he do?

He leaned back in the chair, wearily reviewing everything in a mind that had already gone over it a hundred
times before. Eleven days. Lili had been gone eleven
days, a long time, but not *too* long. Anything less than
that would hardly have seemed reasonable. There had to
be time, after all, for a ransom note to be sent, for
negotiations to be arranged, money to be raised. Yes,
eleven days was to be expected . . . and longer. Everything would be all right . . . as long as no one found out.

He went over to the case where he kept his liquor and
poured out a generous brandy. He detested drinking
alone, but as he wasn't ready to let anyone into his
presence, he supposed it was not to be avoided. It was
absolutely essential that no one guess what was going on;
every appearance of normalcy had to be maintained,
even in front of the servants. If a breath of rumor got
out, it would be all over the city by nightfall. And God
knew what might happen then.

He had, he thought, feeling a little easier as he went
back to his chair, arranged it rather cleverly. Lili's absence had been explained by dropping hints to a few
acquaintances—whom he knew he could count on to
spread the news—that she had been sent off to friends
"in the country" to get some motherly help with her
trousseau. He had been a little afraid that that was going
to be tricky, since he hadn't been in a position to name
names, but he had quickly learned that people believe
what they expect to believe. Everyone had simply assumed she was with this friend or that friend—or the
other friend—and all he had had to do was shake his head
vaguely and take care not to agree or disagree while he
changed the subject.

Later, if they were chatting among themselves and
discovered they had been wrong, they would simply say:
Now, isn't that odd? I could have sworn he said the
so-and-sos or the so-and-sos—but he must have meant
the so-and-sos instead. And that would be that.

Simone, of course, had had to be given specific details,
and that had worried him. Still worried him, as a matter
of fact. The little chit was getting smarter than any of
them realized. It was easy to take her for granted; she
had that mousy way of keeping to the corner all the time.

But she was growing up, and much too fast. If she started to get suspicious . . .

Of course, *he* was keeping her occupied, as they had planned, making sure she didn't have time to gossip with anyone.

Don Andrés frowned as he glanced over at the mantel, but the clock had been broken for some months and he could only guess at the time from the sun. Somewhere around four, he supposed. Maybe later. He didn't like the way that was going either. It made him nervous, the man's boldness with little Simone. It was no more than they had agreed upon, but the child was so gullible, it didn't seem quite right. Still, there was no quarreling with success.

"*Demonio!*" He cursed softly under his breath, reverting without thinking to the Spanish of his youth. He wished vaguely that M'mère was there. He missed the crusty old nursemaid who had come into the household with his beautiful young bride. Somehow, over the years, she had become his confidante, ready to listen when everyone else failed him. He would have felt better if she were sitting across from him now, scolding and badgering.

But M'mère had been the weakest part of the plan. It would have been folly to keep her with him. Not that she would deliberately let anything slip. The woman had a jaw like iron—a prying bar couldn't force it open. But she would never have been able to control her face, her manners, those wonderfully French gestures that expressed so much. One look at her, and even a stranger would have known something was wrong.

Besides, who would ever believe he let Lili go off without her?

He raised his brandy, taking a sip of the warming liquid. It had been a stroke of genius, sending M'mère to the old Ursuline convent. She had worked there once. She knew the nuns and was comfortable with them. And what was more important, they were comfortable with her. They would take her in anytime, without any questions, and not a whisper of it would leak out.

A rumble of carriage wheels passed the window. Don Andrés listened as they slowed down, stopping just beyond the range of his vision. He didn't have to get up and look out to know that Simone was returning with the man who

had been her constant companion these past several days.
And that her small, wistful face was alive with excitement.

A fleeting twinge of conscience pricked him. He had
never paid much attention to Simone. He had taken her
into his home, but half the time he forgot she was there.
She had always been eclipsed by his own livelier, more
vibrant daughter. But she *was* his responsibility. Oughtn't
he to put his foot down? Now? That young *pícaro* was
taking advantage of the situation. It wasn't proper, the
way he was behaving.

But then his thoughts drifted to Lili—his beautiful,
beloved Lili—and everything else left his mind. All that
mattered now was Lili. Picking up the crumpled paper
from where he had dropped it on the desk, he aimed it
with accuracy at the fire.

It held for a moment, still visible in the flames, then
vanished in a burst of yellow.

The sun was just brushing the horizon as the closed
black carriage pulled up in front of the house. The afternoon had been warm, but now the shadows were turning
chilly, and Simone shivered slightly as she stepped out.
The man who had alighted first extended a hand to help
her down.

"Thank you, *monsieur*," she said with a little lilt to
her voice.

" '*Monsieur*'?" He gave her a mockingly serious look.
"What is this '*monsieur*,' all of a sudden? Have you
forgotten? I told you to call me Jean-Baptiste."

"Yes, I know—and I did before. While we were in the
carriage. But here . . . well, here, it's so public. What if
someone overheard? Imagine what they'd think!"

The man smiled, amused by the sudden bout of shy-
ness that brought a becoming pink to her cheeks. Alone
in the carriage, she had indeed called him by his first
name, and been almost completely relaxed. So relaxed,
in fact, she had seemed just the tiniest bit brazen.

"What they would think, *chérie*," he teased, pitching
his voice just loud enough to reach her ears, "is that you
are having a good time with a young man who is quite
taken by your charms."

"More likely"—she gave him a hesitant smile—"they
would think I'm behaving quite foolishly with a young
man who is not the least interested in me."

"Then they would be wrong, because I *am* interested. *Very* interested."

He watched as she dropped her eyes, looking sweet and helpless, as he had thought she would. But when she raised them again, they were unexpectedly steady.

"Are you flirting with me, *monsieur*?"

" '*Monsieur*,' again." He laughed softly under his breath. "What am I to do with you, Simone? Yes, of course I am flirting. Is there anything so terrible about that?"

"Yes," she said quietly, "if you are promised to my cousin."

"Promised?" He looked down at her, fascinated by the combination of confusion and frankness that made her so beguiling. She was a pretty little creature, though hers was not a prettiness that showed at first. It surprised him all over again to see how piquant that heart-shaped face could look. And how dark and remarkably soft her eyes were. He had been more than a little leery when Don Andrés had asked him to keep her occupied, but the task was proving unexpectedly easy. And delightful. "One day you will learn, *chérie*. There are promises . . . and promises."

"Are there?" Simone met his gaze, troubled. He was so exactly what she had imagined, this dashingly handsome Jean-Baptiste Cavarelle—she couldn't help remembering how her heart had stopped beating that first moment she saw him in the hallway—and she *did* have a good time when she was with him. But it made her feel guilty, the intensely physical sensations that went through her whenever he was near. It was not, she was sure, the way a girl was supposed to feel with someone else's fiancé. "I think not. A promise is a promise. I am sorry, *monsieur*— Jean-Baptiste. I enjoyed myself very much today. It's good of you to pay so much attention to me, but I have to go inside now. Please, don't trouble to see me to the door."

A fresh burst of laughter stopped her before she could turn. "Why so timid, Simone? You weren't shy before, when we were riding through the streets of town with the curtains half-drawn across the windows. Are you afraid of me, all of a sudden? Or are you afraid your uncle is going to look out and see you?"

"Well, he'd have reason to be displeased if he did. Don Andrés has always been very generous with me. I'm no kin to him, you know. He didn't have to take me in, but he did. Out of charity and kindness. Don't you think I owe him gratitude for that?"

"And your cousin?" he pressed. "The beautiful, spirited Lili Santana? Do you owe her gratitude too?"

His eyes seemed to change, intensifying. Simone sensed that he was asking something beyond his words, but she couldn't understand what.

"Of course. They have always been very nice to me. Don Andrés and my cousin both."

"You are so devoted to her, then? She truly has been nice to you? And kind?"

Simone caught something like teasing in his tone, and she wavered. It would be so much easier to lie to him, putting him off with a glib answer. But lying was not in her nature. Besides, for all her feelings of guilt, she wasn't sure she wanted to put him off.

"Perhaps not *kind,*" she admitted. "Not always. I don't think she liked me very much at first. And she's so much quicker than I. She torments me terribly sometimes . . . like an older sister. But she *has* been nice, and I do love her. As if she really were my sister. I'd never do anything to hurt her. Just as she would never hurt me."

"I wonder," he said softly, but he did not try to push her again. There was no point pushing when he knew he had already won. "Sisters do hurt each other sometimes, you know. I think it's unavoidable. And anyhow, this is only a flirtation. You can't be afraid of a little flirtation, now, can you?"

"No, I suppose not."

"After all, men flirt with pretty girls all the time. And pretty girls are always flirting back. There's no harm in that."

It's only a little flirtation . . .

Simone was to remember those words often enough in the all-too-brief days that followed. It *was* only a flirtation. But just as Jean-Baptiste had said that there were promises and promises, there were flirtations and flirtations. And she sensed she was deeply over her head in this one.

She tried more than once to put a halt to the relationship she could not control, or at least bring it within more manageable bounds. But Jean-Baptiste Cavarelle made it virtually impossible. Every morning, before she finished breakfast, his carriage would be there in the street. She didn't even have time to gossip with Marie-Louise in the kitchen, or little Lucie, who always seemed to have the latest tidbits on the Blaze or anyone else in fashion at the moment. Suddenly, there he would be, at the front entry. She would hear his voice and rush out before Don Andrés could open his study door and ask in indignant tones why the young man was spending so much time with his ward, when he was engaged to his daughter.

And before she knew it, there would be a wrap around her shoulders, and she would be outside and sitting beside him in the carriage. And at least half a dozen black noses would be pressed against the windowpanes. She could just imagine what the topic of conversation was going to be in the servants' quarters that morning.

"You are ruining my reputation, you know," she said jokingly as he seated her in the carriage and shut the door behind them. It was barely three days since he had called their relationship a "flirtation," but she was already beginning to realize that, for her at least, it was more than that. "Everyone in town is going to be talking about me. And I don't think the things they'll be saying are very nice."

"At least they'll be talking, *chérie*," he said, settling back in the carriage next to her. "Instead of ignoring your existence. And anyway, what does a pretty girl like you need with a reputation?"

He was teasing—Simone knew that—but he had a point, in a way. A reputation was essential for a girl from one of the better families, with a dowry to help her catch the right husband. But as no acceptable man was likely to ask for her, the most sterling reputation would hardly do her any good.

"You're right, I'm sure, Jean-Baptiste. I *know* you're right . . . so why doesn't it make me feel any better?"

He laughed softly, enjoying the closeness they allowed themselves in the carriage. It was refreshingly candid, the way she had of speaking her mind, right out. Not like the usual run of Creole ladies, who had been carefully trained in the superfluities of social discourse. He considered putting his arm around her, but the sun was bright, and even though he had sneaked the curtains a few inches over the windows, someone might peer in. That much of her reputation he could preserve . . . for now. Later, when it was dusk and shadows fell . . .

"Well, then," he said lightly, "I'll have to see what I can do to make you feel better, won't I? . . . How about a ride through the seamier side of town?"

He drawled the words wickedly, and Simone, her natural good spirits restored, had to laugh. It was hard to be introspective for long when he knew just what to say to bring her out of herself. She especially loved it when he offered to show her what he called the "seamier side" of New Orleans. She had heard so many stories about what went on in those tantalizingly disreputable areas, and imagined so many times what the streets and buildings would look like. Now all the rumors and gossip were coming alive before her eyes.

Not that she had been sheltered, like her cousin. Simone was a poor relation, and no one had taken particular pains to protect her. But no one had taken the time to show her anything either, and she was essentially ignorant of what lay outside the walls of the house.

All she really knew was the old French Market, along the river, for it was she and not Lili who had been sent on errands when they were shorthanded or the maids were too busy. But she had always hated it. The bustling levee across from the Place d'Armes, which her cousin found so fascinating, was intimidating to Simone, with its crowds and raucous noises and strange, pungent smells, and she had taken to hiding in bed with a sore throat or head cold when she even suspected she might be sent there. Now, suddenly, it was fascinating, viewing all that color and drama from the safety of a passing carriage, with Jean-Baptiste Cavarelle beside her pointing out all the details she might have missed, and laughing in her ear. Though, she noticed, they never got out and strolled along the riverbank, where someone might recognize her on the arm of a man who was definitely not hers.

Apparently, for all his joking disdain, Jean-Baptiste did not intend to ruin her reputation completely.

In spite of herself, Simone couldn't help enjoying the time they spent together. There was so much laughter in this man, and he gave her so much pleasure. Once in a while she would think of Lili, off somewhere trying on a long white wedding gown trimmed with Brussels lace, and she would feel vaguely guilty. But Lili couldn't be

hurt by a harmless flirtation she didn't even know about.
And all too soon Lili would be back, and Lili would be
Jean-Baptiste's lady then, and appear in public at his
side, and live in his house . . . and bear his children.

And all *she* would have was a few days of happy
memories to sustain her, so she might as well make the
most of it.

The world she glimpsed in passing, through the carriage window, was an intriguing one. They might drive
past the facades of coffeehouses, where young men of
means spent entire days gambling away fortunes, she was
sure, and provoking quarrels that would be settled under
the dueling oaks in St. Antoine's garden. Or the simple
one-story blacksmith shop on Royal Street, run by a man
named Lafitte, who was already gaining a rather unsavory renown, though Simone wasn't quite sure why. Or
just along the edge of certain notorious waterfront areas,
where everyone knew what went on in the converted
flatboats anchored at the shore, but no one discussed it in
front of proper young ladies.

Or the modest little houses along the ramparts, which
were even more notorious—and tantalizing—in their own
way.

"Marie-Louise told me—that's one of our maids—that
all the Creole men have black mistresses. Do you think
that's true? They're supposed to keep them in houses
along the ramparts," she said, turning and craning her
neck to see better. "But I don't see how they could,
Jean-Baptiste. There aren't nearly as many houses as
there are Creole men."

The eager curiosity in her voice brought a smile to his
lips. "Not every hot-blooded Creole has a black mistress,
my silly little Simone. Though it is a convenience in
which many indulge, I concede—especially before they
are married."

"That's what Marie-Louise said. Most men get rid of
their mistresses when they wed—they give them money
or the house they've been living in or something like
that—but everyone's supposed to have one before then."
He saw her give him an odd look out of the corner of her
eye, but she didn't go on.

"And you're wondering if there has ever been a mistress of mine in one of those houses?"

"No," she hastened to say. "Well, yes . . . I suppose I

am. But that's only curiosity, Jean-Baptiste. You don't
have to tell me."

"There isn't anything to tell. No, as a matter of fact,
none of those little houses has ever belonged to me.
Though I have heard rumors of my father's spending a
great deal of time in one of them . . . That one, over
there. The one that's a bit taller than the others."

Simone stared at it, fascinated. But except for an extra
story on top, there was nothing to set it apart from the
others, which in truth were plain and rather disappoint-
ingly ordinary. "Have you ever been inside?"

He burst out laughing. "Actually, I haven't. I spent
most of my youth in France, where I was educated—
away from all the dusky temptations of New Orleans."

"Then you didn't . . . You don't . . ." She hesitated,
suddenly confused. She didn't know why it mattered so
much—he was *engaged* to another woman, after all—but
somehow it did.

"No," he said gently. "There's no one waiting for me
in any of those tidy little houses. I don't have a mistress—
black or white. What do I need with mistresses, *chérie*,
when I've got such a pretty girl to ride beside me in my
carriage?"

The words were no more than playful gallantry. Simone
knew that, but his voice was so sincere that she was
almost tempted to believe him. She leaned a little closer,
not even knowing that she had done it. Knowing only
that there were just a few days left, and she wanted to
make the most of the short time they had together.

Not all their daylight hours, by any means, were spent
satisfying Simone's curiosity about the rougher aspects of
the city. They went to prettier areas too, especially one
along the levee, quite a ways from town, which she came
to think of as "their place," for they could be alone
there, and walk together without fear of being seen, and
sometimes even hold hands. She also found, rather to her
surprise, that she enjoyed riding through the American
section, the prosperous Faubourg Ste. Marie, or St. Mary,
as the newcomers insisted on calling it, just upstream,
with its imposing brick mansions and wide front veran-
das. And farther along the river, prosperous houses were
beginning to rise out of lush green lawns that had been
plantation fields only a short time before.

Simone had no inherent distaste for Americans, despite their exuberant ways and brusque, sometimes rather crude manners. She knew, of course, how Lili felt about them. And because she always emulated her older cousin, she had made a conscientious effort to dislike them, but somehow she never quite managed. Perhaps because they were outsiders, and she knew only too well what it felt like to be on the outside looking in.

It must have been galling, especially to the ones with money, being snubbed by all those fine old Creole families who barely eked out an existence on pride and credit. They had reacted typically, in brash American fashion, and secretly, Simone respected them for it. If they couldn't be accepted in the old neighborhoods, with narrow fire traps crowded one on top of the other, then they would go someplace else and set up magnificent new houses and vast lawns and vividly ostentatious gardens. Castles, almost, that flaunted their wealth.

The buildings might be tasteless, as many had called them; certainly they were gaudy and overornate. But they were big, and they had "money" written all over them, and Simone had to smile as she realized what they were telling the snobbish Creoles. We don't need you, they were saying. We have made our own neighborhoods and our own society. And you can just be damned!

"Oh, look," she cried, pointing to a massive new house that had been erected some distance from the edge of town. Large as it was, the lines were clean and fluid, down to the graceful colonnade that ran along at least three of the sides; and a fresh coat of white paint gave it a sedate, almost conservative air. Not even the most aristocratic Creole nose could pinch with disdain at that. "It's the biggest house I've ever seen. And the grandest! Who does it belong to? Do you know?"

He dismissed the question with a wave of his hand. "It doesn't matter . . . just another rich man. There are many rich men in this part of town. What I wanted to show you is the house next door. Right over there . . . see, it's nearly finished."

Simone turned, curious. The first house had been so impressive, the grounds so broad and sweeping, she had almost missed the only other building in the area, on a corner of its own near the carriage. It, too, was white, though that must have been an undercoating, for it looked like someone was starting to paint it a soft shade of blue.

And while it was also simple, there was at least some ornamentation which satisfied her heart. She had always had the nagging feeling she was more attracted to the garish taste of the Americans than to proper Creole restraint.

"Why, it's even prettier," she said with a rush of enthusiasm as she took in every inch of the charming house and well-tended grounds. "I think you're right. It *is* almost finished. Look, there are curtains in the upstairs windows. I love white lace curtains, don't you? And roses are blooming in the garden. Someone must be ready to move in."

"Someone is ready to move in . . . before another month is up." He touched her arm, coaxing her to look around at him. "And I know who that someone is. You see, this house is mine."

"Yours?" Simone threw a surprised glance back at the small, graceful structure, then turned to him again. "I would have thought . . . Well, I just assumed Jean-Baptiste Cavarelle would have a much grander house. More like . . . like that white palace next door."

"Perhaps Jean-Baptiste Cavarelle is not planning on living here all the time," he said, amused. "Perhaps this is only a second house, and he will spend most of his days somewhere else."

"You mean, a plantation on the river?"

"A plantation, yes . . . or something like that."

It was getting late, and he rapped sharply on the window, eliciting a response from the coachman which Simone could not catch. They were going home, she supposed, and suddenly she felt sad. The time she had left with him was so precious . . . she was so happy when they were together, she hated to see each lovely day come to a close. Soon—how soon?—Don Andrés was going to look up from whatever work was absorbing him so completely and realize what was going on.

And then it would all be over.

She was so wrapped up in her thoughts, she didn't even notice that he had eased the curtains partially shut. *To keep the sun out of our eyes,* he had told her that first time he had done it. But she had known even then that it was not comfort he had in mind. It was privacy.

He slipped his arm around her waist, subtly, possessively, and she allowed him to draw her toward him. He had touched her that way almost from the beginning, and she had not objected. Now it was part of their pattern.

"You shouldn't," she said, half-teasing.

"I shouldn't," he agreed. "But I'm going to . . . and you will let me." He took his other hand and laid it on her breast, lightly, yet not at all tentatively. A slow shudder ran through her body, but she did not pull away.

They rode the rest of the way like that, in silence, one of his hands on her waist, the other on her breast. Simone let her head drop onto his shoulder, not even caring if anyone saw through the gap in the curtains. There was no more thought in her mind of whether this was right or wrong, reasonable or foolish, possible or utterly, hopelessly impossible. There was only her cousin's fiancé, beside her in the dusk, close, as no man had ever been before. And no man ever would be again.

By the time they reached the house, the matter was already settled, and accepted. Whatever he asked, she was ready to give. Whatever he wanted would be his for the taking. That was simply the way it was.

16

Simone and her forbidden suitor returned the next morning to the house amidst the winter-flowering gardens that Jean-Baptiste had told her he owned. He had not said anything when he picked her up, but Simone had known without even looking through the carriage window where they were heading. Just as she had known, when they arrived, that the coachman was going to pull up and that they would get out and go through the door.

The house was well-designed, with an airiness that made it seem even more spacious inside. Morning sun flooded through the east-facing windows, and the central hallway, onto which the other rooms opened, was bathed with light. Someone had been busy during the night. Simone could see draperies at most of the windows now, and a red-flowered carpet had been set in what she supposed was the formal parlor. Windows must have been open somewhere, for a pleasant breeze drifted through the hall, bringing with it the smell of the garden.

"Does this charming little cottage *really* belong to the great Jean-Baptiste Cavarelle?" she asked curiously.

He cocked his head to one side, giving her a deliberately waggish look. "I told you yesterday it was mine. And it is. But it can hardly be called a 'cottage,' *chérie*. There are six chambers downstairs and eight up, and all are really quite large."

"And very pretty," she said, wandering over to the room where the carpet had been spread across hardwood flooring, which looked as if it had never been stepped on. Dark green velvet was hanging at the windows, with gold-tasseled cords to pull it back, and a pair of candlesticks rested on the mantel, but otherwise the room was bare. "It's going to look very nice when it's furnished. A table would be perfect over there—between the windows. With a lace cloth, maybe . . . and a vase of flowers from the garden."

She was prattling—she knew she was—but ever since she had come into the house, she had had an urge to stall for time. The sense of him was acutely physical. She could feel every move he made, without turning to see. She could smell the subtle male scent of his body, even with the distance between them, and she was not sure she wanted him to come nearer.

"Are you afraid of being alone with me, *chérie*?" There was a disconcerting tinge of laughter in his voice.

"Nooo, it isn't being *alone* exactly . . ." In fact, it hadn't even occurred to her that this was the first time they had actually been alone, without even the coachman within calling distance. "It's just that . . . well . . ."

"Just what?"

He was directly behind her. Not touching, but so close Simone was reminded vividly of how boldly intimate his hands had been the day before. She had known then what it meant, her allowing him that liberty. They had *both* known. But now . . .

"I . . . I think we shouldn't be here. Together like this."

"And I think we should. I think we *must*." He took her by the shoulders, coaxing her slowly, firmly around. She tried to resist—she tried to keep at least her head turned away—but his will was so much stronger than hers. "You understood where I was bringing you this morning. And what I would ask when we got here. You understood . . . and you came. Why do you pull away now?"

"No, honestly . . ." she murmured, lying more to persuade herself than him. She *had* understood, at least she thought she had. But she hadn't known how it was going to feel. "This . . . this is crazy! You must listen to me. You have to!" But even as she said it, she knew he wouldn't. His hand had found her breast again, and he was caressing her, daring the little nipple to stand up, rigid beneath her dress. "We mustn't, Jean-Baptiste. We can't. Someone . . . someone might pass by the window! They might look in . . ."

He laughed, hearing the futility in her voice before she sensed it herself. The nipple he had been playing with was so hard he couldn't resist slipping his hand inside her dress to feel it better. "No one is going to pass by, and no one will look in." It amazed him all over again, how luminous her face looked when he touched her. There was nothing plain or prim about her now. He thought he had never seen eyes so dark, so radiantly beautiful. The soft, misty eyes of a woman in love . . . and about to be satisfied by a man.

"But if they did . . ." she protested weakly.

"They won't," he promised, struggling to control his feelings. He had meant only to tease when he put his hand on her breast. He had thought he was going to woo her gently, slowly, taking care not to frighten her. But his own desire had been roused, and it was all he could do not to pull her down on the floor and see if that new carpet was as soft as it looked. "The grounds are large, and the driver is at the gate to see that no one trespasses. But if you'd feel more secure, we could always go upstairs."

"Oh . . . no!" Simone gasped. It was silly—she was in as much danger here as anywhere—but going upstairs was somehow like sealing her fate. "We can't stay long anyway. . . . The house isn't ready for people. There . . . there isn't any furniture."

His laughter had a new sound, confident, seductive. "Not here . . . but there *is* a bed upstairs."

His mouth dropped to the little pulse at the base of her throat; his tongue flicked out, licking it sensuously. Simone felt the dress slipping off her shoulders, felt her breasts popping out, felt the surprising smoothness of his shirt against them.

"This is wrong," she whispered. "You know it's wrong."

"How can it be wrong, when it feels so right?" He had found the fastenings on the back of her dress and was working them open, impudently, one by one. "And it *does* feel right. You know it does."

"Yes . . . but it isn't! It can never be right, Jean-Baptiste! Not when you belong to someone else."

"I don't belong to anyone except myself. Haven't you learned that yet, little Simone? No one ever belongs to anyone. Not really."

"But you're going to marry *her*. Lili. You're going to make her your wife—"

"Shhhh, love. Marriage is a convenience. A kind of . . . business deal." His hands were warm on her bare back, holding her away from him just for a moment. "Especially a Creole marriage. Everything is arranged according to bloodlines and wealth and all sorts of practical matters. It doesn't have anything to do with love."

"Maybe not, but it's more than a business deal! You're going to share your life with her, and your house. You're going to take her to your bed! That *is* part of the arrangement, isn't it?"

He had the good grace to look uncomfortable, if only for a second.

"Just the requisite number of times, to make the requisite number of children. After that, many Creole men have the barest contact with their wives. Surely you didn't think all those little houses on the ramparts were occupied solely by bachelors?"

He paused, letting the echo of his voice linger, low and provocative. He was cupping her buttocks now, pressing her against the hard assault of his groin, boldly, possessively, as if he knew the argument was already won.

"Besides," he reminded her, "I told you—all that has nothing to do with love. And it's the love between a man and woman that counts, is it not?"

"Love?" Simone felt her heart leap with hope. "I . . . I don't know what you're saying."

"But you do, *chérie*. Of course you do. What I am saying is that I love you . . . And I will love you for the rest of my life."

"You . . . love me?"

"And you're surprised? Well, never mind . . . so was I. I didn't expect this to happen, God knows—I wasn't looking to be struck by lightning that morning I asked you out for a drive. But a few days, a few *hours* later, and I was hopelessly in love."

"Oh!"

Simone was intensely aware of everything about him, his hands as they caressed her, his breath, warm on her cheek, tantalizing—that male part of him grown hard, digging into her belly. But even more tantalizing were the words she had always dreamed of and never expected to hear.

"That's all you can say?" he teased. "Just 'Oh!' and that's it. Nothing of love in return? And here I thought you cared."

"Oh, yes, yes . . . I do!" Now that she had said it, the

words came rushing out. "I do love you, Jean-Baptiste. I love you so much. With all my heart. Is that what you want me to say?"

"No, I don't want you to *say* anything. I want you to show me . . . now."

He eased an arm around her waist, turning her before she knew what was happening, and they went up the stairs together. Somehow her arms were around him too, and they were clinging so tight, it was hard to walk. There, in a big empty chamber on the second floor, he laid her on the bed and slowly, wordlessly stripped off what was left of her clothing.

"You know what's going to happen now, don't you?" he muttered hoarsely. "You know I'm going to take off my own clothes and lie beside you . . . and then I'm going to make love to you."

Simone nodded. He was bending over her, his eyes so filled with longing that it would have been impossible to say no, even if she'd wanted to. And heaven help her, she didn't—all the guilt feelings in the world couldn't make her want that. "Yes . . . I know."

"And you know I love you?"

"I know."

He almost tore his clothes, he was so eager to get them off, shirt first, then breeches and socks, leaving only his underdrawers so he wouldn't alarm her with the size to which he had swollen. He had meant, again, to be gentle, but again his own body, his own needs, betrayed him.

This time, Simone did not mind. Whatever lingering doubts she might have had, whatever last feelings of hesitation, vanished as he sank down on the bed beside her, stroking her body with long, sure, hungry motions. Even when he removed the last of his garments, she was not frightened. She wanted this union, wanted it desperately, wanted it as much as he did.

When it came time, it was she whose arms drew him on top of her, she whose legs opened, instinctively, to receive him.

"I'm going to hurt you," he murmured apologetically, "just for a minute."

"It's all right, Jean-Baptiste . . . it's all right. I'm not afraid."

And she wasn't. One of his hands was under her buttocks, steadying, while he used the other to guide himself

into her, but it wasn't necessary, for even as he thrust
sharply downward, she was rocking up to meet him,
instinct taking over again. The sudden swift pain that cut
through her did not matter, for it mingled with another,
deeper, more encompassing agony that swelled and surged
until it seemed to fill her body.

She let herself move with it, flow with it, not thinking
anymore, not caring, mindlessly following the primitive
urges that consumed every part of her being. He was hers
in that moment, only hers, and she was his, and they
belonged together. The intensity grew, pure, exquisite
sensation, so sweet it was almost unbearable. Then suddenly, almost at the same instant, he gave a convulsive
shudder, and she felt herself tumbling, falling, crashing
from dizzying heights into the abyss of his arms.

Afterward she lay exhausted, savoring the warmth of
him next to her on the bed, and the strength, and wondering why she had ever been afraid to give herself to
him. Now all she wanted was to stay beside him, touching him, clinging to him forever. To stay beside him, and
make love with him again and again, and know she
would always be his.

But that, of course, was the one thing she couldn't
have.

She sat up, aware of a nagging sense of foreboding as
she wrapped the sheet around her. Lili. . . . She had
forgotten all about Lili. She had been so caught up in
new, rapturous sensations, she had completely forgotten
that the man who had just guided her across the threshold into womanhood was the man who was destined for
her cousin.

"I think it's time we got dressed," she said stiffly. "I
have to go home."

"So soon, little Simone?" He remained where he was,
lying on the bed, but his hand came up, as if to pull the
sheet from her breasts. "But I have a great deal yet to
show you."

Simone felt her body begin to respond, betraying the
deliberate logic of her thoughts.

"I have no doubt you do, Jean-Baptiste," she said,
stepping over to the window and looking out to cover her
confusion. Bright sunlight turned the lawn into plush
green velvet, and the white palace next door glittered
like an enormous diamond. "You are very handsome,

and very good at making me forget everything else. But I really do want to go home."

"Do you?" He had moved up behind her, his hand resting lightly on her waist. "I don't believe you're being quite honest with me. I believe you're thinking of your cousin again."

"Oh, Jean-Baptiste . . ." Simone's eyes glistened with unshed tears as she turned to face him. "I do love you so much. I will love you till the day I die—and I will always *want* you—but I love her too. Please try to understand. Lili's been a sister to me. I . . . I can't do this to her!"

"You've already done it," he reminded her gently. "You can't go back and change things now."

"I know. And I wouldn't if I could. This is the most beautiful thing that's ever happened in my life, and I will always treasure it. But I can't let it happen again!"

He was silent for a moment, leaning against the window frame, his chest slim and almost hairless, with a faint lacy pattern of light from the curtains.

"You really do love her, then? This young woman you call your sister? You care enough to give up your happiness for her?"

"But it wouldn't be *my* happiness, Jean-Baptiste! It would be hers, and I'd be stealing it." She turned back to the window, feeling vaguely uneasy as she stared at the larger, more elegant house a short distance away. Something about it tugged at the back of her mind—something she ought to be able to figure out and couldn't—but it was an unpleasant thought and she pushed it aside. "Lili was really horrid at first, when Don Andrés took me in. But later . . . well, later she was almost protective. As if I really *were* her sister. I couldn't bear it if I did anything to make her hate me."

"I doubt you could, angel," he said, urging her away from the window. "Stop staring at that formidable mansion, will you? I told you before, it's not important. Nothing that concerns you. And stop worrying that your gorgeous but very spoiled cousin is going to hate you. The lovely Mademoiselle Santana doesn't give a fig about me. Shall I tell you what she said, the one time we met in her father's parlor?"

He could feel her eyes on him, half-troubled, half-hopeful.

"Yes . . . what?"

"She told me—and I quote as exactly as I can remember —'I am here only because my papa ordered me to be.' " He pitched his voice just right, giving a fair imitation of Lili's spirited delivery. " 'I have no desire whatever to marry you, *monsieur*.' "

Simone's lips twitched. "That does sound like Lili," she admitted. It would be so easy to let him convince her, against all reason. She *wanted* to be convinced. "But—"

"But nothing," he broke in. "Good marriages are alliances between two families. Lili's father entered into this arrangement because it's convenient for him. I entered into it because it's convenient for me. And for pity's sake, don't look at me like that! I'm not a monster. Your cousin is going to have an easy, pleasant life, with all the advantages any Creole wife could hope for."

"Sometimes," Simone suggested tentatively, "feelings grow between people. Later . . . after they are married."

"Sometimes," he conceded. "If a man is really lucky, he might even find a wife he loves from the beginning. But there *are* no feelings between your cousin and me, and there never will be. All my feelings are for you, *chérie* . . . and they are growing all the time. And," he added with a wicked grin, "that's not the only thing that's growing."

Simone tried not to look down, but she couldn't help herself. And she tried even harder not to smile, but that was impossible too.

"You're perfectly awful," she told him primly. "You know you are."

If she had said anything else, he might not have wanted her so much. Or if she hadn't looked quite so wistful.

"How would you feel," he said, trying to sound casual, "if I told you you were going to come and live in this house?"

The color drained out of her face.

"You mean, with you . . . and Lili?"

"No, not Lili." He cursed himself inwardly. "This would be *your* house, *chérie*. Yours. Not any other woman's. You, and you alone, would be mistress here. Lili wouldn't come through the front gate unless it was at your invitation."

"I don't understand," she said slowly. But the words were barely out of her mouth when she realized she *did*

understand, all too well. Hadn't he told her he wasn't
planning on living here? She had assumed he meant it
was a town home, where he and his family would come
during the season. Only, of course, he had something
quite different in mind.

This was, for him, like those little houses along the
ramparts, where Creole gentlemen kept their black mistresses. Only it wasn't little, it was quite good-sized. And
it wasn't on the ramparts because she wasn't black!

"You mean . . . you want to keep me here."

"I mean," he said, leading her back to the bed and
sitting her on the edge, "I want you to *live* here. And be
very, very happy. You told me before that you found the
house pretty. I thought you liked it."

"Oh, I do, Jean-Baptiste. I like it very much."

"Then what's wrong? Is it me? Does it bother you,
thinking of spending all that time with me? Hours and
hours every day?"

"No, of course not. I love you very much. You know
that. But . . ."

"But . . . ?"

"But you want me to live here *in sin*!"

He laughed, catching hold of the sheet and beginning,
very slowly, to unwrap it. "It is sin we have just been
indulging in, *chérie*, and unless I'm very much mistaken,
you enjoyed it."

She tried to protest, but it was too late. His mouth was
already there, covering hers, hot and male and urgent.
They spent the rest of the day together, making love
again and then again, and everything was forgotten except the way her body quivered at his touch, and the
hardness of him, deep inside her.

It was not until later, when he had brought her home
and she was alone in her room, that Simone remembered
at last the reasons why she had tried to pull away from
him. The night seemed especially dark, with only a single
candle casting flickering rays over a faded red-and-gold
quilt. His words had been so sweet, his hands and mouth
so persuasive, it had been easy to give in. But all the
sweetness in the world could not stave off reality forever.

Her body was aching as she took off her dress and
threw it in a heap on the floor. Her undergarments were
spotted with blood, and she scrubbed them in cold water
in the basin, wanting to hide her guilty secret, though she

knew the maids would already have guessed and be gossiping. And at any rate, they wouldn't tell Don Andrés.

She loved him so much. She took out a fresh nightdress and sat on the bed, clutching it to her breast. She missed him already. A part of her longed to be with him, to feel his arms around her . . . to make love again despite the soreness from their recent encounter. But another part—the sensible, rational part—warned her to be cautious. She was only asking for grief if she let herself count on things that could never be.

And they never could. Alone, in the night chill of her room, she knew that. Things were so much clearer here. Suddenly the image of that other house came back—the elegant white house she had seen from the window—and she realized why she hadn't wanted to think about it.

It isn't important, chérie, he had told her. *It doesn't concern you.* But, oh, it *was* important, and it did concern her. Desperately. That was his house too! That was why he hadn't wanted to talk about it. The house where he would bring his new bride! Lili was going to live there, so close she would be able to look out her bedroom window and see her cousin in the garden next door . . . with her husband!

"Oh, dear God!" That was a shame she could not bear.

She drew the nightdress over her head, shivering as she slipped in between the cold sheets. Tomorrow he would be back, and she would go with him to the same room in the same house, and there was no denying what would happen there. As long as Lili was gone, as long as she was off somewhere making preparations for her wedding, they would continue to see—and enjoy—each other.

But she would be back . . . and when she was, it had to be over.

The candle sputtered, and Simone blew it out, letting darkness take over the room. She could continue the guilty affair as long as her cousin didn't know about it, but she would never be able to flaunt it in front of her. She couldn't humiliate Lili like that. Or herself.

It was funny, the way things worked out. She rested her head sleeplessly on the pillow. Like Lili, she had grown up in the shadow of the Fleurie curse. When she was little, she had believed it implicitly, the way children always believe fairy stories that give them nightmares. It had saddened—and frightened—her to think of the heart-break in store for her beautiful cousin.

Only the curse wasn't going to affect Lili at all. She realized that now with a grim sense of irony. Lili was the lucky one. She was going to come home in a few days with a beautiful new trousseau and marry the charming fiancé whose little fling she would never suspect, and he would come to adore her in time. Everyone always adored Lili.

It was she, Simone, who would spend the rest of her life dreaming of the man she loved but could not have.

17

The hasty departure from Bellefleur did nothing to assuage Lili's conflicting feelings about Jeremy Blaze. If anything, it intensified them.

"Complex" was too simple a word to describe him, she decided as she stood beside a muddy stream in the early dawn light and watched a small dot in the distance materialize into the hazy silhouette of a man in a boat. Jeremy was capable of warmth, when he chose, and moments of tenderness. But they were moments that almost seemed to be calculated, as if he were deliberately toying with her feelings, deliberately trying to get her to care—then laughing when he succeeded.

She hadn't been surprised, when she returned from her encounter with him in the little open belvedere, to find a trunk standing already packed in the center of her room. He had given her ample notice they were going to leave. Nor had she been surprised when their closed carriage pulled onto the river road with the last waning light of dusk. Criminals frequently concealed their activities under a cloak of darkness. But she had been surprised, an hour later, to be tossed rather unceremoniously on a pile of blankets in the back of an old farm wagon, with another blanket tented over the top. "For your comfort," Jeremy had told her smoothly, "in case it rains"—but she suspected he was more interested in making sure she couldn't see where they were going.

Now, shivering on the shore, after having spent the remaining night hours in a drafty hut, with nothing but a cup of chicory coffee to warm her, she was finding her feelings beginning to crystallize. Jeremy Blaze was an attractive man—she would be a fool if she tried to deny that—but he was a man whose inner thoughts she could never hope to fathom. And a man like that could be dangerous.

"Dare I ask," she said tartly, turning as she heard him come up behind her, "where we are?" The air was crisp, and there was just enough light to see her breath hanging in a cloud in front of her.

"Questions already?" Jeremy flashed her a deceptively amiable grin. He had on an old brown rawhide jacket, with the collar turned up, but his head was bare and a biting wind blew fair hair back from his brow. "I'm glad you've recovered from your uncomfortable night and are back to yourself again."

"And you, I see, are yourself too. Uncommunicative as usual. Does this mean you have no intention of telling me where we are?"

"Ah, and here I thought I was being wonderfully chatty—and communicating all over the place. Yes, of course I'll tell you, though I would have thought you'd guessed. We're on one of the bayous. The specific name wouldn't mean anything to you."

"I already knew that," Lili snapped irritably. She had been on bayous only near New Orleans, but she knew that the term covered all the bays and streams and minor rivers that permitted navigation throughout the area during most of the year. A suitably evasive answer, as usual! "Not that I'm familiar with the swampy depths of bayou country, mind you. From what I've heard, it's not the sort of place that attracts cultivated visitors. Aside from the smell—which, frankly, is vile!—everyone knows it's crawling with alligators. And *snakes*."

Jeremy laughed as he saw the delicate, ladylike shudder she made no effort to conceal. If anything, he had the feeling she magnified it for his benefit.

"Don't be so quick to distrust what you don't know," he said as he stepped up to meet the boat, easing the prow a foot or two onto shore. Seen up close, it appeared to be a canoe of some sort. "The bayous are fascinating if you give them half a chance. You've led much too sheltered a life, *petite*. It's time you got out and saw a bit of the world."

Lili was not at all sure she wanted to see the world. Especially when the lone oarsman scrambled onto the bank and it became clear that Jeremy expected *her* to climb in.

"You needn't stare at it like it's going to attack you," he said, stretching out a hand to help her. "This is not an alligator in disguise. It's called a *pirogue*. The Indians have been hollowing them out of cypress logs for years, and believe it or not, they almost always get where they're going."

It did indeed look like something that had been carved out of an old log. Still, Lili noted gratefully as she set one foot inside, there were at least rough seats, and it did seem fairly sturdy. But the sides were so round, it tipped back and forth every time she moved. And dirty water was sloshing over the bottom.

I'm going to catch my death of cold! she longed to snap testily. But she noticed that Jeremy waded almost to his knees as he shoved the boat away from the bank and jumped in agilely behind her. If he could take a little cold water on his feet without whimpering, then so could she! She wasn't going to give him the satisfaction of seeing how miserable she was, even if it killed her.

And very likely, she thought gloomily, it will!

The sun was just inching up, a great fiery ball, still low in the sky, and for the first minutes of their voyage, the world was a silent blaze of red and orange and gold. In spite of herself, Lili *was* fascinated. Jeremy had seated her in front, and she felt as if they were all alone, with no boats behind them, drifting into a magical dream place where nothing was real.

The wind had died down. The air was so still, the bayou turned into a mirror, broken only by ripples that fanned out from the prow. As the sun continued to rise and the *pirogue* dried somewhat, Lili felt her good spirits returning, and she had to admit it wasn't really all that uncomfortable. In fact, she might even have enjoyed herself if she'd had the slightest idea where they were going . . . and what was going to happen when they got there.

As it was, she kept her eyes glued to the shore, very deliberately avoiding the water. Now that the light was brighter, she was beginning to notice little slithery ripples that did not match the ripples of the boat.

"As you wouldn't tell me where we were before," she

said crisply, "I don't suppose you'll tell me now. Or where we're going."

"A good surmise." He did not break the rhythm of the paddle as he guided them skillfully around the low branch of a tree that trailed long streamers of moss into the water. "No, I have no intention of giving any specific details. I'll leave that to your very active imagination."

It took the better part of the morning to reach their destination, though Lili had no way of judging how much distance they covered. The scenery was a constantly changing kaleidoscope of color and flickering shadow. One minute, everything was open and bright, with yellow sunlight splashing on the murky water, giving it a *cafe-au-lait* appearance, and the banks were so clear, she caught glimpses of frogs hopping among the reeds. Then they would turn into a narrow side channel, and suddenly cypress branches were arching overhead, interwoven with each other and dripping with moss, and only the haziest light filtered through.

By the time Jeremy finally nudged the prow onto a small area along the bank where the vegetation had been partially cleared, Lili was hopelessly lost. She had tried to pick out landmarks as they glided through the water, and several times she thought she had succeeded. But then they passed what she could have sworn was the same dead oak again, the same little inlet where the cane was thicker and farther out from shore, and she was ready to weep with frustration. They might have traveled miles and miles, for all she knew, or they might have been going around in circles and be back where they started!

At least it was a relief to feel earth under her feet again, though the shore was spongy and her shoes made squishing noises when she walked. Civilization had never seemed quite so far away, and she had the sinking feeling her situation had just changed for the worse.

"I suppose," she said, tilting her chin up to boost her courage as he led her away from the bank, "you're taking me to some dreadful little hovel with wind howling through chinks in the walls and a bed of moss to sleep on! Yes, and oiled paper at the windows too, which wild animals probably scratch out in the night!"

But the building that came into view at the edge of a shallow clearing was, if small and roughly sided, at least relatively sturdy. Poles, or stilts, raised it several feet off the marshy soil, and even from the ground, Lili could see that the walls had been properly constructed. And the windows, thank heaven, were glazed, so at least otters and muskrats would be kept at bay, though she wasn't so sure about the snakes.

The interior was unexpectedly tidy, and clean as a pin, with a faint odor of onions and hot pepper, like the smell Lili had come to associate with Dédé Matouse's kitchen. Most of the space was taken up by one large room, plainly intended for both cooking and living, with a rough wooden table in one corner and cots doubling as benches along the walls.

"Dédé will be staying here with you," Jeremy informed her. "And Stevie. They'll see that you have everything you need."

"Thank you," Lili retorted, wondering if he really thought she was stupid enough to believe that Dédé was there to take care of her rather than act as her guard.

There was one other room, a small sleeping chamber. Lili stepped over to the door and looked in curiously. Someone had already brought her trunk and placed it against the wall next to a rustic vanity with a mirror on a stand. The only other furniture was a bed, surprisingly soft-looking, and not as narrow as she might have expected.

She glanced around nervously to see that Jeremy was watching her from across the room.

"Never fear," he said, reading her thoughts. "The bed is intended for one. I have a cottage near the main camp, where the men are bunking, a short distance away." He paused, eyes hooding suggestively as he ran them slowly down her figure. "When, and if, I decide to dally with you, I'm sure I can find something more, uh . . . suitable."

Lili didn't know whether to be relieved or irritated as he swung around and headed toward the door. He had an offhand way of dismissing her that always brought her temper to the tip of her tongue, as she sensed he intended. But when he looked at her like that—when he dared her with those mocking blue eyes—something deep inside couldn't help remembering the way she had felt the first time he touched her. And wondering how she would feel now if he turned around and came back into the room.

The men had all gathered by the time they got back to

the place where they had left the boat. Several other *pirogues* were on the bank now, and everyone was scurrying around, carrying provisions, Lili supposed, and other items back to the main part of the camp.

They were a loud, boisterous group, bold of movement, and almost too theatrical to be real. Not a one of them was the least bit familiar, and Lili couldn't help wondering, as she watched them scramble up the bank and hoist sacks and cartons, why Jeremy had left the other men behind. These were younger, for the most part, and rather flashy, but not as tough-looking, as if they were used to easy living. Flaring shirts had been tucked almost tidily into tight-fitting trousers, and sashes at their waists and bold blue-and-scarlet head scarves showed a love of color.

It's strange, she thought, that there are so many of them. It hardly seemed necessary. All those men to guard one helpless female captive. Why would Jeremy let so many people in on his plan? Unless . . .

"This isn't all because of me, is it?" she said as he stopped next to her. A sack of something that looked like grain was balanced on one broad shoulder. "You didn't come here because you needed a place to hide me until you collected the ransom. You have something else going on."

"I never claimed you were the only thing in my life, *petite*." He tossed her an impudent smile that sent quivers all the way down to her toes, even after everything he had done. "Yes, certainly I have other things going on. Not, of course, that they're as important as you."

Lili ignored the teasing chivalry of his words. Her mind was whirling, trying to sort things out. Jeremy Blaze had been a highwayman on the Natchez Trace, they said—or if he hadn't, he'd gone to great pains to spread the story in town. Only there weren't any highwaymen in the bayous.

But the bayous were a notorious hangout for pirates.

"That's it," she said, her throat suddenly going dry. "You're not a highwayman at all. I doubt you've even been on the Natchez Trace. You're a pirate . . . or a smuggler! That story was just a cover. You have a ship someplace, or ships, and these are your men! They'll do anything you ask, won't they, including cut my throat?"

"If I ask them . . . yes."

The lightness in his voice somehow made the words

more alarming than if he'd snarled them through clenched teeth. Lili started to shiver again, not from the cold this time.

"Oh, sweet heaven." She looked around at the land that seemed to be surrounded everywhere by muddy water. Only that was because it *was* surrounded. They were on an island—and she realized suddenly what island it was! "This is Grande-Terre! We're on Grande-Terre, aren't we?"

Jeremy looked startled, as if he hadn't thought she was bright enough to figure it out. Then, shrugging casually, he shifted the weight of the sack on his shoulders.

"So your active imagination *has* been at work. Well, and what if it is Grande-Terre? Everyone in New Orleans already knows that pirates and smugglers use the island as a base. Its location is hardly a secret. And no one is likely to come here without an army."

"No," Lili said dryly, "I don't suppose they will." She racked her brain, trying to remember what she had heard about the infamous pirate rendezvous. Somehow she had assumed Grande-Terre was farther out, near the Gulf someplace, but her geography had always been fuzzy. What she did know was that it was a good-size island, fringed with trees to screen it from passing ships. And it was inhabited by desperate, vicious, hardened criminals whose notorious brawling struck terror even into the hearts of other ruffians! "And you brought me *here*? To a place like this?"

"The perfect place to keep a captive, don't you think? And to conduct other . . . business. But you needn't be alarmed. Grande-Terre is quite large, and we're in an isolated section. Besides, I'm gaining a certain reputation— and I do have a sizable contingent of men with me."

"Oh? That does reassure me *so* much." Lili was getting her wind back, after the shock of discovering where she was. And how little regard he had for her safety! "I keep forgetting, you're a kind, thoughtful, *trustworthy* man—as you have taken such pains to inform me. You promised nothing would happen to me at Bellefleur, and it didn't, so now I am supposed to be perfectly comfortable on one of the vilest islands in the territory!"

"Why not," he said with infuriating coolness, "since there's nothing you can do about it?"

He tightened his hold on the sack and was just starting

toward a path that led into the scrub when he turned and glanced back.

"Shall I give you a bit of advice, *petite*?"

"Can I stop you?"

"Don't fight so hard when you haven't a prayer of winning. You're like that elderly Spanish gentleman always tilting after windmills. I told you before, the swamps can be a fascinating place to spend a few days. Why don't you settle in and relax? You might even learn a few things that surprise you."

In the days that followed, Lili had to concede, reluctantly, that it wasn't bad advice. The bayous, with their fireflies and deep blue twilights, ancient oaks and cypresses dripping with moss, had a way of burrowing under one's skin, and even the reality of being kidnapped was not unrelievedly awful. True, Jeremy had torn her abruptly from the only life she had ever known, but he had opened whole new worlds in the process. Bellefleur first, with long walks over the grounds, and detailed explanations of things even planters' wives rarely experienced. And now the marshlands, which she might have passed her whole life without seeing.

Nor was Jeremy's company quite as unwelcome as she had a feeling it ought to be. He still treated her the same way, periods of maddening aloofness punctuated by the wickedly lewd innuendos of which he seemed to be a master. But she was getting used to him, and handling it better.

And finding, despite her resolve, that her attraction to him was growing, while her resistance weakened day by day.

Only a foolish little virgin would kiss a man like that, he had taunted that sun-drenched morning in the belvedere, *if she wasn't ready to accept the consequences*. And he had been right . . . then. She hadn't been ready. She had been afraid, and not sure yet what she wanted.

Only she wasn't anymore that same young girl he had dragged so roughly into his carriage. She was a woman, with a woman's body, and a woman's needs she was just beginning to recognize. If he kissed her now, as he had that first night, if he pinned her hard against his body, hands fondling, daring, as they had dared then, would she push him away?

She didn't have the opportunity to find out, for Jeremy, as if he guessed what she was thinking and was disinclined to put her to the test, kept her at arm's length as the days passed into a week, and a week inched on toward two. He was unfailingly attentive—so much so that under any other circumstances Lili would have been flattered—and always entertaining, but he never took that one step beyond the bounds of propriety.

Still, she had to admit she was having the time of her life. There had always been something of the tomboy in her, and she was able to indulge it freely here. Mornings, Jeremy was usually busy, but he didn't object if she stood unobtrusively on the edge of the clearing and watched as the men pulled boat after boat onto shore and unloaded large wooden crates with Chinese characters on the sides. Something illegal, she supposed—the proceeds of a smuggling operation—but it was intriguing all the same, and she found herself staring at the boxes, wondering what was inside. Tea, perhaps. Tea came from China. But the way the men were tossing them around, they hardly seemed to weigh anything. Would tea be that light?

In the afternoons, when the boats were gone, Jeremy had more time, and then they would hike together, covering what seemed like miles and miles. Perhaps he hadn't been exaggerating when he said there was an adequate buffer between them and whatever else lay on the infamous Grande-Terre. Lili was finding it wonderful fun, putting on pantaloons and high boots and sloshing through the mud, or crouching absolutely still behind a tree and watching the otters at play. Or learning how to find possums in the daytime, or paddle a *pirogue* like an Indian along the reedy shore. She didn't even mind that she was turning brown as a quadroon and would be positively shocking when she got home, though she did make a point of watching where she put her feet, and her ear was always tuned for rustling in the grass.

When Jeremy was occupied elsewhere, it was Tin-Tin, and occasionally his sister, who accompanied her, teaching her how to identify the birds by their calls, which even the flighty Vava seemed to get right every time, and where the fish were likely to be biting.

It was from Tin-Tin that she learned about the Cajuns and their way of life.

"We're 'bout the laziest folks you're like to lay eyes

on," he told her one day as he baited a hook and dropped it into a promisingly shady spot. "Born lazy and die lazy, and any man says we're not, I'll punch 'im in the eye."

Lili laughed. "I'm sorry, but you don't seem lazy to me. You hunt for your own meat, and you fish, and you grow your own rice and corn and sweet potatoes. All you pick up in town, according to Jeremy, is flour and powder and shot—and coffee, of course, by the ton. He says you even taught yourself to play the violin."

"Fishin' isn't work. Or huntin'. Or playin' the fiddle and dancin' to the tune. But *work* is work, and us Cajuns avoid it like the pox. That's why we live in little shacks in the swamps and have maybe a change or two o' clothes. There ain't no sense workin' for somethin' you don't need, that's what we always say."

Lili leaned back against the bank, enjoying the jesting banter. The Cajuns *were* lazy, in a way. She had always heard that they could never be depended on—they would drop anything, people said, if a youth came riding along, waving a pole with a red flag on the end to announce an impromptu party. But theirs was a different kind of laziness. They worked long, bone-wearying hours for the things they needed. They just didn't have the same hunger for material possessions.

It was Tin-Tin, too, who taught her the derivation of the word "Cajun," which, as it turned out, was a corruption of "Acadian," referring to someplace in Canada that had once been known as Acadia, though everyone called it New Scotland now—Nova Scotia. It had been French, apparently, but the English had conquered it, and in 1755 they tried to force the colonists to swear an oath of allegiance. The feisty Acadians had refused, quite rightly, as far as Lili was concerned—she couldn't imagine anyone preferring the English to the French—and they had been brutally expelled.

Some of the Cajuns had come directly to Louisiana, arriving the following year, 1756. Others, the ones who had the hardest time, it seemed to Lili, had been crowded into ships and expelled at various points along the Atlantic coast. A few found friendly, compassionate welcomes, but most had met with hostility and suspicion, and slowly, group by group, they had made their way, under the most trying circumstances, to the French-speaking shores of Louisiana. There they had settled in the swamps and

bayous, burrowing deeper and deeper into barely pene-
trable territory and vowing that no one would ever herd
them up like animals and drive them from their homes
again.

"So you see, it isn't just laziness that motivates us,"
Tin-Tin said good-naturedly as he pulled in his line after
a catfish stole the bait. "Governments, especially new
ones, have a way of feeling threatened by folks who own
too much. If you don't have anything, you're not tempting anyone to take it away."

"I don't think, with the Americans, that will make
much difference," Lili said doubtfully, though she had to
admit, in the five years since they had taken over, there
hadn't been any talk of banishing people who refused to
sign loyalty oaths. But then, Louisiana would be empty if
they did!

She enjoyed listening to Tin-Tin, but she couldn't help
noticing that he didn't talk like a Cajun, which struck her
as odd, especially when she learned that he, like the sons
of fine old Creole families, had been educated at Montpellier in France.

"Ain't usual for a young man t' come back from Montpellier," he said, giving Lili a broad wink, "talkin' lak a
Cajun."

Maybe, she thought skeptically. But Cajuns weren't
usually educated abroad either. And graduates of Montpellier weren't usually part of a pirate's retinue in the
bayous . . . at least she didn't think they were. Certainly
not with their parents' blessing! Stevie and Dédé must
have sacrificed a great deal to scrape together the money
for their son's education. She would have thought they
had one of the professions in mind for him. Or maybe a
career in business.

But Jeremy only laughed when she mentioned it to
him.

"What preconceived notions you have, *petite*." He was
sitting on a log at the water edge of the clearing, mending
an old fishing net that had become badly ripped. His shirt
was half-open to the waist, with a frank sensuality Lili
tried not to notice, though it was hard to keep her eyes
where they belonged. " 'Business' to you is an office
someplace, with dark paneling and clerks in eye shades
adding up rows of figures. Well, piracy is business too.
And smuggling. Especially in New Orleans."

"You call *that* business?" Lili stared up from where she sat cross-legged in front of him on the ground. His fingers moved nimbly, finding and repairing tears as if he had been doing it all his life, though he didn't have so much as a callus to show for his toil. "Smuggling? Piracy? But they're . . . they're dishonest!"

"Preconceived notions again?" He laughed as he glanced up from his work, enjoying the companionable moment as much as Lili, though in a different way. It was late afternoon, and shadows brought out a new, intriguing maturity in the exquisitely chiseled lines of her face. She seemed to be growing, right in front of his eyes, taking on new depth and dimension, though she still had some flighty feminine ideas. "You ladies look on business as something open and aboveboard, therefore honest and legal. Has it ever occurred to you, my sweet little innocent, that a man who makes a great deal of money in business might actually cheat at times? Or out-and-out steal?"

"Well . . . yes," Lili admitted. More than once she had heard raised voices coming through Don Andrés' study door, and the word "thief" had been distinctly detectable. "Papa says you have to watch certain men or they'll rob you blind. But—"

"Your papa is a man of business. Who better to know how fine the line is between honest and dishonest in trade?"

"Are you saying he's a thief himself?" Lili twisted her legs around, half-rising to her knees and bristling with indignation. "That's not true! Papa is a fine, decent man. Honor means everything to him."

"I'm sure it does, *petite*. I didn't mean to undermine either your illusions or your very laudable affection." He smiled to himself as he saw the way her chin jutted out, like a little girl again, reminding him vividly of the enchanting creature he had first laid eyes on such a short time before. Rather to his surprise, he realized that her extreme youth was part of what appealed to him. That and the way she had of throwing herself headlong into things, without stopping to think of the consequences. "Don Andrés is well-known for his decency and upright behavior. He's as honest as it's practical to be in the world of business—perhaps more so—and I do, sincerely, respect him. But he'd be the first to agree that integrity and commerce don't always go hand in hand. And good business sense is just as important in so-called illegal operations."

"What a funny way you have of putting things," Lili said, slightly mollified by his profession of respect for Don Andrés. Besides, the breezes were warm, almost sultry, with a tantalizing scent of spring, and it was so much pleasanter sitting and talking than constantly parrying with each other. "Why do you say 'so-called'? Either something is illegal or it isn't."

"At any given time, yes." The light was getting dimmer, and he held the net up, squinting as he inspected a newly repaired section. "But laws are made by men and changed by men. What's legal today might be illegal tomorrow, and vice versa. Take piracy, for instance. The European powers swept the seas clean years ago, but they left a profitable loophole. We call it privateering, to make it sound better."

"Privateering?"

"Legal piracy. Under maritime law, all a privateer has to do is carry letters of marque issued by a nation at war, and he can legitimately attack any vessel flying the 'enemy' flag. To keep his booty, he simply sails into a port of the country to which he swears allegiance and has it approved by an admiralty court."

He turned back to his work, and Lili watched as he ran his eyes over every inch of the net, checking and rechecking the mends, tugging at them to make sure they held. Something in the single-mindedness of what he was doing fascinated her. It was almost as if everything else in the world was gone, and that was the only thing that existed.

The light was fading rapidly, and he looked away for a moment, staring at something in the distance. Streaks of red were deepening in the sky, and his profile was a dark silhouette, intensely strong against that fiery glow of color.

If only it were easy to dislike him . . . or to be afraid. Lili stared at him openly, trying to make something out of his features in the rapidly diminishing light. But there was nothing easy about this unpredictable, enigmatic, maddeningly difficult man. His face might be strong and rugged, etched with the fierce independence she secretly admired, or it might be hawklike, with the innate sharpness of a predator. He might be powerful or savage, ironwilled or unfeeling, dynamic or cruel—it was impossible to tell. He might be the kind of man men listened to and followed—and women adored—or the kind they hated and feared.

One thing was certain. He wasn't a man who faded into the crowd. A man who passed unnoticed anywhere he went. There was an almost animal magnetism about him that drew her eyes and held them, and would not let them go.

"You are watching me, *petite*, as if you didn't know what to make of me."

His voice broke the spell, and Lili found herself smiling.

"Perhaps," she said softly, "that's because I don't."

It might have been Tin-Tin who taught Lili the ways of Cajun life, but it was from his younger sister, Vava, that she learned the infinitely more intriguing facts of life in general. The girl had taken to coming by in the evenings, and often stayed overnight, for her father was increasingly reluctant to let her out of his sight after dark. And in the double bed in the small back room, amidst giggles and whispers that lasted well into the night, Lili found out why.

Poor Stevie. He must have forgotten what it was to be young if he thought a sunset curfew would have any effect on his irrepressible daughter. Like her older brother, Vava had been educated—in her case, in the same convent school Lili had attended before Papa engaged private tutors for her—but beyond a certain fluency in languages, little had rubbed off. She was still more interested in good food than good books, and good toe-tapping music, and a young man she referred to as "my Pierre" in a proprietary tone of voice.

"Papa," she whispered rather smugly, "does not approve."

Lili, knowing Stevie as she did, was inclined to doubt it. If he really disapproved, he would have locked the girl in and posted guards at the door. More likely, all those fatherly scowls were calculated to give the courtship forbidden appeal.

But he most certainly would not have approved of what the two young people were doing.

Lili listened night after night, enthralled, as the girl described in vivid detail exactly what she and her young swain had been up to, and where and how. For someone whose knowledge of lovemaking was fuzzy at best, it was an eye-opening education. Sometimes it got so explicit it was embarrassing—Lili sensed it was improper even *listening* to such things—but she couldn't bring herself to put a stop to that torrent of enlightening words.

Only the more she heard, the more she was sure that this was something she did not want to do with the man she was going to have to marry. Just the thought of it was enough to make her skin crawl. But if that man were Jeremy . . .

Long after Vava had finished and was snoring gently in the darkness, Lili lay awake, her body aching with longings she could now put a name to. Before, her fantasies had centered more around Jeremy's strong searing kisses than that vague, undefined "something" beyond. Now, for the first time, she understood what she wanted him to do with his hands and his mouth, and other parts of his body, which had been only sketchy in her imaginings before. It was unbearable sometimes, feeling all those new, intensified hungers, knowing they would never be satisfied and thinking of flighty little Vava, hotly enclosed in the embrace of a virile young man who would sooner or later be her husband.

It was not that Lili begrudged Vava her happiness. She liked the Cajun girl and wished only the best for her. But she yearned for the same excitement herself, the same passion, the same sheer joy of touching and being touched. She yearned to be a woman, to know how it felt, just once, to lie in the arms of a man she loved.

And the only man she would ever love like that—Jeremy Blaze—didn't seem to be interested anymore.

Or perhaps, she thought late one evening when the house was empty and she was alone, he was just tired of what he considered her silly virgin games. It was so quiet she could hear the rustling of her skirt as she rose and glanced toward the door. Perhaps he hadn't guessed what she was thinking, after all, and didn't know that her feelings were changing. He had pressed his attentions on her rather forcefully that first night in the carriage—and gotten nothing but rejection and a spate of girlish tears. Perhaps he didn't want to put his ego on the line again.

She slipped into the bedroom and pulled one of the dresses out of her trunk. The one Jeremy had admired that first morning in the parlor at Bellefleur. There was a party someplace, a *fais do-do* as they called it, and Stevie had gone with Dédé to keep an eye on their impetuous daughter. From what Lili had heard of Cajun fetes, they could not possibly be back before dawn. She would be unguarded until then, and unchaperoned.

What if she went to the little cottage at the edge of the main camp where Jeremy slept alone? What if they were there together, just the two of them, in romantic golden lamplight? Surely he would kiss her again, if only to tease. And when he did . . .

Lili did not give herself time to think what she was doing. The dress was on in a matter of seconds, and her hair was loose and brushed, dark, shimmering clouds floating over her shoulders. It was not as if she had anything to lose. The man Papa had chosen wasn't likely to believe in her purity when she returned anyway. And she didn't care if he did! She'd rather be an old maid than have to marry him.

But she didn't want to be an old maid without memories of at least one night of love to sustain her.

When she reached the cottage with her lantern, she found to her dismay that it was empty. The door was ajar, but there was no need to knock, for everything was dark and ominously silent.

Stepping inside, she looked around curiously. Jeremy Blaze was a man of simple tastes apparently, for there were no adornments, and not a stick of furniture, not so much as a table or a chair to sit on. The moss she had imagined as a bed for herself seemed to be where he slept, for there was a pile of it against one wall, with a blanket on top and several others in a neat stack to the side.

Lili hesitated on the threshold, wondering if she ought to leave. Then, deciding that was silly, she set the lantern on the floor and sank down on the moss, propping one of the blankets up as a backrest behind her. She had come this far. She might as well wait and see if he returned, or if he was out all night tending to errands she didn't even want to imagine.

It seemed to be the latter, for an hour passed and still he had not come. Lili paced for a while, then settled back, making herself as comfortable as she could on the moss bed. Suddenly she was so tired it was hard to keep her eyes open. Rolling up one of the spare blankets, she

tucked it under her head as a makeshift pillow. Just a few
minutes more, she told herself sleepily as she curled up in
a ball and tugged another blanket over her. Just a few
minutes . . . and then if he wasn't there, she'd get up and
slip back to the house.

She must have dozed off, for the next thing she noticed
was a funny sputtering noise. When she opened her eyes,
the light from the lantern was flickering on and off. Out
of oil, she supposed; she hadn't checked before she left.
And the night was so dark, she couldn't go back without it.

Groggily she slipped out of her dress, easing it off the
bed onto the floor. No point wrinkling her clothes any
more than she had to. It looked like she was going to be
there all night alone.

The irony of the situation did not escape her as she
burrowed deeper into the blankets, pulling them over her
shoulders. All those days agonizing over how she felt,
what she wanted, what she was going to do. Then she
finally decided to give herself to him, and he wasn't even
there.

She let her head sink deeper into the pillow. And fell
asleep.

18

"What in blazes are you doing here?"
Jeremy's voice broke rudely into her reverie. Lili opened her eyes with a snap, trying numbly to bring things into focus. She had been having such a lovely dream: Jeremy had been holding her in his arms, caressing her tenderly, whispering sweet promises of love in her ear. Now here he was, leaning over her with a lantern—and he looked anything but pleased.

"I . . . I must have fallen asleep."

"So I see," he replied dryly. "It doesn't take extraordinary mental powers to calculate that. But what the devil are you doing sleeping in *my* bed?"

"Everybody was gone, and . . . well, it was lonely in the house, and quiet, and I thought I'd come here to see you . . ." Lili sat up, not even thinking, until it was too late, that she was clad only in a sheer linen chemise, which golden lantern rays had a way of turning almost translucent. Hastily she tugged the blanket up in front of her. "There weren't any chairs, so I sat on the bed, and then I got tired and—"

"And you decided you might as well remove your clothes?" Deep blue eyes glinted with sarcasm as he took in the extent of her dishabille. She had let the blanket slip slightly, and he was uncomfortably aware of tantalizing half-moons of dark nipples rising out of the rough gray wool. In spite of himself, something tightened in his groin, and he made his voice unnecessarily gruff. "Hardly the usual behavior for a pleasant social call. Especially from a sweet little innocent whose sensitivities have been so easily offended in the past."

Lili turned crimson all the way down to the roots of

her hair. "I didn't do it on purpose . . . exactly. It's just that the light went out, and I couldn't go anywhere without it, and I didn't think you were coming back . . ."

"If you didn't think I'd return, why did you stay in the first place?" He had squatted beside her, setting his lantern on the floor, but his face was so rigid it might have been carved out of stone. There was nothing to give Lili even the faintest hint what he was thinking. "And that story about the house being quiet doesn't make sense. With your horror of snakes, you'd never venture out in the dark just because you were bored. Why did you really come here?"

Lili gulped. This was not at all what she had imagined. He was supposed to draw her into his arms—gently or roughly, it didn't matter—look at her with such longing it took her breath away, and kiss her with hard, hungry lips. And she would have kissed him back, telling him wordlessly how she felt. Now all she could do was blurt it out.

"I came because I . . . I want you to make love to me, Jeremy!"

That got his attention. His eyes narrowed just for a moment, betraying some depth of emotion Lili could only guess at. Then they glazed over, and he was coldly, brutally in control again.

"So you're still playing little virgin games."

"Oh, no." Lili's eyes welled with helpless tears. "No, I'm not playing games! And I don't want to be a virgin anymore. I'm sick to death of my silly virginity! All it's given me are priggish doubts and a lot of wasted time. I want to get rid of it . . . and I want you to help me."

"Damn!" Jeremy muttered the word softly through clenched teeth. She had swayed closer—unconsciously, he suspected. Perfume rose from her hair and bosom, intoxicating his nostrils. "You may think you're not playing games, but you are—and you haven't considered the price you'd be paying. Virginity, my sweet, is every man's ultimate prize. Prize, hell—it's a basic requirement! There isn't a Creole alive who'd willingly accept 'used merchandise' in his marriage bed."

Lili dropped her gaze, sooty lashes barely shivering against her cheeks. She had him! She realized that with a sudden jolt of surprise. That was desire she heard vibrating in his voice—desire he couldn't conceal.

She had come there to seduce him. She wouldn't have put it quite that way—she had hoped, in fact, that he would be the one to seduce *her*—but the effect was going to be the same.

"And you?" she murmured, daring to look up. "You are a Creole man. Would *you* refuse to take a woman you loved—and wanted—into your marriage bed because she had been possessed by someone else?"

"I don't know," he said, obviously thrown by the question. "I never thought about it. Just once, and then . . . But dammit, we're not talking about me! It's not Jeremy Blaze you're going to have to contend with on your wedding night. Your father has chosen a different sort of husband for you, a pillar of Creole society. And pillars of society are likely to be steeped in tradition."

"And preconceived notions?" Lili lifted her hand, longing, but not quite daring, to lay it on the broad, strong expanse of his chest. "I'm sure he *is* traditional and rigid, and vain enough not to want to be second. But aren't you forgetting something? You've established a certain reputation, especially when it comes to women. Even if you send me back as virginal as you found me, who's going to believe it? Do you really think this Jean-Baptiste Cavarelle, with his tradition and his vanity, will take a chance on a bride who might be impure?"

Jeremy raised one eyebrow. "So you think you're going to be branded anyway?"

"I know I am. Not just by the Cavarelles, but by society in general—whether I'm guilty or not. So it doesn't make any difference, does it?"

Jeremy studied her silently, assessing the alternatives in his mind, wishing for a moment he could ignore the obvious. But she was so blasted young. And she couldn't possibly understand what was happening.

"Purity is a thing that can be proven," he said stiffly. "There are doctors . . . and ways to be sure. If he has any doubts, this Cavarelle fiancé, he can call on someone to check things out for him."

Lili turned away, shuddering. "You make it sound so . . . so clinical. And so horrid!"

"I don't mean to." He leaned forward, touching her lightly on the arms. He was absurdly conscious, as he did so, of the warmth of her, the nearness, as he knew she was conscious of him. "One of us has to show some restraint, *petite*. Loving a man physically is as irrevocable a commitment as marriage, and the results could be more than 'horrid' when your fiancé finds out you're not what he expected. Oh, he might go through with the wedding. There are all sorts of reasons for marriage. But he might resent you for it. And he could make your life miserable."

"Don't you see, Jeremy?" Lili turned slowly, making no effort to hide the tears that were now flowing down her cheeks. "My life is going to be miserable anyhow, married to a man I don't love . . . or even like! At least this way I'd have memories."

She felt his hand on the side of her face, tender, comforting. His thumb was brushing her cheek, and tears were spilling over it.

"You seem to have thought this all through."

"I have . . . and I know what I want. I love you, Jeremy. I want the first time—the only time that will ever truly count—to be with you." She took his hand, holding it for a second, then laid it on her breast. A shudder seemed to run through his body. She could almost feel him surrender.

"You know I desire you, Lili," he said huskily. "You've already figured that out. It would be so easy for me to take you now, to make love to you the way you want to be loved . . ." His fingers had begun to move, tracing her lacy neckline, slipping beneath to caress the soft flesh of her breasts.

"But . . . ?"

Lili held her breath, not daring to let it out. She felt her nipple leap up, erect against sheer linen, aching for his fingers to find it.

"But I want you to be sure. Very sure that it's me—and only me—you want. The act, once done, cannot be recalled. For a woman, there's only one chance."

"One chance is all I need. And yes, I'm sure it's you I want. I love you, Jeremy Blaze—or whoever you are. I know this is a commitment. I know it will affect the rest of my life, and I don't care!"

"You understand what you'd be giving up? Any possibility of finding love in the future, any possibility whatsoever of having a whole, satisfying life with another man."

"I understand."

"And if you're afraid, if you have any doubts—"

"If I'm afraid," she said throatily, "you'll have to kiss me and build up my courage."

She tilted her head back, not even caring how wanton she seemed, coaxing his lips down on hers with a sheer force of will. But she didn't have to coax him to thrust his tongue into her mouth, hot and probing, hungrily demanding the responses she was only too eager to give. It was a hard kiss, with no gentleness in it, an angry surrender, but urgent and longing, and every nerve ending in her body was throbbing with excitement.

"And if you regret it later," he said hoarsely when they had come up for air, "if he rejects you, this choice of your father's, if no other man will have you, and you're sorry—"

"Then you'll have to rescue me," she cried, sure of her hold on him now, sure of the triumph that would soon be hers. "You'll have to come riding through the streets in a darkened carriage on another rainy night, and carry me off, poor unwanted creature, and marry me yourself!"

She felt him stiffen, almost before the words were out of her mouth, and she could have bitten off her tongue. Whatever had possessed her to use that word, "marry," when he hadn't even hinted at such a thing? When she knew he didn't love her as she loved him? All he wanted, all she could expect of him, was this one brief dalliance, and then, like Roger de Courbet Montaigne, he would ride off and never be heard from again.

"I . . . I'm sorry. That was a silly thing to say. I was only joking."

"No, I think not." His eyes darkened, turning almost blue-black in the lantern light. Lili could feel them scouring her face, searching for something he did not seem to find. "I think you meant every word of it—you just didn't mean to say it out loud. You told me you understood. You pretended you were looking at things realistically, but you weren't."

"I *was*," she said miserably. How could she have been such a fool? Everything had been going so well. "Truly I was!"

"You said you wanted me. Just me. A chance to learn about love the first time with the man of your choice. But what you really wanted was me on my knees proposing to make a proper wife out of you. Complete with a ceremony in the cathedral, no doubt."

"Oh!" Lili saw his lips tighten, a thin hard line, like that night in the carriage. Only then she had rejected him, not the other way around. She *had* been unrealistic. She hadn't let herself think about it, but somewhere in the back of her mind there had been daydreams of an elaborate wedding and a life of bliss together, despite the realities of the situation . . . and the Fleurie curse.

But even if she couldn't have that, even if she never saw him after this one night, she wanted to be with him anyway. Somehow, she had to find something—think of something!—to get him to change his mind. She couldn't have come so close only to lose him now.

Then she remembered the way he had looked at her when she first sat up in her skimpy undergarment, the way his hands seemed to have been drawn like magnets to her breast. Perhaps, if she just had the courage, there might still be a chance.

She reached up, trembling as her fingers caught the drawstring that held the front of her chemise together.

"You may not want to make all those pretty dreams come true, Jeremy, but I'm not going to let you cheat me out of my memories."

She jerked the string in one abrupt motion, pulling it loose. The lace-dainty neck held for a second, clinging to soft shoulders, then fell away, exposing both her breasts.

A sharp intake of breath greeted her action, all the encouragement she needed, and Lili felt her heart soar. Jeremy's eyelids drooped, half-closing, one last attempt at resistance, but she already knew he was going to lose.

"All right," he said roughly. "You want memories . . . I'll give you memories. But I'll be blasted if I'm going to ruin you in the process."

Lili didn't have time to contemplate his words, or even wonder what they meant, for he was urging her back, down on the soft, yielding moss, and suddenly the flimsy chemise was no longer protecting any part of her body. Something rough brushed against her back—the blanket, she supposed . . . it was strange how different it felt now that she was naked—and then his hands were touching her again. Rough male hands, not smooth and pampered like her own, frightening in their bold demands, but delighting too, and she quivered as she felt them sensuously sliding down her arms, following the slender curve of her waist, slipping around to the small of her back.

"Oh, my darling," she whispered, "I love you so much. Truly I do. I will always—"

"Shhhh." Jeremy touched his lips lightly to hers, briefly, just enough to still her. He sensed vaguely that he had come to a turning point, a time to decide how he wanted to handle things, what he wanted to say to this woman, do with her. Temptation flickered across his mind, tantalizing, then went away . . . and he let it go. "No promises, *petite*. I can't let you make any promises, when I can give nothing in return."

"Nothing . . . ?"

He laughed softly. His lips had found her neck; teeth were playing with her fragile skin, provocatively, deliberately, half-kissing, half-nibbling. "Nothing but a small lesson in lovemaking . . . and a sense of how it feels to be a woman. If that is enough."

"It is enough." Lili squirmed with pleasure, responding now, no longer reasoning, or even trying to. She could feel his hands, exploring, leaving no hill or valley untouched, running down her sides, rounding her hips, coming to rest with unchecked impudence on her thighs. It *was* enough . . . for now. Later she would want more—later perhaps he would be willing to give it—but now, all she could concentrate on, all she could feel, was the heat that seared through her everywhere those bold hands touched.

"Here, love," he murmured hoarsely. "Lie back . . . like this." She felt him urge her down, felt the bedding sink beneath her weight like a soft feather pillow, felt the edges fluffing up around her. His eyes were hungry as they caressed her, hooded and intense, devouring every inch of her breasts, her belly, the glistening hair between her legs that no man had ever seen before.

He wanted her! She was absolutely sure of that. She sensed his passion as keenly as she felt the irresistible new forces that were sweeping through her own body. He wanted her, and yet, surprisingly, he had made no move to take off his clothes.

"Shouldn't you . . . ?" She raised her hand to his shirt front, just where the open neck ended, feeling suddenly tentative, confused. Now that it was actually happening, she realized she didn't have the vaguest notion how to seduce a man . . . or even if she still had to. "Aren't you wearing too much clothing?"

Jeremy didn't stop her as she unfastened first one button, then the next. But he did nothing to help her either, and she lost her nerve halfway down to his waist.

"Not for what I have in mind." He leaned over impulsively, loosening her hair where it had become tangled behind her, tumbling it in a luxuriant silken cascade over the creamy flesh of her shoulders.

"Which is . . . ?"

"Why, to show you something of love, of course. The physical love that exists between a man and a woman. Isn't that what you wanted?"

A slow shudder ran through her as she felt him claim her breasts, fondling, caressing, cupping them in hard, strong, gentle hands. She had not known a man's passion could be so demanding, yet so tender, all at the same time.

Then he was sliding in beside her, warming her with his own intensely virile heat. He was on the blanket next to her, pinning her full-length against his body, so close she could feel coarse tangles of chest hair on her arm.

"I . . . I don't know how to respond . . . what I'm supposed to do . . ."

"You don't have to do anything. Just lie there and let me teach you what you are longing to learn."

His mouth sought her neck again. His face was buried in thick, flowing hair as he searched for and found the little hollow where it met her shoulder. Lili's arms were around him suddenly, and she was grasping, clutching, not even knowing what she was doing, knowing only that that same audacious mouth was tracing a line of passionate kisses down to the swell of her breasts.

Engorged nipples leapt up to meet his fingers. Then impudent lips sucked them in, only half-playful, exciting one and then the other, teasing with his tongue in ways she had never even imagined. Vava had not told her about anything like this!

"Oh, Jeremy . . . oh, darling . . ."

The longing in her voice was so intense, it drew him out of himself for an instant. He pulled back, every muscle in his body taut, barely under control.

"God, you're beautiful. Have you any idea how lovely you are, or what it does to me to look at you? No, love, don't do that . . ." For she had drawn her arms instinctively across her breasts, suddenly self-conscious. Gently

Jeremy took hold of them, drawing them back, opening
her body to his ravening gaze. "Don't be ashamed of
nakedness, love. You have a beautiful body, made for a
man to worship . . . and enjoy. There's no shame in
being beautiful. And no embarrassment in having a man
notice."

"I . . . I'm not embarrassed, exactly. I just don't
know . . ."

"You will, my sweet . . . you will know. Come here
and let me show you."

He drew her against him, cradling her for a moment in
arms that ached with the effort it took to hold himself
back. Then slowly, so gently Lili was barely aware of it at
first, his hands began to caress her, touching every part
of her body, gauging every reaction surely, skillfully, and
very knowingly.

Lili nestled closer, wondering at how sweetly familiar it
felt as he fondled her breasts upward to meet the hungry
downward assault of his mouth. Already his hands were
sliding lower, blazing a trail across her belly, compelling
her body to arch instinctively upward. Now they were on
her hips, her thighs, the soft skin inside, resting just at
the edge of dark tendrils of hair, moist with her own
desire.

She felt him hesitate just for a second. She knew he
was asking again, mutely, if she were sure . . . really
sure. But it had gone beyond questions now. Beyond
doubts.

"Yes, darling," she said hoarsely. "Oh, yes . . . yes . . ."

Then those same hands were spreading her legs apart,
surely, firmly, provocatively. He was moving at the same
time, his head dropping down, and suddenly his mouth
was there in the space he had just created, and he was
kissing her, incredibly, quite unexpectedly, his lips and
tongue doing even more things that Vava had very definitely not mentioned.

Lili felt a moment of shock, not so much at the boldness of his actions as at the sheer pleasure that coursed
through her. She was sure that what he was doing was
scandalous—something no civilized woman ought to
allow—but she was equally sure she didn't want him to
stop. Her body had a will of its own now, responding
without waiting for messages from her brain, writhing,
twisting, searching, hungering for something that seemed

to be just there, beyond her reach, where she couldn't quite stretch out and grasp it.

Then, just as she almost had it, just as she could feel it swelling and filling her body, he pulled away, jolting her roughly back to reality.

Lili felt a sudden sense of betrayal, anger almost, that it should be over so abruptly. Where was the passion she had been struggling to find, the ecstasy, the longing that had seemed so close to culmination?

"Is that . . . it?" she said, unable to keep the disappointment out of her voice. Was this all there was to lovemaking? A few minutes of sweet intensity, promising so much, and then . . . nothing?

His answer was a soft laugh, deep in his throat.

"Did you think I was going to deny myself the pleasure of sharing this moment with you? Sharing it as much as I can allow myself, at any rate?"

He was easing her into his arms, settling her head against his shoulder, turning it slightly so he could see her face. The feeling of disappointment was already gone, for his hand was there, where his mouth had been before, every bit as bold. His fingers found the same spot his tongue had been playing with, and he was stroking her, slipping inside, guiding her deftly, surely, back to the heights she had climbed before, and beyond.

Lili lost herself in the exciting new sensations he evoked, not even hearing, or recognizing, the little animal whimpers that shivered through the air. Surely this could not go on—her body felt as if it must burst with the sweet pain that raged inside her, spreading out from her thighs.

Then suddenly she *was* bursting, a thousand quivering explosions that healed rather than hurt, and everything she wanted, everything she had been searching for, was there as she collapsed, quivering and drenched with sweat, into arms that closed around her.

Jeremy did not hurry her back from the residue of passion, but continued to hold her, patiently, protectively, making no demands; and Lili was content to lie there, feeling the unnatural heat ebb slowly out of her body. When at last she stirred enough to look up, she saw that he was staring at her strangely, with an expression she could not read.

Then his features relaxed, and faint lines of laughter showed around his eyes.

"And that, my love, is *it*."

She found herself smiling, satiated, but somehow not quite satisfied. For all the very real pleasure he had just given her, it was as if something were still missing. Then she remembered the things Vava had told her, and she realized suddenly what it was that had made him look at her like that.

"No, that's not quite it. It was very generous of you, taking care of my desires first. But . . ." She let her eyes wander down, not the least bit self-conscious now as she caught sight of the hard bulge at his crotch that was just what she had expected to find. "I believe we have a little unfinished business yet to tend to."

His arms tightened, as if in response. But he was shaking his head as he shifted her gently out of his embrace.

"I said when we began that I wasn't going to ruin you. And I'm not."

"But . . ." Lili faltered, staring at him in the lamplight that had begun to mingle with dawn through the windows. "I thought you understood. I want you, my darling, in every way . . ."

She caught her breath, feeling timid for a moment, though heaven knew, there was no reason for it. After what had just happened between them, she could hardly pretend to false modesty.

"I want you, Jeremy, and I know you want me." She slid her hand between his legs, vaguely surprised at how hard he felt. And how exciting it was to touch that part of him.

Jeremy made no effort to stifle the moan of longing that slipped out of his lips. "I do want you, Lili. I want you more than you know. But your head is filled with fairy tales and the bittersweet romance of a fabled curse. You can't possibly—"

"The Fleurie curse? How do you know about that?"

He seemed to hesitate a fraction of a second. "You told me yourself, in the carriage that first night, between sniffles and wails. You're so wrapped up in dreams of mysterious strangers riding masked into your life, you've got it all mixed up with reality. I'd be the worst kind of blackguard to take advantage of that. I promised I was going to see you home safely, and I will . . . daydreams and hymen intact."

He bent down, kissing her gently. Then he took her hand away and raised it to his lips.

"I told you before: when we're together—*if* we're together—it will be because you want *me*. Not some masked stranger, not some fantasy figure you have created in your mind . . . but me."

He got up from the bed, leaving her alone. Lili could hear him moving around the room, looking for her dress apparently, for when he appeared in the range of her vision again, he was holding it in his arms.

"Here," he said abruptly, tossing it in front of her. Whatever tenderness he had felt before seemed to be gone, for his voice was brisk and noncommittal. "I'll wait outside while you put it on, but I suggest you hurry. The sun will be up soon, and someone might come wandering this way. Oh, and *petite* . . ."

He turned in the doorway.

"Next time you curl up in a man's bed and offer your virginity"—he grinned—"ask first if he wants it."

19

Lili spent the next day alternately dreaming of Jeremy Blaze and hating him. Throughout most of the long and increasingly misty afternoon she vowed never again to be tempted by his virile good looks. Not for her a repeat of the insulting laughter that must have echoed all over the island while she stood alone in that little hut and indignantly pulled on her dress! But then darkness came, and with it memories, feelings, sensations, and she was conscious once again of the exquisite pain that radiated out from her thighs, touching—and tantalizing—every corner of her being.

It was an almost eerily quiet evening, with wisps of fog that came and went, twining like wet fingers around her face and neck. She had taken a blanket from one of the cots and wrapped it around her shoulders as she stepped out on the rough wooden porch in front of the cabin. Dédé had come back about noon to prepare the main meals of the day, but she and Stevie had left, separately, after supper, and Lili was alone again. Lantern glow from the windows showed elusive glimpses of tall reedlike grasses and shadowy cypresses, dripping with tendrils of Spanish moss; then the haze closed in again and everything was gone.

Next time you curl up in a man's bed and offer your virginity, ask first if he wants it. The words echoed in Lili's ears, making her angry all over again, her blood boiling, as it had when she first heard them. It was unfair—and cruel!—humiliating her like that. If she had him here right now, face-to-face, she would take great delight in telling him exactly what she thought! Only the basest, meanest, most disgusting sort of man would humiliate a woman like that!

But he wasn't here, and as her temper cooled somewhat, she realized that there was a grain, just a *grain*, of validity in what he had said.

She hadn't asked what he wanted or how he felt. She hadn't even considered it beyond the obvious physical attraction he could not, as a man, reasonably conceal. She had only considered *her* wants, *her* feelings, the fact that *she* had decided it was time to make love.

Once, he had tried to force his attentions on her, and while her body had responded, her heart and her mind had cried no. Was it so different, trying to push that same intimacy on him now?

She wandered restlessly over to the steps. The fog had blown out again, and something faint and shimmery showed periodically in the distance. Like fireflies, she thought, squinting into the darkness—only brighter. Flickers of gold that stayed, just for a second, then vanished as she tried to focus on them.

Lanterns?

She strained her ears, but all she could hear was an occasional plopping sound amidst the moist *chug-a-rhum, chug-a-rhum* of the frogs. In the two weeks since her arrival, she had been disturbed more than once by strange, inexplicable things, especially at night. Lights that shouldn't have been there, noises she couldn't identify. But they had always been vague, like now—nothing she could put her finger on—and in the dark, she hadn't been inclined to investigate. Jeremy was right: she *did* have a horror of snakes.

He had been right about other things too.

She sat down on the steps, grimacing a little as she realized how childish she must have looked. Like a spoiled brat who had always done what she wanted and was used to getting her way. She had barged into his room uninvited in the middle of the night, told him in no uncertain terms what she expected, and thought all she had to do was flutter her lashes once or twice and bare her breasts!

And now she was pouting because he'd behaved like a gentleman and refused to ruin her chances of making a suitable marriage!

She tugged the blanket tighter, pulling it hoodlike over her head. The swamps around New Orleans, like the city itself, could be unbearably steamy in the summer, but winter brought a damp cold that oozed into your bones and crunched underfoot when the frost turned hard. She was tempted to go inside, but glimmers of light still flashed occasionally, bolder now, beyond the edge of the clearing, and she was curious.

The Fleurie curse. He seemed to know all about it, though she could only vaguely remember having mentioned it in the carriage. In truth she *had* been caught up in it lately—perhaps it hadn't been totally unfair to say her head was filled with it—but it was hard when the resemblances between Jeremy and Roger de Courbet Montaigne were so striking.

Lili-Ange's lover had been fair too, with gold streaks in his hair, and eyes that were the most dazzling blue. A coincidence, no doubt . . . but he had been wearing a mask when she met him. A black domino that turned those same eyes violet and accented the sensual curve of his mouth? It had been winter then, as now, late winter, with early roses just coming into flower, like the roses she had purchased that morning on the levee.

And he had been pretending to be a highwayman!

Too much coincidence? But that was silly, and anyway, there was no point fretting over questions that didn't have an answer. Still . . .

She stood up, shrugging the blanket off her shoulders, draping it over one arm. The lights she had noticed before were even more pronounced now. Men moving around with lanterns, it seemed—not caring if she saw. Her ear picked up faint scuffling noises, as if boats were being shoved away from the bank.

Still . . . She was feeling new sensations now. New emotions. New and confusing yearnings for a man she wasn't sure she believed or trusted. Her attraction to him was intense and frightening—she had proved that last night—but she was no closer than ever to understanding who he really was, or solving the enigma of what lay below that handsome, dashingly reckless surface.

He seemed so sincere sometimes, and genuinely decent. Hadn't he kept his promises so far, scrupulously? And hadn't he said he admired Papa for his honesty? But then she remembered the stories she had heard about him, and the things he had almost certainly done. And just what it was that had brought her here.

A splash reached her ears, followed by what sounded like a muffled curse. Someone *was* near the water; she was sure of it now. Ordinarily that wouldn't have surprised her. Jeremy had virtually admitted he was a smuggler. But he had been so open about it before, cartons stacked on the shore in bright morning light, almost as if he were flaunting his activities. What could he be doing now in darkness?

Whatever it was, she was going to find out.

Lili hurried into the empty hut, tossing the blanket on a cot and picking up one of the lighted lanterns. Bringing it back on the porch, she rested it on the rail while she adjusted metal plates over three of the sides so the light would be directed in one steady beam. She would use it as long as she dared. Then she would close it completely, put it down on the ground, and go the rest of the way in the dark.

She had been too frightened before to venture out into the night. Even that one trip to Jeremy's cottage had been along a well-trodden path. She had thought that something was going on—she had sensed it as much as seen and heard it—but she hadn't had the courage to go and see.

She was still frightened. Frightened of boggy holes in the spongy soil, and black snakes that coiled under rocks . . . and what she was going to find when she got there. But she had become much too close to Jeremy Blaze these days—and nights—in the bayou. She had let herself care too much.

She had to find out who he was, what he was really doing, before it was too late.

"Dass de las' dem *pirogue*." A beam of light crept slowly along the shore, picking out indentations in the soil where boats had been loaded and pushed into the water. The wind was faint, but distinct, whistling through mist-shadowed cypresses with a low wailing sound. "Dey clean out de place, lemme tole you. Make fo'-t'ree trip, in an' out ag'in, 'fore dey finish."

"It's all gone, Stevie?" A sudden splash of gold caught Jeremy's features, giving him a gaunt look as he unshaded one side of his own dark lantern. "Everything? Even the storehouse is clean?"

"Clean as Mama's floor w'en she finish scrubbin',"

Stevie said, allowing himself a chuckle, though he kept his voice to a hoarse whisper. " 'Fore I come wit' good ol' bayou mud on my boot, an' make tracks a Canada grizzly'd be proud of . . . Oooo-eeee, do dat git me a tongue-whippin'!"

Jeremy relaxed enough to smile in the brittle lantern light. Dédé, who had been Mama to her husband as many years as he could remember, was renowned for her futile attempts to bring cleanliness into the bayou shanty they continued to occupy despite his efforts to locate them someplace better.

"I'm sure you have, my friend. How Dédé has managed to put up with your muddy boots and still love you all these years, God only knows."

"Mus' be my purty face." Stevie grinned, yellowish teeth looking grotesquely comical against the dark spaces in his mouth. "Us Cajuns, we de damnedest, hot-bloodedest folk you lak t' see. Take more'n a sweet word—I tole you dat, boy—t' win a Cajun woman."

"And more than good cooking to keep a Cajun man at home, I'll warrant. The way your Dédé's managed to rein in your stallion instincts all these years. Though I wouldn't put it beyond her to tie you up like an old fatted hog if you tried to stray." Jeremy was walking while he talked, only half-focusing on what he was saying as he trained his light inch by inch along the hazy edge of the clearing. Here he noted a length of rope the men had left behind; there, some planking that had come loose from the side of a crate. "Help me get this stuff together, Stevie. I don't want to leave it lying around. I don't know if anyone can make anything of it. Probably not, but it's not worth taking a chance."

Stevie obliged. He was a big man, with a belly that showed Dédé's skill with a gumbo pot, but he could move like a cat when he had to, swiftly and silently. Finding a piece of canvas that had been wrapped around one of the bales, he spread it out on the ground and began tossing things onto it.

"Ain't not'ing here I can't manage," he said with a sly sidelong look at Jeremy. "You might want to took you'se'f up t' de cabin. Dat *fais do-do*, it's still goin' strong. Dédé, she's watchin' the young'uns so Tin-Tin can keep his eyes on Vava—if dey ain't too big wit' all dem pretty girls. De l'il *mam'selle*, she been by herse'f long time now. Mus' be gettin' real lonesome."

Jeremy's features tightened wryly. "I think the little *mademoiselle* can survive an hour or two alone," he said, remembering distinctly what had happened last time Lili had been lonesome, and how close he had come to forgetting himself completely. "Anyway, I have work to do here. You know me, I'm never satisfied unless I've checked things over myself."

"Oh, I know you, boy. I knowed you from de time you was jus' startin' to walk, gittin' into more trouble'n a lickin' hound. And I don't t'ink you're here 'cause you got work t' do. Me, I t'ink you scared o' goin' up t' de cabin."

"Scared?" Jeremy looked faintly amused. "What would I be scared of?"

"You'se'f, mebbe . . . w'at's lak t' happen w'en you alone wit' her. She's a real purty l'il t'ing. And don't try an' tell me you ain't sweet on her."

"*Sweet* on her?" Jeremy spotted a longer section of rope stretching half-hidden through the reedy grasses on the shore. Reaching down, he caught the end and began looping it in loose coils around his arm. "What a way of talking. I thought you told me Cajuns were a hot-blooded race. Sweet, indeed! Is that the Cajun way of describing a man's basic physical urges?"

Stevie's grin broadened. The younger man, for all his studied flippancy, was more transparent than he thought. "Sweet" was a pretty good way of describing it, after all. Plainly he was gone on the girl, pretty bad, it seemed. His face had a way of hardening and softening at the same time when he talked about her, as if he wanted to admit his feelings but didn't trust himself.

"It ain't natural, de way you two keep tiptoein' 'round each ot'er. Cajuns *are* hot-blooded. A Cajun man, he see a girl he like, he jus' sweep her off her feet—r'at onto w'atever's handy. And he do it good, she don't make one w'imper o' protest. 'Course he hustles her off to de preacher an' gets hisse'f tied up, but he don't hustle no faster'n he has to. 'Less o' course her paw's on de porch wit' a shotgun. Lak I'm gonna be t'night my Vava ain't home on time!"

"Ah, but hustling the lady off to the preacher is one

thing I can't do," Jeremy reminded him. "Tonight or tomorrow or the next day. You know that, my friend."

"Well, den, I tole you," Stevie replied practically, "you jus' take care o' w'at counts. De preacher, he mostly for de paw anyway, and I don't see no ol' man here wit' a shotgun. You jus' do w'at comes easy, and let de rest take care o' itse'f."

"Would that I could," Jeremy said lightly. He turned away, running his eyes one last time over the bank, pointedly changing the subject. "Everything looks all right, but it's hard to be certain in the dark."

Stevie watched him curiously. Passion for the girl, or love? he wondered. His natural instincts tempted him to tease, just a little, provoking retorts that would give a true indication of how things stood. But he had long ago learned that, with this man, there was only so far you could push, and no farther.

"As r'at as it's lak t' be. Ain't not'ing but ol' ruts w'ere de boats was. An' a few ruts, dey don't matter. You got you' mine made up den? De men, dey gone for good? Dey ain't comin' back tomorrow?"

Jeremy shook his head. He was hatless, and the wind blew his hair, pale ripples that seemed to merge with the thin streamers of fog. "The men have served their purpose. I don't need them anymore. Besides, it's getting to be a problem, keeping them in line."

"You mean, you don't like de way dey lookin' at de girl," Stevie couldn't resist putting in.

The other man didn't rise to the bait. "I can't blame them. She did look winsome, didn't she, standing with those big wide eyes at the edge of the clearing, as if she thought no one noticed? One of men—the big one with the scruffy yellow beard—had drool all the way down the front of his pirate shirt. But, yes, you're right, that's part of the reason I want them out of here. It's all innocent now, but things have a way of getting out of hand. No point asking for trouble. And I really *don't* need them."

Stevie jerked his head around, catching a faint sound, like a cracking twig behind the dense screen of cypress branches. But all he could make out was a faint rustling of leaves and moss in the mist.

"You sure o' dat?"

"Oh, yes, I'm sure." One brow went up, giving Jeremy's face an oddly twisted look in the lantern's rays. "I think I've established my *bona fides* as a pirate."

The older man chuckled softly. "I wouldn't know one o' dem 'bony fides' from an ol' bony hound. But ain't nobody in eyeshot or earshot hasn't seen w'at's goin' on, an' ventured a guess t' de cause. T'ough I reckon somebody'd be real surprised to peek in one o' dem crates an' see dey's not'ing dere."

"And even more surprised to learn that the same empty crates have been moved out night after night under cover of darkness, and brought back with great show the next morning!" Jeremy glanced in the same direction Stevie had, nervously, but without apparent cause, for everything seemed still. "A childish game, I concede. But it was either that or waylay some hapless privateer at gunpoint and come back with real booty."

Stevie pulled the corners of the canvas cloth together, knotting them into a bundle, which he hefted onto his shoulder. "Ain't never knowed you t' take de easy way befo'."

"As a Cajun, you ought to appreciate that. Why go to all the extra effort when it isn't necessary? Take those things back to the camp and make a bonfire out of them, will you? I want to stay here awhile and think."

"Don't be too long," Stevie said with a knowing wink. "Dédé, she gonna be back in t'ree-two hour . . . and I be up to de hut myse'f."

Jeremy grinned as he listened to the other's footfalls echoing clumsily in the darkness. No need for stealth now that everything was taken care of. Stevie had been a part of his life as long as he could remember. It was Stevie who had taken him hunting and fishing as a boy, and sat down for long fatherly talks when no one else had had the time. Stevie knew him as well as any man alive. Knew his hopes and his longings, even his secret fears. But he did not know how he felt about the pretty young woman in the cabin. No man ever knew another man well enough for that.

"What did you mean, you established your *bona fides* as a pirate?"

The voice cut sharply into Jeremy's thoughts. Whirling around, he spotted a slender figure in a burgundy wool shirt and man-tailored moleskin pants at the edge of the clearing.

"What the hell! How long have you been standing there?"

"Long enough to hear that you've only been pretending to be a privateer." Lili stepped closer, away from the cypresses where Jeremy had noticed—and ignored—that telltale noise before. In the light, he could see that her hair was loose, as it had been last night, spilling sensuously down her back.

"What else did you hear?" he asked guardedly.

"That everything has all been playacting. Those men aren't smugglers. They've been ferrying crates back and forth, night and morning, so it would *look* as if they were landing contraband. Where did you get them, Jeremy? Did you hire them for the occasion, or do you keep them for other purposes? And whom are you trying to fool?"

Jeremy frowned, looking vaguely ill-at-ease as he stepped over to the water and stared out into the brooding darkness. But when he turned back, his face had eased into the characteristic amusement Lili was already finding maddeningly familiar.

"So, you've caught me out. You're quicker than I gave you credit for. And bolder. This is the *second* time you've braved shadows and snakes to come out at night. I should have learned my lesson."

Lili caught the mockery in his tone, and it took all her will to bite back the angry, satisfying retort that rose to her lips. "Is that a roundabout way of telling me you're not going to answer my question?"

Her chin had gone up, more bravado than courage, but it was clear she was not going to back down. Jeremy laughed softly as he went over to the place where he had left the lantern, unhooking it from a low-hanging branch.

"Always determined . . . and to the point. It's one of your most charming attributes. Personally, I've never cared for feminine wiles. I like a woman to be direct. In some instances, that is," he added, drawling the words out wickedly. "Yes, certainly, if you want, I'll answer your question."

He squatted down, setting the lantern on the ground and opening the other three sides to release a circle of light. Lili, who had already learned to her regret that this was a man who couldn't be hurried, stood to one side and waited for him to speak.

"What do you know about politics, *petite*?"

"Politics?" Lili made no effort to hide her dismay. She had thought he was going to talk about pirates and the mysterious things that went on in that clearing—she had braved not merely snakes but her own humiliating recollections of the previous night to find out—and all he wanted was to air some stuffy political theory! "I don't know the first thing about governments and wars and treaties, and I don't want to. I've never been the least bit interested in politics."

"That's what I was afraid of." Jeremy gestured toward a spot of ground while he sat down himself, stretching lean legs out in front of him. "I'm going to have to give you a short lesson on the political situation in Louisiana. You know, naturally, that the Americans took formal possession in December 1803. No doubt your papa took you to the ceremony of transfer in the Place d'Armes . . . yes, and judging from the way your nose is curling up, I can imagine what your reaction was! But has it occurred to you that we're better off now, under American administration?"

"Better off? Under the *Americans*?" Lili fairly spat out the word. She could more easily picture a man of ability and intelligence consorting with pirates than defending the boorish occupiers of New Orleans. "But they're . . . they're totally uncultivated, Jeremy! Why, they have no manners at all. They can't even dance decently, and . . ."

She broke off, shuddering as she recalled the American at the quadroon ball, and the gross liberties he had tried to take with her. Jeremy must have sensed what she was thinking, for he leaned forward, resting a hand just for a second on hers.

"I'll grant you the dancing, *petite*." His eyes were twinkling as he drew back again. "And their manners frequently leave something to be desired. But Creole 'cultivation' comes at a price. A young gentleman's formal education might be woefully neglected, but heaven help him if he isn't trained in the social art of fencing so he can wound—or kill—another gentleman in an *affaire d'honneur*. And he'd die of shame before he'd soil his hands working at some petty trade. He'd let his aged mother languish in genteel poverty first. But he wouldn't turn a hair at the thought of marrying a woman he didn't like for her dowry. Now, does that sound 'cultivated'?"

"No," Lili admitted reluctantly. It did seem, sometimes, that the men she met in her friends' parlors were little better than charming parasites, though she would never have had the nerve to say it out loud. "But that doesn't make American brashness any more appealing."

"No. But in the years before those 'brash' Americans took over, business was at a standstill. Only gaming halls flourished, and coffeehouses and bordellos, if you know what they are. Which I rather suspect you do—young ladies seem to be appallingly well-informed nowadays." His eyes were laughing again, but his voice was sincere enough to hold her interest. "Gangs of ruffians roamed the streets, and a decent man took his life in his hands when he went out at night. Now, five years later, lights are well-maintained at every corner, there's a highly capable *garde de ville*, and the voice of the night watchman—the *sereno*—can be heard calling out the hour and the state of the weather. And foolish little girls feel safe enough to venture out on rainy nights."

Lili squirmed uneasily. The ground was damp, but the place Jeremy had chosen was cushioned by a bed of leaves and dead needles. He made no move to touch her again, but she could still feel where his hand had rested before, a warm distraction that would not go away.

"That's not fair," she said. "That's Spanish rule you're talking about. The French held the territory only three years. As for the Americans—"

"Dislike the Americans all you want," he cut in with what Lili could have sworn was an uncharacteristic lack of impatience. "But be objective about them. And Laussat, the colonial prefect, actually had less time than that. He didn't arrive until early 1803, and the tricolor went up for the first time November 30—which gave him exactly twenty days to turn over the territory. But it wouldn't have mattered if he'd had twenty *years*. France has never done well with her American possessions. And now, with these disastrous Napoleonic campaigns—"

"Disastrous? How can you say that, Jeremy?" Lili stared at him in amazement. She had never heard men talk like that in loyally French Louisiana. Except Papa, she thought, with the first vague twinge of doubt. But then, Papa was Spanish, not French Creole, and he was hopelessly old-fashioned. "Napoleon is leading the French to the greatest glories in their history. All the world is falling at his feet. Everyone says so."

"For the time being . . . perhaps." Jeremy's thoughts seemed to turn inward as he stared at the lantern, a steady glow of flame behind its shield of smoky glass. "He has defeated the Austrians and the Russians, and won territory in Italy and Dalmatia and along the Rhine. But he's spreading himself too thin, making mistakes that will cost him dear. The man knows how to conquer, I'll grant you, but can he keep his conquests?" He looked up again, fixing her with shadow-darkened eyes. "Did you know that even now he's setting his brothers up on puppet thrones all over the Continent? Making a dynasty out of peasants, who'll all too soon go back to being peasants again! Revel in the glories of the empire while you can, little girl—it will not last for long."

Lili drew back, not liking the words she knew Papa would call logical and persuasive. Not liking either the fact that she was beginning to remember vividly the things he had done yesterday with his hands and mouth. And wishing she had the courage to slide just a little closer, brushing her shoulder against his, wondering how he would respond.

"You still haven't answered my question," she said, forcing her thoughts back to the matter at hand. "Whom were you trying to fool when you made believe you were a pirate?"

His lips twitched faintly. "Maybe you, *petite*." Then he saw the exasperated expression on her face and laughed out loud. "I'm sorry . . . you make it so easy to tease you. Let's just say there are some men—real pirates—I'm trying to impress. What better way to get their attention than make believe I'm one of them?"

"But . . ." Lili forgot everything else for a moment. "Why on earth would you *want* to impress them?"

"I've told you already how I feel about the Americans. Ill-mannered or no, they're good for Louisiana—and Louisiana is good for them. We belong together, geographically and economically. I want to make sure we stay together."

"But I still don't understand." She burrowed deeper into the leaves, wishing she had had the sense to bring a blanket from the cottage. "How can impressing a bunch of pirates and scoundrels make any difference?"

"Because those 'pirates and scoundrels' hold the key to

our future. You see, I don't believe the European powers are through with us."

"You mean . . . you think Napoleon is going to try to get us back?"

Jeremy shook his head, tumbling gold-highlighted hair onto his brow. "No, he's much too preoccupied with his own battles. I'm not worried about the French—or the Spanish. It is the English and their ambitions that concern me."

"The English? But that's silly, Jeremy! We've never belonged to the English . . . have we?"

"No, but they had the American colonies for a while, and they're still smarting from the loss. Right now they're contenting themselves with trying to humiliate the new nation at sea—just a few months ago they fired on the frigate *Chesapeake*—but war is probably inevitable. When it comes, we're bound to be a target." His voice took on a new note, ringing with subdued intensity. "Consider the strategic possibilities. Solid strength in Canada to the north, a toehold in Louisiana to the south. They could really put a squeeze on the upstart colonials then, couldn't they?"

"Yes, I suppose they could." Lili was intrigued in spite of herself. Politics had always seemed dull and abstract, something to be discussed by old men in rooms reeking of cigars. But here, in the lantern light, as she listened to Jeremy, everything was coming to life. "But what on earth do pirates have to do with future battles against England?"

"Think about it, Lili," he said, sensing her interest and encouraging it. "New Orleans is a port city, strategically located on both the Gulf *and* the river. Any battles here would be at least partially naval, if only in terms of bringing in supplies and defending against blockades. And the best-equipped and best-armed ships in the area belong to privateers."

"So . . . you're going to cultivate them." The thought was strangely disturbing. Suddenly Lili felt cold all over, not just from the night, but from something else she couldn't identify. "You think they'll be useful."

"I'm going to cultivate them, yes . . . and use them if I can. There's one in particular, a man named Lafitte, who has recently opened a blacksmith shop on Royal Street. He's as larcenous a rascal as I ever hope to meet, but he has a rakish sense of adventure. If I can appeal to that, if I can get him to trust me . . . But here, you're shivering. I forget, huddling in front of a lantern isn't the same as warming yourself at a blazing fire."

He removed the lightweight jacket he was wearing, and leaning forward, laid it over her shoulders. Lili was even more conscious of his touch now, as his hands lingered on the collar, pulling it gently together in front. Then, for one heart-stopping moment, she felt his fingers on her chin, tilting her face up to meet the devastating blue of his gaze.

He's going to kiss me, she thought helplessly . . . he's going to kiss me, and I'm not going to stop him. It's going to happen again. Everything this time.

But he held her for only an instant, then let go, easing his hand back again.

"Are you embarrassed, *petite*?" he said softly. "You're looking at me so strangely. Are you remembering what happened between us . . . and wondering if I'm thinking about it too?"

"No," she lied. "Why should I? You made it perfectly clear you weren't interested. And anyway, I only did it because . . . because I was curious. That's all. The whole thing wasn't any more important to me than to you. I . . . I've forgotten it already."

"You haven't forgotten . . . and it *was* important. First loves, first passions, are always remembered. But I think—I hope—you'll have other things to consume your interest on your wedding night with your bridegroom."

So that was how it was. Lili felt as if her whole body were disintegrating, but there was nothing she could do about it. She had thought, irrationally—she had longed to believe—that somehow she had made a mistake and he really did care. But here he was, casually discussing the things she was going to do with another man in her bed!

"That's why you kidnapped *me*, isn't it?" she said suddenly. Things were finally coming clear, just when she was most confused. "That's what the ransom is for—not to line your pockets, but to finance your precious patriotic cause."

His mouth twisted wryly, not quite a smile. "Battles cost money, *petite*. And fortunes aren't always easy to come by. It's a cause, incidentally, of which your papa would approve. I think he might have contributed anyway, if I'd passed the hat. Though he might not have given quite so much."

"And what if he doesn't give you anything?" Lili drew the jacket tighter, trying to ward off the chill that came as much from within as from without. "What if your demands are too high, and he refuses to pay?"

"Oh, he'll pay," Jeremy said quietly. "And he'll pay what I ask."

His voice was so sure, it sent shivers down her spine. Lili got up and wandered over to the edge of the lantern glow, as if somehow a new perspective would make her see things differently. She knew now what had made her feel so cold before. What was it she had thought that first time she met him, when he was still wearing a black domino and she was waltzing in his arms?

This is a man who is capable of anything. This is a man who can kill . . . if he has to.

"I wonder that you are so confident," she said, turning slowly to face him.

"And I wonder that you have suddenly gone so pale." He had gotten up and was standing a few feet away. "Don't you think that's a peculiar reaction?"

"Peculiar? How so?"

"Before, when you thought I was a pirate, you were ready to take it in stride. Now you know I'm a patriot, and it has you visibly upset. What a perverse creature you are." He lifted his hand, laying it on her face again, running it down her cheek and along her chin, as if he knew what effect it was having.

But, of course, he did know, and his ego was enjoying it!

Then, with a light laugh, he was gone, and Lili was alone again.

"Perverse" is exactly the word, she thought as she stood shivering in the light of the lantern he had left behind. Perverse—and illogical. She ought to be grateful that his motives were pure. That he was not a thief, but a man of honor and commitment and purpose.

Only a thief at least had his limits.

Lili slipped her arms through the sleeves of the jacket, but the lining was so cold she started shaking again. All a thief wanted was money, and he would be satisfied. And a thief cared about his own skin.

But the only thing a patriot cared about was his cause. He would risk anything, even his life, for that. He would do anything he had to, and God help the man who got in his way.

Or the woman.

Was Jeremy Blaze a man who could kill? Not for greed or ambition or power, but for the cause he so passionately believed in?

She bent and picked up the lantern, conscious of the warmth as she held it close to her body. Beyond, the night seemed to have grown even darker. She could barely make out the trees, great hulking blots of inky black against the bluer black of a clearing sky. Even the frogs seemed to have gone to sleep. All she could hear was the melancholy moaning of the wind.

It had been so compelling, that brief moment when he wrapped his jacket around her, driving away the cold with the provocative nearness of his body. She could still see his eyes in the lantern light—mysterious, challenging, inviting—and she realized helplessly that there was no way she could resist.

She *would* go to him, even now, if he opened his arms. She knew the risks, and she would go. Deliberately or unconsciously, calculating or playful, he had gotten a hold, not just on her body, but on her heart and her spirit as well.

She started slowly out of the clearing, holding the lantern in front of her. Somehow, without knowing, without realizing what was happening, she had fallen in love with this man she knew only as Jeremy Blaze. She had not meant to, she had not wanted to, but strangely—*perversely*—she had. Now it was too late for qualms or second thoughts. She loved, completely, irrevocably . . . hopelessly. And she would follow wherever love led.

20

Lili tossed her head defiantly, wishing she had left her hair loose to blow out behind her as she hurried down the trodden path that led to the main camp. It was a glorious golden morning, with splashes of sunshine everywhere, but there were still traces of a brief thunder-shower that had pelted the earth at dawn. Droplets of water clung, glittering, to cypress needles and sharp-edged rozo cane, and the ground was so slick in places she had to watch where she walked.

Jeremy would be surprised to see her.

She paused to catch her breath. A little brown bird flitted from branch to branch, trilling a jaunty tune. Surprised, and no doubt furious! She could just see his face, reddening with suppressed anger as he glanced up from whatever he was doing and caught sight of her. He had been avoiding her assiduously for the last day and a half, ever since their midnight encounter by the waterside.

Or, more to the point, he had avoided her since they almost made love on his mossy bed. He would hardly be pleased to see her now.

Well, he could be pleased or not . . . she was going to him, and that was that!

She started down the path again, humming a little melody as she recalled the foolish nightmare fears that had almost gotten the better of her. She had been so frightened when he told her what he was; the craziest images had flooded through her mind. Jeremy, the pa-triot, as a cold-blooded killer. Jeremy, a man who would do anything to make his idealistic vision of the world a reality. Jeremy, whose passionate existence was a threat to her very life.

It had all seemed so vivid in that darkened setting. The lantern, casting moodily sinister shadows; unidentifiable sounds somewhere out in the night; the fog closing in, damp and cold as it penetrated the thin jacket. But here in the sunlight, with silver-green leaves shivering in the wind and the song of the bird harmonizing with her own sweet soprano, such melodramatic suspicions seemed the height of silliness.

It wasn't that Jeremy was not dangerous. He was— wildly dangerous. But Lili sensed that the danger he posed was more to her heart than her life or her safety.

And when it came to her heart, she was ready to take a chance!

She laughed out loud, enjoying the warmth of the sun on her cheeks, the cool kiss of the wind as it caught her hair and attempted to pull it out of its combs. She had never felt quite so alive in her life. There was something wonderfully exhilarating, just being out by herself, dressed in the kind of low-necked gown she had never been allowed before—with not a thing underneath!—thinking what it was going to be like when she encountered the man she loved again and got past that initial phase of anger.

There was a break in the shrubs, and Lili cut through, across an open expanse of blowing grasses. Moisture penetrated her shoes; she could feel it drenching the hem of her dress. Maybe Jeremy *didn't* love her the way she loved him. Maybe his feelings weren't as deep as hers . . . now. But feelings changed. If she could just be with him, if they could spend time together, the way a man and woman were meant to, surely she could win him over.

She reached the clearing where the camp was located just in time to see Jeremy coming out of the main building with a bucket in one hand and an oversize paintbrush in the other. He must have been whitewashing, for there were chalky smudges all over his clothing and on one side of his nose, giving him an engagingly boyish look. Lili had the sudden irrational urge to run up and tell him she adored him and that all she wanted was to be his!

But that was exactly the wrong thing. Adoration was not what he wanted. Not now. Maybe later, when they were entwined in each other's arms and passion had brought them so close their hearts and bodies were one.

What was needed now was a more devious approach. Feminine wiles, and no backing down this time. No letting him distract her with one of those superbly timed barbs that always got a rise out of her. Heart pounding, palms coated with sweat, she stood there and pictured the look in his eyes when he turned. Widening at first—that would be surprise—then they would darken with anger and scorn, and it would be up to her to get him to change his mind.

But when he did turn, Lili saw only the surprise. And behind it, a flicker of something that came and went in an instant, which she recognized unmistakably as pleasure.

Why, he wanted me to come! she thought with a rush of elation. His silly ego made him protect himself, and his sense of honor wouldn't let him use me! But he wanted me all the same, and he's glad I'm here.

She was going to win! Without the no-holds-barred fight she had imagined! All she had to do was let him know how she felt. Let him know that it was he—Jeremy Blaze—she wanted, and not some stranger in a domino mask.

And, naturally, she'd reassure him that she didn't expect anything beyond this one brief dalliance.

Of course, later, when they were together in bed, after what she had been waiting for finally happened, she might just *hint* that she would be willing to give up everything and run away with him. And by that time, he would be so enamored, he might just agree.

She took a step forward.

"Hello, Jeremy."

Breathlessly she waited for him to throw aside the bucket, splashing whitewash over the porch as he hurried down the short flight of steps to catch her in his arms. But now that that brief moment of surprise was over, he seemed to have regained his composure. Looking unsettlingly sure of himself, he set the pail down deliberately and stood at the top, arms akimbo, eyebrows faintly cocked.

"Hello, pretty girl. Did you come to distract me?"

"More than that, I hope."

The comment did not come out as boldly as she had intended, and Lili felt herself falter. There was a distinct look of amusement on his face as he sauntered down the steps, making no effort to move quickly. Damn him. How could she have forgotten that trick he had with his eyes, taking in her figure, not at all discreetly, but insolently, boring through the pale rose dimity of her lace-trimmed dress. Sweet heaven, he looked as if he knew she wasn't wearing any undergarments!

"You look busy," she said hastily. "What are you doing?"

"Obviously"—he sent those impudent eyes up the steps to the place where the bucket and brush were resting— "I've been lounging around, relaxing in the sun and catching up on my reading. *Poor Richard*. Have you read him? Ah, but I forget. You have a distaste for things American."

"And a distaste for sarcasm," Lili snapped, feeling her temper starting to simmer. The only thing that was obvious was that he was trying to distract her, and coming very near to succeeding! "You needn't be so smugly patronizing. I meant, of course, why are you whitewashing a building that's already served its purpose? Your fake pirates are gone—I'm sure everyone on the bayou has seen and admired them. You don't need a place to bunk them anymore."

"There *are* other uses for buildings," he said, not unkindly, but not exactly warmly either. "Even in the bayous. If you wanted to use that pretty head of yours for something other than daydreaming, I'm sure you could come up with at least a dozen." The wind had risen, blowing blond-highlighted hair over his eyes. He reached up without thinking, leaving a white streak as he brushed it back. "Much as I'd like to stay and chat, and fetching as you look in that dress—pink becomes you; you should wear it more often—I'm afraid I have to get back to work. Now, if you don't mind . . ."

And that was that. Lili watched helplessly as he started back up the stairs. A dismissal, as cool and polite as if she'd been in a business office and was taking up somebody's precious time! The temper she had been holding in came to the tip of her tongue, and she let it go.

"You are the most infuriating, maddening, *confusing* man I have ever met in my life!"

"Confusing?" Jeremy stopped midway up the steps. That was the one word he had not anticipated in whatever tirade she might treat him to. "In what way am I confusing, *petite*?"

"In every way! And you do it deliberately—I swear you do! Look at that silly name you chose. Jeremy Blaze! You know I can't possibly believe it, yet you dance a jig around the subject every time I bring it up! If you're really a patriot, the way you pretend, and not the pirate you were before—or the highwayman before that— why do you have to be so mysterious? Sometimes I think you keep things from me just for the sake of doing it! Why, you've never even told me where you're from."

"Haven't I?" The brows went up again, almost imperceptibly. Lili sensed that it was not an involuntary reaction. "I may not have mentioned it in so many words, but a clever minx like you ought to have figured it out. A man gives away his background, however subtly, by the way he speaks. I come from here, of course."

"Here? The *bayous*?"

He laughed. "Am I so sophisticated you can't accept that? Or is my accent too polished? I meant, I come from Louisiana—New Orleans—but in a way, you were right. A good part of my boyhood was spent in bayou country. In fact, Stevie virtually raised me."

"Stevie?" Lili was so startled she almost forgot everything else. "But that's so improbable, Jeremy. Why, you're not like the Cajuns at all!"

"Or the Creoles, though I am one. After my father died, when I was eight, my mother found herself—perhaps 'purchased' would be a better word—a considerably younger husband. He wasn't a nice man, I'm sorry to say, but he seemed to make her happy. She never found out about his many flagrant indiscretions, so I suppose he earned the generous allowance he was given on her death. At any rate," he added dryly, "he didn't live to enjoy it. His excesses did him in."

There was a singular lack of bitterness in his tone. "You didn't mind?" Lili said curiously. "Disliking your stepfather so much?"

"Actually, no." He reached for the bucket, which was still sitting at the top of the steps. An unnecessarily brusque movement that gave Lili the feeling he had said more than he intended. "I was left pretty much to myself, which was all right with me—especially after the child came along, my half-brother. Stevie had already taken me under his wing. His father was a farmer, one of the tenants on my father's land. In his home I grew up naturally, free of Creole prejudices and preconceived notions."

"You mean," Lili couldn't resist putting in, "like mine?"

"Let's just say I kept an open mind. When it came time to go to the university, I chose Harvard, mainly because I was fascinated with American law and politics. But later, I attended Montpellier too, so I experienced both worlds. Now I'm at home in either."

Lili frowned faintly. The way he was talking, it was clear he came from money. Yet she could have sworn she knew every family of wealth and prominence in New Orleans, and there was no one even vaguely matching Jeremy's description. Or his younger brother, for that matter, who must be about her age.

"Are you telling me the truth, I wonder. You did give the impression, once before, of being something you're not."

"I gave the impression," he admitted, "but I didn't lie. I may not mention things from time to time, when the occasion demands. But I never out-and-out lie . . . unless it's absolutely necessary."

Lili caught the wry edge to his voice. "And you're not lying now?"

"No, I'm not lying now."

He swung around easily, heading up the last couple of steps, a pointed cue that as far as he was concerned the conversation was over. Lili could have screamed in exasperation. She *would* have screamed if she'd thought it would do any good. But he was perfectly capable of striding right on inside, as if he hadn't even heard. She had to do something quickly or he was going to get away. And heaven knew when she'd have a chance like this again.

Feverishly she cast about in her mind, seizing on the first thing that came to her.

"I know all about you, Jeremy Blaze. You're a fraud! You accuse *me* of playing games, but you're the one who hasn't been honest. You're not what you pretend."

His back stiffened, as if that random thrust had hit home. But when he turned, his face was controlled.

"What do you mean, I'm not what I pretend?"

"I mean you're a man of feelings, of course." Lili smiled to herself, though she was careful not to let him see it. Apparently he couldn't resist a challenge to that arrogant male ego! "You pretend you don't care about anything, but you do. You care . . . and you *want*. Every time you think I'm going to scratch that brittle surface and see underneath, you hide behind a cutting comment or turn around and walk away. You're so blasted sure it'll make me lose my temper! Up until now, it has."

"And now?"

"Now I know that what you want is me. As much as I want you. Only you're too proud and stubborn to admit it. I'm not going to let you get away so easily, Jeremy."

"I don't think," he said, his voice unexpectedly gentle, "that the choice is yours."

"Oh, but it is." For all the brashness of her words, Lili felt her confidence flag. His eyes had not left her, but everything in his manner was unutterably cool. She had the terrible, helpless feeling he was going to turn and saunter inside. "I know it is, because you really *do* want me."

"Do I?" Jeremy's face was a taut mask as he took in the pastel-and-white softness that provided such a provocative contrast to her dark, sultry beauty. An aching hunger, too long reined in, gnawed at his insides, as impossible to deny as it was to control. All he could do was keep her from recognizing it.

God, had she chosen that absurdly innocent dress, the one he liked least of all the outfits he had had made, because she knew how sweetly pure it looked? And what effect it would have on him? Had she stopped, when she fastened all those little white buttons that ran up the front, to think how easy they would be to undo again?

Probably, he thought wryly. And she probably knew that his fingers were itching to touch them now, to ease each pearly orb out of its casing, slipping the soft fabric away from her pliant, sensuous body. Just for an instant he let himself think about how it would feel, taking her at her word, removing that frilly pink dress, carrying her inside . . .

"Wanting has nothing to do with it," he said gruffly. "What a man wants and what he does are not always the same thing. Just as what a pretty girl wants isn't always what she gets, no matter how spoiled she might be. Though that's a lesson you don't seem to have learned."

Lili felt her heart sink. It was not so much the harshness in his tone that alarmed her as the cold, deliberately calculated finality. If she couldn't think of something, he *was* going to leave. And there was nothing on earth that would stop him. Unless . . .

She remembered suddenly the way he had reacted that one night they had almost been together in his bed. He had been maddeningly cool then too, completely in control of his emotions—until she had exposed her breasts to eyes that could hardly wait to devour them! Hot, surging passion had consumed him then. She had seen it in his face, his body, heard it in the deep, vibrating huskiness of his voice. Yes, and it would have gotten the best of him, too, if she hadn't blurted out all that folderol about getting married.

If she could just find the nerve to do the same thing again! If she could get his blood boiling, as it had that night, he would never be able to resist. Especially if she had the sense to keep her mouth shut!

She was surprised at how free she felt, like the little bird in the branches of the tree, as she lifted her hand to the top button on her bodice, half-hidden beneath a snowy ruffle. Free and unafraid. There were no doubts now, no fears, no qualms. They belonged together, she and this man who had stolen her away in the darkness. What was about to happen between them was as right as it was inevitable.

"You *are* mine, Jeremy, and you know it. Not forever maybe, but for this afternoon." She raced her fingers down, quickly, lithely, undoing the front of her gown.

Another second. Just one more second, and she would slip out of that subtle veil of dimity and lace and be standing in front of him clad only in a golden burst of sunlight.

But this time he was ready for her. Whitewash splashed over rough wooden boards, as Lili had imagined before, and Jeremy was hurling the bucket aside, charging down the steps, taking the last several in a single leap. She had not even managed to unfasten the last button when his hand closed over hers, so hard it hurt.

"What the hell do you think you're doing?"

His voice was rough, like a slap in the face. Lili struggled to free herself, but his grip was too tight. "Ow— Jeremy, don't! I'm just doing what you want . . . what we both want!"

"The devil you are! You're doing what you want, as usual! I told you before, I have no intention of taking you to my bed. Not as things stand now. Do you think you're so beautiful, all you have to do is tear off your clothes and I'll fall madly in love? Or do you have so little respect for yourself, you only want to arouse the animal lusts any man might feel for a naked woman?"

"No!" Lili couldn't let herself listen. "That's just your pride talking, Jeremy. You can't let something like pride stand between us."

"It isn't pride, you little fool! Why do you persist in making me hurt you? Pride *is* stupid, and whatever else you may think of me, I'm not stupid. There are other, more compelling reasons for not doing what you're, uh, suggesting." His eyes ran down the half-open front of her gown, lewd, even now, habitually arrogant. Defiantly Lili tilted her chin up.

"Name one!" she dared.

To her discomfort, the look in his eyes turned to amusement.

"Have you stopped to think that I might not be *able* to make all the pretty promises your heart craves?"

"You might not be able—or you don't choose to? Isn't that what you asked me, that first time when you nearly ravished me in the carriage? You can't—or you *won't*?"

"In this case," he said evenly, " 'can't' is the word. I am not, as it turns out—at the moment—free to make a commitment."

"You're not free?" Lili felt as if all the air had been kicked out of her. She took a step backward, and he let her go. "You mean . . . Oh, *mon Dieu!*"

The one thing that hadn't occurred to her! The one very logical reason he hadn't pursued her, beyond that initial wild attraction in the carriage. Her knees turned to jelly, and she was so weak for a second she was sure she was going to swoon. Jeremy was already committed to someone else. He was engaged. Or married.

"Damn you!" she cried, the pain so acute it was a burning physical sensation shooting through her body. "Damn you—I hate you! You played with me. You knew how I felt, and you *played* with me! It was all for your ego. The looks and the innuendos! All for the fun of it!"

"Be fair, Lili—"

"No!" she cried out. She didn't want to listen. She didn't want to be fair. "I'm not going to stay here another second! You've already had enough laughs at my expense. You're not getting the ransom too. I'm going home to Papa, where I belong. And you can't stop me!"

She spun around, taking advantage of his startled reaction to get away. Not even thinking, she headed down the path, cutting abruptly to the right, out of sight for a moment. She didn't know how she was going to elude him. She didn't even know where she was going or which direction led to home. And she didn't care!

Surprise sounded in the voice that called after her.

"Wait, Lili—don't be a fool! For God's sake, the marshes are riddled with bogs and quagmires. It's not safe."

Not safe? She could have screamed in frustration. He had kidnapped her, brutally, arbitrarily picking her as a pawn in his sinister plot. He had toyed with her heart and her body, he had used her as no man ever had before, and now he was telling her she wasn't safe! Just because she might be sucked to her death in the mire!

Nothing, *nothing*, could be worse than what he had already done.

He was married. She pushed her way through a heavy screen of prickly shrub, not even noticing when it tore her pretty gown and drew blood from her arms. She had to escape. She could not bear the humiliation she would suffer if he caught her and she was forced to look into that mocking, scornful, cruel face again.

He was married! She had taken off her clothes and lain in his arms, begging him to make love to her; she had squirmed with delight while he did unspeakable things with his mouth and fingers—and all the time he had been married to someone else! Like Gabriel Dubois with her pious, gentle, gullible mother.

Only she had the horrible feeling that Jeremy really cared for his wife.

She paused for a second, ears straining. The footsteps she heard thrashing through the brush seemed to have gone past. She had fooled him, then, darting into the shrubbery. He was still heading in a straight line, following the course of least resistance.

Her breath came in sharp, painful gasps. She had thought he was such a gentleman, because of the restraint he had shown with her. But he hadn't been thinking about her at all. He had been thinking of his wife!

And intending to remain faithful, no doubt. Which he had managed disgustingly well, except for that one brief flare-up of passion.

A wave of nausea flooded over her. It was all she could do to keep from retching. Would he confess the truth when he got home? Would he embrace his beautiful Paulette or Denise or Hortense in their marriage bed and coo sweet love words in her ear . . . and tell her how close he had come to betraying her with the spoiled little rich girl who had thrown herself at him?

And how glad he was he had stayed true?

Damn, she thought helplessly. Damn, damn, *damn*. Tears blinded her eyes, and she started to run again, mindlessly, unable to see where she was going, everything a golden blur in the mist of her pain. She had loved him, truly and deeply, and he didn't have any feelings for her. He had only been passing time until he could return her to her father and collect the small fortune that was all he had ever been interested in.

She did not realize, until she had rounded a dense clump of wild myrtle and looked ahead, that he had tricked her. She *hadn't* fooled him when she ducked into the shrubs. He had simply known where she was going to come out.

He was there now, a few yards ahead, feet braced firmly on the ground, hands slightly out from his sides, poised to catch her.

Lili didn't think. She simply reacted. Whirling around, she raced back the other way, into what looked like an open field. But the ground was treacherous, more mud than grass. The first few steps, and she was up to her ankles, but she kept on, not even caring about snakes and frogs and God knew what other slithery things. She hated him. Hated him more than she had ever hated anyone in her life, and she was going to get away!

Then suddenly her feet hit a slick patch, and she was sliding, sliding . . . out of control.

21

Her arms flailed out, fanning the air in a desperate attempt to regain her balance. Then, just as she was falling, fingers caught her wrist, strong, bruising fingers jerking her roughly back. A sharp pain flashed out from her shoulder, racing down her arm.

Jeremy! Already blind with tears, Lili sobbed out her frustration. He had caught her. She had thought she was so clever, and he had been waiting all the time! Now it was too late to escape.

With one last frantic, irrational burst of energy, she struggled to free herself, twisting away from that vise-hard grip, writhing and kicking, futilely, for her slippers had been lost in the slime, and bare toes had no effect on legs that felt like iron. Jeremy clutched at her other wrist, but the ground was slippery, and he miscalculated. Suddenly his feet were all over the place, and he was going down, taking her with him.

The mud was cold and horribly clammy, oozing through the back of her dress, but Lili barely noticed. All she could feel were Jeremy's arms tight around her, his body grossly, insinuatingly pressed against hers. Her thigh had gotten wedged between his legs, and something hard and unmistakable pushed out from his groin. With a rush of horror Lili realized that the passion she had failed to rouse before was throughly inflamed now.

And incredibly, shamefully, her own body was stirring, remembering things she had vowed to forget.

Angrily she tried to push him away, tried to slide out from where he had her imprisoned, half beneath the weight of his muscular body. But he seemed to have different ideas, for he was holding on to her, twisting her up with him, out of the mud and onto firmer ground. Tall grasses, wet from the recent rain, bristled around them, cutting off the rest of the world.

Drawing himself up on both elbows, Jeremy pinned her shoulders to the earth as he stared down at her. The beauty that had moved him the first time he saw her was even more bewitching now, sweet innocence mingling with fiery anger and a mounting passion she was only beginning to recognize herself. The struggle had loosened silken wisps of hair, and they flared out, disheveled, around her exquisitely lovely face, lending a sultry sensuality that made his blood burn.

His eyes dipped lower, taking in the open front of her bodice, the swell of firm young breasts rising out of mud-spattered lace, the faint outline of her nipples, and his groin throbbed and ached until he knew he had to have her.

He sank down, body crushing hers, full-length against the earth, face only inches from the quivering softness of her lips and cheeks. He didn't want this. God knew, he hadn't planned it this way. But his inhibitions had been lulled away by days of flirtation, nights of almost making love, and his will was no longer his own. Passion consumed every nerve, every sinew of his body. He could no more have denied it than he could have denied the air that flowed into his lungs.

The sharp ejection of hot breath on her cheek told Lili more eloquently than words that the anger and humiliation in this capitulation were as much his as hers. She could feel the rage that vibrated through every tautened muscle of his body. But she felt the urgency too, and she knew he was not going to stop.

Let me go, she tried to cry out. Let me go! You're dreadful and deceitful, and I hate you—and I don't want this to happen! But it was already too late, for his mouth was on hers, stifling all but a helpless moan that ended somewhere deep in her throat.

It was not a kiss, but a command. There was no tenderness in him now, no gentleness, nothing of the thoughtful, teasing lover she had imagined when she dared to put on a frilly pink dress with nothing underneath and come to find him. His lips were hard, arrogant. She had not known that lips could be like that, almost violently ravenous as they assaulted the frail fortress of her mouth.

Now, treacherously, it was opening—why hadn't she fought harder?—and his tongue was inside, raping that warm moist cavern, relentlessly and very thoroughly.

And, heaven help her, a part of her—the part she could not control—was thrilling to it, reveling in his strength as she had reveled before in sweeter passions, and she longed for nothing so much as to suck him deeper into her mouth.

Desperately she doubled her fists, tearing her head away as she beat an angry tattoo against his chest. She couldn't let him do this to her. She couldn't! She had come like a whore to claim a man who could never be hers. If she let him see how much she still wanted him, how desperately her body ached to accept his caresses, he would think that was exactly what she was.

But all the frantic hammering in the world had no effect. Whatever masculine urges had caught him up, he was their prisoner now. A shudder ran through Lili's body as she felt his weight rise, felt bold, demanding hands sliding down from her shoulders, skillfully, provocatively—felt trails of mud smearing creamy ivory breasts as he found that last little button and ripped it open.

No! every instinct in her heart screamed out. No! But her body had developed a will of its own, moving and responding by itself. Somehow her hands had stopped fighting. One minute they had been beating against his chest; the next they were clutching at his neck, his back, trying to pull him closer.

He seemed to sense the completeness of his mastery over her. His mouth grew harder, hungrier, draining away the last of her will to fight. Lili had not thought his hands could be any bolder, but they were. He was ripping her dress now, roughly, casting aside the last shreds that impeded his approach. And her own hands were helping, her mouth glued to his as together they exposed her flesh to the rugged body that hovered above.

There was no need to urge her legs apart. They were spreading already, and he was thrusting down, sharply, driving into her.

The pain was almost instantaneous. Lili felt her body contract as it stabbed through her, searing and unexpected, like a flame-burned blade, and she let out a strangled half-sob. Sick with horror, she realized what she had allowed, what she had shamelessly encouraged him to do.

He must have heard the muffled sound, for he stopped, rigid and motionless, still buried deep in her body. Or perhaps he had felt the tearing of that delicate barrier, and been startled into remembering how young and inexperienced she was.

When he didn't move, Lili dared to hope that whatever he expected had happened, and the terrible shame was over. But then he started again, slowly at first, long, even, in-and-out strokes that, surprisingly, hardly hurt at all. Something strange was happening inside her, something warm and throbbing that seemed to take the last of her resistance and turn it into the most exquisite agony.

His motions were defter now, and quicker, and she was moving with him, her hips struggling awkwardly to keep up. His hands slid under her buttocks. She could feel him helping, guiding, and suddenly they were following each other's rhythm, ebbing and flowing in perfect unison, dying a little with each hard, deep, satisfying lunge.

Everything else was gone now. The pain that had racked her before, the shame, the desperate need to get away. There was only the hardness of him, filling every corner of her being, compelling her body up again and again to meet him, to search for the release only he could give. When it finally came, the soft cry that slipped out of her lips mingled with a deeper masculine groan as Jeremy surrendered with her.

Nothing, *nothing*, could ever be so perfect again. Lili lay alone on the ground, some minutes after he had left her, lost in the lingering, blissful satiation that still warmed and satisfied her body. How could she ever have questioned whether this was right or wrong? How could she have tried to fight him off? It didn't matter who he was or what had happened before. It didn't even matter that the words of love she longed for had never been spoken. The sheer magic of their coupling was enough to leave her dazed and glowing.

It was only slowly that she became aware of a cold breeze wafting over her body. Sweat chilled to a wash of ice water, and she felt herself descending unpleasantly to earth. Even before she opened her eyes, she knew that

Jeremy had left and was standing some distance away. And that he wasn't looking at her.

Dear heaven! He hadn't even taken the time to remove his clothing. Waves of humiliation flooded over her. Even his trousers were fastened again as he turned to face her, a nice tidying operation, as if nothing had happened. He had thrown her on the ground like some cheap trollop and satisfied his basest urges without so much as a pretense of nicety.

And he hadn't even cared enough to stay and comfort her when he was through!

"You raped me!" she cried unreasonably.

To her surprise, he did not seem angry. If anything, Lili sensed pain in his troubled blue eyes as he came over and squatted beside her. Pain and regret. Could it be that he had a conscience after all?

But his words dispelled that illusion.

"Ah, and here I thought it was you who unbuttoned all but the last of those little pearls on the front of your bodice."

The cad! He had taken advantage of her innocence, and now he was trying to make it look like everything was her doing. "Yes, but I . . . I changed my mind! You know I did! I was trying to run away from you. How could you be arrogant enough to think I still wanted *that*?"

"Was it arrogance that made me feel your arms around me, clinging?" There was amusement in his tone now. "Or the very eager and surprisingly knowing way you were sucking my tongue into your mouth? Forgive me, love, if I'm a bit confused. Those hardly seem the actions of a woman who doesn't want *that*."

"Noooo, I suppose not, but . . ." Lili faltered, trying not to let him see the tears that had risen to her eyes. "I didn't want it to be like this. Not some . . . some casual affair on the ground! You didn't even take off your clothes. Oh, Jeremy, I thought it was going to be pretty. And nice."

"If you were more experienced, you'd know that the first time for a woman is rarely nicer than this . . . or more satisfying." He smiled, half wryly, with a mockery that seemed to be directed more at himself than at her. "But it could have been prettier, I confess. Though, to be fair, *petite*, that wasn't altogether my fault. You did tempt me beyond all reason." He laid his hand on the side of her face, running gentle fingers down her cheek, tracing the line of full, sensuous lips. "Still, I knew what you wanted. I understood the romance your heart craved. And, God forgive me, I didn't give it to you."

Lili lay absolutely still, not even daring to move. She had no idea where it had come from, this unexpected new tenderness, but she wasn't about to question it. He was talking now the way she wanted him to talk. Treating her the way she hungered to be treated.

"You could make it up to me," she said hopefully.

"And how is that, love?"

"Oh, I don't know . . ." She felt her body begin to writhe inwardly with anticipated pleasure. If all those things Vava had told her about especially virile men were true, there might be quite a number of delights yet in store for her. "But I'm sure you can think of something."

"I can . . . and I will."

He cast a rueful glance at the place where her dress lay, torn and ruined on the ground, then commenced to tug off his shirt, which was nearly as muddy but at least intact. Lili gasped, unable to tear her eyes away as he exposed a rugged upper torso.

Even inexperienced as she was, she knew he was superbly built. His shoulders were strong and broad, straining with muscles that continued down his arms and rippled across his chest. Darkish curls matted enticingly, and she followed, mesmerized, as they narrowed into a thin, even darker line along his belly, disappearing into the top of his trousers. If that hard bulge she spotted at the front was any indication, Vava had not been wrong about a man's capacity for desire.

Then, before she could think about it any further, his arms were around her and he was lifting her up. He did not attempt to dress her in the shirt, but simply wrapped it around her, and Lili felt deliciously naked as he carried her in long strides back to the camp. Her head sank on his shoulder, and she forgot everything else except the physical sensations that swathed and enveloped her like a rough, warm blanket. The smell of him was acutely sensual, the man-odor of sweat and tobacco and leather. His chest hair prickled against her cheeks, lightly, tantalizing, just touching and teasing her lips.

When he laid her down at last on the mossy bed in the

small hut, the rest of the world was gone, and Lili longed only to feel him beside her again. Yet even as the yearning was most intense, something disturbed her—something faint and nagging in the back of her mind—and she couldn't seem to let herself go.

It was a moment before she realized what it was. When she did, everything came back suddenly and joltingly. The reason she had run away from him in the first place, the very real, terrible reason this love between them could never be.

To her embarrassment, the tears she had managed to hold back before came rolling down her cheeks.

"What?" Jeremy hesitated, half-kneeling beside her, looking, for the first time since she had met him, vaguely uncertain. "I thought you wanted this, love. Isn't this what you've been begging for? Now all I see are thundershowers. If you're not sure, tell me . . . I will not force myself on you again."

"It's not that," she said miserably. "I do want this . . . I want *you*. But I can't help remembering what you said before. About not being free to make any promises. Oh, Jeremy, you're married! You have a wife somewhere waiting for you. Or a fiancée."

His lips twitched faintly at the corners. "No, love, I am not married. You needn't worry about that. Nor have I ever asked any other woman to be my wife. But I do have certain . . . commitments."

"Commitments? Oh, your silly *cause*!" Lili felt as if a weight had fallen from her shoulders. It wasn't another woman, after all! He didn't love someone else, so there was still a chance for her!

"And you don't fear causes?" He raised one brow as he looked down at her.

"No. I don't fear anything now."

"How very young you are," he murmured gently. "But perhaps you're right. You *don't* need to fear anything . . . now."

Lili lounged back into the pillows, her eyes closing as she waited breathlessly for the feel of bristling chest hair against her own smooth breast, which was bare again, for the shirt had somehow fallen away. Or had she shrugged it off? She smiled a little at her own wantonness, imagining the choice words that would have spilled out of her mouth just a month ago if she'd heard of some young lady behaving in such a wildly improper manner.

But to her surprise, Jeremy made no move to touch her. Aware of a faint chuckling sound, she opened her eyes warily.

He was standing over her, looking down with a mingled expression of amusement and tenderness.

"I *am* going to give you what you plainly desire, love. And what I desire most passionately. But I think right now I'd better clean you up. I doubt you've ever been so filthy in your life."

It was not quite true. Having been a willful child, Lili had taken perverse pleasure in coming home so soiled from head to toe she was barely recognizable. But she had never gotten dirty in quite such an intriguing manner, and she contented herself with remembering every delicious detail, leaving out only the explosive anger at the beginning, as Jeremy left the room, tending to something outside. When he came back, he was carrying a smallish pail in one hand and a large sponge in the other.

"It's fortunate I was heating this bathwater for myself. It looks like you need it more. If we don't get that dried mud off soon, I fear it will be a permanent appendage to your very lovely skin."

Lili's lips turned up at the corners as she eyed the bucket. "A bath? In that? I know you call me *petite*, but I'm really quite tall for a woman. And even if I were the littlest bit of a thing, I could hardly fit into that."

"I didn't expect you to," he replied, a surprisingly rakish edge to his voice. "In fact, I don't expect you to do anything at all. Just lie back and imagine you're some dusky queen floating on a barge down the Nile, and I am your faithful slave."

"Oh." The look on his face, only half-teasing, made her feel warm again, a slow burning sensation that started in her belly and oozed outward until it filled her entire body. "I think I could get used to being spoiled."

"I think you already are." Reaching out impulsively, he ripped away the combs that still half-held her tousled hair. A spill of tresses tumbled silky-dark and free over the pillows, trailing onto the floor. Her hair was one of the first things he had noticed about her, and desired— that glorious red-black hair and the high spirits that had made him sense, even then, that he would be taking a wildcat to his bed. "I think you are much too used to it. But never mind. You've earned the right to be outrageously spoiled today."

He dipped the sponge into the water, making a faint splashing sound. As Lili watched, he rubbed it across a cake of fine white soap, releasing the fragrance of French perfume.

He has expensive taste, she thought, vaguely surprised. It seemed funny in a man who had relinquished all other pleasures for the life of a renegade patriot. But then, he had been raised with money, and it was hard to leave everything behind.

She sighed as the warm soapy sponge touched her cheek, and she felt him caressing away the smudges and smears. Slowly, gently, he began to move downward, taking care not to spill any more than a few drops on the blanket-covered moss.

He did not hurry, but took his time, thoroughly sudsing her shoulders, relishing every bone and hollow, as he knew she relished his touch; following the ripe young curves of her breasts, lingering on nipples that seemed to push of their own accord into the slightly rough surface of the sponge. The rich scent of soap hung provocatively in the air as those sweetly seductive movements continued to her belly, the outer roundness of her hips, sliding down her legs, and finally her feet, which he cleansed as thoroughly as everything else, teasingly separating each toe and washing it tenderly.

Lili heard rather than saw him soak the sponge in the bucket again, heard the sound as he squeezed it out and applied a new coat of lather. She could have screamed with the familiar, exquisite, aching yearnings that flooded over her as he urged her legs apart and she felt him lay it lightly between. Wetting each dark, matted curl, he eased them apart, then delicately swathed her inner thighs, wiping away the dried sweat and blood.

He winced as he drew the sponge back and caught a glimpse of the dark red discoloration. "I hurt you, love. More than I needed to. I'm sorry. But it only hurts the first time—I promise."

Lili, remembering the severity of the pain that had ripped through her, was inclined to doubt it. But remembering, too, the intense sensations that had followed, she was more than ready to forgive. "It doesn't matter, my darling. I don't mind." She would endure anything, suffer anything, to lie beside him again and feel that same wonderful, terrifying, all-encompassing delight.

"But you should mind, *petite*. No woman should accept pain as a matter of course. Or indifference. From now on, there will be only pleasure for you in the act of love, as there is for me." He was taking a clean silk handkerchief out of his pocket as he spoke. Moistening it, he began to dab away the smooth, strangely sensuous residue of soap. Then, surprisingly—for Lili could have sworn he was not a patient man—he turned her, protesting faintly, onto her stomach.

"Hush, sweet. You're as dirty in back as in front. Nay, dirtier, I swear! I shall have to cleanse every part of you, and I assure you, you will find it most interesting."

It was not an empty promise. Jeremy was a skillful lover, experienced enough to know how to touch her, even in seemingly the most innocent ways, and caring enough to want to. The sponge had just the faintest hint of scratchiness, not uncomfortable, but tantalizing, making Lili's skin tingle, and the silk handkerchief that followed was so smooth it felt like a lingering whisper. Then he had put them both aside, and she could feel his hands fondling, soothing, massaging. Every taut muscle in her neck succumbed to those wonderfully potent fingers; the tension eased out of her shoulders and back, even the soft flesh of her upper arms.

A long slow shiver sighed through her as he took her buttocks in both hands, cupping them firmly, possessively, not even embarrassing her when his fingers slipped intimately into the crevice between. Then he was caressing her thighs, perilously close to the center of the fire that had begun to rage through her body.

By the time he was finished, no part of her had been left untouched, and Lili was glowing with a curious combination of expectation and sheer, utter relaxation. A strange sense of lethargy seemed to have overtaken her, and he had to slide one hand under her hips, the other resting on her waist as he coaxed her gently onto her back again.

"I think, love," he said, smiling at the look on her face, "you are ready for us to renew our pleasure in each other."

Lili chided gently, "I think I have been ready for some minutes now."

"You mustn't be so impatient. There are many joys in lovemaking, and not all of them come from the act itself. Give yourself time to notice—and savor—each special moment."

Matching his actions to his words, he moved at a careless pace, rising almost languidly as he began to remove his clothing. It was a simple, natural gesture. Having been raised among the earthy Cajuns, there was no self-consciousness in him, no sense of shame at his own nakedness. And with the degree of intimacy they had just shared, he did not feel the need to shelter Lili from her first glimpse of his body. The boots came first, finely tooled black leather, turned almost brown under a thick coating of mud. Then his belt; then he was slipping out of tight-fitting black pantaloons with an easy, graceful motion which showed that, like Lili, he had not worn anything underneath.

Only in his case she sensed that he routinely disdained such niceties as drawers and other body garments.

She stared, fascinated by the sheer maleness of his body, now that she could see it in its entirety. Like his chest, his legs and hips were muscular, but leaner, lithe as well as powerful, and his buttocks were sinewy and strongly molded. But she barely noticed any of this, except as the vaguest impression to be stored away in her mind and enjoyed later at leisure. Now all she had eyes for was the visible proof of his manhood, thrusting out, ramrod hard and arrogant, from a nest of surprisingly dark curls between his legs.

Thank heaven she hadn't seen it before! The size alone would surely have made her swoon. But now that she knew how expertly he could fit that part of him into the softness of her own, more pliable flesh—and how her body responded when he did—the sight brought not alarm, but haunting reminders of a rapture so compelling she would die to feel it again.

He must have understood, for he made no attempt to cajole away imagined fears as he came over and knelt with infinite tenderness beside her. Bending, he touched his lips, not to hers, but playfully, once on the tip of each rigid, rosy nipple. Then suddenly his mouth was between her thighs, and there was no more teasing, and he was kissing her completely, boldly, in the most intimate way possible.

A wave of shock shivered through her—she was still too new to love not to be startled—but even as she stiffened, her hands were already tangling in his hair, urging him closer. Every instinct in her body tensed, remembering and anticipating the wonderful, dazzling, bewildering sensations that had swept over her before.

But he only laughed, a strange choking sound deep in his throat, as he pulled back.

"Not this time, love. Later I will do that for you again, and I will teach you how to pleasure me. But that first sweet initiation was just for you, a tender introduction to the rites of love. Just as that last rough tumble was mostly for me. Now it's time to share our passion."

He lay down beside her, so near she could feel his warmth, but still not touching. Then he was drawing her closer, and somehow their bodies were together, full-length against each other, and she was beneath him.

"Jeremy—"

"Shhh, sweet, shhhh. This is not the moment for words."

"But I have to tell you. I want you to know. It really *is* you I care about." Sensing his startled reaction, she hastened to add: "You said you were a fantasy figure for me, a silly daydream I made up out of all those stories about the Fleurie curse. But that's not true. Not anymore."

"I know that, my angel. I knew it before, or I would never have let passion get the better of me."

"You knew? But you seemed so angry."

"I was. But not angry at you or at what was happening between us. I was angry because it was turning into a hurried spill on the ground. I wanted our first time together to be beautiful and lingering, and exquisitely tender. Like this."

He penetrated her slowly, with one long, even stroke, sliding his hardness and warmth into her body. For all his pretty promises, it did hurt, but only slightly, not the sharp pain she had experienced earlier, and discomfort was soon lost in other, more consuming sensations as he commenced the deft, knowing motions she had come to recognize and understand. Her hips followed his, not at all clumsily now that their bodies knew and were familiar with each other, but easily, surely.

Our first time together. The words washed over her

with the sweetness of a soothing balm. Our *first* time . . .
as if there were times and times yet to come. Lili let her
hands slide down to his buttocks, feeling and marveling
at the muscles that tensed and released as he drove
himself into her again and again. This was all she wanted,
all she needed, all she would ever ask in her life. Jeremy
accepting and desiring her.

She had not been lying to him. All the wonder, all the
passion, all the gentle yearning seemed to merge into one
overwhelming flood of emotion. The Fleurie women and
their silly legend—and masked strangers with roses in
their hands—were so unimportant now. This was Jeremy,
warm and real. Jeremy, the man she loved . . . and she
would love him forever, no matter what the future brought.

She clung with her arms, her legs, wrapping them
around him, whimpering softly, not even aware of the
sounds she was making as she moved with those hard,
rhythmic thrusts, faster all the time, more urgent, until at
last they reached the peak they had scaled before and
were safely down again.

"Oh, my dear, I do love you," she murmured as they
lay, separate but together, warmly enclosed in each other's arms, drifting slowly on a sea of contentment. "I love
you so much . . ."

She broke off, remembering suddenly that the word
"love" was forbidden except as an endearment, which,
like "sweet" and "angel," might be whispered in moments of passion. But when she looked up apprehensively, she saw to her surprise that he was smiling, not
just his lips, but his eyes, his entire face filled with a
gentleness she could never have imagined.

"You don't need to be afraid of speaking your feelings.
I'm not going to throw you out of my arms—or my
bed—for being honest."

"But you never wanted to hear them before," she
reminded him. "You said I shouldn't talk about love, or
promise anything, because you couldn't make promises
in return."

"I still can't." His muscles contracted, a subtle tauten-
ing, but he did not pull away. "That's something you
must understand and accept as a condition of our being
together. Promises are beyond me, but not the sweet
words of love you hunger to hear. And I do love you, my
darling Lili angel. I love you with all the passion in my

body and all the power and depth and aching of my soul. Will that satisfy you?"

Satisfy? Lili felt as if her heart were spilling over. Her whole body seemed to be flushed with fever, and the coolness was wonderfully refreshing as he dipped his silken handkerchief in the water and ran it expertly along her temples, her breasts, even between her thighs, where the reminders of their lovemaking were still moist and somewhat sore. She smiled a little as he set it down, and she caught sight of the initials embroidered in one corner. J-B. So her first instincts had been right. His name really was Jérème Blaise, or something of the sort. It seemed she knew more about him than she had thought.

Not that it really mattered. She knew the most important thing. She knew he loved her.

"It's quite pleasing, I admit, and *almost* enough. But I was thinking . . ."

Jeremy caught the teasing in her tone and matched it. "You were thinking . . . what?"

"I was thinking it would be nice if you didn't just tell me how you felt, but *showed* me. In a very . . . physical way. If, of course, you can manage it again."

She had already made sure with her eyes that he could. And she had made sure that he saw her doing it.

He pretended to be shocked. "What a brazen hussy you're turning out to be. And greedy too."

"And you don't like that?"

He ran his hand slowly, tantalizingly, down her body, as she had known he would, warming her all over again, all the way down to her toes.

"I love it."

22

Damn! Jeremy slammed his fist down on the old-fashioned schoolmaster's desk, which stood by itself at one end of the long empty room. Lili, asleep after hours of exhausting lovemaking, had barely stirred when he slipped her gently out of his arms and made his way to the large building in the center of the camp. Somehow, he had thought the solitude would calm him. But now, standing alone, glaring down at his own handwriting splashed across a sheet of parchment, he realized it was having the opposite effect.

"Damn!"

This time he uttered the word aloud. Anger, mingling with remorse, tensed every muscle as he cursed himself for that ill-timed spectacle this afternoon. The girl had been totally inexperienced. There was a soft vulnerability beneath all that dazzling fire, and he had known it! She hadn't deserved the clumsy groveling that had put such an abrupt end to her virginity. Or even the somewhat gentler attempt at atonement that had followed. She should have had what he sincerely wanted for her, an idyllically romantic wedding night between clean white sheets, with a bridegroom who appreciated both her beauty and her innocence and took the time to bring her slowly, tenderly, to womanhood.

Brows knitting together until they formed a dark line across his forehead, he glowered down at the paper in front of him. Neat, terse sentences, everything spelled out in businesslike terms. Just what Don Andrés was waiting to hear: the time and place he could expect his daughter to be returned to him tomorrow.

Jeremy could almost see the look on the old don's face, relieved and smugly self-satisfied—if the missive had been delivered this afternoon as planned.

Glancing up from the desk, he stared dully at the room, faintly illuminated in the light of a crude oil lantern. It was a simple place, stripped of the bunks that had lined the walls, and completely bare save for the desk and its chair. The smell of whitewash was still pungent, and a faint odor of wood dust came from the floor. It would do, he thought wearily. It would do very well, but all that mattered little now.

He wandered over to the window, peering out into the night, but like everything else, it seemed to elude him. He had had so little to do with innocence for such a long time. He had nearly forgotten what it was. Not since Maria . . .

The darkness was impenetrable. Nothing showed behind the glow of light on the glass, yet he knew the area so well, he could see without eyes. There, to the left, was a stand of cane. And just in front, an ancient cypress, with streamers of gray moss forming a cavern where he had loved to play as a boy, and where he had enjoyed his first passionate kiss with a girl whose name was long forgotten but whose lips he could remember in vivid detail. Beyond, on the other side, a path led to the water, passing through what had once been woods but was now cleared and held the hut he had just come from.

Maria. It had been months since he had thought of her, or wanted to. He had long since assumed the hurts had healed, easing with the passage of time and fading memories. But he had been wrong. There was still a lingering pain, or perhaps only a sadness, all the more poignant because it no longer ran deep.

He allowed his body to ease as he leaned against the window frame. She had not been the first woman for whom he had felt affection; certainly she had not been his first sexual experience. Years of living with the Cajuns in the swamps had seen to that. But she had been the first to truly touch his heart. Perhaps, he thought, that was why his mind was drifting back to her now, at the very moment he had acknowledged his love for another woman.

And though he did not delve into it, that was part of why he was feeling so squeamish. Not just because of what had happened with Lili. But because of what had happened—and not happened—with Maria.

He stared out into the darkness again, conscious of a

restlessness he couldn't shake. Theirs had been a very usual relationship, the kind that occurred again and again in a city where ladies were supposed to be pure, men felt the need to prove their virility, and a convenient racial group existed to pick up the slack. He shouldn't by rights have taken it seriously. No one ever took these things seriously. But, oh God, she had been very lovely—a little like Lili, but duskier, with darker eyes that only occasionally showed flashes of yellow, and hair that had the barest hints of red.

He had met her on a dare. Someone had seen her and challenged him, and he had gone to one of those *pensions* run by "sympathetic" hostesses, which even then had disgusted him, for they had the same slave-auction aura that was later taken over by the gaudy quadroon balls. He had gone condescendingly, sure he was not interested, and he had taken one look and been captivated. After meticulous financial arrangements with a shrewd and ambitious mama—which he had abhorred, but accepted because his blood was boiling in his veins—he had begun the affair that lasted eight years.

She had been barely fifteen, his beautiful Maria, though he had not known it at the time. Fifteen, and as innocent as Lili when he had brought her to his bed. But he had been infinitely more patient with her, infinitely kinder, though he had never once evoked the same wild passions that had erupted in his arms this afternoon.

In fact, he had always had the rather guilty feeling that he never excited, never satisfied her. But she had sighed and cuddled contentedly in his embrace, and he had never asked. He didn't want to embarrass her, he had told himself then. Now he suspected it was his ego that hadn't wanted the answer.

There had never been a question of love between them, at least not on his side, though he suspected that she had loved him. But he had had a feeling of responsibility for her, and an inherent distaste for the way he had had to treat her in public. That, as much as anything, was the reason he had gone to France. And that was where she had died, trying to give birth to his child.

The pain that racked his body now was keener, more immediate, dulled by time, but intolerable all the same. Damn her, she had known she shouldn't have children! There had been several miscarriages early in their relationship, and the doctors had warned her not to get pregnant again. He had tried to be careful, tried to withdraw in time and leave her safe, but he had been young and impulsive then—*then*, hell, he was impulsive now!—and he hadn't always succeeded.

And she, treacherous nymph, had not made it easy. She had deliberately seduced him into imprudence, and then, triumphantly, succeeded in carrying the child within three months of term. He had thought then she wanted a baby, and with the arrogance of youth and masculinity, he had assumed he understood. Now he realized she had wanted the child as a way to hold on to him.

It would have worked, too. The pain intensified, twisting like a knife in his gut, recalling the searing anguish of that night they had told him she and the boy were dead. He had wanted his son. He had realized it then with a terrible surge of helplessness. Wanted and ached to hold him, to watch him grow to manhood, to be to him the father that he himself had never had. Raw anger had swept over him, anger that this thing could happen, and loss, and a deep, irrational sense of betrayal.

And guilt, because he was grieving more for the boy he did not even know than for the gentle woman who had just bled her life away.

Jeremy turned uneasily from the window. Somewhere, beyond that veil of darkness, Lili was sleeping, lovely, passionate Lili, dreamily unaware that he had left her. Even now, there was a possibility, however slight, that she could be pregnant with his child. Beads of perspiration broke out on his forehead. Blast the Fleurie curse, but there *was* a family history of fecundity at the most inappropriate times!

And his own personal history included the destruction of a woman he had cared about, as the direct result of his physical passion.

The thought was idiotic, and with every rational part of his mind he knew it. Lili was strong and healthy. Even if she was pregnant, which was highly unlikely, she wasn't going to die in childbirth. He knew it, and yet the idea sent cold prickles down his spine. Damn. He had thought he was over that by now. It was silly superstition, clinging to the past—as silly as Lili's confounded legend—but he couldn't help feeling an overpowering urge to hurry back and clasp her in strong, protective arms.

Sitting down at the desk, he picked up the paper and ran through it with a quick, cursory glance. Then, abruptly, he ripped it in two. No sense telling Don Andrés he was going to send his daughter back in the morning, because he wasn't. He *would* return her—in time for that farce of a wedding the old man had set up, and hope to blazes his clumsy passion hadn't ruined everything—but he wasn't ready to give her up now.

In spite of himself, his thoughts kept flicking back to France, those last two years, after Maria had died. He had remained, tending to family business, or so he had said, but in reality he had been setting things straight in his mind. God, he had been cocky when he came home! So blasted sure he had it all figured out! Time to settle down, he had told himself. Time to lead a normal, conventional life, with normal, conventional obligations.

Conventional, hell! No sooner had he returned than he had thrown convention to the winds. First with his political stand, bound to be unpopular. Then this insane scheme, which had a fifty-fifty chance of blowing up in his face. If he had any sense, he'd get out now, while he still could.

But he had given his word.

His lips tightened as he held a corner of the torn document to the top of the lantern, waiting until it caught fire before dropping it in a ceramic tray on the desk. He had given his word, and a man's word was his honor. He would not break it. But he was damned if he was going to let her go like this.

Opening the drawer, he pulled out a new sheet of parchment, expensive but unmonogrammed, the simple good taste he had always favored. The old don could damned well wait to get his daughter back! He wouldn't like it, but he didn't have a choice.

Jeremy dipped the pen into the inkwell. He had cheated Lili out of the sweetness of a wedding night. At least he could give her the honeymoon every young woman dreamed of. A few days in New Orleans before he turned her over to her father. A few deliriously happy days filled with everything she wanted . . . and then perhaps it would not matter so much. He owed her that.

And—he touched the nib to the smooth surface of the writing paper—he owed it to himself.

23

New Orleans was a brash, bustling city. If anyone had had the effrontery to point that out to Lili, especially a despised American, she would have retorted with typical Creole passion that it was elegant, charming, and sophisticated—and supremely gracious! In that, she would have been partly right. There *were* elegantly gracious elements, but they existed primarily behind the high walls of private homes. For the most part, New Orleans was rough and colorful and raucous, and that was part of its appeal.

It was impossible to stand on the street and not feel the throbbing pulse of the city, not hear it in the vibrating din all around. The constant creaking and groaning of wagon wheels as goods were transported to and from the docks and canals; the high-pitched whinnying of horses and the sharp, brittle snap of the drivers' whips; the clanging of church bells at almost any hour; a sudden blare of horns and drums, announcing the arrival of fresh shipments of oysters along the riverfront; the rattle of chains as a gang of blacks set out from the *calaboso* each morning to sweep the gutters and repair the levee; the cries of vendors, calling out their wares in a mingling of French and English, Spanish and the soft, lilting patois that was native to the area. It was a rhythm that, once experienced, could not be forgotten, and Lili felt an almost physical thrill at being home again.

She had assumed, when they got to the city, that Jeremy would keep her locked up, and while she hadn't exactly despaired at the thought—he was making it abundantly clear he had no intention of going back to his original, maddening aloofness—she hadn't been pleased either. But beyond a rather rough journey from Grande-Terre, over some secret route apparently, for she had been blindfolded part of the way, things were turning out much pleasanter than she had anticipated.

In fact, far from being shut away, she found that Jeremy expected her to come with him while he went around town on various errands.

"I'm not going to have to worry, am I," he said with a bawdy wink, "that you'll try to get away?"

Lili made a halfhearted attempt at indignation. "You think I'm so enamored, I wouldn't even be *tempted* to leave? What an arrogant man you are!"

"And right?"

She had to laugh. "And right."

She would not have been the least surprised if they'd gone everywhere in a closed carriage, perhaps with the curtains drawn, for as he had pointed out himself, she was well-known and made a conspicuous figure. But with a careless "I much prefer to walk when the weather's fine and the occasion permits," he'd chosen instead to make her less noticeable. She already had a wardrobe of bright gowns, not unlike the outfits worn by pretty quadroon mistresses or sultry temptresses from Santo Domingo, who peddled sweetmeats in front of the Cabildo. Now he completed the costume by bringing home several vivid *tignons*, the turbanlike head coverings women of color were required to wear on the street.

It took Lili forever to coax a square of vermilion madras into the traditional arrangement with its seven graceful upturned points. But when she finally succeeded, adding a pair of flashy gold earrings, she had to admit she looked exactly like the women she had glimpsed so often—and envied—on the street. Still . . .

"Aren't you afraid someone's going to recognize me?" she said. "An associate of Papa's, who's called at the house? Or someone I danced with at a soiree?"

He laughed easily. "Are you worried, *petite*, that I might lose the ransom I've set my heart on? How generous of you. Or are you afraid you'll be torn prematurely from my arms?"

Lili's cheeks colored, nearly matching the *tignon*, but she managed to hold her ground. "You needn't make fun of me, Jeremy Blaze. I've confessed my love for you, but you've done the same, so I think we're even! And I do wonder that you're so comfortable, letting me wander about the streets where I could be seen."

"*Touché*, my sweet." He kissed her teasingly on the nose. "I do love you . . . and don't fret so much. People see what they expect. Sun-bronzed skin, a yellow calico dress with white dots, a flaming scarlet *tignon*—obviously, underneath must be a lady of color. If, by chance, someone looks more critically, and I very much doubt anyone will, all he's going to say is: By God, what an amazing coincidence! That girl bears a startling resemblance to young Lili Santana!"

"Vermilion," Lili said. "The *tignon* is vermilion, not scarlet. If you're going to come out with bold statements, at least get your colors straight. And I hope for both our sakes, love, you know what you're talking about. You're risking the ransom, which means a great deal to you. But if I'm caught in an outfit like this, roving the streets on the arm of a notorious rake, my reputation will be ruined—and that's far more serious!"

"So it is," he agreed. "Virtue beyond rubies, and all that. But it isn't going to happen."

As it turned out, Jeremy knew what he was talking about. If she had any doubts, they were laid to rest the next morning when she accompanied him to the old French market along the levee. They had been there perhaps an hour when he left her briefly to greet a flamboyant-looking man with long black hair and a neatly trimmed beard. Lili didn't think much about it. In fact, she was so engrossed in the magnificent selection of cashmere shawls a peddler was showing—and wishing she had a servant to send home for the fifty dollars the woman was asking—she barely noticed anything else. Until she looked up and saw, not five feet away, a colleague of Don Andrés'!

Her first reaction was to freeze. Then, remembering what Jeremy had said about appearances, she forced herself to turn back, assuming the sensuous grace of a refugee from the islands as she continued to examine the shawls. To her amazement, the ploy worked. Out of the corner of her eye she saw the man staring at her, but it was not the puzzled look of a person who thought he saw someone he knew. It was the quite lascivious leer of a man who was plainly wondering if she attended the qua-

droon balls, and whether he could manage the price her
mother would negotiate.

Gliding away languidly, she took care with each indo-
lent movement to let him know that she had noticed and
that she felt nothing but disdain. It was all she could do
to keep from laughing when that worked, too! Jeremy
was right: people *did* see what they expected. A look, a
gesture, a simple change of dress was more effective than
the most elaborate disguise in the world.

Once Jeremy saw how much she enjoyed the market,
he made a point of bringing her there every morning.
Wandering up and down the aisles, rubbing shoulders
with servants from better families and housewives in plain
dark dresses carrying straw baskets, Lili almost felt as if
she were a little girl again, as fascinated as ever by the
sights and sounds and intoxicating smells.

Everything was in its place. One section held fish and
crustaceans, freshly trapped in the ocean or river, or
brought down the canal by boats early that morning from
Lake Pontchartrain. Redfish gaped up from long count-
ers, and funny flat flounder, and snapper and catfish and
pompano, releasing an unmistakable odor into the air.
Lili paused to watch as men in rubber boots and aprons
plunged bare hands into wire boxes squirming with live
crabs and crayfish. Just beyond, cut pieces of turtle had
been heaped into large, moving mounds, wriggling and
twitching, as they would until long after sundown.

The meat came next, mutton and sausage and huge
chunks of smoked bacon, and then the chickens, squawk-
ing in their cages or tied in threes by the legs. As Lili
passed, one was just being removed for the inspection of
a sharp-tongued country grandmother, who poked and
prodded and pinched from beak to tail, paying particular
attention to the craw. Lili chuckled, remembering M'mère
in those marvelous days when the thrifty old woman had
dragged her along like an extra basket every time she
went to market. She had poked at the craw too, feeling
for an excess of rocks, and muttering under her breath
that dealers fed their chicken small pieces of gravel to get
the weight up before bringing them to market. Which no
doubt they did, since she always seemed to find an inordinate amount.

Color and variety were everywhere, from the green of
the peas and cabbages and wild peppers to bright red

radishes, and beet-roots, and potatoes, both Irish and sweet. Nutmeg and cinnamon provided a spicy contrast to the distinctive sweet aroma of bananas just beginning to turn brown; and the delicate fragrance of early-spring violets was overwhelmed by a mouth-watering whiff of gingerbread as a black woman wove through the crowd with a basket on her head. There were bottles of beer, and brandy and wine, and huge kegs of *tafia*, or sugar-cane rum. And animals, too, monkeys whose constant gibbering added to the exotic cacophony of sound, and screeching parrots in startling shades of red and yellow and almost violet blue, and alligators, looking benign and lazy at the bottom of their cages, though Lili knew their jaws were powerful enough to snap a man's arm in two.

Jeremy was spoiling her outrageously. Lili had not one, but two of the lovely cashmere shawls after he caught her glancing at them. And innumerable gaudy earrings, which looked wonderful with a *tignon*, and even a plain but very pretty tortoiseshell comb, not at all what a lady of her station usually wore, but something she confessed she had always wanted. And roses, too, a fresh bouquet every morning, one with a handful of violets thrown in as a *lagniappe*, the charming local custom of giving something "extra" for a favored customer.

He would even have bought her a parrot if she hadn't put her foot down.

"You told me once I was much too spoiled," she said, laughing delightedly. "You're not doing anything to remedy the situation."

"No," he replied, giving her an amused look. "I'm not—but it's my pleasure. And you're going to have to indulge me."

Lili was hardly likely to argue. In truth, she adored the way Jeremy was treating her, and when she didn't stop to think about the future—the long days that would be so empty after she had lost him—she was blissfully happy. Willingly and quite unashamedly she took everything he offered—except the parrot. It was a wonderfully exquisite creature, all hauteur and scarlet feathers, and she loved to stare at it in the cage, but it had a distinctly mean-tempered look, and she could just imagine it spitting seeds all over the carpet!

They finished the morning, as usual, in the small stalls near the pillars, where steaming cups of coffee could be enjoyed, flavored with chicory, and all manner of deliciously tempting *morceaux à goûter*. Oysters, just arrived from the docks, and baby strawberries, the first of the season, and little ginger cakes, quaintly known as "mulattos' bellies." And, of course, big bowls of gumbo, filled to the brim, and jambalaya, with spicy chunks of *andouille* sausage emitting an enticing aroma.

Lili might have been able to resist had not the sweeter scent of sugar and freshly grated nutmeg caught her nostrils as a melodious voice called out: *"Belles calas, tout chauds*. Get your rice calas here." Lili ordered a double portion of the deep-fried patties and sank her teeth in, while Jeremy, pretending to be shocked, teased her mercilessly as she licked every bit off her fingers—though she noticed that he did the same with his own.

They were hardly hungry after that, but they went home for the noon meal anyway, as they always did about one or one-thirty each day. The shuttered dining room was dark, and Lili lit candles on the table while Jeremy went to the rear to pick up a kettle of crawfish bisque from the cookhouse out back. None of the servants was allowed inside, except in the mornings to tidy up, and Lili, after her initial surprise at the odd way the household was run, had to agree it was a sensible arrangement. The things they had gotten in the habit of doing right after lunch, or before lunch, or sometimes even *during* lunch, would hardly have occurred so spontaneously if there had been someone around.

"You *are* spoiling me," she said after they had decided not to bother with the bisque, but let it get cold next to a basket of bread on the sideboard. Jeremy had just shown her once again that it wasn't necessary to have even a blanket-covered layer of moss to experience the delights that were usually associated with a bed, and she was balanced precariously on his lap, not even embarrassed that they'd been in too much of a hurry to take off their clothes, but were still half-dressed in a state of great dishevelment.

"Spoiled, indeed!" He tweaked one nipple, which had dislodged itself temptingly from the front of her gown. "You want everything—and you manage to get it! Come, now, you've distracted me enough for one day. Let's see if we can find your *tignon*, which seems to have disappeared somewhere, and make you presentable to go out. I have an appointment I don't want to miss."

"Couldn't you be a little late?" Lili slipped one hand inside his shirt, already partially undone. Coarse hair teased her fingertips, reminding her enticingly of the sensations that had just passed between them, and which she was sure he was as reluctant as she to leave behind. "Whoever he is, this man . . . will he wait for you?"

"I think he'll have to," Jeremy groaned, feeling his resistance ebb. He was used to being his own master, used to controlling his feelings, but somehow, since he had seen her, *wanted* her, he had changed and softened in ways he would never have thought possible. Lifting her impulsively, he carried her through the door, not at all sure whether he had the patience to bring her all the way upstairs or was going to stop at the sofa in the parlor. And not giving a damn.

And Lili, feeling wonderfully, shamelessly wanton, didn't care either.

It was late afternoon by the time they finally went out. If Jeremy regretted his missed appointment, Lili could see no signs of it as they set off at a comfortable pace. No doubt he thought that the man, who had already waited some hours, would wait a few minutes more. And considering the force of his personality, such arrogance was probably justified!

They turned the corner at St. Ann, heading toward Royal Street. Lili realized with a vague sense of disappointment that he was taking her to one of the many coffeehouses where a good portion of the male population of New Orleans spent their waking hours, settling business and arguing over politics, or just whiling away the time with a heated game of backgammon or chess.

She had been surprised at first, and a little intrigued, to be allowed into those bastions of male privilege. Most Creole wives considered them "safe" territory, being blissfully unaware that an occasional woman did wander in, and exactly the sort of woman they wanted to keep away from their men! But after her curiosity had been satisfied, she found herself growing bored with the darkly good-looking young gentlemen who swaggered in, impeccably cravated and gloved, sword sticks swinging at their sides. It seemed they didn't have anything better to do than wager money they could ill afford. And complain endlessly about the Americans, with such silliness even she found it tiresome.

Which, she suspected, was part of why Jeremy had brought her there in the first place.

They had just crossed St. Philip, stepping gingerly, for a light rain had fallen the night before and the ground was still damp, when a blast of hot air came out of a squat one-story building on the corner. Peering through the open doorway, Lili spotted a reddish glow in the otherwise dark interior. The rhythmic ringing of a blacksmith's hammer echoed down the street.

For a moment Jeremy seemed to pause, and she fancied she saw him incline his head in the faintest hint of a nod. But there was no acknowledgment from within, and as they went on almost immediately, she decided she must have imagined it.

The coffeehouse was halfway down the block. A murmur of masculine voices was audible even before it came in sight, punctuated by the clatter of domino tiles on a wooden tabletop. As they entered, Lili saw that the few men present had bunched together in a small group at one end, arguing loudly and calling out comments while they watched the players and placed bets of their own on the side.

Jeremy seated her at a table and strolled over to join the others, more for appearances than anything else. Although the games themselves intrigued him—he thrived on competition, and while he preferred chess, dominoes was lively enough to hold his attention—Lili knew he was as contemptuous as she of the idleness and waste. But he made a point of blending in whenever they went out together.

Ordinarily she would have stayed where he had put her, enjoying the pleasing contrast of bitter and sweet in a cup of strong black coffee. But the afternoon had turned unexpectedly warm, and the smoke from a half-dozen red-tipped cigarillos, mingling with the natural mustiness of the place, had turned the air almost unbearably close. Thinking that a breath of coolness would feel good, she went over to the door.

It was not until she was actually outside that it occurred to her she was alone. For the first time since they had come to the city, Jeremy had let her out of his sight! The thought gave her a strange, almost heady sensation, as if she had put something over on him. Ridiculous, of course, but still . . .

She stared down the street, squinting into the dazzling brightness of a half-round setting sun, visible over the tiled rooftops. What would happen, she wondered, if I walked away? If I just wandered casually to the corner and across the street? Would I be allowed to go? Or is someone watching from behind a shuttered window?

It was not a serious thought. She didn't truly want to escape from Jeremy. Indeed, she would have panicked if someone had appeared to take her away. But the impulse had a certain impish appeal, and she couldn't resist moving a little farther from the door.

At the very least, she'd find out if he really trusted her.

She did not hurry, but sauntered nonchalantly down the street, trying to be surreptitious as she glanced over her shoulder. No one was there; not a whisper of movement showed in any direction, even when she reached the corner. The blacksmith's hammer had ceased, and soft strains of guitar music drifted down from a second-story window. Lili was not sure if she was disappointed or pleased. Jeremy did trust her, apparently—but he didn't seem overly devastated at the possibility of losing her!

She had just about tired of the game and was turning to go back when she caught sight of a slim man who seemed to be coming out of the blacksmith shop. Something about him was unpleasantly familiar, and she paused for a second, trying to figure out what there was in those narrow, sloping shoulders and oddly stealthy movements that set her teeth on edge. He, too, hesitated, as if looking around. Then he started toward her, and suddenly she remembered.

The mulatto. The man she had seen talking to Jeremy at the plantation. The one with the self-indulgent yellow eyes that turned to mirrors in the sun. He had sent shivers down her spine then too.

Instinctively she stepped back into a narrow alleyway that cut between two buildings. She was not afraid that this was the man Jeremy had stationed to guard her . . . at least she didn't think so. Those empty yellow eyes hadn't seemed to register anything when he glanced in her direction. But then, with eyes like that, it was hard to tell.

Worrying that he might see her, she moved deeper into

the passage, a dingy, rather unpleasant place, though it opened onto a court with a charming garden at the rear. She couldn't help thinking that she had spotted him in front of the blacksmith shop. In almost exactly the place she could swear Jeremy had stopped a few minutes earlier and given a nod toward the interior! Of course, she might be making something out of nothing—the man might actually have emerged from the building next door. But the coincidence was unsettling.

If she was right, this had to be the person Jeremy was meeting. The appointment he had been loath to miss. Yet, remembering the man's face—the sneer that seemed to be permanently twisted on his lips, the evil way he had leered at her before—she found that hard to believe. Surely it was impossible, incredible, that Jeremy would have dealings with someone like this.

Unless the man *did* have a hold over him. Unless there was something Jeremy wanted enough to give up all qualms. Something he *needed*.

Lili was so wrapped in her thoughts, she didn't even notice that a middle-aged man in snuff-colored pantaloons with a matching coat and striped Marseilles waistcoat had just come out of a door facing the garden and was heading toward the passage. His head was down, and he was looking at a paper of some sort, as unaware of her presence as she was of his.

They saw each other at the same moment. The man had just reached the passage, and Lili, almost at the end herself, had to stop abruptly to keep from running into him.

A flicker of surprise showed in light hazel eyes. Then the man's face relaxed into a vaguely pleased expression, and he tucked the paper into his pocket.

"Well, what have we here? Such a pretty *mam'selle*. If you were looking for the servants, you'd be at the carriage entrance, so it must be me you want, *n'est-ce pas*? I was about to go out, but I think I could make a little time . . . for you."

The words were harmless enough, but something in his voice didn't go with the gray-streaked hair and conservative clothes, and Lili felt herself growing uneasy. Despite the French that peppered his sentences, he was speaking English, with an unmistakable American drawl.

"I, uh, I glimpsed your garden from the street," she

said. "It looked so nice, I longed to . . . to see it closer. I didn't know anyone was here. I'm sorry. I . . . I'll go now. I apologize for disturbing you."

She started to leave, backing away. The man reached out and caught her wrist, not roughly, but too tight to shake him off.

"Nice try, honey, but the garden's not visible from the street. You have to be halfway down the passage to see it. If you came, you came to see me. And since I don't see a basket of goodies on your head, I think I can guess what you're peddling."

"Oh, no . . . really." Lili gasped, horrified, as she realized what he was thinking. "I . . . I didn't even know who lived here! Truly, I just wanted to see the garden!" She tried to wrench her arm away, but although he was not a big man, barely taller than she, he was surprisingly strong. "I've been here before, some . . . some time ago, and I remembered the garden . . ."

Even to her own ears, the faltered protests sounded feeble. She already knew, before those pale eyes flicked down her figure, giving her an insultingly quick once-over, that he didn't believe her.

"Come on, sugar, don't be shy. You haven't been doing this for long, is that it? Hell, honey . . ." He pulled her toward him, their faces on a level, so close she could feel the heat of his breath against her mouth. And smell, to her disgust, that he had been drinking whiskey in the middle of the day! "You've come for money, and you're going to get it. You don't have to pull this act to drive a bargain. I'm not tight with my purse when there's something I want."

"Sir, please . . . you misunderstand." Lili twisted desperately, trying to work free. What was there about these Americans that made them think it was all right to insult Creole women? Here she was, just starting to believe they weren't so bad after all, and another Mordecai Braddock turned up!

Then she remembered that this man, like Braddock, didn't know she was a Creole. With her gaudy gown and sun-bronzed skin, he assumed she was a quadroon.

"Let me go," she said, deciding on bolder tactics. Reasonable arguments were wasted on an animal like this. "You're all the same, you Americans! *Sales cochons—*

a bunch of filthy pigs! You think your purse is all that's needed, and you can have anything you want!"

"Misunderstanding, hell." The man's voice roughened, and his features took on an angry redness. "What's the matter? Now that you've seen me, you've changed your mind? Come, come, I'm not ugly. And little girls who sell their bodies for cash can't afford to be choosy. I'm a married man, but that doesn't matter to you darkies. And since my wife's back home visiting her dear simpering Mummie, it can't matter to her either, now, can it?"

Lili grimaced as he forced her full-length against his body, filling her with nausea. Sick with revulsion, she recalled the terrible things Mordecai Braddock had done, the awful, humiliating ways he had touched her.

She had not fought back in time with him. She had not cried out until his hand was already over her mouth, and she had nearly paid for it. She was not going to make the same mistake twice. Screaming as loud as she could, she jammed her knee into his groin.

He let out a howl and fell back, reeling as much from surprise as from pain. Lili gaped, fascinated, as his eyes glazed over, and she realized suddenly that he had been telling the truth. He really had thought that she came as a prostitute and that all those protests were a bargaining ploy. She might have been able to reason with him if she'd tried a little harder.

Now it was too late. Unwittingly, in her desperation to push him away, she had forced him toward the street. Now, as she watched, he pulled himself painfully erect, effectively blocking her only means of escape. There was no way she could get past him.

And if he had been angry before, that was murderous rage she saw in his eyes now.

"Help!" she cried desperately. "Please, *please*, someone help me!"

Terrified, she took a step back, trying desperately to control her breathing, which was coming in sharp, painful gasps. What if no one heard her? What if the street was still empty, and the blacksmith had started up again, and the sound of the guitar muffled her cries! Then, just as she was gauging her chances to lunge past him—and perhaps deliver another incapacitating kick in the process—a hand came out of nowhere, catching the man by the shoulder, whirling him around, and slamming him with a loud *whomp* against the wall.

Lili could only stare, stunned, at a broad expanse of back, clad in white cambric, with a shock of black hair above and coarse workman's breeches below. Then a face emerged from under one iron-rigid arm, pop-eyed, and so comically twitching she felt an insane urge to giggle.

Just for an instant she thought the stranger was going to squeeze the life out of her miserable attacker, and she didn't know if she was glad or horrified. But he only shoved the man away carelessly, like a dog that had been making a nuisance of itself.

"I believe, *monsieur*," he said in softly lilted French, "that the lady has expressed disinterest in your attentions. Perhaps you would find it preferable to pay court elsewhere."

The man seemed to understand, though he answered in English.

"She's a tricky little slut . . . but never mind," he grumbled. "I've no desire to risk my neck over a bit of baggage who comes looking for money, then cries rape when the price isn't to her liking!"

"Good," the stranger replied, switching to the same language as he eased the man back toward the courtyard. "I think we understand each other, which is always pleasant. But I seem to have torn your shirt, sir, in my enthusiasm to explain my point of view. Perhaps you'd like to go inside and change."

He waited quietly at the end of the passage, his tall muscular body blocking Lili's view. Faint scuffling sounds told her the man was making his way across the court—painfully, she thought with satisfaction—and then a door slammed somewhere.

As her rescuer turned, Lili, whose mind was still whirling, barely had time to form the vaguest impressions. His shirt was immaculate and freshly pressed, as if he had just put it on, but sooty smears showed on his breeches, and sturdy boots looked as if they had seen considerable use. The black hair she had noticed before framed a neatly trimmed black beard, which in turn framed dazzling white teeth as he flashed her a gallant smile.

"I think, *madame*, you have seen the last of the gentleman. I trust you are uninjured."

"Y-yes," Lili said weakly. Except for a bruise where he had been holding her wrist, she was unhurt, though she was shaking so badly she had to put her hand against the wall. "But if you hadn't come along when you did, I . . . I don't know what would have happened."

"Ah, but I did come," he drawled easily, "and from what I saw, it looks like you were defending yourself admirably. But what in God's name are you doing here? There's only one house at the end of this walkway."

"I just stepped in . . ." Lili hesitated, remembering the clumsy mistake she had made before. "To, uh, to get out of the way of a carriage that was careening down the street. The *banquette* is narrow, and I was afraid I'd be spattered with mud. Then I . . . well, I saw the garden and wanted to have a look. I didn't think anyone would object."

"Didn't you?" He was studying her so intently, Lili had the uncanny feeling he knew exactly how many carriages had—or had not—passed that spot in the last several minutes. "Well, now you know better, so perhaps you'll be wise enough not to trespass on the property of others again."

Lili nodded, feeling contrite and very foolish. Now that she had recovered somewhat, she realized to her surprise that she had seen this man before, in front of the old market on the riverfront. This was the bearded acquaintance Jeremy had been speaking to while she busied herself with shawls and a small matter of avoiding undue attention.

She did not have time to digest the coincidence, for running footsteps echoed abruptly on the boardwalk. Turning apprehensively, she saw Jeremy, wild-eyed and breathless, fair-streaked hair blown back from his brow.

Lili's heart contracted. His face was darker than she had ever seen it, clouded with an expression that could have been alarm or rage, though she suspected the latter. She squirmed uneasily, only too aware of how things looked. Jeremy thought, of course, that she had been running away—and gotten herself into trouble! And whether his ego or his passion was most affected, he wouldn't be quick to forgive.

Bracing herself against angry questions, she tried to

focus her mind, to sort out the silly story she had already started to tell. But she didn't even get a chance to open her mouth. Those clear blue eyes lingered just long enough to make sure she was all right, then darted back to the other man.

"I owe you one, my friend."

A gleam of white showed again between the generous mustache and small dark beard. "I shall remember that. It is always good, having a man like you in my debt."

"Though not always comfortable for the debtor."

"Ah, well, one cannot always be comfortable." Turning back to Lili, he swept her a low bow. "Lafitte at your service, *madame*. Jean Lafitte. That is my blacksmith shop, just down the street. And the debt would be mine if I could but have a smile from the lips of so lovely a lady."

"Monsieur Lafitte." In spite of herself, Lili managed a wobbly smile. There was warmth beneath that blatantly outrageous flirtation, and charm, which she suspected had won over many a feminine heart. So his was the smithy down the street. That would explain the breeches and rather scruffy boots. But *Lafitte*? She racked her brain, trying to think where she had heard that name before.

Let's just say there are some men—real pirates—I'm trying to impress. One in particular, a man named Lafitte . . . as larcenous a rascal as I've ever seen, but he has a rakish sense of adventure.

Oh, God. Was this the same Lafitte? The man Jeremy wanted to sway to his cause? The man he wanted in *his* debt, and not the other way around? If so, he must be doubly furious with her.

She stole a glance through lowered lashes. But whatever inner fury Jeremy Blaze was feeling, she could not read it in his face. Without looking back at her, he took the other man's arm, moving with him to the rear of the passage. Helplessly, Lili listened as the murmur of voices drifted back, urgent, half-whispered. Talking about her, she sensed, but she couldn't make out the words.

Unshed tears glistened in her eyes, forming a halo around the men as she stood and watched. Two tall, strong men—she couldn't help thinking how alike they were, their physique, their bearing, the easy confidence and cool, arrogant style that made them a match for each other. Except one, if Jeremy was right, was a notorious pirate and smuggler. And the other, heaven help her, was the man she loved, though she might have damaged their relationship forever with what she had just done.

She stepped back to the place where the walkway met the street, but made no attempt to move out into the inviting sunlight that slanted down from the rooftops.

He had kept her with him much longer than she had expected, longer than it could possibly take for a ransom to be collected, and she had dared to hope that he was as reluctant as she to give up the joys they had discovered in each other's arms. But angry as he was—and worried about the money that was so important to his precious cause—he could hardly be expected to keep her any longer. She had the sinking feeling that the urgent business the two men were discussing, their heads so close together, was her return to Don Andrés.

A carriage rolled down the street, the sound coming first, a slow, even clopping of hooves and the faint hiss of well-oiled wheels. Lili glanced out of the shadows, not really interested, but grateful for the distraction. As she did, she saw a little heart-shaped face staring with haunted eyes through the darkened windowpane.

Simone. Lili stiffened, forgetting everything else as she sensed the pain and helpless anguish in those unnaturally bright eyes. At first she thought the girl must be worried about her—about the kidnapping that had taken place nearly a month ago now—and that was why she was so distressed.

But then a hand reached out, drawing the curtain closed, and she had a brief but devastatingly clear glimpse of the man beside Simone.

Sick at heart, Lili turned away, unable to watch any more as the carriage rumbled down the street. It was not worry she had seen in the girl's eyes. It was remorse. She had thought, the afternoon he came to propose, that Jean-Baptiste Cavarelle had tarried to flirt with her cousin in the garden. Now, plainly, the affair had gone beyond flirtation. He and Simone were lovers . . . and guilt had driven her to the brink of despair.

Lili swayed against the wall, closing her eyes, trying but failing to blot out the terrible, tormented look on Simone's face. It did not for a minute occur to her to blame her little cousin. Always the naivest of creatures,

Simone was too malleable, too trusting, to be a match for devious masculine ploys. Besides, who knew better than she what it was to love a man—even the *wrong* man—and be so consumed with passion that reason and will no longer existed?

But she did blame the man who was slated to be her husband. Blamed and hated him, with all the dammed-up fury and frustration in her heart.

I can't marry him, she thought helplessly. I can't. *I can't* marry this monster who has so little respect for me, he's carrying on an open affair with my cousin!

Yet even as the bitter words galloped across her brain, Lili knew there was nothing she could do. Easter Monday would come, as it always did, and she would find herself at the altar—unless this man she loathed had decided to call it off, which was looking less and less likely, or unless Papa, for some wildly unexpected reason, had taken pity and changed his mind.

Or unless Jeremy had come to the conclusion that he wanted her more than the ransom, that his love was so fiercely intense he could not deny himself. But after what had just happened, that was the slimmest hope of all.

She listened as the sound of hooves and rolling wheels lessened until finally they were gone, and only the guitar remained, the same monotonous phrase over and over. The tears she had been fighting got the better of her, and she let them slide down her cheeks. They had already made up their minds, these men who held her destiny in their hands. Papa had decided, and Jeremy had decided, and Jean-Baptiste Cavarelle had decided. And she, being a mere woman, had no say in the matter.

24

It would not in the least have eased Lili's distress if she could have peered through the curtains of the carriage that had just passed and was turning the corner from Royal Street onto St. Philip. Her philandering fiancé might not be quite the heartless scoundrel she had painted in her imagination, but the expression on his face as he gazed at the dark curls on the little head resolutely turned away from him would have unsettled her even more. This was not the casual lust of a man adding one more woman to his large and indiscriminate collection. It was a look of genuine and very tender concern.

And, at the moment, exasperation, for he had planned what he considered a perfect surprise to climax a delightful afternoon. But it was beginning to look as if a degree of finesse would be required to carry it off.

Leaning forward, he let his lips play with her hair as he coaxed her gently around.

"Here, here—what's this?" He cupped her chin between his thumb and forefinger, noting but not commenting on the dewy moisture that brightened her lashes. "Sadness on such a beautiful day? You know how I love it when those pretty lips turn up."

"I know, but . . ." Her voice was soft, with the hint of hesitancy he had come to know and adore. "I don't feel much like smiling."

"But, *chérie*, what has come over you? You seemed so happy a minute ago. We were laughing and having fun, and I thought you were in the best of spirits. What happened to change your mood?"

"I don't know," she replied honestly. "I *was* having fun, but then . . . well, I looked out the window, and something came over me. It was almost as if I could feel *her*. Lili. And then I remembered she's coming home soon, and it will be all over for us."

"Hush, *chérie*." His finger played with the slightly pouting line of her lower lip. "We've discussed this before. You know that nothing has to end between us. Not now. Not ever. I love you, and you love me, and our love will endure."

"Even after you're married?" Simone's voice rang with uncharacteristic bitterness. "Sharing your home—and your bed—with someone else? *Mon Dieu*, Jean-Baptiste! Do you really think I'd sink to such shame?"

"Shame? And here I thought there was love between us. When a man and woman truly love each other, they share everything—even their bodies. Where is the shame in that?"

Sweet, beguiling words. Simone leaned back, her head turned to the curtained window, shutting him out. It would be so easy to let him lull away her inhibitions, to listen to the sensual lilt in his voice. But somewhere deep inside was the cold fear that had started two days ago and never quite left her thoughts. It had come into her consciousness subtly, bit by bit, little things that weren't quite right, slowly adding up. Even now, she wasn't sure . . .

"It doesn't work that way, Jean-Baptiste," she said, pushing the other, more disturbing thought out of her mind. "There *is* shame in hurting someone you care about. And an open alliance between us would hurt Lili."

"Lili again!" He settled back, almost petulantly, a little surprised at the way she was taking things, though there wasn't anything he could do about it now. "It seems to me you spend an inordinate amount of time worrying about your spoiled and very self-centered cousin."

"She gave me a doll once," Simone said unexpectedly. "I was very ill, with the fever that comes in the sickly season, and they thought I was going to die. When I got better, Lili sneaked into my room and gave me the most beautiful doll, with jet-black hair and a red lace dress. She had gone to the church and promised God she would give it to me if I lived."

"Very sweet and touching, I'm sure." He choked back a few choice comments, having learned from experience that there was no point challenging her intense loyalty to

her cousin. "But I daresay our pampered little Lili had
an ample collection from which *one* could be spared."

"Yes, but you see, this was her favorite. God would
never have granted her prayer if she hadn't offered something she loved. She *is* my sister. I call her cousin, but
she's my sister. And she always will be."

Her lips were quivering, but her little chin tilted up,
and he let out a long, involuntary sigh. The day had been
perfect; he had had such pleasant plans. Now, unless he
could come up with something quickly, it looked as if a
certain basket was going to remain where it was on the
seat by the coachman.

And a certain small package was going to bore a hole
in his pocket.

"So, because of a doll, you would reject my love. Even
though I've told you over and over that this marriage is
simply a convenience."

"But it *will* be a marriage, Jean-Baptiste. You will
stand before the priest and all those people in the *cathédrale*
and speak your vows. And the sin, which is bad enough
now, will be a thousand times worse when it becomes
adultery. It's not just Lili, but God himself who will not
forgive me then."

"Ah, is that what you're worried about?" He smiled,
feeling considerably easier. The attachment to Lili, he
could not fight. But God was another matter, especially
if things came off as he had planned. "God is everywhere, dearest, not merely in the cathedral. And 'all
those people' are not necessary for a marriage of the soul.
They're there to witness the binding of two prominent
families. That has nothing to do with true marriage . . .
or love, which is the only natural union between a man
and a woman. Besides . . ."

Simone tried to keep her eyes down, but something
teasing in his tone forced her to look up. It was hard,
being sensible, when she was with him. And he knew so
well how to get around her.

"What . . . what are you up to?"

"You'll see."

Opening the door, he shouted something she couldn't
make out to the driver, then flopped back on the seat
again.

"I had planned a party at the house, just the two of us.
There's a picnic hamper and a bottle of the finest cham-

pagne in the city. But I told the chap to head for our
special place on the levee instead. We'll have dinner there,
and watch the sun go down. Then we'll go *home* . . .
together."

There was no question what he meant by "home."

"But Don Andrés—"

"Don Andrés knows what's going on. He is not blind
or dim-witted. Naturally, he does not like it. But being a
reasonable man, he will accept it."

"And he'll let you marry Lili anyway? Even *knowing*?"

He laughed softly. She was such a child sometimes. "I
have told you over and over and *over*, and you have not
listened. This match Don Andrés has made for his daughter is based on *practical* considerations. That's just the
way the world is. Marriage is marriage, and love is love,
and only for a fortunate few do the two ever come
together. Here, curl up in my arms"—he coaxed her
closer, with only a minimum of resistance—"and enjoy
the surprise I have planned. Of which, I may hint, to whet
your curiosity, the smoked ham and oyster pâté and
deliciously sweet pink champagne are only the smallest
part."

The sun had mellowed to shimmering amber, the color
of a perfect afternoon, by the time they reached the
levee. The driver made his way clumsily up the steep
bank, not even grumbling about the weight of the basket
he was carrying, or all the extra work. Chuckling under
his breath, he spread out a carriage blanket, topping it
with Brussels lace and a pair of white candles. He had
been young once himself, and there had been an agree-
able respite or two he was fond of remembering—though
it would never have occurred to him to serve dinner at
sunset on a deserted part of the levee.

Nor, he thought with a knowing grin as he set out the
various dishes, would it have occurred to him to provide
such a sumptuous repast. He liked this young rascal's
style. If he knew anything about ladies—and despite the
passage of years and a wife who had eyes in the back of
her head, he rather fancied he did—he had a feeling the
girl was going to be cooing and cuddling in a matter of
minutes.

He was still meditating on that, and other, more obvious ways the pretty dark-haired *demoiselle* might show
her gratitude, as he returned to the coach and pulled a

discreet distance down the road. Glancing over his shoulder, he saw the young couple scrambling up the slope, the girl's skirt blowing in a gentle puff of wind, the man stretching out a hand to steady her.

When they reached the top and Simone saw the last light of the dying sun settling over the earth, she was glad she had put off her trepidations and agreed to come. They had never been here at quite this hour before. The breeze had stopped, and everything was so silent she could hear the cries of the keelboatmen far down the river.

"It's so beautiful," she whispered as she gazed at the water, a mirror-shiny arc flowing like molten gold between high levees into the distance. "I've never seen anything so beautiful in my life."

"It is beautiful. The whole world is beautiful today . . . and you're the most beautiful thing in it. Did you know, your eyes absorb the sunglow, and then they turn blacker than ever. How can that be, *chérie*?"

"I'm sure I don't know, Jean-Baptiste." Lowering her gaze, she turned away, hoping he had not heard the catch in her voice. She couldn't bear it when he looked at her like that. It made her remember how much she loved him and wished this sweet interlude could go on forever. "But this dinner you've provided—it's really lovely. Look at the lace tablecloth . . . and candles too, though they aren't lighted yet."

"It's not the candles I want to discuss," he said, catching her little pointed chin and forcing her to look back at him. "Or the tasty dinner you and I are going to enjoy together . . . later. I brought you here this afternoon for a special celebration."

"I don't understand." Something in his voice, the intensity of the way he was looking at her, made her heart do flip-flops in her chest. "What do we have to celebrate?"

He smiled, a little patronizingly, very conscious of the advantage a few years in age gave a man.

"Do you remember, before, I told you there are different kinds of marriages. And the only kind that matters is a marriage of the spirit, which has nothing to do with social contracts and all that mumble-jumble in a church. That's the kind of marriage I want us to have, Simone. Those are the vows I want to exchange with you today. Here, in this special place, just the two of us. No priests, no crowds of people watching from the cathedral, only

God and the river and the sky to witness our commitment to each other."

"Jean-Baptiste—"

"Shhhh." He laid his finger on her lips, a light, sensual
touch, silencing her as effectively as if he had drawn her
into his arms and kissed her. "You're confused, but you
won't be for long." Reaching into his pocket, he pulled
out a small box covered with wine-red velvet. "I brought
this as a token of my love for you—proof that I intend to
keep my promises."

He opened the lid with a snap. Simone gasped as she
saw a dainty circle of gold set all around with tiny rubies,
nestled in a bed of crimson satin. On closer glance, she
realized that each flawless gemstone was cut in the shape
of a heart.

Like a make-believe wedding ring, she thought—the
perfect gift from the perfect lover.

"You are right," she said softly. "Everything about the
world is beautiful today."

"It will be even more beautiful when I have spoken the
words I came here to say. And you have made the same
vows to me and I can call you my wife at last." He saw
the look on her face, and smiled. "You *will* be my wife,
Simone. In my eyes, in my heart—and what else matters?" Putting his arm gently around her waist, he guided
her to the water edge of the levee. "Come over here.
This is the prettiest spot, don't you think?"

Simone stared dizzily at the water, which had gone
from gold to orange to crimson, deepening with each
change, reflecting the rich colors that streaked across the
sky. She felt very small in the vastness of the world, and
very safe with him beside her.

"I don't think there has ever been any place prettier.
Or ever will be. But—"

"No buts now. No hesitation." He had taken the ring
from the box and was holding it up to the light, each tiny
faceted heart catching and refracting the fire of the sun.
"Give me your hand and listen very carefully to what I
am going to say."

Every reasoning instinct warned Simone not to do this,
not to leave herself so vulnerable. But then her hand was
in his, and the little gold-and-red circlet was slipping onto
her finger.

"Take this ring, sweet Simone, as a symbol of my

eternal devotion. You are mine, now and always, as I am yours, to death and beyond. I promise to love you and adore you, to laugh with you and weep with you, to provide not just for the needs of your body, but for your mind and your spirit as well . . . to keep you safe and smiling and cherished. You are the wife of my heart, and the wife of my soul, and nothing that matters will ever come between us. I swear that, before God and everything I hold sacred."

Before God and everything I hold sacred. Simone stood beside him, keenly aware of the unaccustomed coolness of the ring on her finger, and wondered how it was that life could be so glorious and painful all at the same time.

If only this were real, she thought helplessly. If only she could truly be his wife. She would give her soul, and everything *she* held dear, for that.

"I, Simone," she heard herself saying, "take thee, Jean-Baptiste—"

"No, no," his voice broke in, chiding gently. "Not words you have heard somewhere and memorized. That doesn't mean anything. Tell me in your own way what you feel."

In her own way? Simone panicked as she looked up into eyes that seemed to be asking so much of her. No one had ever encouraged her to be herself before, to *express* herself.

"I do love you, and I will always love you. Is that what you want from me? But I don't need to promise that. It's a part of me, my feelings for you—like the air I breathe and the food that nourishes and sustains. You are my sun and my earth and my stars. I could no more deny my love for you than I could deny the beating of my heart. And yes, I will be your wife . . . tonight."

"Not *tonight*, darling Simone. Always."

Oh, God. It was a sin. The worst kind of sin, but she loved him so much.

"Always," she whispered. "Always . . . until the day I die."

She didn't know if he drew her closer or if it was she who went to him, but suddenly her head was tilted back and he was kissing her slowly, tenderly, draining the honeyed sweetness out of her mouth. The earth was a deep, luminous red, one last burst of glory from a dying sun, when at last he released her.

"Now, my dearest wife," he said, smiling as he led her over to the place where Brussels lace and pale candles, pink-toned from the sunset, were waiting, "I think it's time for that celebration I promised you."

Still somewhat in a daze, Simone allowed him to seat her on the edge of the blanket. The picnic dinner he had assembled was superb, and she admired it enormously, but for the first time she could remember, she had no appetite at all. Even though he spread oyster pâté, with his own hand, onto lightly toasted French bread and held it to her lips, she barely managed a nibble. Paper-thin slivers of ham lay nearly untouched on her plate, and extravagantly expensive vermicelli with a lovely herbed sauce, even the little cakes he had bought, which would ordinarily have tempted her well off her diet.

She did, however, manage a glass of wonderfully pretty pink champagne, which, she quickly discovered, had a peculiar warming effect on her stomach and a strange way of doing something she was not quite sure about to her head.

"I think," she said, embarrassing herself by giggling, "that I am quite giddy."

"Good," he replied indulgently. "I don't approve of women drinking to excess. But every once in a while a pretty girl ought to get giddy. Especially on her wedding day."

The sun had settled beneath the horizon, and the candles were lighted, though it was so still they barely flickered in the gathering darkness. The warmth had gone with the sun, but the chill of night had not yet come, and Simone was quite comfortable when he moved closer and put his arm around her.

"Everything is so unreal," she said, staring at glowing candle flames, mellowed by the very definite glow of the champagne. "It's like something out of a fairy tale."

"It *is* a fairy tale," he told her, laughing gently. "Once upon a time, there was a gallant young prince—that's me—who had been searching far and wide for the will-o'-the-wisp of his dreams. Then, just when he decided she didn't exist, he came home and—guess what? He found a very beautiful . . ." He kissed her lightly on the lips. "Adorable . . ." And then again, taking her breath away, making it hard for her to think. "Very sexy princess—that's you—on his doorstep."

"I don't think, Jean-Baptiste," she said, struggling to collect her wits, "I like being picked up from a doorstep."

"On a moonbeam, then. He found her sliding down on the rays of a rising moon, and his heart was bewitched forever. Is that better?"

"Yes," she said, shivering slightly, for the night was getting cooler. "It's much better. I just wish the story didn't have to end."

"But you have forgotten, *chérie*." He smiled as he helped her to her feet, leaving the basket and blanket for the driver to pick up, and started with her down the slope. "The end of a fairy tale is the best part. And the prince and the princess were married—that's what they always say—and lived happily ever after."

"Always?" she asked softly.

"Always."

They continued the rest of the way in silence, still holding hands, still enveloped in the magical aura of a fairy-tale world. When they reached the carriage, he helped her up, playfully touching his lips to her hand before releasing it.

"And now, sweet Princess Simone, I want you to wait here like an obedient wife while I go back and make sure the coachman doesn't miss anything. Then we'll go home, and I'm going to show you the best part of a wedding. The honeymoon."

Left by herself, alone in the carriage, Simone felt the cold even more. She found a fur throw and wrapped it around her shoulders, but even that didn't help. As long as Jean-Baptiste was with her, as long as she was in his arms, she could forget the fear that had been clutching her heart in icy fingers these past two days.

But the minute he was gone, it came back.

Was it true? Could it possibly have happened? She tried not to think about it, but the more she tried, the more it tormented her. She had dared to confide in only one person, Marie-Louise, the pretty quadroon maid who sometimes, grudgingly, worked miracles with Lili's stubborn tresses. But Marie-Louise lived in a different world. Even if she hadn't been wildly jealous of her beautiful young mistress, she would never have been able to comprehend Simone's anguish or the terrible, consuming guilt that overwhelmed her.

What different does it make? sly sidelong glances seemed

to say. You love this man, and he cares about you, and you're not going to catch a good husband anyway. So why are you worried?

At least she was practical. With a sigh, Simone snuggled deeper into the fur. There were ways of proving these things, apparently, people who could be seen discreetly if enough time had passed. Wait another week, Marie-Louise had advised. Then, if she still wasn't sure, arrangements could be made.

Another week, and she would know. Another week, and the icy fingers would either give up their grip on her heart, or . . .

Or the fairy tale would turn into a nightmare.

She watched numbly as Jean-Baptiste scurried down the bank, holding up a lantern to illuminate the path for himself and the coachman, who was struggling behind with the hamper. *And the prince and the princess lived happily ever after.* That was how fairy tales always ended, he had said—only he was wrong. That wasn't the ending at all.

The end came when you closed the book, and set it aside, and were jolted back to reality.

25

Lili woke up the next day feeling miserable. Sunlight peeked through cracks in the drawn draperies, and church bells were ringing, telling her it was a beautiful Sunday morning. But all she could think of was the terrible cold expression on Jeremy's face as they had ridden home in the hired carriage he summoned from down the block.

She had tried, haltingly, to explain, but every word that tumbled out of her mouth had only made things worse. And even she had to admit, it *was* a flimsy story, especially that part about ducking into the passage to avoid a sinister-looking "someone" on the street. But she didn't dare mention the mulatto she had seen with him before.

When they had arrived home, he stayed only long enough to make sure she was inside. Then he had gone again, wheels rattling against the cobbled drive as the carriage pulled out into the street, and Lili had been left by herself to brood. He had returned in time for dinner, in a considerably softer mood. But she noticed, although he spoke freely—and even told several amusing stories as they enjoyed an excellent roast duck with seasoned rice and a side dish of aubergines and wild peppers—that the usual intimacy in his manner was gone. And for the first time, he had remained downstairs while she went to bed—alone.

It didn't help in the least to look over now and see a shadowy indentation in the immaculate whiteness of his pillow, and realize he had been there, lying next to her for a while.

He hadn't tried to wake her. He hadn't pulled her into

his arms and kissed her tenderly and made long, leisurely love, as they had every night since they had been together.

She put on one of her prettiest dresses, a loose emerald silk that flared around her ankles, and jammed a couple of combs in her hair to create the tousled effect he liked. But when she got downstairs, the parlor was empty, and she spent most of the morning alone. Or nearly alone, for every time she peered through the shutters, she saw a man standing in the street, making no effort to conceal the fact that he was staring at the house.

Apparently Jeremy still didn't trust her.

Not that he was likely to. Miserably, Lili realized that this man she had come to love more than anything else in the world was wildly furious with her. Worse, he was furious with *himself* for having let his ego lull him into risking the small fortune he expected to get for her.

And wounded ego was something a man like Jeremy Blaze would not countenance gracefully. She could just imagine him now, out negotiating her return to Don Andrés. And if, in his haste, he came up with a little less cash, he'd be furious with her for that too!

Lili was only partly right about Jeremy's anger. He *was* furious, but it was a fury that was directed inward, with a violence he had never felt, or would feel, for any external enemy.

Nor had she understood the reasons for the tension that now held his body rigid as he alighted from a coach in the stableyard and stood for a moment on the cobblestones, collecting his thoughts. It was not thwarted ego that was gnawing at his gut, or any lack of confidence in the depth of Lili's passion. He was inclined to believe the clumsy story she had blurted out in the carriage, though, disturbingly, he sensed she was holding something back. But he was bitterly aware that what had nearly happened was his own blasted, careless fault!

Beads of sweat broke out on his forehead as he recalled the way he had felt when he turned around in the coffeehouse and saw that she was gone. He had not been alarmed, not then, for he had noticed the stale air himself, and how uncomfortably close it was. But he had panicked a second later when he went outside and heard screams coming from down the block.

He had reacted then as never before in his well-ordered life. Fear had taken over, blotting out every vestige of

reason as he pounded down the *banquette*. All he could
think was that something was happening and he didn't
know what it was, that it might be too late by the time he
got there.

Then he had found her, pale and trembling, but unhurt, and this time his reaction had been completely
characteristic. A hot river of anger flooded through him.
Not the relief a weaker man might have felt, but pure,
instinctive rage. Rage that he had experienced such fear;
rage that he, whose self-assurance was his armor, had
been reduced to utter helplessness; rage that he had let
himself care about a woman, love a woman so deeply,
that his heart was open to pain.

The rage had continued well into the evening, blocking
out feelings that were too uncomfortable to think about as
he paced the streets of the city like a restless, prowling
panther. Wearing himself out at last, he had returned,
relaxed enough to behave civilly—even charmingly, he
hoped—over dinner with a contrite and unusually quiet
Lili.

But he had not relaxed enough to let down his guard.
Or to give in to the urgings of his body as he lay beside
her, rigid with longing, that last hour before dawn. It had
been a mad impulse, going to her like that. It had taken
every ounce of strength he possessed to keep from running his hand lightly over the smooth skin that had always excited him so much, to keep from brushing her lips
with the aching hunger of his own hard, demanding mouth.

But if he had let himself touch her just once . . .

Jeremy broke off his thoughts abruptly, and signaling
the driver to wait, headed for the rear door of the small
wooden cottage. Lili had been right about one thing, at
least: he had been spending the morning arranging her
return to Don Andrés.

Or *trying* to arrange it, for the messenger had come
back with the sealed missive intact. Incredibly, the good
don had picked this particular afternoon to go out, and
was not expected home until evening.

Lili looked up as Jeremy entered the parlor, her face
so wistful it tugged at his heart. Partly because the way he
had been treating her was beginning to make him feel
guilty, an unprofitable emotion he rarely indulged in, and
partly because he could not trust himself to spend these
last hours alone with her, he had decided that one final

outing would not hurt—a small diversion to while away the hours and leave her with pleasant memories.

"Have you ever heard of Congo Square?" he asked, trying not to notice the mingled hope and appeal in her eyes.

"Congo Square? Well . . . yes, of course." Lili hesitated, not knowing what he expected. The square on Rampart and Orleans was known throughout the area as a place where blacks gathered on Sunday afternoons to "dance Congo" under strict supervision, until sundown put an end to their revelries. "The servants talk about it all the time. But naturally, I've never been there."

"Then I think it's time we remedied that." Jeremy gestured toward the door, then held back. Too many misunderstandings had already been caused by a lack of openness on his part. It was only fair to be honest with her now.

"This is your last afternoon as a quadroon, *petite*. And your last time in emerald-green silk, becoming as it is with that exotic suntan. You'll be wearing modest white when I bring you back to your father . . . tonight. For the little time that's left, I thought you might like to see something you've never seen before, and never will again when you take your place as a proper Creole wife."

He was trying to be kind. Lili knew that as he helped her into a small closed coach, privately hired apparently, for it was a far cry from the vehicles that usually lined up along the Place d'Armes. But all she could feel, all she could think about, was the bitter realization that they were going to part soon and she would never see him again.

The city had a festive Sunday air as they drove through the streets, jangling harness and prancing hooves adding to the lively cacophony of sound. The Americans, with their underlying puritanism, had been shocked when they saw how the people of New Orleans celebrated the Sabbath, for while Creoles were intensely devout in their own snobbish way—and many answered the church bells that pealed out from the cathedral tower—Sunday, even during Lent, was essentially a holiday. Everyone with horses and a cabriolet was on the rutted spring-muddy streets, coming or going from visits with friends; parasols twirled gaily; and shiny sharp-heeled boots clicked along the boardwalks. Smiles showed everywhere as master and slave, banker and journeyman, dressmaker and doctor and parlor maid, enjoyed the bright sunlight and pleasant cool breeze from the river.

In spite of herself, Lili felt her pulse quicken as they approached the square and the sounds of a milling crowd drifted toward them. She had not forgotten what Jeremy had just told her. She knew he was sending her home tonight, and she minded dreadfully. But she was young and intensely curious, and already there was a faint beat of drums, and exotic smells were mingling with the dust that turned the air to a yellow haze.

They arrived a minute later. Craning her neck, Lili saw carriages lined up all around the square, so thick in places she could hardly make out the boat basin, which bounded one side and was linked by a narrow channel to Bayou St. John. On the ground, in front of and all around them, people were laughing and circulating, a swirling mass of colorful motion.

Breathlessly she leaned forward, impatient as their coach jockeyed into position, somewhat behind the others. This was the infamous Congo Square, or Place des Negres, as it was sometimes called, or Congo Plains—though never, oddly, Circus Square, which was its official name.

The crowd surprised her, not because it was large and gaudy, but because of the wide range of racial diversity. She had not realized it, for Don Andrés was extremely straitlaced, especially when it came to his daughter—and M'mère would have fainted dead away if she'd even talked of such a thing—but this was not merely a gathering place for blacks. Quite an astonishing number of whites were here as well, including, if appearances were not deceptive, some of the monied elite of the city.

Jeremy took her arm, half-lifting her down from the carriage, and Lili sensed, as the crowd jostled them back and forth, that he was already beginning to be sorry he had brought her. But if she had learned one thing about this man and his stubborn male pride, it was that he never backed down. Especially in front or her.

There was an earthier feeling here, mingling with the crowd, and skin tones were darker. Mulattos brushed shoulders disdainfully with griffes, and griffes with quadroons, with only an occasional white, and that a man strolling with his dusky mistress. Lili tried not to gape, but she couldn't help herself. Favored slaves strutted about in last season's gray-striped trousers and the cast-off coats of their masters, and women who ranged from cream to *cafe-au-lait* and darker showed off pretty calico gowns and bright silk or madras *tignons*, though a few brazenly left their hair loose in flagrant disregard of the law.

Everything was raucous, and vivid with color and sound. The hot smell of people massed together mixed with a pungent aroma of peppers and spices as shrill cries of hawkers rose above the din of laughter and conversation. Here, Lili saw a slender girl weaving through the crowd, a basket of gingery mulattos' bellies balanced on her head; there, an old woman, stoop-backed but tall as a man, calling out the virtues of small pies on the tray that was slung by a cord from her neck. Portable tables seemed to be everywhere, shaded from the glare of the midday sun by garishly dyed cotton awnings. On some, she spotted bottles of ginger beer; one others, cooling pitchers of lemonade.

Maybe, she thought, amused, "Circus Square" was not a bad name after all. Certainly it had a rowdy carnival atmosphere.

The dancing itself took place in an area in the center, a rough dirt tract, deeply rutted into primitive patterns by the stamping and shuffling of countless feet. Here, separation by color continued, with only the darkest, for the most part, indulging in the action. The music had already begun, dominated by a prolonged rattling that seemed to come from the head of a large cask, rhythmically beaten upon by massive beef bones. Other instruments joined in haphazardly—various crude drums, and something that looked like long-necked banjos, and calabashes studded with brass nails, which were played by striking two sticks against them.

Curious, and completely forgetting that the ivory tones of her skin set her apart from the much darker Africans, Lili made her way to the edge of the large open space. The excitement was keener here, a kind of anticipation that seemed to sizzle through the air. The men, as if they couldn't wait, were already prancing out into the center, bare-chested for the most part, or clad in loose open-fronted shirts, legs encased in tight breeches with shimmering pieces of metal on ribbons around their ankles. Some of the women were dancing too, but most were still on the sidelines, tucking skirt hems into waistbands, as they often did when they worked in the fields. On the fringes, children in drab outfits, brightened with feathers and bits of ribbon, were frolicking in uninhibited dances of their own, their shouts mingling with the drums and the clanking of the anklets and the chants that had begun to rise from the crowd.

Lili was so engrossed, she didn't even notice a tall, elegantly gowned woman standing in almost exactly the same position on the opposite side. But the woman noticed her, and dark eyes narrowed speculatively as they took in the flashy green silk dress, the low neck that displayed nearly all of her bosom, the auburn-highlighted hair, carelessly arranged with a pair of combs on top of her head.

The gaze was so steady, and so intense, it finally penetrated Lili's subconscious. Feeling vaguely uneasy, and not at all sure why, she looked up.

Her blood froze as she recognized her father's beautiful, arrogant mistress—Chartreuse.

Lili had a sudden wild impulse to turn around and pretend she was occupied with something else, as she had that morning on the riverfront. But what had worked with a casual acquaintance would not work with this woman. Chartreuse was shrewder, and more observant. She and Lili had never met—they had seen each other only from afar—but one was the daughter and the other the mistress, and they had been interested enough to mark each other closely.

And, of course, she had to know that Lili had been kidnapped. And that Don Andrés was worried to despair.

For one split second Lili's heart stopped beating. She knew it was irrational. There was nothing Chartreuse could do, not with the bustling crowd and all that noise. And even if she could, wasn't Jeremy sending her home anyway? What did it matter if the process was hurried a few hours?

Then, unexpectedly, the woman's gaze shifted, seeming to scan the area behind Lili, and with a slow, deliberately insolent languor, she turned away.

Stunned, Lili stood and stared as Chartreuse dissolved into the crowd. Did she hate her so much, this woman who had been barred from their home? She didn't even

seem shocked to see her lover's daughter dressed in
gaudy silk in the square.

Or was there a reason she wasn't shocked? There *had*
been that moment her eyes seemed to focus on something just behind Lili? Jeremy? Did they know each
other? Could they have been in on this from the beginning?

Lili did not have time to dwell on that disturbing
thought, for a sudden blare of sound broke her concentration. As she turned, she saw that the dancers were
forming into pairs, male and female, some with small
circles around them. The entire area was filled, but it was
the couple in the center, a bronze-skinned man and extremely dark woman, that caught her attention. He was
handsome, in a common way, dressed in a white shirt
and trousers that emphasized his lean male form. She
was neither young nor beautiful, coarse-featured and almost gawkily bony, but as she began to move, twisting
and gyrating slowly, with sinuous grace, not a person
among the watchers could tear his eyes away.

The music, too, began slowly, a primitive beat that
picked up as the crowd continued to chant, clapping their
hands and stamping in unison. Caught up in the infectious rhythm, Lili felt her body begin to sway with the
others. This was music as she had never heard it, raw,
vibrant, compelling. A primal force that seemed to be
drawn from the heart of the earth and the soul of everyone listening.

Fascinated, she kept her eyes glued on the center of
the square.

The dancers followed the tempo, sometimes a fraction
of a beat behind, as if pulled along on the current of the
drums. Lithely they circled each other, every languid
motion of their hips, their shoulders, their chests sending
out sensuous vibrations, though their gazes never met.
The scent of sex was in the air, mixing provocatively with
dust and sweat and cheap perfume as the dancers skillfully maneuvered around each other, acting out age-old
mating rites with none of the superficial fatuity of a
drawing-room flirtation. The beat picked up, and their
pace with it, nimble feet and gyrating bodies echoed in
the somewhat more subdued movements of other couples
scattered around the square.

There was nothing subtle about the dance they were
performing now. No pretense at anything other than

what it was, and Lili could understand the fascination that brought all those *voyeurs* in their carriages from other parts of town. It was frank, earthy, sensual. More than sensual, it was erotic and explicit, every swing of the hips, every motion of the body blatantly, openly mimicking the act of lovemaking.

The music reached a wild crescendo, climaxing abruptly when the woman's body jerked back, holding for a moment, as if suspended on strings, then collapsed in a heap of calico and long, loose hair in the dust. Almost before she had been helped away, another woman leapt in to take her place, and the dance began again, slowly at first, pulsatingly, building to the same frenzied peak.

Dancer after dancer replaced the original couple, the woman surrendering most often, for it was she who seemed to abandon herself most completely to the primitive rhythm. But sometimes the man, too, stepped aside, while the crowd stamped and chanted its approval. Lili stared transfixed, wondering how it would feel to dance like that, just once, wishing she had the courage to dart out into the center of the ring and test her skill.

And I could do it, she thought rebelliously. I *could!* The motions were simple, instinctive rather than learned, and she could improvise as she went along. Her toes were tapping, her mind toying daringly with the provocative impulse. Jeremy would be livid, of course. He would hate it if she made a blatant display of herself.

But did it matter what Jeremy Blaze thought?

And what could he do about it anyway? Lili tilted her head back, unaware of the way the sun blazed in her hair, seeming to set it on fire. Threaten to send her home to Papa? But he was doing that already!

It was the thought of Jeremy as much as the sensual beat of the music that proved too much to resist. Almost before she realized what she was doing, Lili had moved forward, hovering just at the edge of the place where the others were dancing as the music rose once again to a wild fever pitch. Then, just as it broke in one last tumultuous crash, even before the woman had dropped to the ground, Lili was there, taking her place, her body already poised in the first slow, sensuous motions of the dance.

The gasp that shivered through the crowd told her she was behaving in a wildly unconventional manner. Ivory-

skinned women in emerald silk dresses did not take part
in the dancing, but she no longer cared. The drums
paused, as if startled, then began again, and Lili kicked
off black satin slippers, letting the dust ooze through her
toes as she marked the beat with her feet. She had been
conventional all her life. She had done what she was
supposed to do, said what she was supposed to say,
behaved in all the proper conventional ways—and what
had it gotten her? An unwanted engagement to a man
she didn't even like.

Her arms began to move, rising as that other woman's
arms had risen, seeming to beckon to the dark strutting
figure who was barely a haze on the fringes of her vision.
He was a small man, shorter than she, a bantam cock
showing off to the barnyard, male ego aroused because
this incredible vision of cream and auburn and green had
chosen to dance with him. Lili laughed, a guttural sound
low in her throat, as her body moved instinctively, following the rhythm of the drums. She was not one woman
anymore, dancing for one man. She was all women,
dancing for all men, seducing all men with the supple
grace of her body.

Her hair suddenly felt heavy, and she reached up impetuously, spilling chestnut-brown and dark fire-glinted
red in rich cascades over her shoulders. Shamelessly she
realized that every man there was imagining those same
luxuriant tresses sprawled in a tumble across his pillow.

Every man . . . and especially one.

She had not glanced at him, but even without looking,
she knew Jeremy's eyes were on her. And she knew they
were burning with mingled rage and desire.

Something seemed to burst inside her, erupting like a
torrent of molten lava. Jeremy had always been in control of everything. It was he who made all the decisions.
He who gave the orders. He who offered or withheld the
love that was so vital to her existence. He who *let* her
stay with him, or told her in a few devastating words that
he was sending her away.

It was time someone gave this maddeningly arrogant
man a dose of his own medicine. Time someone turned
the tables on him and showed him how it felt to be
manipulated.

She spun around abruptly, teeth flaring white against
the almost unnatural red of her lips as she saw exactly the

look she had expected. He was surprised by her sudden
wantonness—and shocked, she realized with a surge of
dark amusement. He hated the spectacle she was making
of herself in front of all those other men. And yet he
loved it too, with a reluctance that was torn out of him.

She was dancing just for him now. When she flung her
hair into the wind, she was calling back memories of the
musky fragrance that half-suffocated him every time he
buried his face in it. When her mouth parted, she was
inviting his tongue to reexplore in imagination the enticing pleasures of that warm, moist cavern. When her hips
began to writhe to the throbbing pulse of the drums, she
was defying his own hips not to respond to each evocative
gyration, not to hunger for the deep penetrating thrusts
that joined them together.

She was not just teasing him now, not practicing the
flirtatious art of seduction. She was ravishing him, as
totally and relentlessly as he had ever ravished her with
his eyes, his mouth, and finally, eventually, his body.
And the haunted expression on his face told her he knew
it.

She gave herself up to the final throes of the dizzily
escalating dance, enjoying for one last moment the sweet
savor of a revenge she had not even known she wanted.
The tempo grew faster, harder, louder, tinny strings and
drumbeats melding into one solid pattern as Lili twisted
and turned, barely aware of anything else in the cloud of
yellow dust that swirled around her. Just once—just
once—in their brief time together, she and not Jeremy
was in control of their separate destinies.

Then the music ended, and she felt her body snap
back, drawn as if against her will. But she did not collapse
as the others had done. She remained standing, staring at
Jeremy, challenging him with her eyes.

Come to me, she cried wordlessly, triumphantly. I dare
you to come and claim me—now!

His eyes answered with a flash of blue fire. Angry
again, but so caught up in the spell she'd created, he
couldn't get away. His body coiled with the tension of a
tightly wound spring, he started forward, moving on the
balls of his feet, like a jungle cat poised to strike. Lili
stretched out her arms, every sense heightened as she
waited for him to pause a short distance away and begin

swaying with her to the renewed *tap-tap, tap-tap* of the drums.

Instead, he scooped her up and threw her over his shoulder! Like a caveman with his booty!

The crowd, apparently, loved that masculine assertion. Laughter rang out, loud and spontaneous, as he started to carry her off. Wild with fury, Lili flailed and pounded on his back, shouting for him to let her down. But nothing could induce him to give back even a shred of pride and let her walk the rest of the way on her own. The last thing she was aware of was the humiliating sound of applause as the crowd parted to let them pass.

She could gladly have kicked him as he tossed her into the carriage like a sack of laundry and signaled the driver to pull out. She *would* have kicked him if he hadn't gotten a hold on her and pinned her against the seat.

"Now," he said, his voice taut with restraint, "would you mind telling me what that little scene was all about?"

Lili's cheeks flamed. Damn the man. He had just embarrassed her in front of half the city, and now he was treating her to his usual sarcasm. *That little scene* had been her bid for independence. Her way of trying to prove, at least for a few minutes, that she, and not he, was in control of her life.

"You have no right to question me," she said, fury lending strength to her efforts to get away. If he had released his grip, even for a second, she would have thrown open the door and leapt out of the moving carriage. "You have no right to ask for *anything*. You tore me away from my home—you abducted me by brute physical force! And all you wanted was my father's *money*." She spat out the word. "Oh, yes, and the base amusement you could extract from my body in the meantime. You are the lowest, slimiest, most despicable—"

"Lowest? *Slimiest?*" To her disgust, he started to laugh, though his eyes were grim as he wrenched her wrists in both hands, holding her hard against the leather-upholstered seat. "What a catalog of my sins. Do you expect me to apologize for 'amusing' myself with your body, when you clearly amused yourself with mine? Or was it an apparition, that night I came back and found you half-naked in my bed?"

"Oh!" He really was a low, slimy cad for reminding

her of that! "I was still a child then. I didn't know what I was doing. You can call me a fool if you like—"

"Oh, I think you knew what you were doing, all right. I think you knew *exactly* what you were doing. Just like you knew what you were doing a few minutes ago when you flaunted your body in front of me."

"I didn't *flaunt* my body. I was just dancing, like the other women. You didn't object to what they were doing. As a matter of fact, you seemed to enjoy it. Why is it all right for them and not me? Because they're black and I'm white, I'm supposed to sit in the parlor doing needlepoint and never go out and have any fun?"

There was enough logic in her words to make him uncomfortable. "You weren't just dancing," he said gruffly. "You were putting on a show, especially for me. And we both know what you were after."

Pinning her wrists together with one hand, he used the other to search greedily for the rounded softness of her bosom. Lili gasped as a sound of ripping silk mingled with hoarse breathing. Incredibly, he had already freed her breasts, trapping and fondling them until her nipples turned into hard little peaks rigid with the longing she could no more control than he could control the swollen throbbing in his groin.

"Wasn't *this* what you were looking for?"

No, Lili tried to cry. No! But the word was lost in the fury of his mouth as it came down on hers with the sudden violence of a rushing tornado. No, this wasn't what she wanted! Not this mindless, animal brutality. She *had* wanted to feel his arms around her. Heaven help her, she had wanted it more than life itself. She had wanted to feel her body wedged so hard beneath his that she couldn't move. But she hadn't wanted it like this.

Where was the tenderness she craved so desperately? Where the half-gentle, half-angry capitulation she had expected after she proved once and for all that she was a match for him? She had sought, boldly, to dominate him, but she had longed to be dominated *by* him too. Longed for the sheer masculine vitality that swept her along on untamed torrents of rapture, washing everything away, like the thundering waves washed the sand from rocks on the shore.

Only it was supposed to happen with love, not unbridled lust!

"No!" She was startled by the sharpness of her own voice as the words she had struggled for finally came. Pushing him aside, she somehow managed to right herself on the seat. "No, I will not let you take me like . . . like some *fille de joie* on the floor of a cheap hired carriage. I love you, Jeremy. I would do almost anything you ask, but I am not your whore. And I will not let you treat me like that!"

The color drained out of his face. For a second Lili was terrified she had angered him more. Then, to her amazement, the corners of his mouth twisted up.

"I wasn't aware that I was treating you like a whore. I don't think of you as such, but then, I haven't been very good at communicating my feelings. Maybe it's just as well you're going back this afternoon."

He turned toward the window, grimacing as he stared out at the streets, almost empty now, for the afternoon was latening and rain clouds had begun to gather in the east. She had been playing with fire, the minx. And she knew it. But she had always been a spoiled creature, used to getting away with the most outrageous tricks. And wasn't that part of what he loved about her?

"I am sorry, sweet." He turned back with a self-mocking half-smile. "You do have a way of bringing out the unexpected in me, but that's no excuse. It's been a long time since I've had anything to do with youth and innocence. I should have remembered that pretty little girls need their hearts courted as well as their bodies."

Lili tugged the torn silk over her bare breasts as she stared at him helplessly. He was being gentle now, but it was not the kind of gentleness she longed to sense in him. And how could she forget the words he had uttered?

It's just as well you're going back this afternoon.

But it wasn't as well! Not for her. She was going to be desperately lonely after she lost him. She would remember him, yearn for him, every day for the rest of her life.

And she had a terrible feeling that after the first few nostalgic weeks he wouldn't think about her at all.

"I . . . I didn't mean to make you angry, Jeremy. Truly I didn't. At least, not like that."

"How did you intend to make me feel, *petite*?"

"I don't know. I . . . well, I wanted to make you notice me. Not just *look* at me, but really pay attention. Don't laugh, Jeremy—I wanted you to know I was there!"

He wasn't laughing, exactly, but she could see he wanted to. "I should think, my dear, that I've done nothing *but* pay attention to you since the day fate brought us into each other's lives. Though I will confess to having looked too."

"Yes, but you only saw what you wanted! Oh, Jeremy, you've always been in control. Everything I've done, everything I've felt, everything I've *thought,* has been a reaction to you. It's like some terrible tug of war . . . and I'm always losing. Just once, I wanted to win! I wanted to *make* you feel something, the way you manipulate my feelings."

"Oh, God, is that what this is all about? Control?"

He leaned back against the leather upholstery, trying to think, but finding himself strangely unable. He was keenly aware that there were still choices, still directions he could go with this relationship if he listened to his heart.

But he had always been a man who listened to his head.

"What kind of games are we playing with each other, Lili? Love doesn't have anything to do with control or 'making' someone feel something. Love is enjoying and giving . . . and sharing. And I do love you, my sweet little innocent. I love you with all the adoration in this unworthy, rather jaded heart."

He put his arms around her, with the tender affection she had longed for before, and Lili nestled against the comforting warmth of his chest. Not that she regretted that wantonly brazen dance. For all Jeremy's justified condemnation of game-playing, there had been a satisfying gleam in his eye as he stood there watching her, and she knew she would never feel quite so bold or free again. But she was glad he had decided to forgive her, and their last hours together would not be spent in bitter recriminations.

Fortunately, there was a blanket tucked under the seat, for her dress had been badly torn, and she could hardly stroll across the yard looking like that. The carriage must have been a private hire, after all, she thought, as she felt the surprising smoothness of cashmere against her skin. Coaches that picked people up on the street were never so well-equipped.

Her slippers had been lost in the dust of the square,

and Jeremy wrapped the blanket around her and carried her inside. In his arms this time, thank heaven! She kept her eyes pointedly on one bare toe, peeking out from the edge of brown wool, as they passed the servants' quarters, over the kitchen. Maybe, if she was lucky, they'd all be out.

Or maybe—considering where most of the blacks spent their Sundays off—she'd be luckier if they weren't!

Jeremy carried her through the darkened side hall and up a narrow flight of steps to the second floor. The door to the bedroom was open, and there, amidst old-fashioned blue-flowered wallpaper and frilly feminine curtains, he laid her on the bed and began, gently, to remove her torn clothing. It was an impersonal action, as tenderly solicitous as a parent undressing a child for the night, but it brought a warmth that flowed through Lili's body until her skin was flushed and tingling.

She watched warily as he folded the lustrous green silk and placed it on a chair. Every irrational hope in her heart was wishing—praying!—he would profess his love again. And every rational thought in her brain was certain he was going to go to the wardrobe, pull out a blandly proper muslin gown, and tell her, still gently, and very kindly, that it was time to get dressed and go home.

But he did not move. He simply stood there, for the longest time, staring down at her with an aching hunger he made no effort to conceal. Then something seemed to give inside him, an inaudible sigh she could feel, but not hear, and he began slowly to unfasten his shirt. He made no effort to hurry, but took it off almost languidly, then started to loosen the waistband of form-tailored silk jersey pantaloons.

"What . . . what are you doing?" she asked tentatively.

He laughed softly, a low, light sound with no mockery in it.

"You said you wanted to win, *petite*, just once. It seems you have. I am going to take my clothes off and come and lie beside you. Then I am going to make love to you slowly, tenderly, savoring every moment."

Lili barely dared to breathe as he finished uncovering his tanned, muscular body. The shutters were open, but the light that filtered through the curtains already held hints of dusk, and long shadows emphasized the strong

lines of his chest, the breadth of powerful masculine
shoulders, the lean hardness of his hips and thighs.

"You're . . . not going to send me back tonight?"

"Damn you," he groaned as he came to her. "You
know I'm not."

"And tomorrow?" She hated herself, but she couldn't
help asking. She didn't want to know, and yet she had to.

His body stiffened just for a second. Then he relaxed
and touched his lips lightly to the little throbbing hollow
at her temple.

"Tomorrow is another day," he said gently. "I make
no promises for tomorrow. But tonight, I am yours—
wholly, slavishly yours—and I am going to give you everything you desire."

26

Jeremy did not send Lili home that night, nor was he feeling any inclination to return her to her father in the morning. In a small back room, which he had fitted out as a study, he spent a few quiet minutes by himself, and there, for the second time, tore up a message that had been intended for Don Andrés.

He was ironically aware, as he stared down at the scraps of parchment in his hand, that only chance was keeping her with him. Chance, and the old don's one weakness. Had the man not had an affinity for horses—and had not the solemnity of Lent been broken by an impromptu race the day before—Lili would be sitting in her front parlor at that very moment.

As it was, she was still in their bedroom, greedily wolfing down croissants and sweet black coffee richly flavored with chocolate and cinnamon, which Jeremy had fetched himself from the kitchen. And no doubt feeling very smug! He had weakened enough, seeing her there, beautiful and shamelessly naked in his bed, to tell her she could stay one more day. Eyes brimming, as much with mischief as tears, she had pleaded for a month, and he had weakened again, compromising on a week.

That farce of a wedding Santana had planned was to take place two weeks from this afternoon. From what Jersey knew about women and the preposterous lengths they went to on such occasions, seven days would hardly be enough, but he was finding, rather unexpectedly, that that was all he was willing to give. He had made certain promises to Lili's father, which had been reiterated several times in hand-delivered missives, and his promise was his honor. He would keep it. But he was blasted if he was

316

going to give up the astonishingly sensual pleasures they
were discovering in each other's arms until the last possible minute.

Having no choice, Lili had gone along with the arrangement. And not altogether reluctantly, for she was at
an age when a week seemed forever and she still believed
in improbably happy endings. Surely, in that time, she
told herself confidently, Jeremy would decide he loved
her so much he couldn't bear to lose her.

And even if he didn't, one week before the wedding
meant she had passed *five* weeks in the company of the
notorious Blaze. Jean-Baptiste Cavarelle might have been
willing to ride out some minor tongue-wagging, but that
would be total scandal. At the very least, there had to be a
possibility he would call off the marriage.

She didn't even mind that Jeremy insisted on remaining inside. After the way she'd behaved on the last two
occasions when he had taken her out, she couldn't blame
him. Besides, it was scarcely a hardship, spending all
those tender hours in his company, especially since the
servants were still banished, and they had the little house
on the ramparts all to themselves. Jeremy was an experienced, skillful, exceptionally attentive lover, as eager to
give as to receive, and under his sensitive tutelage Lili
felt herself blossoming and maturing, changing from a
spoiled little girl to a woman of growing warmth and
depth.

Not that he had lost his sense of the outrageous. Except in moments of the most consuming passion, there
had always been welcome touches of humor in their
lovemaking, and Lili was finding now that he took an
almost puckish pleasure in trying to shock her—and occasionally succeeding. One of the first things he did was
rummage through the drawers in the chest in their room
and pull out every hand-embroidered silk chemise and
delicate lacy undergarment, which he claimed to take out
in the yard and burn! Lili supposed he had left at least
something for her to wear home, but if so, she couldn't
find it.

"If it weren't too dark with the curtains closed," she
accused teasingly, "I expect you'd make me go around
naked."

"And if it didn't get chilly occasionally," he agreed.
"Your body is glorious, and I love it, so I don't want

anything but the absolute essentials coming between it
and me."

Having been primly brought up, Lili knew she ought to
be horrified. But in truth she loved the freedom almost
as much as she loved feeling her body sensuously nude
beneath thin silk or calico. She loved it when he slid the
dress off her shoulder to reveal a creamy pink-nippled
breast, which his mouth seemed always ready to suck in.
And she loved it when he caught her in the hall or on the
stair landing—or halfway up or down—taking her right
where they were standing, her buttocks pressed against
the wall, the hard pressure of his loins grinding into her.

Nor did he content himself with merely possessing her
in unconventional places. He picked the most unconventional—and sometimes embarrassing—times too.

Late one morning, Lili was standing at a high side
window, calling down to a vendor who had appeared in
the narrow carriageway that led not only to their stableyard
but also to another house in the rear. The girl had a tray
of juicy spring strawberries, and Lili was haggling as
shrewdly as M'mère ever had, when she became aware of
something brushing her legs.

An instant later she felt teasing kisses. Then his tongue
was out, licking the smooth skin of her inner thighs,
pointedly moving up.

"Jeremy!" she hissed. But the only response was a
faint sound of laughter, muffled first by her skirt, then
her body, as his mouth found and began tenderly to
assault that most intimate center of her desires.

A current of shock jolted through her. Desperately she
tried to focus on what the girl was saying, tried to remember the price they had just been bargaining. But he
was kissing her even more intimately now, his mouth
forming around those other, softer lips, his tongue slipping inside. She held out as long as she could, concentrating fiercely, staving off the yearning that had begun to
burn in her belly, spreading outward to her breasts, her
limbs, even her cheeks, which she was sure must be
scarlet.

Giving up, she called out an absurd price, and telling
the girl to get the money from the kitchen, collasped,
half-laughing, half-sighing, on the floor. Jeremy was incorrigible, absolutely incorrigible, but, oh, it was amazing what he could do to her body. The last thing she saw

was his face, tangled in colorful madras and seeming to wear a beard of her own downy curls. Then his tongue had plunged deeper, and wave after wave of the most delirious sensation was sweeping over her.

She was still sighing when it was over and he had drawn her into his arms.

"You are terrible," she said, trying not to giggle. "You know you are. You're a thoroughly disgusting man."

"Thoroughly," he agreed, pleased with himself. "And you adore it."

"I do," she admitted, "but I hate myself for it."

He laughed as he cuddled her closer, slipping the dress all the way up and over her head.

"Why?" he teased. "Because you're not in control?"

"No. Because women aren't supposed to be happy if they're not married. And maybe even if they are. There was a man once—the kitchen maids gossiped about it for weeks—who sent his bride home on their wedding night because she responded too ardently to *his* caresses."

Jeremy caught the laughter in her tone, but he sensed she was not altogether joking. Cupping one hand under her chin, he tilted her face up.

"Don't be afraid to be happy, *petite*. Or passionate. No one is ever going to send you back because you're too deliciously responsive in bed. And . . ." He broke off, grinning suddenly. "Don't be embarrassed about relishing this interlude of ours. Neither you nor I will ever know such privacy again. We'd be fools if we didn't make the most of it."

As if to emphasize his words, he picked her up and carried her to the comfortable, if rather unfashionable couch at the side of the room. After what he had just done for her—albeit in a quite startling manner—Lili considered it only fair to offer to reciprocate in kind. But although he had taught her to give him the same acute pleasure, and encouraged her burgeoning skills with the most flattering response, he refused gently now, preferring the joy of sharing, and longing suddenly for the soft, moist satiny feel of her enveloping and enclosing his hardness.

And because that was what she herself wanted, Lili was in no mood to argue.

Being confined to the house offered another, different advantage, which Lili had not anticipated. All those hours together gave them time, not just for love, but to talk as well. To share all the trivial, funny, intimate details of their lives.

Lili found herself telling Jeremy things she had never told anyone before. And in the course of exposing her feelings, she began for the first time to understand herself. Having thought of her childhood as happy, it came as a surprise to realize she had been lonely too, growing up without the love and tender guidance of a mother. Even that silly attachment to the Fleurie curse—which she was finally coming to recognize as the epitome of foolishness—had been her way of trying to belong, as if somehow those colorful stories could make up for the family she had never had.

In his turn, Jeremy began to open up. Lili had already heard about adventures in the bayous and things that had happened at Harvard and Montpellier, but now he talked about people as well. The stern, unapproachable father who had died when he was young . . . the mother who seemed to have been a hopelessly flighty creature, but for whom he had had genuine affection . . . even his stepfather, a wildly incorrigible wastrel, and his younger half-brother.

But among all those people, Lili couldn't help noticing he never mentioned a girl he had cared about. One particular woman to whom he had been attached.

"One would almost think you were a monk," she teased one lazy afternoon. "You sound as if you'd taken vows of holy chastity."

"Good God." He looked up in mock horror. "Of all the things I've dabbled in, that's one I never thought to try. Chastity has never seemed to me the least bit holy. Surely *you* ought to realize that." He paused rakishly. "Or have I learned so little in all those years of debauchery that I appear an inexperienced lover?"

"How should I know, sir?" she said primly. "I am not experienced enough to tell the difference. But surely, in 'all those years' of lechery—"

"Debauchery," he protested, laughing. "You make me sound like a dirty old man."

"In all those years of *debauchery*, there must have been one special woman. Yet you never speak of her."

The question seemed to strike a responsive chord. Jeremy got up and went over to the window, slipping on

a shirt as he stared out at a sky so blue it almost looked
artificial. Lili was afraid for a minute she had annoyed
him by pressing too hard into personal feelings.

But when he turned back, his face was unexpectedly
gentle.

"There was someone once . . . a long time ago. I see
no reason why you shouldn't know of it. And yes, before
you ask the obvious, she was a woman of color and I did
keep her in a house on the ramparts, though not this
house. I would never dishonor you—or her—that way.
Her name was Maria, and she was almost as beautiful as
you."

"Did you . . ." Lili felt something tighten in her throat.
It was silly, being jealous of the past, but she couldn't
help herself. "Did you love her?"

He seemed to think for a moment. Then, shaking his
head, he came back and sat on the edge of the bed. "No,
I was fond of her. Very fond, but I didn't love her. If I
had, I would have married her."

"*Married?*" Lili gaped at him, scandalized. "But, Jeremy! You said she was a quadroon. Things like that are
against the law!"

"I said she was a woman of color. Actually, her mother
was an octoroon, and her father was a Spaniard, one of
your father's older contemporaries. Her skin was as light
as yours. And there wouldn't have been any problem in
France, where I took her to live. The French are not so
rigid about these things. I could have married her there,
if I'd wanted to."

"And you didn't?"

"No, I didn't." Jeremy paused, vaguely uncomfortable. These were thoughts he had never expressed out
loud. "I may not have loved her, but she was deeply
attached to me, and as long as we were together, I would
never have felt free to marry someone else." He ran his
hand lightly down the side of Lili's face, aware that the
delight he was taking in her now was something he had
never felt for his docile mistress. "She was my responsibility, Lili. I didn't know that when I began the liaison,
but she was. I could never have sent a polite letter of
dismissal, or bought her off with a payment of cash."

"What happened to her?" Lili asked, curious in spite
of herself.

His jaw tightened just for a second, and a faint tic

showed in his chin. When he went on, however, his voice was steady.

"She died. I stayed in France for a while, tending to family business. I had sent for Tin-Tin by that time, and my younger brother. When I came home, I was fully convinced I had sown my wild oats and was ready to get married and take my place in society. A proper, orthodox marriage, mind you. And a proper, orthodox place in society."

"And you ended up as a fake pirate and a real kidnapper!" Lili tried not to laugh, but it was hard. "I'm sorry, Jeremy, but it does sound wildly improbable. How on earth did you get sidetracked like this?"

"Oh, Lord." His lips twisted wryly. Lili couldn't tell whether he was bitter or amused. "I suppose I saw a will-o'-the-wisp I wanted and went half-crazy chasing after it. That's the trouble with will-o'-the-wisps. When you have your eye on them, you don't see anything else. Now I'm afraid I'm committed. Utterly, irrevocably committed."

He said it lightly, but there was a quiet edge to his tone that told Lili he meant it. He *was* committed—to his precious patriotic dreams, which were as silly in their own way as the Fleurie curse. And to sending her back to Don Andrés, as he had agreed. What was there about proud, strong men that made them think they had to do something simply because they had said they would?

And yet, had he been another kind of man—had his rigid sense of personal honor been any less—would she have cared so deeply?

"Do you know something, Jeremy Blaze?" she said softly. "I love you. I am never, *never* going to be sorry for the time we have had together. And I will always love you."

"I hope so," he said, eyes clouding over with something unexpected, almost troubled. "My sweet, sweet love, I do truly hope so."

The words were gentle, and flatteringly sincere, but Lili was left with a sense of something disturbing, something unspoken between them. That night she awoke to find the sheets around her drenched with sweat, even though the room was cold; and fragments of dreams kept coming back, strange, haunting images, all the more unsettling because she couldn't quite catch hold of them. She only knew they were about Jeremy, and every time she tried to focus on them, something hard and unexpected knotted in her stomach.

The feeling was still there the next morning, and she found herself dwelling on those first confusing, frightening days after she had been kidnapped.

It wasn't that she had forgotten the unusual circumstances that had brought her here. It was more that she had pushed them to the back of her mind, like so much clutter covered with cobwebs in a dusty attic. Now, suddenly, spurred by her subconscious, she was noticing things she had overlooked before—and worrying about them. Like the men who slipped through the rear door from time to time to see Jeremy in his cubbyhole of an office in back.

She couldn't say the men were exactly *menacing*. In themselves, there was nothing alarming about them. But there was something strange in the way he received them, never bringing them to the front of the house—and pointedly suggesting that Lili remain upstairs while they were there. She hadn't thought much about it before. After all, he'd admitted he had dealings with smugglers and other questionable characters. That overbearing protectiveness could be his way of shielding her from some of the more unsavory aspects of his various operations.

Still, it did occur to her that the one operation she was sure he had going at the moment was her kidnapping! Could these men who stole in and out at all hours have something to do with her?

Could it be that he was protecting not her, but his own dubious schemes?

She hated herself for her doubts, but try as she would, she couldn't shake them, just as she hadn't been able to shake her dreams on that morning she had awakened after Jeremy's apparently tender comment. All she could remember was how urgently he had insisted on sending her home, and how she had gotten him to relent only by appealing to his baser, more primitive urges. Now she found herself wondering—without any real reason, just an unpleasant instinct—if it wouldn't have been wiser, and safer, to have done as he wished.

She ventured downstairs only once while Jeremy was entertaining a caller, and that once she lived to regret. It was an impulsive act. She had just paused at the head of the stairs, hesitating as her ear picked up the sound of voices. Not that she was eavesdropping exactly, but she didn't back off either, especially when she heard a door open and realized Jeremy was showing someone into the parlor.

Then she caught the soft edges of a familiar voice, and without thinking, she hurried down to greet the visitor.

"Monsieur Lafitte—"

The man turned just as he was about to enter the parlor. In a dark green morning coat with a black velvet collar and pearl-colored kerseymere pantaloons, he looked every bit as dashing as he had when he so gallantly came to her rescue. Though now that she knew who—and what—he was, Lili fancied she saw something restless and vaguely ominous beneath that immaculately tailored surface. Especially when he smiled, white teeth strikingly accented by the blackness of his beard.

And when his eyes sparkled with an appreciation that told her, rather unsettlingly, that he had not failed to notice how fetchingly sapphire-blue silk became her dark, upswept hair and the coppery tones of her complexion.

"A pleasure, *madame*," he said with an unusually deep bow. "I had not anticipated such charming company."

"And here I thought you'd come to let me repay your kindness." Lili dimpled prettily, determined to show Jeremy that she could be a good hostess and was not the least bit intimidated by his choice of associates. "But you will permit me to send for coffee and sweets, won't you? Or perhaps some delightful spring strawberries, which we have in abundance these days."

Lafitte declined, thanking her graciously, and Lili, more to be polite than anything else, preceded the men into the parlor. Carrying on a bright stream of social banter, to which their visitor responded in kind, she opened the shutters and let in a burst of sunlight.

Only when she turned and saw the look on Jeremy's face did she realize she had made the worst kind of blunder.

He could not have been angrier if she'd deliberately set out to provoke him. Lili faltered, noting the tightness around his mouth, the hard set to that virile, square-cut jaw, and wished fervently she had not defied him and come downstairs. Apparently recognizing a familiar voice wasn't an excuse to force her way into his private masculine world.

She had just stepped away from the window when she saw the way his eyes were taking in her figure, with almost the same conflicting passions that had blazed through them as she danced for him in the square. Horrified, she realized that the sheer sapphire gown, without a modest backup of undergarments, was semitranslucent. And the light coming from behind gave both men more than a teasing glimpse of her legs.

She had forgotten how she was dressed—though it must seem quite ordinary in that nefarious sector of town!—and it hadn't occurred to her that her lover might be jealous. If it weren't for the violence of his reaction, the taut, icy anger she had hoped never to see again, she might almost have enjoyed the sensation.

As it was, she could hardly wait to get out of the room. Choking back her embarrassment, she managed—heaven knows how!—to carry on a brief, desultory conversation before effecting a graceful exit. Fortunately, Monsieur Lafitte didn't seem to notice anything, either in her behavior or in Jeremy's, for beyond that one furious glare, he had not so much as glanced her way again. But it was a relief to be out in the hall and on the stairs, where she could let her cheeks flame crimson.

Why did she always seem to do something wrong? Even when she was trying to be accommodating. And why did Jeremy have to be so impossible? All she wanted was to please him. But how could she, when he never told her what he wanted?

He must have bidden his guest an extremely perfunctory good-bye, for Lili had barely gotten upstairs when she heard footsteps thundering behind her, and Jeremy burst into the room.

"What a pretty way you have with visitors," he said harshly. "So warm and welcoming! You couldn't wait to get downstairs, could you, and renew your acquaintance with the notorious Jean Lafitte?"

"Well, he did save my honor, if not my *life*," Lili retorted hotly, her temper flaring. She loved this man with all her heart—she hated it when they quarreled—but there was a limit to how much she was willing to put up with. "And what's wrong with a warm welcome? I was trying to be gracious. I thought Monsieur Lafitte was your friend."

"So you decided you'd pop downstairs and say hello.

Even after I told you explicitly that I didn't want you there when anyone was around."

"You didn't *tell* me, explicitly or otherwise. You just sort of implied it."

"Told or implied, you got the message. My God, Lili, the man is infamous. He may have opened a quasi-legitimate business in the city, and he may be charming enough to talk his way into some of the wealthier drawing rooms, but he's still a criminal. And a shameless rake with the ladies. To come out, in front of a man like that, wearing a diaphanous little bit of a nothing . . . Dammit, woman! Where's your common sense?"

He turned away, having revealed more than he intended. Lili, watching wide-eyed, couldn't resist the faintest hint of a smile. He *was* jealous. He hadn't liked the way that "rake" was looking at her. And because his silly male pride wouldn't let him admit it, he hid behind thunderbolts of anger.

"I'm sorry, my dear," she said, dark lashes quivering contritely on her cheeks. "I won't do it again, I promise."

She could have laughed out loud when she saw how well it worked. It was amazing, the way even the most virile man responded to a dose of feminine weakness. He still made a show of being angry, mumbling something under his breath about not wanting her *ever* to associate with Monsieur Jean Lafitte again, and he went downstairs to tend to "some business I've been neglecting." But the situation was defused, and she knew that when he came back he would be in a gentler mood.

She was not wrong. Never had Jeremy been more loving than he was that evening, and Lili sensed with each tender kiss, each sweet lingering caress, that he was trying to tell her he was sorry. And because she wanted things to be right between them—and because more than half their week was already gone—she did not press, but took him as he was.

It was not, perhaps, the wisest thing she could have done, for the seeds of suspicion, once planted, found fertile soil in Lili's imaginative brain. Much as she fought the impulse, she caught herself peeking out of the window more than once when hoofbeats echoed on the carriageway, or hovering at the top of the steps after Jeremy had gone down. And standing there, her body rigid, every muscle straining—terrified that a groaning floor-

board or faintly moving shadow would give her away—
she realized she was afraid.

Not of Jeremy. Never of Jeremy. She loved him and
knew he would not hurt her. But of something she could
sense, could *feel*, but could not understand.

It was on that stairway, late in the day, a dismal Friday
with storm clouds gathering, that Lili saw the one person
she dreaded most.

Even then, she might have missed him, for most callers
went directly to the small room at the rear of the house.
But this man had a kind of petty arrogance that made
him swagger into the hall as if he owned the place, and
she had a clear view of his face.

It was the same man. The mulatto who had frightened
her so badly before.

Lili's already frayed nerves tensed, dulling her reac-
tions, and she failed to draw back. Mercifully, his focus
was on the hall. He looked around insolently, almost
stupidly it seemed, never once glancing up. Then Jeremy's voice snapped out sharply—Henri, the man seemed
to be called—and, his lips curling in a sly half-smile, he
turned and sauntered back.

Lili did not let her breath out again until after he had
gone. Even then, her hand was trembling so badly she
had to hang on to the railing. What was he doing here?
Twice before she had seen him—once with Jeremy, and
once in the immediate vicinity—and both times she had
had the unpleasant feeling there was something evil about
him. What if her first instinct had been right? What if he
was a vital part of Jeremy's plans? Or had some kind of
sinister hold over him?

What if the reason he was here now had something to
do with her?

With an effort, Lili forced her fingers to release the
rail. It would be risky, but she had to find out. She was
even more frightened now, as she started slowly down
the stairs. She had no idea how Jeremy would react, or
the other man, if they caught her, but that was a chance
she had to take.

Every step seemed to creak, and her heart was thumping so wildly she was sure they would hear. But somehow
she managed to get down. From there it was a matter of
sliding along the hall, taking care that the thin soles of
her slippers never left the polished floor.

She hesitated when she reached the study door. If Jeremy was about to come out . . . if the man had his fingers on the knob . . .

But there was only one way she was ever going to learn the truth. Moving closer, she laid her cheek against the wood.

A faint sound of conversation was audible within. Lili tightened her brow, puzzled for a moment, thinking someone else had joined them. Then she realized she had never heard Henri's voice before.

She had been expecting something affected, with a lisp perhaps, matching his gaudy, rather dandified clothes. But he spoke in the guttural tones of a common workman.

"We can't take no more chances," he was saying. "It's too risky. The danger's greater, every hour we wait. We gotta dispose of 'er. Now."

"Dammit." Jeremy's voice came through the door, loud and strangely petulant, not forceful with his usual self-assurance. "You know I'm not going to allow that."

"You got no choice. You let yourself get too attached to the bitch. I warned you when I came to see you in that fancy place you was staying. But you wouldn't listen. You let it go too long."

Jeremy must have turned away, because his reply was muffled. Lili sensed something like anguish in those low, vibrating tones. Bitch. The man said that Jeremy had gotten too attached to the bitch. They *were* talking about her. And in the cruelest way possible.

"It's too late for anythin' else," Henri was saying, apparently in answer to some remark of Jeremy's she had missed. "Maybe if you handled it different, from the start. Maybe if you kept 'er isolated. But she's a threat now. She has t' be destroyed."

Destroyed? Lili's blood turned to ice. He sounded so cold, so matter-of-fact, as if he were speaking of some diseased animal. She strained her ears to hear Jeremy's response.

". . . I still have tonight," was all she could catch. She could almost feel his urgency through the heavy wooden door. "It's possible things will work out. Good God, man, I don't want to do it. I *won't* do it if it isn't absolutely necessary."

"That may not be your decision," the other replied

grimly. "But sure . . . all right. I'll give you till tomorrow. If things don't look no better then—"

Jeremy seemed to be answering, arguing. Oh, God, she hoped he was arguing, but she couldn't make out the words. And Henri was cutting him off.

"If things don't look better tomorrow, I'm gonna tie a stone round 'er neck myself, and take 'er down t' the river an' drown 'er."

27

Lili's entire body went rigid, every nerve tingling with apprehension as she listened to that cold, cruel voice graphically foretelling her doom. As if it were an everyday chore for him. As if he didn't mind in the least his part in the heinous act that was about to be committed. She did not need to see his face to know he meant every word he had said. She had become an inconvenience, a liability to these men who were holding her, and because of that, she had to be eliminated.

No, not eliminated . . . *destroyed*.

She shuddered as she pulled back from the door. Now more than ever it was essential that she get away from there without being caught, without the two men knowing she had overheard their plans. Instinctively she moved, not toward the stairway, across that treacherous stretch of open hall, but to the narrower confines of the rear entry. She was going to be destroyed, like some barnyard animal that had outlived its usefulness! And Jeremy was not going to express anything more than regret.

I don't want to do this . . . unless it's absolutely *necessary*.

Oh, dear heaven. Lili turned fitfully, staring at the door that led to the backyard. Vaguely she sensed that she had come the wrong direction, that she wasn't safe here, but her brain was so numb with shock, she couldn't focus. Something was going to happen tonight. They had both mentioned it. And whatever it was, it had to do with her.

Something concerning their negotiations with Papa? Her mind started to clear, and she remembered the way Jeremy had always talked around the subject whenever she brought it up. A man doesn't keep all his assets in cash, he had told her. It takes time to raise money.

But what if it wasn't just money they were after? What if something else was involved?

Dizzily she realized that that was the only explanation that made any sense. If this were an ordinary kidnapping, even the most exorbitant sum would have long since been raised and turned over. What if they were after something else? Political favors? The right kind of connections? And what if Papa wasn't in a position to deliver? Would they be merciful and let her go if they didn't get what they wanted?

Jeremy, perhaps, she thought, shivering. But the others? Remembering the malignant undertones in Henri's voice, she was inclined to doubt it.

She was a risk to these men. Icy fear clutched at her heart. Every hour she was here was another hour she might stumble onto something, see something she could talk about later, overhear something at the closed study door. Jeremy *had* kept her too long. He must have realized a week ago that they weren't going to get what they wanted. He had been ready then to settle for cash and send her home.

And she had talked him out of it!

A faint noise came from the direction of the study. Whirling, Lili stared at the empty hallway, understanding suddenly what it was that had made her nervous before. The men would be coming out soon, and when they did, they were going to head straight for the back door. She didn't dare slip outside. The servants' quarters opened into the rear yard, and the servants were all in Jeremy's pay. But there wasn't so much as an alcove or a shadowy corner in which to hide.

She hesitated, calculating her chances. If she was swift enough, and silent enough, she might be able to make a dash up the stairs before they realized she was there. That at least would buy her a few hours to figure out what to do.

But to get to the stairs meant passing the study door.

How could she have been so stupid! Bitterly she berated herself for the foolishness that had gotten her into this mess. How could she have let herself forget, even for a moment, where she was and what kind of men held her life in the palms of their hands? She loved Jeremy, and because she loved him, she had talked herself into believing that he loved her too. And she had assumed his love would protect her.

Only Jeremy Blaze was a man who lived on the razor edge of danger. He had said that himself, the night they met. She had thought he was teasing—she had enjoyed the aura of danger he exuded, believing it an illusion—but he had been deadly serious. He was ready to take the most reckless chances with his own life. Why had she thought it would be any different with hers?

The sound of a latch broke into her thoughts. The study door? Sick with fear, Lili realized she had waited too long. She couldn't get to the stairs now. Any minute, any second, the door would creak open, and they would be out in the hall. She had to do something quickly or she was going to be discovered.

Looking around frantically, she searched for something to give her an idea. But there was only a pair of Jeremy's muddy boots by the door, and a wooden wall rack with a couple of old jackets and a russet-brown greatcoat of some shiny woolen material. Henri's, no doubt. It was cheap, but flashily cut, the sort of thing that looked like his taste.

Henri's greatcoat?

Her ears strained as she listened tensely. No footsteps, not yet. They were lingering, then, just inside the door, but that couldn't go on for long. Impulsively Lili pulled the coat down and slipped her arms into the sleeves. It was longer than it looked hanging on the peg, and she saw with a surge of relief that it came almost to her ankles.

If she tucked her skirt up so shimmering blue wouldn't show at the hem—if she raised the collar to hide as much as possible of her face and hair—would she look enough like the man who had come in half an hour ago to escape notice?

It was a gamble, but she knew she had to take it. Hands trembling, she fumbled with her skirt. There was no sash on the high waistband, so all she could do was knot up the slippery silk on both sides and hope no telltale trace peeked out.

Buttoning the coat, she glanced down, taking stock of herself. Her slippers looked odd beneath that bulky mannish garment, but at least they were black—and would anyone look at her feet? Then the door opened, a jarring sound that sent her heart into a somersault, and she realized suddenly there were no options left.

Without giving herself time to think, she slid the collar up and stepped into the yard.

No one was in sight, but Lili knew someone was there, and she knew that Jeremy had given strict orders to keep an eye on the house. Fortunately the weather was turning raw, and everyone seemed to be inside. Clouds were massing on the horizon, giving the air a greenish cast, and it was so dark it felt like dusk.

It took all Lili's willpower to keep from hiking up the long coat and racing wildly across the cobblestones. But that was the one thing she couldn't do. She hadn't a prayer of outrunning Jeremy's men. Her only chance was to slip past them unnoticed.

Remembering the way she had blended into the crowd before, in her pretty quadroon dresses and colorful *tignons*, she forced herself to play the same game again. Jamming her hands into her pockets, she sauntered insolently across the yard, mimicking Henri's mincing steps as she headed for the unpaved drive. Apparently that was the way he had come in, for there was no sign of a coach or horse. At least she hoped so, for she didn't dare call attention to herself by peering into the stable.

Her collar had come halfway down, and she turned it up, grateful for the wind that made the gesture natural. It was even harder not to run when she reached the carriage drive. Only the windows of the house looked onto that narrow passage, and she could be reasonably certain no one was watching. But what if the man Jeremy had on guard in front ambled that way? Or ducked inside for shelter!

Forcing herself to maintain the same slow, steady pace, she continued down the dirt lane. Not until she finally reached the street did she allow herself a breath of relief.

She had made it! She knew she had as she passed one shadowy doorway, then another, and nothing happened. Whoever was watching had seen exactly what he expected— the same slim, foppish young man who had come that way before. She had made it, and she was safe. All she had to do was turn right at the corner, and right again, and she would be on her way home.

She felt a little twinge. Not regret exactly, but loss.

Would Jeremy be secretly glad when he went upstairs in a few minutes and discovered she was gone? Would he be relieved that she was safe?

Angrily she forced the thought out of her mind. Her hands still in her pockets, she quickened her pace, now that she was sure it was safe. Jeremy had used her horribly. He had toyed with her affections, taking what he wanted—indulging his own considerable lusts, even when he knew it could cost her her life! She was a fool, thinking about him now. She was going home, and that was what counted. Home to darling, doting, desperately worried Papa, who would be beside himself with joy when he saw her.

The first raindrops fell, light but cold on her hair and face. She flipped the collar up again, but it was loose and kept falling back. At least Papa loved her. At least she had him. The one constant in her life. The one person who had always been there for her . . . and always would be.

She had just come to the corner when some instinct caused her to turn and look back at the house. To her horror, she saw that all the shutters were open. Lights seemed to be everywhere, flickering behind every curtain, like people with lanterns searching for something.

For her?

Her breath caught in a painful gasp as she realized suddenly that Jeremy had already found out she was gone. And if she'd been thinking, she would have known that that was exactly what *would* happen. What had she expected when they got to the hall and Henri discovered his coat was missing?

They were searching, but it would be a quick, cursory search, for Jeremy already knew what he was going to find. Within minutes, dark figures would be swarming out of the house, the gang of henchmen he had no doubt packed into servants' quarters in the back. She didn't dare go home now. It would take half an hour to get there, even if she ran all the way.

And in half an hour, Jeremy could have every street, every approaching lane, blocked off with horsemen and carriages.

More likely carriages, Lili thought with a sinking feeling. Dark closed coaches like the one in which he had taken her captive that first night. It would be a bit conspicuous, even for Jeremy Blaze, to carry her off kicking and screaming on the back of a saddle horse.

She was out of the house, she had gotten to the corner without being spotted, but she was a long way from safe. She couldn't stay where she was . . . and she couldn't go home. Nor could she take shelter with friends. Jeremy knew her too well. She had told him too much about herself. He would anticipate her every move.

She was free, but she was trapped. There was no place she could go.

28

Along the riverbank, several miles away, where Lili's cousin had left the carriage she had hired in town and was heading toward the path that led up the levee, the rain was more a mist, falling, but lightly, like the spray from a summer fountain.

Simone tilted her face up as she walked, letting the moisture collect in little drops that ran down her cheeks and teased her full pink lips. She had always hated the rain before, and the fog. They had terrified her as a child, making her run inside crying and burying her head under the pillow. Now, strangely, she found herself almost eager to experience the sensation.

Perhaps that was because, although she had not yet crystallized the thought, she already sensed that this was the last time she would ever feel the cool, natural kiss of the rain.

The ankle-deep grasses were drenched by the time she reached the path, and she had trouble making her way up the slippery slope without Jean-Baptiste to hold out a strong helping hand. Something caught in her throat, and she tried to swallow, but she couldn't. Suddenly she realized why she was here, what it was she had come to do, and the enormity of it made her stop and look down at the road, a faint red-ocher ribbon below in the mist.

She was not afraid. It surprised her a little, but she felt no fear. Either of the pain or of what would come after. But then she thought of Jean-Baptiste, picturing how his dark hair would look in the rain, his dark laughing eyes, spiky lashes glinting with moisture, and the lump came back to her throat. She could bear anything, accept anything . . . but oh, it hurt to realize she would never see him again. Never taste the sweetness of his mouth, never feel his naked body pressed in shameful bliss against hers.

She started up the levee again, not pausing to rest until she reached the wide flat space on top. The wind was brisker here, howling up from the river, and her breath came in short, painful pants. She had never been robust, even as a little girl, and these past few days, the slightest exertion left her wobbly and light-headed.

She pulled the fringed silk shawl tighter around her shoulders. A pretty thing, a gift from Jean-Baptiste, but so frivolously light it offered no protection.

Not that that mattered. She was hardly going to catch her death of cold from the storm. She would never catch a cold again. Soon it was all going to be over, and nothing would matter anymore.

She cringed as the events of that morning came flooding back. It had been truly horrible, even worse than she had imagined. She had had to make an excuse—Jean-Baptiste had been increasingly reluctant to let her out of his sight, even for a few hours at night—and it had been all she could do to convince him she was exhausted and needed some time to lie down. Fortunately, the pallor in her cheeks had lent credence to her story, and though he had looked worried, he had finally left. And she had gone to the place down the block where she had arranged to meet Marie-Louise.

What happened in the hours that followed was something she longed to blot out of her mind. The long walk down narrow streets and garbage-strewn alleyways in a part of town she had not even guessed existed. The horrible woman in that horrible room, smelling of herbs and dead things.

The shades had been drawn, and Simone had barely been able to pick out objects across the room, but even then, she had seen that the woman was very black and very old. Her hands had been gnarled, like dried-out ginger roots or the talons of a bird. But her eyes had been sharp. Small, beady eyes that seemed to take in everything at once. And those claws had required only minutes to complete their embarrassingly thorough examination.

Simone had not needed the confirmation that came out of thin lips. She had seen it already in the faint, unconscious nod of that elderly head. And she had understood then, though she had not put it into words, that everything was over.

The mist thickened, swirling like tendrils of wet hair around her face, reaching out to caress her cheeks with icy fingers. She had never had more than the sketchiest knowledge of human reproduction. It was not that she had been sheltered. No one had minded, or even seemed to notice, if she curled up on a bench in the kitchen and listened to the servants gossip. But no one had explained things either, and while she knew where babies came from, and how they got there, she had no idea of the subtleties of the process. She had not known if one time with a man was enough, or a dozen—or whether one missed period was cause for alarm.

But she had known this morning as she stared into dark, penetrating eyes in that foul-smelling room. One missed period was more than sufficient. She was pregnant, with the child of the man her cousin was going to marry. And she had known, with all the certainty in her young heart, that she could not live with the shame.

There were, apparently, things that could be done. Potions that would produce the desired effect . . . for a price. She had sat there quietly, listening, her hands clasped in her lap while the woman assured her it was all quite common, and safe enough. As safe as carrying a baby to term and risking hemorrhages and childbed fever. And, of course, the man could be counted on to help with the money.

Simone had not tried to argue, promising instead to think it over. All she had wanted was to get out of there. But she had known, even then, that she couldn't go through with it. Even if she had the courage to ask Jean-Baptiste for the money—and even if he consented, which was unlikely—how could she calmly prepare a potion in a cup and drink it down . . . and will her baby to die?

She closed her eyes, feeling the rain on her lids and lashes. She was aware, vaguely, that the effect would be the same. The little life inside her was going to end this afternoon. But somehow it didn't seem quite so terrible this way.

Lili . . .

She opened her eyes, wishing she didn't have to keep seeing the image of her cousin's face. Wishing she could somehow avoid this final humiliating confrontation with the sense of her own betrayal. For betrayal it was. She had known Jean-Baptiste was Lili's. She had known the pain her self-indulgence would cause, but she had gone to him anyway.

Beautiful, high-spirited, fun-loving Lili, whose friendship had grown from such unpromising beginnings . . . Lili, who had teased and bullied and comforted, who had shared her secrets and eventually her affection . . . Lili, who had cried when she thought her cousin was dying, and given up her favorite doll without a whimper . . . Lili, who was going to come home tomorrow and expect to look her in the eyes . . .

Pour l'amour de Dieu, how could she possibly face her? How could she watch, day after day, as luminous gold-brown eyes took in her thickening waistline? The fullness in breasts that had always been small? How could she bear it when speculation turned to horror and the truth became clear? An affair was one thing, a small secret share of happiness no one need ever know about. But a child would be a constant, living reminder of sins too vile to forgive.

It was strange, the twists fate took. All those years growing up, her heart had ached for Lili and the bittersweet romance of the Fleurie curse. Only, curses had a way of following their own unpredictable courses, and it was she who had fallen in love with the man she couldn't have. She who had surrendered to his sweet words, and even sweeter caresses, and was going to bear his child.

But it would end with her. This was it. No baby daughter to make the same mistakes all over again. No pretty image of an ill-fated mother to perpetuate the wickedness and shame.

The wind gusted, ripping the shawl from her shoulders, buffeting it like a pale blue butterfly down the slopes to the road. Simone watched dispassionately, making no effort to catch it. She did not even feel the cold now as she stared down at the dark waters of the river, half-veiled in mist and rain.

Beckoning, they were beckoning . . . swirls of blackness, capped with wispy white, like combers on the shore . . . and she was going to them.

It had been nearly the same hour then, that last time she had stood in this spot—but, oh, it had felt so different. The sun, setting in the west, great streaks of red and orange casting a rich glow over the levee and the river beneath. His hand had been in hers, the ring sliding onto her finger, that same ring she had hidden in a drawer under piles of serviceable white lingerie with hardly a hint of lace.

What would they think, she wondered, when they found it and saw all those tiny ruby hearts set in gold?

At least she had been his for a little while. And he had been hers. For one beautiful, deliriously happy week they had been husband and wife, and she would not give that up for anything in the world. Not even to save her life.

She started down the slope, moving mechanically, like a puppet with neither sense nor feeling. The river, after swelling and receding for the past few days, was on the rise again, but the level was still low, and she stumbled several times as she half-climbed, half-slid to the bottom.

She loved him so much. Every breath in her body, every shred of emotion belonged to him. She hesitated at the edge of the water, staring out, wondering what it was going to feel like. Lili was a good swimmer. Don Andrés had insisted that his daughter be taught, for her safety, at the summer villa on Lake Pontchartrain. But Simone had screamed when they tried to coax her into the water too, and no one had pressed.

Just for a moment, remembering those childhood summers, she felt something tight and hard in the bottom of her stomach, and she knew she was going to be afraid. But she had no choice now. She had made her choices already. She had reached out and taken what she wanted, and it was time to pay the price.

She slid one foot tentatively down the bank, cringing back as icy wetness oozed through the seams of a delicate kid boot. Somehow she had not thought it was going to be so cold. Jean-Baptiste would forget her after a while. He would be sad at first, for he had a genuinely caring heart, but time would ease the pain, and he would forget. And after a while he would fall in love with the beautiful woman he had married.

It was always like that with Lili. People always loved her, responded to her, even if they didn't mean to.

She waded out slowly, letting the water splash up around her ankles until the hem of her gown was soaked.

29

The broad, loose collar of the russet greatcoat had fallen again, but Lili gave up struggling, plunging her hands in her pockets instead. The rain seemed to have grown heavier just in the last few seconds. Her hair was saturated, and she could feel rivulets of water trickling down her neck.

Reaching the corner, she veered arbitrarily to the left. Not for any reason, just because it was the opposite way from home. She still hadn't formed any kind of plan. She didn't know where she wanted to go or what she was going to do. But she couldn't stand still and wait for her pursuers to close in.

A loud clopping of hooves broke the silence on the empty street. Jumping tensely, Lili flattened herself against a stone wall. Just behind . . . It seemed to be coming from somewhere just behind . . .

Taut with fear, she edged back to the corner and peered out.

A man was galloping full speed down the street, coatless, long loose sleeves plastered rain-drenched to his strong, muscular arms. Jeremy. Lili felt herself tremble like a leaf in the river-chilled wind. He was pushing his mount mercilessly, a superb gray Arab, flanks and mane, like his own white shirt, darkened by the unrelenting downpour. Even from a distance she could see that his face was drawn and gaunt.

For one brief instant she dared to hope that he was worried about her. That he was thundering down the street like a wraith out of hell because he was desperate to find her before the others did.

But then she remembered that Jeremy Blaze was only

worried about his own passionate schemes—and about what was going to happen if she got back to Papa before he caught her.

He reined in at the corner, abruptly, horse and rider rearing in one magnificently fluid motion. Gasping, Lili realized she had left herself much too exposed. If he turned and squinted into the rain, he would see her. But she didn't dare draw back. Even the slightest movement might catch his eye.

He remained absolutely motionless for one heart-stopping instant, head up, nostrils flaring, as if testing the air. Then, seeming to pick up a scent, he wheeled around and raced down the street in the opposite direction.

Just the way she had hoped he would go. Weak with relief, Lili clung to the wall a moment longer. All that male arrogance had played him false. He thought he knew her so well. He was so sure she was frightened out of her wits and charging headlong for home!

Well, she *was* frightened. But she was far from witless. And until he figured that out, she had at least a slender advantage.

She started down the *banquette* again, unable to keep from glancing over her shoulder every few seconds. Instinctively she stuck to the wall, so close she could feel her sleeve brushing damp stone. It was only a second before more hoofbeats caught her ear, underscored this time by the sound of wheels sliding through the mud.

The coaches were out as well.

Ears straining, she listened, trying to judge distance and direction. So far, they didn't seem to be coming this way, but that couldn't last long. When they didn't find her on the lanes around the Santana house, they would broaden their search.

Her eyes darted ahead, scanning the darkening street, looking for a recessed door or service alley where she could hide if she had to. She was halfway down the block before she found one, and then not a second too soon. The sharp crack of a whip came from the corner, and suddenly one of the vehicles was turning toward her.

Apparently Jeremy was not quite as arrogantly sure of himself as she thought.

She drew in her breath, not even daring to exhale as she stared out from her shadowy hiding place. The car-

riage that rolled past was not moving at the same wild
pace as Jeremy and his sleekly powerful Arab, but it was
still too fast for the street and the hazy half-light. Tingles
ran down her spine as she recognized the same closed
black coach with curtained windows that had taken her
prisoner. Obviously Jeremy's men were out in full force.

Or were they *Jeremy's* men?

Lili pulled back into the shallow passage, a slim crack
between clapboard buildings, too narrow to accommodate a carriage or even a man on horseback. The smell of
decaying garbage, mingling with garlic and other cooking
odors, told her she had stumbled on the back door of a
restaurant, or maybe a hotel or boardinghouse.

It hadn't occurred to her to wonder if Jeremy was in
charge. She had simply assumed it, though not, she realized now, for any reason. True, he had given all the
orders while she was around, but that only showed he
was in charge of her. Who better to handle a female
captive than a devastatingly handsome man with a proven
way with women? The conversation she had overheard
with Henri indicated he was part of a larger gang. But
just because he was forceful and dynamic didn't mean he
was their leader.

She continued to hold her breath until the carriage had
gone and the street was quiet except for a steady patter
of rain. As she slipped back onto the *banquette*, it seemed
to her the storm had intensified. The wind gusted savagely, and she lowered her head, tugging her collar up
again, though she knew it wouldn't do any good.

Blast this ridiculous coat anyway! She had been glad
enough to have it when she stole across the yard, but now
its cheap fabric soaked up the rain, making it cold and
uncomfortably heavy. Jeremy had no doubt given a detailed description to the small army of searchers fanning
over the city. In Henri's coat she would be an easy
target.

But without it, in sapphire silk, with absolutely nothing underneath, the rain plastering the flimsy fabric against
her body, she would be even more conspicuous.

Footsteps echoed behind her on the boardwalk, faint,
but clearly audible. Her heart leaping into her throat, Lili
whirled around. But it was only a man caught in the
storm, shoulders up as he braved the wind, his head, like

hers, buried in the high collar of his coat. He seemed not to notice her as he passed, muttering under his breath, and disappeared around the corner.

Lili followed more slowly, her shoes so soaked it was hard to walk. She was still hugging the walls, though none of her pursuers seemed to be on foot, so at least she could hear them coming. When she got to the corner, she slowed down and glided out cautiously.

The man was already gone, and no one else was in sight. Lili hesitated a moment, trying to decide where to go, which direction to take. Darkness was settling eerily over the street. Dusk perhaps, or maybe just the storm. Either way, night was coming, and her peril would be even greater.

It might be harder for her pursuers to spot her, but it would be harder to see them too. If the searchers dismounted, she would have no way of knowing where they were or what they were doing. They might be anywhere—in a doorway, an unshuttered window, even standing stock-still in the middle of the street.

And every time she passed a corner, every time she was caught for a few seconds in the yellow rays of a streetlamp, she would be visible for blocks.

Right or left?

She turned her head helplessly, searching for something to give her a clue. One way or the other, it could be disaster. Right or left . . . she might be walking into a trap.

The wind rippled the dark surface of the water, sending it up to lap around Simone's ankles as she stared out into the emptiness. The rain had stopped, and the mist was drifting inland. Across the river, the last gray light of dusk softened the shore until it melted into the horizon.

So pretty, she thought, feeling the cold for a moment and shivering. It was so pretty when day drifted off into darkness, and she had been so happy here. But all the happiness was over now. She had taken her share in one greedy gulp, and there was nothing left.

Nothing but shame and the terrible humiliation of knowing that the whole world was going to find out what she had done.

She stirred a little, breaking the reverie. She had already been standing much too long at the edge of the icy water. Her feet were so numb she couldn't feel her toes. It was time now. Time . . .

She never had a chance to finish either the thought or the movement she had started. A hand reached out abruptly, bruising her arm, and she felt herself being dragged roughly onto the bank. Turning back, startled, she saw the distraught features of the man she loved.

"*Mon Dieu*," Jean-Baptiste cried out. "What are you doing? Are you crazy?"

Simone made no attempt to answer. They both knew that for a few brief moments she had indeed been mad. The thought of facing the disgrace had driven her temporarily out of her mind. But her sanity was back now. She was sure of it as she felt his arms around her and looked up into his eyes.

"I love you," she said. "I love you more than anything else in the world."

"You *love* me?" His voice was strained with emotion. "For God's sake, if that's true, what are you doing here? How could you consider *this*?"

He choked, unable to utter the words he was thinking. Simone clung to him, suddenly frightened again. He was asking questions, and he deserved answers. But what could she say? Her mind whirled dizzily, trying to find some easy way to break the news she had been hiding, to tell him what she had to.

There was no easy way, but if she didn't do it immediately, she knew she'd lose her nerve.

"I . . . I'm going to have a baby!" she blurted out.

"A *baby*?"

His face, in the dying light, was a kaleidoscope of emotion. Surprise first, then disbelief, then—incredibly, impossibly—joy. Simone could see it in the way his eyes widened, the light that came into them. Then his mouth wa open, and he was laughing.

"A father? I'm going to be a *father*." He started to swing her up in the air, then stopped, tender concern showing as he drew her like a china doll into his arms. "But you're shivering, *chérie*. Were you so afraid to tell me the truth? Did you think I wouldn't be pleased? And why . . . ?" He paused, suddenly turning serious. "If you're going to have a baby—my baby . . . I thought you meant it when you said you loved me. Don't you *want* our child? Would you really have ended it? Like this? Here?"

No, Simone thought as she rested her cheek against the comfort of his shoulder. No, she wouldn't have ended it—here or anywhere. That was the wonderful, surprising, unexpected secret she had just discovered. She had been desperately unhappy, and unhappiness had brought her to the brink of self-destruction. But she had been standing for a long time in the same place. Half an hour at least. And she had known, as she watched the distant shoreline fade away, that she was not going any farther.

Someday she would tell him. Someday they would talk about it, and she would try to sort out the complicated feelings she still couldn't understand. But now all she wanted was to swathe herself in the warmth she saw in his eyes. The solicitude she heard in his voice.

"Oh, Jean-Baptiste, I do love you. And I do want your baby. But I'm not your *wife*. Soon I'm going to be so fat, everyone will look at me and know. It was the shame. I couldn't bear the shame!"

"*Nom de nom*," he cursed softly under his breath. He was the one who should be ashamed, and he was bitterly aware of it. He had been so sure that that mock wedding— and the ring with the little rubies, which he noticed she wasn't wearing now—would be enough. Was it inescapable Creole vanity that every man thought he had only to flash his charm and make a declaration of love and no woman would be able to resist? "There are things I should have told you long ago, *chérie*. It is my sin, and not yours, and I am going to make up for it now."

"I'm sorry, I don't understand . . ."

"You will, soon enough. Suppose I could promise that things are going to be better. Suppose there are plans— very special plans—which you know nothing about. Would that make you happy? Would that put the smile back on those pretty lips? And the pink I love so much in your cheeks?"

"I don't know . . ." Simone hesitated, wanting to believe him, longing to believe. But he was going to marry Lili. And how could things be better then? "Can you really promise me that, Jean-Baptiste? Can you *really* make me happy again?"

"Oh, yes," he said, confidence returning. "I think I can."

He lifted her in his arms and carried her back up the levee, stumbling a little on the rain-wet slope, but never so badly she was afraid they would fall. It was almost dark by the time they reached the top. The squarish outline of a carriage could barely be distinguished on the road below. Setting her on the ground, he placed his own warm jacket around her shoulders and began, very softly, to speak.

The coachman, waiting patiently, watched as their silhouettes merged slowly into the oncoming night. The horses pawed the earth, shaking their heads restlessly, and he had to pull on the reins to steady them. They weren't used to being out, poor creatures, after dark. They didn't like it, but that was all right. They'd be going soon.

He had been worried himself, an hour before, when the young gentleman had come charging out of the Santana house, his face as black as the storm, and leaping up on the high seat beside him, ordered him to drive like hell for the levee. He hadn't understood what was going on, but the tension had been a physical thing, tangible between them, and remembering uneasily how dark and deep the river could look sometimes, he had pushed his horses to their limit.

Then they had arrived, and it had been there—that bit of a blue shawl, wet with the mud and the rain, lying like a broken bird on the ground.

Ah, well, it was going to be fine now. Relief settled through him as he climbed down, slowly, for his joints ached from the damp, and lit the lanterns that were hanging on both sides of the carriage. Whatever their quarrel, whatever had happened between them, clearly they had patched it up. Light was shining on their faces as they approached, and he could see that the girl was smiling.

The darkness was even more impenetrable on the narrow streets of the city. Lili had to use her hands now, groping along the walls and fronts of buildings to feel where she was going. The storm seemed to have passed, but fog was rolling in, great cold billows that added to the gloom.

A streetlamp flared suddenly, perhaps twenty yards

away. Jumping. Lili stared at that faint circle of diffused
gold. Someone had lighted it, obviously. Yet she hadn't
known he was there. Even now, peering intently, she
could barely make out the vaguest pinprick of light slipping off in the haze.

And that was a man with a lantern! How could she
hope to detect someone who was trying to be stealthy?

She jammed her hands back in her pockets, balling
them into fists to try to get some warmth into them. The
fog was nearly as wet as the rain, and she was chilled to
the bone. Even if she'd been able to see the houses that
fronted directly on the street, with an occasional shop
beneath them, what could she have done about it? She
could hardly bang on the door of a stranger, dressed in
the sort of gown a quadroon might wear to a ball, skin
bronzed, hair in shambles, and expect anyone to believe
she was the kidnapped daughter of Don Andrés Santana.

She wished now she had paid more attention to Papa's
business associates when she encountered them in the
hall outside his office. Some, she knew, maintained homes
on this side of town, even though it wasn't strictly fashionable. But it had all been polite small talk, a way to
pass a few minutes, and she had never thought she'd
care.

Lights began to show in some of the windows. The
mist was blowing out, and tantalizing glimpses of faded
wallpaper and high-ceilinged rooms were visible behind
lacy curtains. Here and there, a shaft of yellow spilled
onto the street, highlighting brass name plates next to
some of the doors.

Lili eyed them as she passed, searching for one she
recognized. If she could only find someone she had met
before, someone who knew her by sight, then surely
everything would be all right.

Or would it?

She realized suddenly how well Jeremy knew her . . .
and how little she knew of him and his plots. She was
certain there *was* a conspiracy, but she had no idea how
far it extended. Almost anyone could be involved. A
casual colleague of Don Andrés', a servant in their own
home, even an intimate friend. She might go to the one
place she thought she was safe, and find she had stumbled into their hands.

And yet . . . she had to do something.

She shivered as the utter hopelessness of the situation swept over her. She couldn't turn to a stranger, she dared not search out a friend, but she couldn't keep on walking either. Sooner or later she was going to have to trust someone. Sooner or later she was going to have to take a chance and turn to someone for help.

But who . . . and when? And what if she chose wrong?

30

L eClerc?
   Lili stared at the rather ostentatious name plate on a nondescript house in the middle of the block. Not an uncommon name, but it wasn't all that common either. A lighted lantern dangled from a hook next to the door, casting a glow into the gloom, but there was nothing else particularly welcoming about the place. It had a grayish look, as if the paint had weathered from neglect, and wrought-iron balconies along the first and second floors appeared to be caked with dirt and mold.

Could it be the same LeClerc who was a business associate of Papa's? Ramon LeClerc—or was it René?

Lili racked her brain, trying to recall the man who had sat tight-lipped across from her in the carriage that day she returned from the levee with a rescued puppy in her lap. A slight, bland-looking man, thirtyish, it seemed to her, with thinning sand-colored hair and watery brown eyes that had bulged slightly as he looked at her.

Yes, it could be, she thought, glancing up again. This was exactly the house she would have imagined René LeClerc might own. He had been neatly dressed the few times she had seen him, but the lining of his coat was shabby, and she had noticed that his fingernails were not quite clean.

And if it was the same Monsieur LeClerc, then she might have stumbled onto the one place she could feel safe. Impulsively she ran up the steps to the front door. He was a mousy man—not scrupulously honest, she was sure—but hardly the sort to be attracted by the thrill of adventure. Or to risk his neck for a cause.

And hardly the sort Jeremy and his friends would include in their gang.

Letting the knocker drop with a loud clang against the door, Lili listened to the sound that seemed to echo through the house. When nothing happened, she knocked again, and then again, but still no footsteps came from inside, and her heart sank. Lamps had been lighted—she could see them through cracks in the shutters—but no one appeared to be home.

Then, just as she was about to give up, she heard a faint click, and the door swung open.

The man who appeared on the threshold was so large that he loomed up from the shadows. Light, coming from behind, made his jacket an almost phosphorescent white, his skin deep blue-black.

Lili started nervously.

"I apologize for the interruption. I know it's close to the dinner hour, but I wonder—is Monsieur LeClerc at home?"

"You wish to see the *monsieur*?" The man seemed to hesitate, though, strangely, his expression was not unkind. It was almost, Lili thought uncomfortably, as if he wanted to tell her something.

"Please . . . if it's not too much trouble. This is the house of Monsieur *René* LeClerc, is it not?"

"It is." As he backed away to let her into the shallow entry hall, Lili realized why she hadn't heard him approach. He moved like a cat, soundlessly across the floor. "May I tell him who has come to call?"

"Uh . . ." Lili's hand went up, instinctively patting her hair. Her name would get her in, but was that really wise? She didn't know the first thing about this man, except that he looked more intelligent than his master. "I . . . I'd rather not identify myself. It doesn't matter anyway. Just tell the *monsieur* that a lady wishes to speak with him. If he doesn't seem interested, tell him . . ." She hesitated, recalling the American who had accosted her on the street, and the way he simply assumed that a dark-skinned woman approaching his house wanted to sell something. "Tell him I'll make it worth his while."

"As you wish." The kindness vanished from the man's eyes, replaced by frank disapproval as he turned and melted into the shadows. Lili knew what he had to be thinking, and it made her feel cheap and dirty inside. But

she couldn't take the chance that Jeremy had been re-
cruiting among the slaves.

An icy draft blew across the hall. Didn't LeClerc have
the money to purchase fuel? she wondered, shivering. Or
was he too tight? Probably a little of both. The entryway
was comfortably, if sparsely furnished, but the upholstery
on the side chairs had worn through in places, and the
mirrors cried for polishing.

The man was back in a few minutes, his eyes blank,
though she still sensed disapproval. "This way, *mademoiselle.*"

The room into which he ushered her was as cold as the
hall, though a fire flickered feebly on the grate. René
LeClerc was seated in front of the hearth, enjoying a
warming sherry from the surprisingly elegant painted china
decanter on a table beside him. He looked much as Lili
had remembered, only his brow seemed to be higher, his
hair lighter and thinner, his eyes a slightly duller shade of
brown.

Those same eyes widened as she came into the room,
surprise and pleasure mingling with a curious kind of
revulsion. Lili shuddered with disgust. Obviously her message had been delivered as stated, and he had translated
it into the most graphic terms in his mind.

And obviously he disliked her. Disliked the color of
her skin, her station in life, everything she stood for. But
that didn't keep him from imagining exactly what he was
going to do to her if she didn't put a stop to this
immediately.

"You don't recognize me, Monsieur LeClerc?" She
stepped forward, tossing her head to let him see she
wasn't intimidated.

"Should I?"

Lili cringed. She had forgotten how thin and reedy his
voice was. "We have met. I am Lili Santana . . . Don
Andrés' daughter. Surely you know me now. I realize I
look a sight, but I was kidnapped by desperadoes! Oh,
monsieur, they've been holding me for ransom. I've been
in their clutches for weeks! I barely managed to escape
with my life, but I can't get back to Papa!"

The words came out much too fast, sounding wild and
hopelessly improbable. She could see the disbelief in his
eyes, changing slowly to . . . What? Amusement? Surprise? A little bead of saliva appeared at the corner of his

mouth, and she realized suddenly that her coat was open. Damp silk clung to every curve like a translucent second skin, and his eyes were creeping up her legs where the skirt had been tied.

"No, don't clutch at your coat like that," he said petulantly. "You're dripping water all over the carpet. It can't be comfortable anyhow. Take it off and warm yourself by the fire." When she did not respond, but continued to tug the bulky fabric awkwardly over her breasts, his voice grew harsher. "I said take it off!"

There was just enough emphasis to make Lili obey. She had the feeling he was capable of ringing for his manservant to come and wrench it away from her.

"You don't believe me, do you?" she said, trying to sound defiant as she stepped over to the fire and dropped the wretched garment on the hearth. Even closer, the flames were not bright enough to warm her. "You think I'm making it up."

"Making what up? The part about being Lili Santana? Or that ridiculous tale of crazed desperadoes? Oh, I know you, *mademoiselle*. I should have recognized that arrogant demeanor immediately. But you must think I'm dull-witted. If the only child of Don Andrés had been abducted, wouldn't he have set up a cry that could be heard all over the city?"

"But surely he has!"

LeClerc's thin lips twisted into a hint of a smile. "Surely he has not, and that says something, doesn't it? Not a breath of any such story has gotten out. But perhaps 'abducted' is not the term. Perhaps you ran off of your own accord, and now you're sorry and want to go home. And you need my help."

"But that doesn't make sense." Lili struggled frantically to figure out what he was saying. Don Andrés hadn't told anyone about the kidnapping apparently—but why? She would have thought he'd move heaven and earth to get her back. Or had that been a condition of her safe return? "Even if you were right—and you're not—how could you possibly help with Papa?"

"Why, by going to him, of course, and repeating the absurd tale you just told me. I might even imply that I came to your rescue, as I had to once before when you were behaving hotheadedly on the levee. It *would* make things more persuasive, especially in light of the demean-

ing circumstances of your captivity." His eyes slid down
her body, ostensibly calling attention to the state of her
dress, but not missing an inch of exposed flesh. "I am not
unwilling, you understand. Don Andrés, naturally, would
show his gratitude. But there are certain risks. I'd need
to be assured of other . . . compensations."

"*Compensations*?" Lili watched warily as he poured a
generous portion of sherry and took a sip.

"Are you aware, *mademoiselle*, that I did you the
honor of asking for your hand in marriage? No? I thought
not." He let out a sharp sound, halfway between a snort
and a laugh. "Your father obviously didn't consider it
worth mentioning."

Jerking up from the chair, he began to pace back and
forth, hands clasped behind him, long neck angled out in
front.

"You are nothing. The bastard child of a bastard mother.
Tainted blood, all the way back. Black, from the looks of
you, even before! Now it might as well be branded on your
forehead. He should have been grateful that I wanted
you. He should have been grateful *anyone* wanted you!
But no, Don Andrés Santana is too proud for a poor
bank clerk. And now he's spreading rumors, the fool,
that you're engaged to the Cavarelle heir."

"Those aren't exactly rumors—" Lili ventured, sensing
he was getting much too worked up. She had to calm him
before things went too far.

But he cut her off.

"No one's seen him, you know," he said contemptuously. "Not for years. The Cavarelles never mixed with
the hoi polloi. Too good for the rest of us. The young
one, this Jean-Baptiste, spends little time in the city. I
doubt he's even here now." He snorted again. "And
we're supposed to believe he's the eager bridegroom of a
girl with tainted blood! A flimsy cover, that's what I call
it . . . because you ran off with a man! Just like your whore
of a mother!"

Lili listened in stunned amazement to the tirade. Drawing back as far as she could on the hearth, she stared at
the hatred that blazed out of his eyes. He had thought he
could have her, this poor puny man with neither physical
appeal nor social standing. And he had been bitterly
wounded when Don Andrés turned him down.

"I'm afraid Papa is not always as tactful as he might be. I imagine he didn't refuse you kindly."

"Kindly? You think that would have made it all right? If he'd done it kindly?" Something seemed to tense in his body, straining until Lili was terrified it would snap. "He shouldn't have refused me at all. I wanted you. Oh, I wanted the money too—your papa's money is very appealing—but I wanted *you*! Ah, well . . ." The tension seemed to break, and suddenly he was smiling unpleasantly. "It looks as if I'm going to have a share of both, and without having to marry you. I did say, didn't I, that I expected a compensation?"

"You must be mad," Lili cried, not even making an effort any longer to placate him. "You've concocted some fantasy in your head, and you're convinced I'm going to go along with it. But it's not true! None of it. I was kidnapped, whether you believe me or not. Papa *will* compensate you, generously . . . if you bring me back unharmed. But if you do anything to me . . ."

"If I do *anything*?" He stopped pacing and moved closer, eyes almost on a level with hers. "How charmingly vague. You mean if I sully that sweet innocence Papa holds so dear."

Lili felt the color drain from her face. She had been so afraid of Jeremy and his men when she fled into the rain-cold dusk. But this was a thousand times worse. "I wouldn't have put it that way, but yes. Papa does prize my innocence. And you said it yourself: he is a proud man. If he thought you had disgraced me, he wouldn't hesitate to call you out. He may not be young anymore, but he's strong, and skilled with a sword. If the two of you were to meet under the dueling oaks in Père Antoine's Garden, I wouldn't bet on you."

"Nor would I, *mademoiselle* . . . but I hardly think your Papa will do anything rash. Imagine the scandal. Besides, I rather doubt you'll be inclined to mention this little incident. After all, it was you who came to my door—dressed like a whore."

"Because I was frantic to get away from the men who were chasing me. I had to find help!"

"And did you have to make explicit promises to get it? You did tell my man, Claude, that it would be 'worth my while.' And you made it very clear what you meant. He will swear to it if he has to. And Don Andrés will believe him. Claude is a man of honor . . . for a black."

"Oh, dear heaven." Tears of frustration stung Lili's eyelids. What was there about men that made them think every woman in a vividly hued gown was easy prey? That the Americans behaved so grossly was disgusting enough. But Creole men were always so chivalrous in the ballroom. "And for that—a subtle innuendo you didn't hear yourself—you would condemn me? Do you really have so little regard for my virtue? Just because of the way I'm dressed?"

"And the way you behaved. You left your coat open, knowing how you were clothed underneath. And you took that same coat off, *mademoiselle*, with just the slightest prodding. But then, you're used to displaying your body, aren't you? What is one man, more or less? Looking at you . . . touching you . . ."

Lili gasped. "You can't mean that!" He really was mad. She might have been foolish, turning to someone she barely knew, but she had done nothing to deserve this.

"Oh, but I can . . . and I do. I might have more regard for your 'virtue' if I believed you had any. But you see, I was there. In the square, this weekend. I saw that *very* interesting dance you performed.

"You were . . . there?"

Oh, God. He had seen her dance, seen her body pick up the sensuous beat of the music, her hips swaying shamelessly, uninhibited. He had seen her eyes meet Jeremy's, sharing secrets that were reserved for the bedroom! He hadn't recognized her then, in colorful quadroon garb. But when she'd showed up on his doorstep, revealingly dressed, hair spilling onto her shoulders, he had made the connection. That was the expression she had seen in his eyes when she uttered her name. And that was why he was treating her so despicably.

And in a terrible, grotesque way, she almost understood. Any Creole woman who behaved with such abandon in public knew what she could expect.

"Yes," he said calmly, enjoying the expression on her face. "I was there. And I know what you are. So, please—no more coy protestations. Let us simply discuss what it is you want from me. And how far you are willing to go to get it."

"Oh, *monsieur* . . ." Lili sank down on the hearth weakly, knees buckling under her. "I *was* kidnapped . . . several weeks ago. I don't know why Papa has kept it a secret, but I'm sure he has his reasons. Only . . . I fell in love with my captor! I loved him so much, I would have done anything. I thought he loved me too, but then . . . something went wrong. . . . If I have to go out on the street again, they'll find me. And they're going to kill me!"

"A most diverting story." He stared down at her, thin nose pinched with disdain. "I might have believed you if you'd told me that in the first place. But you've been piling lie upon lie since you came in here."

"I haven't lied," Lili broke in. "Exactly." She *had* pretended to be innocent, but that was just because she hadn't known she'd be caught. "I may not have told you everything, but what I said was true!"

"Well, it doesn't matter, does it?" Squatting down, he peered into her face, reddened by the faint glow of the fire. These girlish qualms were getting tiresome, and he was beginning to lose patience. "As you mentioned, you can't go back on the street, even assuming I'm ready to release you. And I'm not."

Lili felt fear rising from her stomach. "You can't keep me here! Not against my will. And if you . . . if you hurt me, you'll be sorry! When I tell Papa—"

"When you tell Papa what? That I defiled your lovely virgin body? You're going to find it hard to prove that nasty little allegation, since there wasn't any virginity to defile."

"Yes, but Papa doesn't know that!" Lili flung it out as a challenge. She was clutching at straws, but she had to do something before this went too far. "I'll say you were the one who did it to me! I'll say I escaped from my kidnappers unharmed, and came to you for help. And met an unspeakable fate! My lack of virginity, as you so grossly pointed out, will be all the proof I need. And, of course, the bruises on my body, since you'll have to take me by force."

"Ah, but I am not going to force you. There will be no marks, except a little redness at the wrists." He got up, lips tightening as he sidled over to the door. "I abhor violence. And you look like the kind of hellcat who could do serious damage with your nails. Do you think I'd risk having my eyes scratched out? No, I prefer that you come to me voluntarily."

"I would die first!"

LeClerc glanced back, noting flashing eyes and the rise of color in her cheeks. Nauseating really, but that sort of trashy behavior had always had the secret power to arouse him. "I think not, but that, of course, will be your choice. Claude," he called through the doorway. "Fetch another glass. The *mademoiselle* is going to join me in some sherry. Oh, and a length of rope too. Three feet should do."

Voluntarily? Lili gaped in horror and disgust. He was going to tie her up. That was what he meant by red marks on her wrists. And he talked about voluntarily!

Every hair on the back of her neck prickled as she watched the man Claude slither into the room and set the glass on a table. He barely looked at her, but she knew he hadn't failed to notice the way she was dressed. And she knew it confirmed the opinion he had formed of her before. LeClerc gestured toward her hands, and he came over, tugging her roughly to her feet as he wrapped the cord around her arms.

He's done this before, Lili thought helplessly as the rope gouged into her flesh. He's done it before . . . and he knows what's coming next.

She tried desperately to meet his eyes, to plead for help, but if he even noticed, there was no response. His hands slid up her arms, a little too insolent, and she cursed herself bitterly for having lost his respect before. If she managed to resist LeClerc—if he didn't work out his gross passions on her body after all—would she be tossed like a bone to his manservant?

Or even if he did?

Shivering, she realized that there was something of the voyeur in this mousy little man. He was the sort who would enjoy watching her be used by someone else.

"You remember Eveline, that ungrateful girl who ran away, don't you, Claude?" LeClerc was saying, lips twitching, as if in acknowledgment of his own cleverness. "And I had such lovely plans for her. Ah, well, fortunately I kept her papers. Here she is, back again—I'm sorry to say, recalcitrant as ever. We'll have to do something about that, won't we?"

Lili tensed, not knowing what he was talking about,

but sensing it spelled trouble. She threw a confused look at Claude, but his eyes were averted as he tightened one last knot so hard her wrists ached. He had to know she wasn't this Eveline they were talking about, but he didn't say anything. Didn't even register surprise.

"That will be all, Claude." LeClerc waved the man away with an oddly effeminate flick of his hand. "Oh, and, Claude, make sure the front door is locked. We wouldn't want our lovely Eveline trying to escape again, especially when her hands are tied. She might fall down the steps and hurt herself."

"As you say, sir."

He glided out of the room as silently as he had come. Lili stood absolutely still, trying to figure out this latest development, not quite grasping it. All she knew was that she had, somehow, to make LeClerc see reason.

Forcing herself to turn, she met his eyes steadily.

"I'm not this Eveline who ran away from you. You know that perfectly well. And so does that toady of a servant, for all that he hasn't got the guts to stand up to you."

"He's not a servant. He's a slave. And you *could* be Eveline. Five-feet-seven, as I recall, black hair, yellow eyes, and a tongue like a viper. A perfect description, wouldn't you say? It really is a miracle, having the dear child back again after all these months."

"And you think because you call me Eveline, because I match some vague general description, you can *treat* me like Eveline? You think you can do anything you want to me?"

"But *I* am not going to do anything. Dear, dear, and here I thought you understood. *You* are going to do it all. Perhaps you'll even repeat that charming little dance. Didn't I tell you I expected you to come to me? Voluntarily?"

"And I told you I'd rather die first!"

"Ah, yes, so you did. But that might not be exactly the option." He wandered over to a small writing desk and, opening the drawer, began to rummage through a sheaf of papers. "Now, where did I put that? . . . Here it is. Eveline. . . . I seem to have been slightly mistaken. Five-feet-*five*—but I don't suppose the discrepancy will be noted. Value two hundred and fifty dollars. Much too high, but she was a pretty thing . . . *is* pretty, I mean."

He turned slowly, fixing Lili with an oddly feverish look.

"This paper gives me absolute power over a woman called Eveline, whose description is recorded here. *Absolute*, you understand. A slave is a piece of property. Bought and *sold* at will."

Lili's blood ran cold as the truth began to dawn on her.

"You mean . . ."

"Exactly," he said with a quiet emphasis more frightening than all his previous ranting. "Claude, who is very understanding for a black, will have a carriage waiting at the back door. You will do what I say—you will do *everything* I say—or I'll take you to the Exchange tonight and put you up on the block."

31

"You'll . . . what?" Lili stared at him numbly. The room seemed to be spinning, and it was all she could do to keep from collapsing back on the hearth.

"You heard me. I said I'll take you to the Exchange and turn you over for public auction. It would be a pity, of course, disposing of such a lovely creature, but I'm sure the 'gentlemen' who handle these things will understand. Especially when I tell them how difficult you've been. Slave sales are held every Saturday, I believe. How convenient that that's tomorrow. Ah, well, if I must lose you, at least I'll be consoled by a handsome profit. I imagine you'll fetch considerably more than the two-fifty I paid for, uh, you."

"But this is insane! Surely you don't think you're going to get away with this!"

"Why not? The description on the papers matches perfectly. Except I doubt you're much of a seamstress, but then, I don't suppose that's what you'll be purchased for." He laughed unpleasantly. "What are you going to do about it? Stick your nose in the air and tell everyone you're Lili Santana? Look at you. The dress of a trollop and the brown skin of a mixed-blood beauty. Who'd believe a story like that?"

Helplessly Lili realized he was telling the truth. Just as no one had recognized her on the street, costumed and acting like a quadroon, no one was going to see her now as anything other than what she appeared. If only she hadn't spent all those weeks in the sun.

"You're very sure of yourself," she said, stalling for time. "But do you think everyone else is going to be so confident? Don't forget, Don Andrés Santana is a powerful man. What if somebody gets nervous and decides to check with him?"

"Oh, I doubt that. Your dear papa *is* powerful. But he's rigid too, and he's made a lot of enemies. If the men I turn you over to give the slightest thought to your story—which I don't for a minute think they will—I suspect it will only make things more diverting. And, of course, there's always the possibility that *they* were in Congo Square last Sunday too." Going over to the table where Claude had set the glass, he picked it up and filled it from the decanter. "Won't you take a drop of sherry? To seal our bargain?"

"You are a monster," Lili said, horrified. "You look like a timid little mollycoddle, but you're the worst kind of beast!"

"And you, my dear, are an extremely haughty woman." The barb had struck home, and he drew back, spine stiffening. "You're no blood kin to Santana, but you seem to have absorbed his arrogance. It will be interesting to see how proud you are when you come to my bed tonight."

Lili looked him in the eye. "And if I continue to refuse . . ."

"If you continue to refuse, I am prepared to carry out my threat." He took a step toward her, then stopped, balancing the glass to keep from spilling it. "But why are we talking of unpleasant things, when we both know they're not going to happen? I'm sure, after you've had time to think this over, you'll come to the only sensible conclusion. Apparently you don't know much about slaves, or the routines involved in selling them. You would be with the men in charge for only one night, but I assure you, you'd find that night extremely long. They would, naturally, examine you. It's their duty to make note of any physical deformities, and, of course, to check for diseases, such as yaws or syphilis. What a pity you weren't wiser about doling out your favors."

Something in his voice made Lili wary. "What . . . what do you mean?"

"Why, didn't you know? Virginity is as highly prized among pretty slaves as among their mistresses. Had you been, shall we say, intact, every effort would have been made to keep you that way. It has an effect on the price.

But since you have already been damaged . . . Well, damaged goods *are* damaged goods. It doesn't matter how many times penetration has occurred. I'm sure the men will find you attractive . . . assuming you haven't picked up something unmentionable from one of your lovers."

Lili shivered. She might not have had much experience with slaves, but she sensed he wasn't exaggerating.

"You truly are despicable."

"Perhaps," he agreed. "But I am only one man . . . and there will be several men where you are going tonight."

He came closer, leaning forward, the wineglass tilting in his hand. As Lili's eyes dropped, she saw with revulsion that the front of his breeches was bulging out.

"They, at least, won't expect me to feign enthusiasm."

"No, I daresay they won't." He extended the glass, an invitation. "I don't suppose it will make any difference to them, one way or the other. But don't worry. They won't leave any bruises either. They'll want you to look good when they put you up on the block."

Lili stared at the glass, dark gold liquid catching and holding the light. All too bitterly, she realized the choice he was offering her. A night of unutterable degradation at his gross hands . . . or a night with any number of men pawing her body.

"I can hardly accept the sherry, *monsieur*," she said evenly, "with my hands tied behind me."

He smiled, a slow, mean smile that told her he was sure he had won. And by all that was sane and rational, he ought to have.

"You must allow me to help you."

He held the glass to her lips, tilting it forward. Sucking in deeply, Lili filled her mouth, then pulled back and spat in his face.

She had one moment of swift satisfaction as she watched wine spattering over his nose and dribbling down his chin.

"I would sooner submit to a horde of barbarians than let you lay one filthy finger on my body!"

"Bitch!" He raised his hand as if to strike her. Then, pulling himself together, he drew back, glowering at her with the most intense hatred she had ever seen. "You think you're too good for me. You and your father . . .

and all your kind! Well, we'll see how good you are after that 'horde of barbarians' at the auction house finishes with you." He turned angrily and stomped out of the room.

At least, Lili thought as she watched him disappear, his face was not the only part of his anatomy that had been affected by her assault. His manhood, like his smug self-confidence, seemed to be more than usually fragile.

He came back a few seconds later, wearing a long dark greatcoat of some excellent fabric, though Lili noticed that the hem was fraying. No doubt the profit he expected to turn on his $250 investment would come in handy.

Claude was waiting in the hall as they left the parlor and turned toward the rear of the house. Something in his expression caught her eye, and Lili realized she had misjudged him before, as he had misjudged her. Her resistance apparently told him he had been wrong, and she sensed pity in the dark eyes that followed her into the shadows.

Not that it would do her any good. Claude would never defy his master, and in all fairness, she couldn't blame him. He was a slave—a real slave—totally at the mercy of the man who owned him. What was happening to her could happen to him at any time.

Only for Claude it would be a thousand times worse. His humiliation was for a lifetime.

LeClerc's anger had eased somewhat by the time they reached the coach, and he was beginning to be sorry he had acted so hastily. He had desired the girl deeply, with a passion he rarely felt, and he sensed now, vaguely, that he might have been a little precipitate. True, she had spat in his face, and spitting revolted him. But perhaps if he had taken more time with her . . . Perhaps if he had spelled out, with a bit more clarity, exactly what she might expect, she would have been more amenable to what was clearly the lesser of two evils.

He glanced over at her face, proud and defiant as she seated herself in the carriage, staring straight ahead. She was an arrogant slut. But it was her arrogance that made him want her . . . and sluts had always held a certain appeal. He had gone to a whore once, not an octoroon in one of those fancy houses Creole gentlemen frequented, but a real whore, in a boat along the waterfront, with curtained cubicles in the hold. It had disgusted him, but it had been the only truly satisfying experience he had ever had with a woman.

If he had just been a little more patient . . .

He settled back as the carriage pulled out through a darkened passage into the street. But he hadn't been patient, and now it was too late. He couldn't tell the driver to turn around and go back. That would be exposing his weakness.

Maybe when they got where they were going. Maybe, when she saw that he meant to go through with it, she would come to her senses. Maybe then she would beg him to give her another chance.

The ride in the cramped coach for hire took less than half an hour, though it seemed considerably longer. The silent streets were empty, the only sounds coming from their wheels, with an occasional low curse expressing the driver's opinion of the road and the miserly sum that had been negotiated for risking his life thereon. The rain had stopped, but a smell of mud was in the air, mingling with garbage and excrement from the open gutters.

The Exchange was a rambling, rough wooden structure fronting on Chartres Street. The doors were open when they arrived, allowing glimpses of tables inside, which showed that it was a kind of coffeehouse for a commoner, more raucous crowd. Auctions were just beginning to be held there, informally on weekday afternoons, with various commodities for sale. Only on Saturdays were the tables shoved back and a place cleared along one wall for the display of human goods, an increasingly popular alternative to slave shops and yards in other areas of the city.

It was not in front of the Exchange itself that they pulled up, but a squalid one-story building down the block. LeClerc glanced over, trying in the light of the carriage lantern to gauge Lili's reaction. He didn't know what she had expected. He rather thought she didn't know herself. But whatever it was, the reality of this shabby storefront, with peeling paint and shutters permanently nailed over the windows, had to be grimmer.

He climbed down first, then reached out and grabbed her arm, half-helping, half-jerking her to the ground.

The sound of the carriage must have heralded their approach, for a door swung open abruptly, spilling shafts of yellow light onto the *banquette*. The odor of mildew and sweat was almost overpowering.

The man who ushered them in was a taciturn hulk, tallish and overweight, in a loose shirt with sleeves rolled up to the elbows. By contrast, the shadowy figure that rose from a table in the corner and sauntered toward them was almost appealing, a crooked smile and twinkling blue eyes belying the fact that he was one of the meanest bastards in the business. LeClerc noted with satisfaction that the other two men, who had been seated with him, looked as if they were his match for coarseness and brutality.

And, judging from the bored expressions on their faces, there wasn't anyone in the little cages out back they found even slightly interesting.

"I've come to put a woman up for auction," he said, opening his coat and drawing out the papers he had secreted in an inner pocket. "Her name, as you see, is Eveline. There's a complete description of her—including the fact that she manages some rather indifferent work as a seamstress. As you see, she's not unattractive, even in her present condition. I expect to get five or six hundred dollars for her. With the usual commission to you, of course."

"Of course." The man who had come over from the table squinted down at the papers, then shifted his gaze to the merchandise. "Could be right," he said after a moment. "We ain't got nothin' to compare, that's for sure. 'Less somethin' better shows up th' next few hours. You'd be asking more, I reckon, if she had more t' offer?"

His expression made it clear what he was asking. LeClerc answered slowly, choosing his words with care, as much for Lili's benefit as for the man's.

"You'll find that out for yourself, I'm sure. When you check her over. But I don't think the little something you'll find missing will disappoint you . . . if you get my drift."

The man chuckled nastily. "I get it. I get it."

"We're all gonna get it soon enough," one of the other men chimed in from the table, which was strewn with filthy plates and half-empty whiskey glasses. "What d'you say—eh, Danton?"

The first man agreed with a lopsided grin. "You got yourself a deal, LeClerc. Yeah, yeah . . . sure I recognize you. You're a scoundrel, but this time it looks like you brought somethin' good. This little slave here . . . what's her name?" He glanced down at the papers. "Eveline? Yeah, Eveline looks real good. Let's jus' see what we can do with 'er."

Throughout this brief exchange, Lili remained absolutely silent, standing a few paces from the door, her hands still bound behind her, her bearing as arrogant as ever. LeClerc was aware of a feeling of disappointment. If she couldn't be intimidated into groveling for her freedom, at least he had wanted the satisfaction of seeing the fear grow in her eyes.

But she'd just been standing there like a piece of stone, as if she hadn't seen—or understood—what was going on.

Now, suddenly, she stepped forward, and LeClerc felt a twinge of anticipation. So, she was going to make a fool of herself after all! Her nose was in the air, just as he'd imagined, and she looked so haughty she might have been dressed in imperial satin, with plumes in her hair.

"This man is a liar," she said coolly. "A liar and a snake. I am no more this Eveline he is referring to than you are. Eveline ran away months ago, and he's trying to recoup his losses by putting me up for sale in her name. I am a free woman. I would have the papers to prove it, but he took them when he captured me. They are ashes now on his puny hearth. My name is . . . Ange." She threw her head back boldly. "Lili-Ange. And you'll live to regret it, sir, if you lay a hand on me."

In spite of himself, LeClerc had to admire her. He had underestimated the bitch. If she'd claimed to be the kidnapped Santana heiress, the men would have been all over the floor now, rolling with laughter. But this story had a ring of truth.

"Don't listen to her, gentlemen," he whined. "It's she who is the liar. I'm afraid she's become totally unmanageable. She *has* run away. More than once. See . . . look here. I brought the advertisements I had to place last time. That's how I recovered her. I paid a pretty penny, let me tell you."

"I don't know." Danton scratched his head thoughtfully as he glowered down at the papers LeClerc had handed him before. "I don't want no trouble. It says here your Eveline's five-feet-five. This one, she looks taller."

"Five-five . . . -six . . . -seven—what's the difference?" LeClerc tried to sound as if it were a matter of no consequence. "Who knows how they measure these people? Or what they write down."

"It also says that Eveline is a seamstress," Lili pressed. "And I very much doubt it adds the word 'indifferent.' I, personally, have never sewn a stitch in my life. I am a musician . . . and an artist. I was educated at a school for young ladies near Montpellier. By my father—who, incidentally, is a man of means."

The reference to a well-placed papa was not lost on Danton. Such things were not unusual in New Orleans, where color lines were frequently crossed. "You're sure you know what you're doing?" He turned to peer at LeClerc. "She don't sound like no seamstress to me. If she comes out with these wild claims tomorrow—"

"And I will," Lili cut in. "I'll come out with more claims than you ever dreamed of. And I'll substantiate them, too! If there's one of those new upright pianos in the vicinity, or a sketchpad, I can prove my abilities aren't those of a slave. And if you think no one's going to pay attention, you're very much mistaken."

She was good. LeClerc gaped, openmouthed. He had to give her that. She was good. Every gesture, every flip of her hair, every disdainful glance from those curious yellow-hazel eyes bespoke the aristocratic breeding she claimed.

"If she pulls that nonsense tomorrow," he said sharply, "you'll just have to laugh it off. Come, come, Danton, I've seen you operate. I'm sure you've handled this kind of problem before."

"Maybe," the other agreed, "but nobody ever played it like this. All the others, they was bluffin'. You listened to 'em, you knew it. But this gal . . ."

"She is convincing," LeClerc conceded. He ran his finger along the inside of his collar, feeling the sweat. "She's quite the little actress, though she's never been onstage a day in her life. Must be something in her blood. Still, I think you'll be able to manage her tomorrow . . . if that's still necessary. But there's probably a way or two to knock the cockiness out of her tonight."

He paused, looking around to make sure they caught his meaning.

"I'm not too concerned, you understand, how you go about it. Anything you do is fine with me. She's not my worry anymore. Unless, of course . . ." He turned back, almost hopefully, to the girl. "Unless you're ready to mend your ways and would like to come home."

He knew as he looked at her it was no use.

"Are you planning on passing this way as you leave, *monsieur*?" she said softly.

"Passing that way?" he echoed, puzzled.

"Yes. The closer the better. I'd love the pleasure of spitting in your face again!"

The sound of masculine laughter was still audible on the street minutes later, after he had made the final arrangements and taken his leave, sidling the long way round to the door. His ears were burning as he picked up the top hat he had left on the carriage seat and popped it on his head. It was a crude, coarse sound, the kind of blatant male crudeness that always turned his stomach.

Well, maybe it would turn hers too.

He had lost her. He knew that as he dismissed the carriage and headed home on foot, even though a faint drizzle had started in again. There would be no last-minute screams for help from that ugly little hovel. He had lost her . . . and the knowledge was like gall in his mouth.

Maybe he should have tied her hand and foot to the four posts of the bed and forced himself on her. That's what any other man would have done. That's what those men inside were going to do if she resisted. But he'd tried that once, with a coal-black bitch who had cursed and kicked and bitten, and he hadn't gotten any satisfaction. Hell, he hadn't even been able to get it up!

It wasn't that he wanted real emotion from the women he possessed. Real emotion—a demand for mutual satisfaction—would have terrified him. What he wanted was the practiced pretense of a whore.

And Lili Santana *was* a whore, deep down inside where it counted. Wild and unconventional, full of fire beneath those affected ladylike manners. He had seen it that day on the levee, with her hair tumbling down, flashing in the sun. He had heard it in the string of curses any harlot would be proud of.

It was that harlot he wanted . . . wanted so badly he could taste it. And he had lost her.

At least he would have his revenge. Lili Santana would suffer. That proud spirit would be dragged through the dirt for the humiliating way she had rejected him.

But once again, there would be no satisfaction, because he wouldn't be there to see it.

32

Lili tried to keep her head high as she stood in that small, smoky room and faced the four men who held her fate in their hands, but it wasn't easy. She could be brave if she had to. She had found out in the last few hours just how much inner courage and strength she possessed. But courage alone wasn't going to help her now.

"I told you," she said, forcing herself to eye them steadily, "that you'd be sorry if you laid one hand on me. And I meant it! You'd better think twice about any nasty little plans you have."

"Sure. And who's gonna make us sorry? You?" The man who had butted in before rasped the words with a sneer. If he was the least bit intimidated, Lili couldn't see it. The other man who had been seated with Danton was as silent as the overweight flunky at the door, but all four were on their feet.

And they were all staring at her with looks that sent shudders down her spine.

"Hardly." Her mouth was so dry it hurt. "I'm not a threat to you. But don't make the mistake of thinking I'm alone in the world. I may have wandered out foolishly on a stormy night, but my absence hasn't gone unnoticed. Even now, someone is looking for me."

"And that's supposed to scare us?" The man chuckled unpleasantly as he moved forward, eyes running down the front of her dress. "I 'spect that's your 'Papa' you're talkin' about. He's gonna be real mad, is he, when he finds out where you are?"

"Why not? Papas have been known to take affront when their daughters are treated with heinous incivility.

They've even been known, at times, to hold female off-spring in lofty esteem."

The man's brow tightened, annoyed, Lili sensed, because he couldn't understand the polysyllables she had deliberately thrown out. Danton laughed good-naturedly.

"Sure, sure . . . you don't talk like no slave. But if your papa held you in such *lofty esteem*"—he pitched his voice high, mimicking her haughty tone—"wouldn't he take better care of you? Wouldn't he know, right now, where you are?"

"He might . . . and he might not. Did your papa always know where he could find you when you were young?"

"No. But my pappy didn't hold me in esteem, neither. I reckon he'd as soon have left me as found where I was." He winked broadly, waiting for the laughter to die down. "Jest who is this papa we're s'posed to be worried about? Might make a difference, we had a name to set us quiverin' in our boots."

Lili drew in a deep breath. That was the one question she had hoped to avoid. Anyone she named, any member of a prominent New Orleans family, might well be someone whose every foible had been thoroughly dissected in masculine gossip. Someone about whom *everything* was known.

Except . . .

"Have you heard of the Cavarelles?" she said impetuously.

"The Cavarelles?"

The man at the door turned, uttering aloud the question that was on everyone's lips. From his actions and speech, she sensed he was slow, but even for him, the name had penetrated.

"You're telling us your father is a Cavarelle?"

Danton's milky blue eyes narrowed, and Lili could almost feel the wheels spinning in his head. No one ever saw the Cavarelles—LeClerc had said as much—so he wouldn't have any point of reference. But even he must know that the old man had died years ago. Long before she was born. And the young one, Jean-Baptiste, was too close to her own age.

If only she were better-informed! If only she'd been curious when Don Andrés told her she was going to marry into that illustrious family. How much would people be likely to know about them? Could she make up an uncle or a cousin and hope to get away with it?

"Not exactly," she hedged. "My father wasn't a Cavarelle, but he was connected with them . . . intimately. Do you remember the widow? Marguerite?" His expression told her he did. "You might say my father . . . belonged to her. Though, obviously, not quite as exclusively as she might have liked."

Danton whistled through his teeth. "Lorenzo Lafourchette. The second husband. I did hear he liked a little on the side. But . . . Say! He's been dead a coon's age. How the hell's a dead man gonna take care o' his little girl?"

"He may be dead . . . but his successor isn't."

"His successor? You must think I'm stupid. There ain't no successor. The lady died first."

Lili gulped. A mistake. A stupid mistake. She'd have to be more careful.

"I meant his predecessor, naturally. Marguerite only married Lorenzo after my father got tired of her. And he didn't get tired until he'd acquired enough of her inherited assets to set himself up handsomely." The lies came spilling out, fluently but dangerously, and Lili half-wished she hadn't started the whole thing. But she had to keep talking, had to keep them from thinking of anything else. "I don't claim that my father is the nicest man in the world. Or that his methods are exactly . . . scrupulous. But then, nice, scrupulous men aren't alarming—are they?"

"I don't recall anyone before Lafourchette," Danton said thoughtfully. He was watching her intently, trying to see if she was bluffing. " 'Course, I was a boy at the time. And the Cavarelles, they stick to themselves. What'd you say his name was?"

Lili forced herself to meet those cool, pale eyes. "His name doesn't matter. And it's not my father you have to worry about. It's some of his younger associates, with whom I am—shall we say?—very *close*. You know of a man called the Blaze?"

Danton's mouth twisted, not the way she had imagined. "I heard tell of 'im," he admitted. "But I ain't never laid eyes on the fella. Lots o' stories drift into town. Mostly, they're bigger'n the men that come after 'em."

"This one isn't, let me assure you. You haven't seen him because he's been careful to stay out of sight. Until now. But he's here. In the city."

She hesitated, sensing that she was getting nowhere. She had to do something to make her story believable. But if she told them too much, mightn't that be jumping from the frying pan into the fire? One word, one hint of this leaking out, and Jeremy and his deadly band would know where to find her.

But with Jeremy, at least there was a *chance* he would protect her. What chance did she have with these brutes?

"If you're curious, you might find him at a certain blacksmith shop on Royal Street. Run by a man named Jean Lafitte. And his brother Pierre."

"The Lafitte brothers." The man who had moved up before shuffled back clumsily. "I don't know, Danton. I don't like this."

Lili looked from one to the other, daring for the first time to hope. The whole town had been buzzing about the Blaze before she was kidnapped, but apparently Jeremy had been too busy in recent weeks to add kindling to the fire. Fortunately, the dashing black-haired Lafitte didn't seem to maintain such a secretive existence.

"I don't know neither," Danton conceded with a speculative scowl. "She could be runnin' a bluff. She's a sly bitch. But I don't like it myself."

"You'll like it considerably less if you harm me—in *any way*." She put the emphasis on the last words, making her meaning abundantly clear. "Lafitte is capable of breaking you in two, like a twig from a dried-up tree. And so is the Blaze!"

"I wonder . . ."

"Wonder all you want. But while you're wondering, ask yourself this. Why do you suppose that snake LeClerc was in such a hurry to dump me here?"

Danton smiled. "He wanted the money."

"Oh, yes, he wanted money. And I do match the missing Eveline's description, after a fashion. But surely he could have brought me to the auction himself. It would be different if I were a burly male, likely to cause trouble, but why would LeClerc pay someone a commission for handling a securely bound woman? . . . And the sale isn't until tomorrow. Yet he brought me here to-

night, to you, instead of keeping me for his own enter-
tainment."

That got them. More than anything, Lili sensed that
that blatant allusion to men's grosser instincts had set
them thinking. Even the dull one was looking uncomfortable.

She hastened to press her advantage.

"René LeClerc might be enamored of money, but he's
not about to risk his neck. And neither will you—if
you're smart."

"It seems to me," Danton said slowly, "the little bastard's already stuck his neck out. *If* what you say is true.
Jest bringin' you here was takin' a helluva chance."

"Maybe. But remember, LeClerc isn't the one who's
going to drag me kicking and screaming to the block
tomorrow. And *he* hasn't touched me."

"He tied your hands together."

"He didn't tie them. His manservant did. But I wasn't
talking about that, and you know it. If you want to touch
me enough to untie my hands, that's fine. I'd be grateful.
But try anything else, and be prepared to pay with your
life!"

Fire flashed out of her eyes, but inside she was terrified, and it was all she could do to keep them from seeing
it. Especially when Danton drew a long, mean-looking
blade out of the waistband of his breeches. Cringing, she
saw it coming toward her, but he only lashed out harm-
lessly, severing the cords that bound her, without drawing a drop of blood.

Sheer relief ran through her as she drew her arms
forward, stretching aching muscles and rubbing her wrists
until the circulation returned.

But the relief was short-lived. What followed was a
nightmare more hideous than anything she could have
imagined. Coarse hands removed her dress, not roughly,
but carefully. Almost gently. Lili sensed with sickening
revulsion that the men were more interested in watching
her reaction than keeping the fragile silk intact for tomorrow. Coarse eyes took lewd note of the fact that she
was not wearing anything underneath. And coarse mouths
opened frequently to describe in obscene detail exactly
what they liked about her body, and why.

Standing there totally nude, shivering with cold and

disgust while they took their time looking her over, Lili
was certain she had sunk to the depths of humiliation.
But in that she was mistaken.

What was to come next was all that LeClerc had described, and more. The examination given to slaves going
up for public auction was nothing if not thorough. Every
part of her body was poked and prodded, every inch of
tender flesh subjected to the grossly personal scrutiny of
foul male hands. The plumpness of her breasts was observed and commented on, the firm, round lines of her
buttocks explored, her nipples pinched until she winced,
though she bit her lip to keep from crying out.

Waves of nausea flooded over her as she felt them
probe each bodily cavity, her mouth first, counting the
teeth, or so they said, and her rectum, checking for signs
of disease. Even that sweet special place that had been
known—and touched—by only one man. Loathing and
despair overwhelmed her as she felt crude fingers insinu-
ating themselves into every private part of her body.

Was this what it was to be a slave? This terrible degradation every time a piece of human property was exchanged or sold? The awful fear, if you were young and
pretty—or handsome—that you'd be used like a barnyard
animal for unspeakably foul purposes? Was this what it
was like to be born with the wrong color skin? Never to
have control over your life or destiny?

Or your dreams?

Bitterly Lili was reminded of Don Andrés and the
sympathy he had for blacks, refusing to keep slaves in his
house and treating even casual workmen with respect.
She knew now that he was right. She had never thought
much about it. The quadroons on the street in their
pretty dresses and bright *tignons* had always looked glamorous and exotic, and it hadn't seemed to matter. Now
she understood that it *did* matter. It mattered horribly.

Don Andrés had been right about other things too.
But she had been young and cocky, and so sure she knew
best. She wished now—oh, how she wished!—she had
listened. He only wanted to take care of her. To protect
her from all the danger and ugliness in the world.

Lili had no idea how long she spent in that room,
perhaps thirty or forty minutes, perhaps an hour or two—it
all went by in a blur of fear and humiliation. She only

knew, when they finally led her, still naked, out into an open yard in back and pressed a filthy scrap of wool into her hands, that she had been spared the final, brutal degradation of having body after coarse male body forced on her.

She was so exhausted, she hardly noticed the foul-smelling yard, with metal-barred boxes lined up in rows between what appeared to be brick or stone walls. It was almost pitch dark, the only light coming from a smoky lantern one of the men was carrying. Lili could barely make out shadowy figures crouched like animals in some of the cages, or curled up in the fetal position because there wasn't room to stretch out or sit upright.

Vile odors came from the blanket, and she could hardly bear to hold it in her hands. All she wanted, when they shoved her into one of those hideous boxes, was to roll it up and push it as far away as she could. But there was no flooring, only rain-damp earth, and the cold was so intense, she was forced to wrap it around her.

Shivering, she tucked her knees up to her chin, like those dim forms she had glimpsed before, and tried to sleep, knowing she would need her wits about her tomorrow. But the darkness was bitter, and she could still feel with agonizing clarity every terrible lewd thing they had done to her body. From all around came sighs and whimpers, telling her that others, too, were afraid and lying awake in the night.

Her brain was so numb, it was hard to focus. Impossible to make any plans. All she could think was how horribly, cruelly, these men had treated her . . . and how close they had come to something she couldn't even bear to imagine. Soon—how many hours now?—they were going to drag her out in ropes again, or chains, and sell her to some man she had never seen.

And what would he do, this man, when he brought her home with the papers that made her his Eveline? Would he be intimidated by stories of imaginary papas and smugglers with blacksmith shops in the city?

Or had she only put off the inevitable for one night?

In the thin light of dawn, the yard seemed even more squalid. The cells were smaller than Lili had realized, rough wooden boxes, barred in front and jammed to-

gether. Those nearest her were empty, so at least she was
spared the agony of having to watch other human beings
in misery. And seeing the pity in their eyes as she tried,
humiliatingly, to cover her nakedness with a scrap of
blanketing.

Sometime late in the morning, a guard she hadn't seen
before slopped a bowl of watery rice gruel flavored with
rancid bacon grease on the ground in front of her. Just
the smell was revolting. Retching, she turned her head to
the side, trying not to let herself think, not to imagine
what was going to happen next.

It must have been well past noon by the time the men
returned. The sun was surprisingly warm, intensifying a
sickening stench of vomit and urine, and Lili clenched
her jaw as she heard them come into the yard. She
couldn't see anything, but sounds told her that slaves
were being taken out in groups of twos and threes. Sharp
grunts from the guards were punctuated by an occasional
faint murmur or a whimper of pain, but surprisingly, no
one wept, no one begged—no one cursed the brutal
bastards who were hauling them off.

Nausea welled up from her stomach. Were they so
resigned to their fate, these men and women who were
owned like cattle and pieces of furniture, that they took
this barbaric degradation as a matter of course?

The yard was nearly empty when a pair of mud-spattered
black boots stopped in front of her cage. Shivering, Lili
knew her turn had come. The barred door creaked open,
and male hands gripped her arms, pulling her out, painfully, for every muscle was stiff and cramped. Desperately she clung to the blanket, but it fell away partly,
leaving her back and buttocks exposed.

Inside, her gown was returned to her, dry now, but
stiff and badly wrinkled. There was no privacy. All she
could do was turn her back as she dropped the blanket
and pulled it on, fingers trembling so badly she could
hardly work the intricate fastenings. Danton wasn't there,
but three other men were—two she didn't recognize, and
one the sullen hulk who hadn't spoken a word the night
before.

She was shuddering as she finished dressing and turned
around.

They were leering openly. Lili panicked as she realized

what she must look like, the dress too low-cut, too form-fitting, the skirt tied up to expose ankles and shins that were nearly as tanned as the rest of her. One of them was almost drooling, his tongue flicking out to moisten his lips. For an instant she was terrified that the thing she had been so afraid of last night was going to happen now.

But before they could do anything, the door opened and Danton ambled into the room.

He stopped just inside, leaning against the doorframe. Something smoldered in his eyes too, as in the others', only more controlled, and somehow more degrading.

"Now, ain't that a cute trick, tyin' the skirt up like that. I think we'll jus' leave it. A little leg never brought the price down. Sure is a pity . . ." He grinned slowly, almost boyishly, one side of his face twisting up. "It would 'ave been nice . . . real nice. We could 'ave had a good time last night. Myself, I think you was bluffin'. But, shit! Ain't no gal worth riskin' a man's life."

Lili had assumed she would be tied again, if not chained, but her hands were free as Danton and one of the others walked her down the street, each with a firm hold on one arm. The noise from the Exchange was audible for some distance, growing louder as they approached. Shuttered wooden doors had been opened all along the front, and the place was so crowded, men spilled onto the *banquette*.

Lili had never seen so many people crammed into one room in her life. Most of the tables had been removed. Those that were still there had been pushed back against the walls, and men were standing on them, jockeying for a better view of the large wooden crate that formed an impromptu stage at one end. A slave was there now, a muscular youth with ebony skin and intelligent eyes, but despite a few halfhearted bids, the audience seemed to be paying little attention. There was a raucous carnival atmosphere, a kind of Mardi Gras feeling, as if these men in their top hats and shirt sleeves had come not for business but to see a good show.

Were they waiting for her?

Lili's blood ran like ice in her veins as she stood in the doorway, as yet unnoticed by the men inside. Surely this wasn't the usual crowd for a Saturday auction. Had word been put out that a pretty light-skinned female was going to be placed on the block?

One by one, the men turned and saw her, and an animated hum of conversation swept the room. Bitterly Lili realized she had been right. They *were* waiting for her. They could hardly wait for the bidding to begin.

The man on the block was disposed of, and several others, but Lili barely noticed. All she could think was that she would be standing there soon. She would be exhibited in front of serious buyers and ghoulish curiosity seekers, and have a dollar value placed on her soul!

And if that many men had gathered for the privilege of making an offer, it wasn't because her papers stated she was a seamstress.

Lili had thought—she had promised herself—that when her time came, they would have to drag her to the block, kicking and clawing every inch of the way. But she realized suddenly, as fingers gouged into her arms, thrusting her forward, that that was just the kind of circus this crowd had come to see. They'd be talking about it for months. The fiery mixed-blood beauty who had screamed and scratched and had to be subdued by all those big strong men!

Well, she wasn't going to give them the satisfaction! Head high, spine as stiff as M'mère's had ever been, she glided forward, maintaining her dignity even as she was hoisted onto the oversize packing crate. Let them try to break her spirit or her pride, she thought defiantly. She'd show them what she was made of!

Some of the excitement seemed to go out of the crowd, and Lili felt a brief flush of triumph. Even the auctioneer, beside her on the platform, looked as if he had been taken aback. He was a burly red-faced man, not as tall as she, but broad-shouldered, with powerful arms and a barrel chest.

He recovered quickly, face contorting into a well-practiced smile.

"Ah, gentlemen . . . do you see what I see?" Smoothly oiled tones contrasted jarringly with his stocky peasant appearance. "Here it is, what we've all been waiting for. The climax to this afternoon's proceedings, the *pièce de résistance*, so to speak. And what a delectable *pièce* it is, don't you think?"

It? Lili cringed as hoots of approval went up from the crowd. Whatever little advantage she might have had, this man had maneuvered it away with a few glib words. The smell of the room was stifling, an ever-present odor of dampness mingling with tobacco and perspiration . . . and the pungency of raw whiskey, which told her at least a fair percentage of the buyers were American. Creoles, content with coffee and an occasional sherry or brandy, had nothing but contempt for anyone who overimbibed in public.

"Yes, yes, gentlemen," the auctioneer broke in, raising both hands for silence. "Yes, I see you're appreciative of the little treat we've brought you. But we wouldn't want to keep the, uh . . . *lady* waiting, now, would we? The sooner we conduct our business, the sooner one of you can claim this lovely treasure and carry it off. Now, let's see. What do we have here?" He ran a quick eye down the paper which Danton had thrust toward him. "Eveline . . . nice little name. And a seamstress, so it's claimed. Excellent at tailoring." He looked up, playing the audience. "Now, gentlemen, I do admit there's no proof she can stitch a straight seam. But then, I don't suppose that'll bother any of you . . . too much?"

He winked lewdly and was rewarded with a coarse burst of laughter.

"Hell, no," one of the men called out in a harsh northern accent. "What I see, that little miss can stitch my seams, straight or crooked, any day."

Another round of laughter, which the auctioneer tolerated only until it tapered off. Then he started to read again.

"Eveline, seamstress . . . light-skinned . . . yellow-eyed. Like a cat," he interjected, winking again. "Five-feet-five, they say—but it seems to me there's a couple more inches of pride and insolence to be tamed here."

"Turn her around," someone shouted. "Let's get a good look. Wouldn't want to buy a pig in a poke."

In a daze, Lili felt hands on her shoulders, not rough, but strong enough to let her know they could be. Feeling as if she were floating in a foggy dream, she began to move, rotating slowly to the sound of whistles and bawdy comments.

This can't be happening, she thought. It *can't*. But it was, and there wasn't a thing she could do about it.

"Nice legs." One voice rose above the others. "How 'bout we see a little more of 'em, eh?"

The auctioneer leaned forward, but before he could oblige, one of the men in front had clutched her skirt in a coarse attempt to rip it off. Jolted out of her lethargy, Lili raised one foot, ramming it against his shoulder.

"Get your filthy paws off me!"

The man's face reddened, and she thought for a second he was going to lunge at her. But companions on both sides caught him by the sleeves, choking with laughter as they held him back.

"Hot-tempered, ain't it?" came an amused cry.

It again! Something snapped inside her. Not a one of the men who had preceded her to the block had uttered so much as a word of protest. Nor had the slaves in the yard. But she was Lili Santana! She had not been raised to submissiveness and degradation. She wasn't going to march meekly to her fate without telling each and every one of these swine exactly what she thought of him!

"How dare you talk about me like that?" She tossed back her head, shaking the auburn-tinged tresses that were already tumbling over her shoulders. "I am not an *it*. I am a *she*! A human being, with a right to pride and self-respect. And dignity. The law says you may own a fellow creature if his skin is another color. You may demand his loyalty and his labor. But nowhere is it written—in either the laws of man or the laws of God— that you may rob him of his humanity! Or *her*!"

A brief hush had fallen over the crowd. Not shame, Lili sensed, but surprise. She hastened to make the most of it.

"You bring us here and treat us like barnyard beasts. Like sheep and cows and horses set out for your inspection. No, less than beasts! Your horses—your dogs, by God!—meet with more kindness than most of your slaves. Look at me! My skin is fairer than yours, sir." She pointed at random, knowing the accusation fitted half the men in the room. "Or yours. Or you, on the table in the back—with the swarthy complexion! How would you feel if someone came along and decided *you* were black because it looked like there was indiscretion in your background? Am I any less deserving of the right to human dignity than you?"

Several men glanced at each other sheepishly, and Lili knew she had them thinking. At the very least, she was spoiling their fun.

"Ooo-eee, but she's feisty!" The speaker was standing on one of the tables, next to the dark-skinned man, who, Lili was pleased to observe, was looking uncomfortable. "Hot as Cajun pepper! Wonder if she's got them fancy ideals in bed!"

The auctioneer laughed, a sound that seemed forced. "I doubt that, sir. I doubt it very much. A good point . . . and I'm glad you brought it up. I feel bound to point out that an examination of the merchandise has shown that the little lady here no longer retains her virginity."

He waited just long enough for a murmur to go up from the audience, then quelled it quickly.

"A tiny flaw, a *tiny* flaw—which lowers her price to a manageable range. And, of course, a little experience makes a woman more, uh . . . interesting. If you're going to buy a 'barnyard beast,' gentlemen, might as well make it a good one. You wouldn't bid on a wild dog, now, would you? Or a horse that hadn't been broken in."

"Damn you!" The words burst out of Lili's mouth. She looked from face to face, hating each and every one of them. "You call yourselves men, but there's not a man among you! A real man wouldn't have to buy a woman or force himself on her. A real man could find a woman who *wanted* him. I'm no longer a virgin because . . . because I'm married!" The lie tumbled out of her mouth, all the more easily because no one was there to refute it. "I don't expect you to believe that, but I am. I'm also a free woman. I was kidnapped and brought here with papers from someone who really *is* a seamstress and five-feet-five . . . though I don't expect you to believe that either. But you had better believe, if you buy me and try to use me for any foul purpose, I will personally make sure you have reason to regret it!"

There was enough vehemence in her tone to bring a sigh to the auctioneer's lips. He, too, was paid by commission, and he could see Lili's price going down with every vitriolic word that poured out of her mouth.

"I don't think you're in any position to do anything," he said wearily. "Now, gentlemen—"

"You may have taken my freedom," Lili cut in, "but I still have my fingernails. And my teeth, which I know what to do with!" Anger had gotten the better of her, and, caution forgotten, she went on in graphic detail to describe exactly where she would aim her fingernails if

anyone tried anything, and what she would attempt to
bite off with her teeth. The vulgarity seemed to have an
effect, for several of the men went pale.

"Then, may I suggest, gentlemen," the auctioneer said
dryly, "you consider removing her nails and her teeth,
which are hardly essential for what I'm sure you have in
mind."

Only the barest titter met his comment. Lili sensed she
was getting through. "You had better take my life too,"
she said, fixing first one man, then another, with intensely probing eyes. "Because as long as there's a breath
left in me, I'll show my disgust for any man who thinks
he can abase me." She remembered LeClerc's reaction
when she had expressed her contempt so vividly before.
"Keep me from biting or clawing if you will, but I can
still spit in your face! And if you bind my mouth, then I'll
laugh with my eyes at your pathetic attempts to prove
your masculinity. Let's see how much of a *man* you feel
then!"

"Yes, well . . ." The auctioneer gave up, turning to
the audience with a shrug. "Tiresome, but a gag might
help. Shall we start the bidding at two hundred and fifty?
Two hundred, then? Come, come . . . bind her mouth
and her eyes. Look at it this way, sirs. It will be a
challenge, taming all that fury. Or don't you feel 'man'
enough to try?"

That got the first genuine laugh in several minutes.

"I'll give you one hundred," someone called out from
the back. Almost immediately, one-fifty was heard, then
two hundred, and the bidding was off.

Lili listened with sinking heart. She had almost dared
to believe she had a chance. But all she had done was
give these odious barbarians a moment's pause. And not
a very long moment at that. LeClerc might not make the
profit he had hoped for, but she was going to be sold
anyhow.

And her spirited outburst only meant that whoever
purchased her would be on his guard, making it harder to
escape.

If only I'd listened to Papa, she thought, realizing how
futile regrets were now, but wishing with all her heart she
had been an obedient, sensible daughter. She didn't want
to marry Jean-Baptiste Cavarelle, God knew. She would

never *want* him . . . but anything was better than being placed on a packing crate and sold like a slave.

The bidding slowed around four hundred dollars, and Lili realized with a tightening in her stomach that it would be over soon. She looked around helplessly, trying to figure out who had made the last offer, but amusement had returned to all those faces and she couldn't guess. The level of conversation was up—the men were having fun again—and she was too tired, too discouraged, to fight anymore. Whatever was going to happen would happen. All she could do was try to endure it.

She was so wrapped up in her own sense of futility that she didn't even notice that a woman had slipped in through the open doors. Even when she turned and saw her, Lili was surprised not so much by that feminine intrusion as by the elegant hooded mantle that covered her completely, casting her face in shadow.

It's too warm for a long velvet cloak, she thought.

Then the woman took a step forward, shrugging back the hood at the same instant she started to speak, and Lili realized suddenly who it was.

Chartreuse.

"I bid one thousand dollars." Her deep, sultry voice rang through the room. "I have cash here to pay for the girl. Accept it, and we'll call the auction over."

Lili could only stare at her, stunned like everyone else. The room had gone so silent, a faint shuffling of feet in the back stood out distinctly. How on earth had Chartreuse known she was here? She wouldn't just have happened by with all that money in her pocket! But none of those men last night had had any way of connecting her with Don Andrés Santana or his beautiful mistress. And LeClerc would hardly have mentioned the matter.

The Exchange suddenly came to life, buzzing with questions and speculation. The men hadn't been planning on pushing the bidding anywhere near that high, Lili was sure. Even had she been sweetly docile, one thousand dollars was far too much to pay for a woman who wasn't even pure. But now their curiosity had been roused, and several made moves as if to continue.

But just as the first opened his mouth, a powerful man in a sweeping black hat and neatly trimmed black beard slipped up behind the woman.

"I would not suggest, gentlemen," he said, laying a hand on her shoulder, "that you bid against this lady. The price she has offered is more than fair. Surely you wouldn't wish to be the cause of her disappointment."

Such was the presence of Monsieur Jean Lafitte that not a word was heard from any of the men. The presence—and the reputation, which Jeremy had told her was making itself felt throughout the city.

Jeremy . . .

Lili stared at the man numbly, realizing suddenly that if Lafitte knew where she was, then Jeremy had to know too. And Jeremy's men. The thought ought to have filled her with alarm. The danger was even greater now—her very life might be in jeopardy—but she couldn't bring herself to care. Jeremy had feelings for her. She knew he did. He even said he loved her. Surely he would protect her.

And if he couldn't . . . well, at least he'd see to it that things were done cleanly. She'd rather be killed outright than suffer the thousand deaths that would be hers if one of these men took her home.

The transaction was quickly completed. While Chartreuse counted her thousand dollars into the auctioneer's hand, Lili scrambled down from the crate, refusing the assistance of several of the men who suddenly turned gallant and offered to help. Her face was composed, but her mind was in a turmoil, trying to figure out everything at once.

It was Lafitte, then, who had learned where she was. That made sense. She had told Danton and the others she knew him. One of them must have decided it would be prudent to check out her story.

But what did Lafitte have to do with her father's mistress?

She watched nervously as Chartreuse turned away from the auctioneer and came toward her. An open carriage was waiting outside, and they climbed in together, not speaking, though the older woman slipped off her cloak and held it out. Lili accepted gratefully, thankful for the thick velvet folds that hid her shame from curious eyes as they started down the street.

Where was Chartreuse taking her? she wondered. To Don Andrés . . . or the blacksmith shop on Royal Street? Or had Lili's instinct been right that afternoon in Congo

Square? She tensed as she recalled the way Chartreuse's eyes had seemed to slip behind her . . . and the suspicions that had flashed through her mind. Did her father's mistress resent her enough to have joined in the kidnapping plot with Jeremy and his men? Was it back to them they were going now?

But Chartreuse, it seemed, had ideas of her own. She settled back in the seat, waiting until they rounded the corner, then turned to study Lili with an unsettlingly steady gaze.

"I am taking you to my house," she said, "It's time we got to know each other."

33

"We have never been friends, you and I, but we aren't enemies . . . though I suspect you haven't always realized that." Chartreuse made an elegant figure as she stepped over to a small mahogany side table and poured out a steaming portion of coffee, releasing a heavenly fragrance into the air. "Perhaps you don't realize it now."

Lili took the cup that was handed to her. She had just gotten out of a warm, soapy tub and was wearing a crimson satin dressing gown, not the color she would have chosen, but wonderfully luxurious as it caressed her skin. Beyond a few embarrassingly explicit questions—designed to find out whether she had been harmed or merely frightened—Chartreuse had left her alone, giving her the privacy she needed to pull herself together. By the time Lili ventured down in her borrowed robe, a coffee service had been arranged on the table, with cold meats and cheeses and little frosted cakes.

Hardly, she had to admit, the actions of a woman who intended her harm.

"I'm not sure what I realize at the moment." She had just started to feel human again, though her hands were still trembling as she balanced the cup on its saucer. "But, no, I don't think I look on you as an enemy. How could I? I don't know why you came with all that cash to rescue me at the slave auction, but you did. And just in time! For that, you'll always have my gratitude."

"Perhaps I did it out of respect—and affection—for your father."

"Perhaps. But a thousand dollars is a great deal of money, even though I know Papa will repay you. And you didn't *have* to do it. You could just have told everyone who I was—and let me be horribly humiliated in public. I expect it would have served me right."

"You think I would have enjoyed that? Teaching you a lesson?"

"I think you must hate me . . . very much." She looked up, meeting the other woman's eyes. "Because of me, you've never been able to come to my father's home, even in costume at a masquerade. You must have wished many times I wasn't in the picture."

Chartreuse smiled, half to herself, as she rose and drew open the draperies. She had always been an intensely private person, unaccustomed to voicing her feelings. "It would have been easier, I agree. But you *were* in the picture. I knew that from the beginning. And I have never hated you."

The room, flooded with late-afternoon sunlight, showed an abundance of richly polished wood Lili had not noticed before, and warm colors, crimson and vermilion and gold. Everything, from the exquisitely embroidered firescreen to the candelabra on mosaic-topped tables, the carpet and mirrors and brocade-upholstered chairs, was elegant and understated. Exactly the kind of room a woman like Chartreuse would have. And a room where Don Andrés would feel comfortable.

"Then you're more generous than I deserve," she said. She had grown up enough in the last few weeks to be able to look back on her previous behavior with some objectivity. "It must have been extremely unpleasant, being barred from the house by a little brat who couldn't bear the sight of you."

"It was disappointing, of course. I would have liked to be a bigger part of your father's life. But you're forgetting, the difference in our stations would have precluded all but the most clandestine visits anyway. And your hostility was natural. You were just a child."

"A very spoiled child." Lili drained the last dregs from her cup and cast an eye on a crayfish salad. She had been too nervous to eat before, but now her stomach was beginning to rumble. "I always got my own way. I thrived on it. Generosity, I'm afraid, wasn't a big part of *my* nature."

"I didn't expect it to be . . . then. Now, as a woman, I would hope you'll understand. Not my feelings so much as your father's. He has always been a strong, virile man. Hard for a daughter to comprehend, I suppose—and accept—but it's true. For such a man, being without a woman is against nature."

"I do understand." Lili fought back the sudden image of Jeremy that rose to her mind. There were men like that, men whose very essence spelled masculinity, and it tore at her heart to realize she might never see him again. She no longer felt she was in danger—plainly Chartreuse intended only kindness—but freedom from danger meant losing the man she loved. "I always did, in a way. My mother was very beautiful, but there was something . . . lost about her. Even when I was little, I sensed Papa was lonely and needed somebody. Though, of course, I didn't know exactly *how*. Only, somehow . . . well, it seemed a betrayal. As if by caring about you, he didn't love her anymore. And I suppose," she said thoughtfully, "he didn't."

Chartreuse took Lili's cup and refilled it. Then, seeing the direction her eyes were going, she dished up a plate of salad and added several tinned biscuits.

"I think perhaps it's time you learned about my relationship with your father. So you know the way things are between us."

"Oh . . . no." Lili stopped, the fork halfway to her mouth. "No, truly, I didn't intend to pry. How Papa feels about you—and you about him—is nobody's business but your own."

"And yours, for he loves you and needs you to understand. Maybe you will when you realize he loves me too. Not the wildly romantic love he once felt for your mother, but a quiet constancy that fills the empty spaces in his heart. And I love him . . . though heaven knows I didn't plan to. Or want to. For me, at first, it was an arrangement of convenience. But perhaps you know how it began?"

Lili shook her head, mouth too full of salad to respond.

"No? Gossip has a way of spreading. I wasn't sure." She had remained standing, acting the part of the casual hostess. Now she busied herself at one table, using the platters and spoons and china saucers as an excuse to keep from looking around. "I didn't have an easy life when I was young. I don't say that to win your sympathy, but because it's a fact. My mother was a free woman, but we were poor, and money was always a problem. They didn't have quadroon balls then, but there were other ways of meeting men of substance, *white* men, and I was just fourteen when I was exposed to them. I was pretty enough to attract attention, and young enough—and foolish enough—to pick the handsomest man who wanted me."

"He didn't treat you well?" Lili caught the irony in the other woman's voice.

"About as well as could be expected. He wasn't cruel, but he wasn't kind either. Like too many good-looking men—especially the very pretty sort—he had been overindulged, and his world revolved around himself. The affair continued, as is usual, until he got married. Then he wanted to renege on our agreement, and because the contract had been carelessly drawn, he got away with giving me only a small monthly allowance. Even that ended a year later, when he died."

"How awful!" Lili set the plate down and rose to refill her cup. "I can't imagine how you got by without any money. Did you . . . did you have children?"

"Only one." Her face softened for a moment, glowing from within, then reverted to the cool mask she customarily wore. "A girl. He was bitterly disappointed when she was born—he had longed for a miniature reflection of himself—but I suspect he would have liked her better as she grew. She was very beautiful, even as a youngster. Much more beautiful than her mother. And her skin was as light as yours."

"Oh." Lili sensed where the story was going. "When she got to a certain age, and it was time to make a match for her, you presented her with the same choices you had had yourself."

"I didn't want to, but what else could I do? I thought about sending her north. She was fair enough to be accepted there. Or to Europe. But where would I have gotten the money? I barely brought in enough as a milliner to make ends meet. Dances for the *gens de couleur libres* were becoming popular—white men attended all the time—and one night I took her."

Her face tightened, and she stared blankly at the wall. Bright shafts of sunlight, which had splashed so brilliantly only an instant before, had disappeared abruptly in a wash of shadow. "She hated it! God, how she hated it!

She was beautiful, but she was talented too. She wanted to be an essayist or poet, not the concubine of some spoiled rich man . . . and I wanted it for her. But there was no way I could arrange it. All I could hope was to strike a better deal for her than my mother had for me. At least her daughters would never be put in that same cruel position. The vicious cycle would end with her."

That was something Lili could understand. Like the curse on the women of her own family, going on and on generation after generation, until someone finally broke out of it.

"So you took her to the ball on Condé Street, or wherever such dances were held then," she said, putting herself in the older woman's position. "And you felt horribly guilty—you were sure you were the worst mother in the world—and every minute was an absolute misery."

"I did take her to the ball . . . and yes, I did feel guilty. But I wasn't exactly miserable. You see, it was there that I met your father."

"There? At a ball for the *gens du couleur*?" Lili could not conceal the shock in her voice.

"Does that surprise you? Your father was a very dashing *chévalier*. He still is . . . in my eyes. He loved dancing. But your mother was alive at the time. He couldn't have held a gay *soiree* in his home, nor could he in all propriety have gone without her to other private galas. The balls were a good compromise. Men of all sorts attended, and no one asked too many questions."

"But did he . . . ?"

Lili faltered, unable to imagine Papa, who believed with such passion in the dignity of all people, participating in something so degrading to women. But Chartreuse *had* pointed out that he was an extremely virile man . . .

"Did he go to choose a young lady for himself? No. He attended only to dance, though I didn't know that at the time. In fact, I had him picked out for my daughter."

"Papa? For your *daughter*? But he must have been quite old at the time!"

"He was, if you look on fifty-something as old. But you must remember, I had selected a young, comely man for myself once . . . and learned a hard lesson. I knew Don Andrés Santana by reputation. He was kind and honorable, and I had reason to believe he would be generous. When he approached me, I thought he was going to ask for my daughter, and I was prepared to drive a hard bargain. Imagine my surprise when I learned it was *me* he wanted!"

She started to laugh, genuinely. Her face crinkled up, making her look like a girl again, and Lili caught a glimpse of what it was that had captured Don Andrés' interest, and held it all these years.

"I told him it was out of the question! I was too old—I was nearly forty myself—and my previous experience had been much too unpleasant. There was nothing, I assured him, *nothing* he could offer that would make me change my mind. But he was shrewder than I thought. A house would not have tempted me, and he didn't try. Or security. Or a large cash settlement. He offered instead to take care of my daughter! A very clever man, your papa. He would educate her if I wanted, he would send her to France, where her spirit could find a home—and she would never have to offer herself for sale to the highest bidder."

Lili shuddered, understanding only too well. The auction today had been coarser, more obvious, but the principle was the same. "You sold yourself instead . . . so she wouldn't have to."

"That was what I thought, though your father was extremely attractive, and it wasn't an altogether unappealing arrangement. Naturally, he hadn't expected anything to come of that evening's dancing. There was no place we could go. I lived in a small boardinghouse, in the same room with my daughter, and his wife was at home. We rode in a carriage all night, holding hands—kissing sometimes—and by morning I desired him as much as he desired me. Three days later I moved into the house he bought for me, and we have been together ever since."

"And you have never regretted it?"

"Never."

"And your daughter?" Lili asked curiously. "What happened to her? Did she go to France as she dreamed?"

"No." Chartreuse shook her head, smiling faintly. "The situation was much too unstable. You don't remember the Revolutionary government, of course, but there were reasons why it was known as the Terror. I sent her instead to Quebec, where excellent tutoring ought to have prepared her for a brilliant career. But, being headstrong and contrary, she fell in love with a young *canadien*, a dancing master of sorts, long on charm and short on practical skills. Thank heaven your father provided an ample dowry. Now I'm the grandmother of three small boys."

Slipping over to the window, she looked out. It had begun to rain again, lightly but steadily. Water glistened on the wooden *banquettes*, and drying streets had turned once more to mud. Dark clouds massing above the rooftops hinted at wintry gales in other parts of the city.

"I don't suppose I will ever see them—or her—again. It's too long a trip for me now, and she can never come here, married to a man of a different race. He knows about her background—it makes no difference to him— but no one else does, and I suspect it's better that way."

She stared out at the deserted street, forgetting Lili for a moment as memories flooded back, feelings that still had the power to hurt. She had not been completely honest before. There *were* regrets sometimes. Not for the relationship with Don Andrés, which was pleasurable and satisfying, but for the loss of her only child. She was very much aware that her lover was old now. Soon she would be alone. But she was aware, too, that if she had it all to do over again, she would not change a single minute.

She was still there, a few seconds later, when a carriage appeared at the end of the street, rounding the corner at breakneck speed. Wheels slid to a halt in front of the house, and a man leapt out, his clothing damp, as if he had been in the storm, fair hair plastered like a cap to his head as he hurried toward the door.

Glancing back, Chartreuse saw that Lili was as yet unaware. Murmuring a hasty excuse, she slipped out of the room. There were times for talk and explanations, and times for a tactful retreat, and this was one of the latter.

Lili barely turned her head as the other woman left. She was so tired that every muscle in her body screamed with exhaustion, but she had discovered, to her surprise, that she was ravenously hungry. She had just picked up a plump ginger cake, temptingly iced in white with little sugared violets, when the sound of hurried footsteps came from the hall.

Jumping nervously, she saw the figure of a man materialize in the doorway, powerful shoulders nearly filling the narrow space.

Jeremy. Her hand tightened around the cake, crumbling it into pieces that fell unnoticed to the floor. He was hopelessly disheveled. His shirt was saturated and badly soiled—one sleeve was torn, showing glimpses of tanned skin beneath—and his hair was a terrible mess, but he had never looked so wonderful.

Whatever doubts Lili had had about this man vanished as she stood in the center of the room and gazed at him. His face alone declared the depth of his passion. Gaunt hollows showed beneath his cheekbones, and there were dark circles under his eyes, telling her he had been up all night, frantic with worry.

Not for the ransom he stood to lose, not for dreams and personal ambitions, but for *her*. Because she was as much a part of his heart as he of hers.

She opened her arms, but he was already there, catching her by the shoulders, holding her back for a moment to scan her face with anxious eyes.

"You're all right? They said you were . . . The message I got . . . But are you sure?" His voice rasped with emotion. "If anyone has harmed you, I swear I'll kill him with my bare hands!"

"No, no . . . I'm fine. Really. They terrified me half out of my mind, but they didn't . . . they didn't *do* anything. Oh, Jeremy, it was awful!" Panic returned, making her knees weak, and she started to shake all over as the hideous details of that experience came back. "I thought they were going to sell me. They said . . . they made me believe . . . when someone took me home . . ."

Jeremy pulled her against him, his lips on her hair, not kissing but comforting, longing to take away the pain and the fear.

"Oh, God, Lili. I've been a fool, such a damn fool! This is all my fault. Can you ever forgive me, my darling? I love you so much. I don't know what I would have done if you'd been hurt."

Lili raised her face to his. *Forgive?* All she wanted was to feel his arms around her, to know he cared with the whole of his heart. She touched his cheek, aware at the same moment of sticky icing on her fingers and the moisture that was flowing down the back of her hand.

Tears? Was he weeping? Her strong, proud Jeremy, who never let down his guard?

"No, love, I'm the one who's a fool. I should have known . . . I should have trusted . . ."

Then his arms were around her, lifting her gently, carrying her upstairs, finding somehow the room where she had changed, with the water still cooling in the tub. It didn't matter anymore whose fault it was, or who had played the fool. It didn't even matter what happened tomorrow. They were together and in love, and this night at least was theirs.

34

The door closed softly. Lili curled up on the bed, where Jeremy had placed her, nestling back in a pile of down pillows. It was a small room, fitted out for guests, though the furnishings were old-fashioned, and she suspected no one used it except for freshening up.

It appeared, however, that it was going to be used today.

Jeremy turned back from the door, his face enveloped in shadow, for it was getting late. Eyes glowing out of the darkness told her wordlessly once again that he loved her. Lili marveled, as always, at the way his very presence seemed to fill the room. His body appeared even larger in that cramped chamber, a potent masculine force, trapping her breath in her throat and making her pulse quicken just at the thought that he was going to come to her.

But he did not move. Surprisingly, he stood there, hesitant, almost tentative, as if he weren't sure of himself.

Jeremy unsure? Lili resisted the smile that rose to her lips. It seemed a contradiction in terms.

"Don't you think you ought to get out of those wet clothes?" she said huskily. "You'll catch your death of cold."

"I'd be happy to oblige . . . and to relieve you of that dressing gown, which, incidentally, is extremely fetching." He came and sat beside her on the edge of the bed. "I'd like nothing better than to free my body from its restraints, and yours, and lie beside you all night long."

His voice vibrated with emotion, making Lili's heart flutter like a caged butterfly in her breast. It seemed strange to think she had ever been afraid of this man. So afraid she had been ready to risk the most horrible dangers to run away from him.

"If that's what you want, what are you waiting for?"

"I think, love, I'm waiting for your permission."

Her *permission*? "Is this arrogant, aggressive Jeremy Blaze, who has never asked permission from any man or woman in his life? Since when do you *ask* for what you want?"

"I had some of the arrogance knocked out of me last night . . . and the better part of today. Do you have any idea how I felt when I discovered you were gone? How desperate I was? Besides, love . . ." His voice took on a teasing tone. "I'm not quite the blusterer you make out. I've been playing the part of a pirate and a highwayman, and the drama has gone to my head. But I do, on occasion, behave in quite a gentlemanly manner."

Turning serious, he took hold of her hand, keeping it for a minute before reluctantly letting go.

"I want you, Lili . . . I want you like hell. But I'm not going to lie to get you. What I'm asking for is tonight only . . . nothing beyond that. I sent a message to your father as soon as word reached me that you were safe. I promised he'd have you back first thing in the morning. That's a promise Chartreuse will see that I keep."

"Chartreuse?" Lili looked back at him uneasily. "Then she *was* in on it. But why? If she really loves Papa, how could she cause him such pain?"

"Pain is sometimes unavoidable, *petite*. There are things you don't understand. Things you *can't* understand. But Chartreuse does, and because of that, she acted as she has . . . even if it was sometimes against her will."

He was talking of his cause again. Lili sensed that, and she remembered suddenly how Chartreuse had spoken of sending her daughter north. The Americans, in some places at least, were abolishing slavery. Wasn't that a cause a black woman might sell out her heart—or her lover—for?

"Then . . . this is good-bye?"

"I've given my word, *petite*—I will keep it, if it tears my heart to shreds." His body ached, groin hardening and throbbing until he longed to crush her in the bruising pressure of his arms. Damn, what a fool he was! And what a mess he'd gotten them both into. "I need you to love me, Lili. Love me totally, with no doubts, no reservations, no fears—or hopes—for the morrow. I need to know that you belong to me. As . . ." His voice deepened, low and throaty. ". . . I belong to you."

Lili felt as if his face were melting in the shimmering haze that swam across the surface of her eyes. She *did* belong to him. She had from the moment she first saw him, though she hadn't known it. And she did love him. Loved him so much that nothing else mattered. Not even the aching loneliness that would be hers for the rest of her life.

"I believe you asked my permission to remove my dressing gown. I grant it now."

Slowly, almost humbly, he lifted his hands to the neck of that satin garment, playing with the edge, brushing lightly against skin that was already tingling. His eyes were questioning, as if he thought she had only been teasing and might pull away. A new emotion, humility—one he was not accustomed to—and it sat strangely on him, like a new coat that had not been cut to his size.

Lili would have smiled at that uncharacteristic awkwardness if he had not opened her robe just then, tenderly, very sensuously, and begun to slip it off her shoulders.

The fabric felt incredibly sleek as it slid away, catching briefly on the swell of her breasts, teasing nipples that were already erect with longing.

Then his eyes were questioning no longer. They were bold, as she was used to seeing them—as she loved to see them—a sultry violet-blue in the shadows. Still he did not reach for her, but rising, took a slow step back. Not touching, never touching, but playing, fondling with his eyes, caressing with looks that were both torture and exquisite delight.

Oh, the force of that deep, smoldering gaze. Longing seared through her—his longing mingling with her own—and she sensed that he was holding back, prolonging the sweetness, less for himself than for her.

Shivering with pleasure, she felt those hot, impudent eyes pass over every part of her body, dipping into the hollows of her shoulders, circling ripe, round breasts, lingering. Like brands searing into her skin, they blazed a trail down her belly, her hips, the soft inner skin of her thighs, darting boldly to where dark hair curled between her legs.

Never had she felt like this before . . . never had it been so right, so perfect. Her legs parted unconsciously, an aching, instinctive invitation for him to come to her. He held back one last moment, body taut with longing. Then he was there, devouring mouth clamped hard on hers, skin against feverish skin, and he was inside her.

Their excitement peaked quickly, surging and pulsating with each deep, sliding motion. So much had happened between them, love and longing and the threat of loss, but all that was gone now. They were just two lovers, two people who had somehow, miraculously, found each other and shared a secret destiny. Lili felt her passion rising to meet his—or was he rising to her?—and they surrendered at the same time, losing their separate identities in the whirlpool of sensation that both drained and filled their entire beings.

He did not withdraw immediately, but shifted his weight gently off her, kissing and whispering sweet words of love to ease the moment nature forced him to retreat from her body. Even then, he lay beside her, clinging as tightly as she, cradling her in arms that never wanted to let go.

It was some time before he allowed the world to intrude. When he did, he pulled himself up on one elbow, looking down at her with a face that seemed to be filled with sadness.

"I've made many mistakes with you, my darling. So many mistakes. And I have regretted them deeply, though never, I admit, when you're in my arms and we're making love. Many times I've wished I could go back and change things, start over again and make it all different."

"It seems to me," Lili said, half-teasing, "your greatest mistake is letting me go."

"I know."

"You *know*. And yet . . ."

"And yet." He traced the full, sensual lines of her lips with his finger. "I don't do these things by choice, love. I do them because my hands are tied . . . now. I cannot promise what you want to hear, but I can tell you this. If it were in my power to give you everything you desire, if I were free to marry you tonight, I would. That's more than I've ever said to any woman."

And more than she had hoped to hear. Lili knew that as his arms tightened around her again, and she tried not to think that it wasn't enough. Tried not to remember that whatever commitments Jeremy had made were stronger than his feelings for her. And for a few sweet moments, lost in the skill of his lovemaking, she succeeded.

There was time to talk later, propped up on pillows as they leaned back, still tangled in each other's arms. Haltingly Lili told him everything that had happened, from the time she had knocked at René LeClerc's door, seeking shelter and a sympathetic ear, to that horrible moment she found herself standing naked in front of four leering men, terrified that they were going to rape her.

Jeremy listened in silence, only the tautness of his arm betraying his tension, until she had finished. Only then did he finally ask the question she had been dreading.

"Why, in God's name, did you do it? Why did you run away?"

"I . . . I was afraid, Jeremy." Lili forced the words out, painfully embarrassed, but knowing he deserved an answer. "It sounds silly now, but I was just so afraid!"

She tried to explain, telling him how she had felt those first two times she saw the mulatto, in the fields at Bellefleur and later outside the blacksmith shop. When she got to the part about the conversation she had overheard—was it really only yesterday afternoon?—her voice was shaking.

"I should have realized you'd protect me. I should have had more trust. But, oh, it was awful, the way that person was talking about me. As if . . . as if I were some kind of animal! A bitch. That's what he called me. 'I'm going to tie a stone around her neck myself'—those were almost exactly his words—'and take her to the river and drown her!' "

Jeremy had drawn back as she spoke, mouth open, eyes glazed with an expression she couldn't read. Then, just as she was certain he was going to berate her for eavesdropping, he threw back his head and laughed!

"You ran away because of *that*?"

"I . . . I don't see what's so funny." Surprise mingled with indignation. "It was silly, not trusting you. I've already admitted that. But when I heard that horrible, evil man—"

"Oh, sweet, I'm sorry. I don't mean to be unkind." He controlled his amusement, but just barely. "You do have the most extraordinary imagination. It never fails to dazzle me. That 'horrible, evil man'—his name is Barnaby, by the way—sounded like he was talking about an animal because he was. Literally a bitch. A female dog. One of my prize breeding stock who had fallen ill."

"You're saying—"

"I'm saying that Barney, as the keeper of my kennels, felt the bitch ought to be destroyed. I obviously did not agree." His face twisted wryly. "As it turned out, he was right. He usually is. The crisis came last night, and she was beyond saving. Unfortunately, I had neglected to isolate her soon enough, so now it looks like I'm going to lose not one valuable animal, but several."

"A dog? This was all about a dog?" Lili shuddered as she thought of the horrors she had gone through. The degradation. The long, cold night, shivering in a cage in the yard. And the unspeakable things that would have happened if she hadn't been quick-witted enough to throw Jean Lafitte's name into the conversation. "You mean it was a *misunderstanding*? But, Jeremy, he seemed so sinister. His eyes. They're like vacant mirrors. As if there's nothing behind them."

"In a way," Jeremy said gently, "there isn't. Barney is what's kindly referred to as 'slow.' All his wits weren't there when he was born. People tend to be frightened by differences they don't understand, but he's wonderful with animals, which is part of why I bought him. He's the only slave I own—I don't believe in the institution—but I can protect him more easily this way. And he's not so dull of wit, incidentally, that he didn't manage to save you this afternoon."

"*He* saved me? No, wait a minute. It was Chartreuse—"

"Yes, but how do you think Chartreuse knew where you were? And what kind of trouble you were in? It was the purest bit of luck, love. That weasel LeClerc—God help the slimy bastard when I get my hands on him!—has an exceptional manservant, a slave—"

"Yes, Claude. I know. He actually seemed sorry about what was happening. But, of course, there was nothing he could do."

"Not directly, no. But like many a restless bondman,

he has made the acquaintance of the Lafitte brothers. Not all the smugglers of Grande-Terre were born free. When LeClerc made sure he was out of town this afternoon—on an unscheduled 'pleasure jaunt'—Claude headed for the smithy on Royal Street. Ironically, the men were all out helping to search for you."

"Except . . . Barney."

"We had left him to take messages, fortunately. He recognized Claude's description and was instantly distraught. You may not think much of him, sweet, but he is quite taken with you. Like many a simple creature, he responds to beauty, and you are very beautiful. Claude remained to pass on the word—neither man can read or write—and Barney went for Chartreuse."

And that was how she was rescued? Not because of the wonderfully clever way she had thought to mention Lafitte, or anything she had done for herself? Just because a slave had taken pity on her, and a frightening-looking man thought she was beautiful?

Her sense of humor returning, she started to laugh.

"Things aren't always what they seem, are they? You can't count on anything. Not even your own ill-founded assumptions."

"No." He turned solemn eyes on her face. "No, things *aren't* what they seem . . . at all. But . . ." His mood lightening, he grinned rakishly. "Some assumptions are safer than others. And some you can *definitely* count on."

Lili followed his gaze downward.

"You are insatiable," she teased, trying to look shocked.

"And you aren't?"

He attempted to draw her closer, but she wedged both hands against his shoulders, playfully holding him back. There was something wonderfully tantalizing about being called insatiable, making her feel wanton and reckless. Making her long to do things, dare things . . .

"Perhaps," she conceded, meaning yes, and enjoying the fact that he knew it. "But why all the hurry? Aren't you the one who taught *me* to take time and savor every sweetly sinful moment?"

"Sinful? What an intriguing concept."

"And just look at you! Why, you must have been riding like a demon through the streets. You've gotten hopelessly mud-spattered—right through your clothes! I seem to recall, under similar circumstances, you felt the need to clean me up." She threw a glance at the high-sided copper tub in the corner. "It's too bad we took so long with, uh . . . other things. The water is quite cold. I would have dunked you in and scrubbed you from head to toe."

"You could saturate a cloth, as I did for you, and sponge me off. As thoroughly as you like."

"Could I?"

"You *could*."

Lili eyed a thick, soft towel where she had dropped it on the floor. He had been teaching her, slowly, to become familiar with his body, casting aside the inhibitions that had been drilled into her, and she was an avid learner. But there were moments, like now, when she was still tentative, not exactly sure what he wanted, or how much she ought to do.

Only this was their last night together. The last time she would ever feel free—and loving—with a man.

"Yes, you're right—I think I could."

She picked up the towel, and kneeling by the tub, dipped one end into the water. It gave her a giddy feeling to know he was lying there motionless on the bed, just waiting for her. She had wanted once before, that afternoon she danced in the square, to guide the course of their lovemaking, to control for a few brief moments his destiny as well as her own. But she had gone about it clumsily, trying to force his responses.

This time she was going to seduce him slowly, tenderly. And this time she was going to succeed.

The water was cooler than she had imagined, but the sultry heat of the afternoon lingered in the small room, and the shudder that ran through his body as she drew the towel across his naked chest had nothing to do with the chill. She was a little amused to realize she had not been exaggerating before. He *was* dirty . . . all over. Mud was caked in the strangest places—the nape of his neck, his thighs, behind his knees, even his ankles, which had been covered by high riding boots—and it gave her great pleasure finding every one.

Never before had she given herself the luxury of exploring his body with the undistracted attention he always gave hers. At his encouragement, she had kissed and fondled, her hands increasingly bold, and even her lips, but her eyes had always been surreptitious. Now, unashamedly, she devoured him visually, studying and memorizing the tantalizing differences that made him so virile and unique. The varying patterns formed by powerfully etched muscles as they strained across his arms and shoulders, hugging his thighs, bulging out from the back of strong calves . . . the leanness of his lower torso, hips sleek and compact, buttocks firm, with sinew hard as bone . . . the provocative line of hair that ran down his belly, teasing her to follow . . .

Was this what it was? The mastery he had always had over her? Not the force of a dynamic personality, but the sheer pleasure he took in her body? The way he reveled in every part of her?

The towel was losing its effectiveness, but she couldn't tear herself away, even for a few seconds, to moisten it in the water. It was barely damp as she brought it to his groin with an intimacy she had never dared before. She had held him sometimes, there, she had done the things he taught her, but she had never felt quite so free to look . . . or feel.

"Is it all right?" she said, suddenly shy. "To touch you like this?"

"It's all right," he replied huskily. "You can touch me any way that pleases you."

"But I want it to please you too."

"God, yes . . . it pleases me. *You* please me . . . very much."

Lili dropped the towel, letting her hands do the touching now. It was amazing, how hard he had grown in such a short time, ramrod stiff beneath that thin layer of skin, coarse hair at the base contrasting tantalizingly with the smoothness of the tip. This was the essence of him, the maleness. She didn't ever want to forget how he looked, how he felt in her hand.

Then, unable to bear it any longer, she eased him back, pressing him into the pillows as she positioned herself above him.

"I am going to make love to you now, as you have made love to me. And you are going to let me do it."

"Am I?"

"You said I could do anything that pleases me . . . and this pleases me."

She plunged downward, forcing that hard male member deep into her pliant softness. The response that surged through him seemed to ripple directly from his body into hers. With a quivering sigh, Lili eased back, almost losing him, then pushed down again, back and down, back and down, finding a rhythm that inflamed and provoked. He was hers now, as never before—completely hers—and she abandoned herself to a wild new boldness that swept away the last inhibitions, making her for the first time completely and absolutely a partner in their love-making.

Teasing, she pulled back again, leaving him briefly, her fingers running down the shaft of his manhood, their bodies not quite touching. Jeremy stirred, but he didn't try to move, sensing and enjoying the unexpected wantonness that thrilled him as much as her. She had always been beautiful, and exciting, but hers had been the challenge of dormant femininity waiting to be awakened. Now she was a sultry temptress any man would adore.

She sank down, engulfing him again, and he groaned with pleasure.

"Ummm, love . . . I think I was wrong. I haven't made any mistakes with you." Her full breasts dangled down, brushing his lips as he spoke. "I'm sorry you've been hurt, but I'm sure as hell not sorry I kidnapped you. I like the way it's turned you into a woman."

She let her tongue play teasingly with his ear, sensing from his reaction that it was driving him mad. "You think I wouldn't have become a woman anyway?"

"Not in a Creole setting." His hands itched to form around her buttocks, forcing the swift, sure movements that would lead to culmination, and it was all he could do to lie still. "There are too many rules, proprieties . . . all that damned baggage a woman has to carry. You can't step out of the parlor and into the bedroom, and take those ladylike manners off with your gown."

"Not even with a man like you?"

The minx. She was using her tongue again, darting along the edges of his lips, too quick for him to catch her in his mouth.

"Maybe, in time. But who the hell wants to wait until

he's middle-aged to have a wanton in his bed? You needed this, Lili—this break with everything you've known. You needed it to dare to be yourself. And no matter what happens—God help me, *no matter what*—I'm glad I gave it to you."

He gave in at last, his hands going where they longed to be, his hips coaxing hers to the frenzy that could no longer be staved off. She was not making love to him now . . . or he to her. They were making love *with* each other, and all the rapture of the world was theirs.

35

Madame Jean-Baptiste Cavarelle . . .
Lili stared dully at the ornate gilt-edged mirror.
Damask draperies had been pulled across the windows,
muffling the sounds of the busy Place d'Armes, and
banks of candles cast a softening glow on her reflection.
Any minute now they would be calling her to the
cathédrale. Hairdressers had been busy all morning, arranging stubborn tresses into a pair of thick braids, twined
with strands of pearls around her head, and delicately
shimmering lace floated over her shoulders.

Or perhaps it ought to be *Mrs*. Jean-Baptiste Cavarelle.
New Orleans was an American city now. No doubt that
was how she would be known in the new house on the
outskirts beyond the Faubourg Ste. Marie.

She took a step back, ironically aware that she made a
picture-perfect bride. Her gown was the most exquisite
imported satin, copied from the latest Parisian illustra-
tions; her veil had probably blinded half a dozen lace-
makers in a convent in Belgium; her slippers were so
thinly soled they would not last to be worn again. Even
her hair, modishly tamed, showed flashes of red only in
the ringlets that tumbled onto her forehead, and her
skin, which had already begun to lose its tan, was liberally dusted with pearl powder.

Perhaps too liberally, she thought as she turned from
the mirror and glanced toward the hall. For the first time
in her life, she had had to dab rouge on her cheeks to give
them a healthy glow.

Voices spilled through the half-open door. Lili stood
just behind it, picking out her father's baritone as he
greeted various friends and colleagues in the small house

that had been put at their disposal across from the cathedral. A thoughtful gesture, for although it was only a few blocks from home, the rains had stopped for the season, and dust had a way of seeping even into closed carriages.

No girlish giggles mingled with the hum of masculine conversation, and Lili realized, rather guiltily, that Simone had already left. She had not been particularly kind to her cousin in the week since she had come home. With the flurry of preparations and last-minute fittings, it had been easy enough to avoid her at the house. But just a few minutes ago, she had burst into the room, bubbling with excitement and eager to help. And Lili, unable to forget what had been going on while she was gone—what was still going on, if the girl's flushed looks and secret smiles were any indication—could not bear the sight of her.

It was not that she hated Simone. She didn't even mind that the girl seemed totally unrepentant, as if somehow she had managed to justify what was soon going to be an adulterous affair with her cousin's husband. Simone was as much a victim as she. Barely more than a child, she had been caught up in pretty daydreams, trapped by a man's honeyed words.

And if their positions were reversed—if Simone were the bride today, the dashing bridegroom Jeremy Blaze— would *she* be any different?

Oh, God . . . Jeremy.

She turned away from the door, panicking for a moment, aware suddenly of what she was about to do . . . and what she was leaving behind. They hadn't even had time to say good-bye to each other. It had been just dawn when the carriage had pulled up in front of the Santana house. Such a short trip—it had gone so fast, she hadn't even realized they were there—and suddenly the door had been open, and he had been leaping out, lifting her down.

Just for a second his face had seemed as stricken as hers, and Lili had thought he was going to say something. But he only bent his head, kissing her lightly, not on the lips, but on the cheek. And then the street had been empty again, with only the sound of carriage wheels echoing in the distance . . . and he had been gone.

Lili turned back to the mirror, trying not to think of the love that was lost forever as she checked her gown

and veil one last time. Like it or not, she was beginning a
new life, a life that depended, at least in part, on her own
resilience. She couldn't afford to dwell on regrets.

A black velvet jeweler's box rested on a table in front
of the glass, and she laid a hand on it tentatively. Jean-
Baptiste Cavarelle. A handsome man, charming . . . a bit
amoral perhaps, but not unreasonably so by the standards of the day . . . and generous. And rich. There was
only one thing wrong. She didn't love him.

She had hoped, foolishly, that morning she had slipped
back into the house, that she would arrive to find everything in disarray and the wedding postponed. But all the
preparations had gone on anyway, as if Papa was sure
she'd be back in time. The gown was ready, except for
last-minute touches, and even the trousseau; and arrangements had been completed for the ritual in the cathedral
and the elaborate party afterward, which would last for
several days.

And all of this had been accomplished without M'mère,
who, to Lili's surprise, had been packed off to the
Ursulines, apparently so she wouldn't give away the secret. Poor, darling Papa. In the midst of all that frantic
worry, he had thought to protect her reputation. No one
was going to know that his little girl had been kidnapped
by a notorious rake!

Oddly, though, he hadn't *looked* worried. Lili picked
up the case, running her fingers idly across the velvet. He
had been overjoyed to see her, of course, and relieved.
But it didn't look as if he had been pining the weeks
away. In fact, he seemed to have gained weight, and
several times she had actually caught him whistling! Papa
had never whistled in his life.

She had tried once, with the only argument she could
think of, to get him to call off the wedding. Working up
her courage, she had gone to his study and forced herself
to hint, subtly at first, that things had happened during
those weeks which made her a somewhat less-than-
"suitable" bride. When he had densely refused to catch
her meaning, she had made things clearer and clearer,
until at last, knowing it was her only chance, she had
blurted the truth in words no one could possibly misunderstand.

But instead of looking shocked, his face remained
impassive.

"We anticipated that . . . naturally. This man, Blaze, has a certain reputation. But Monsieur Cavarelle has generously agreed to overlook any little . . . problems. Especially as you don't seem in the family way." He studied her coolly. "You aren't, are you?"

Lili shook her head. She had had proof, the very morning she arrived home, that that part of the legendary curse at least was broken.

"No, I'm not, but—"

"Well, then, it's settled. And fairly so. Under the circumstances, it would be most unchivalrous to hold something like that against you. It's hardly your fault, what that brute did to you."

Lili swallowed hard. "It's not what *he* did to *me*, Papa. It's what we did to each other. He never forced me. Never. I went to him willingly. And I was . . . I was happy in his bed!"

That brought the reaction she had expected. His face went ashen, all the color ebbing away, but somehow he managed to compose himself.

"My mind is made up, daughter. You are going to marry Jean-Baptiste Cavarelle in the Cathédrale de St. Louis Monday next. There's no going back. Especially now. And may I suggest," he added dryly, "you curb that impetuous tongue when you converse with your new husband. We wouldn't want your marriage getting off to an awkward start."

An awkward start? Lili jolted back to the present with a bitter laugh. The man was having an affair with her cousin, and she was desperately in love with someone else! How could things be more awkward than that?

She glanced down to see that she was still holding the jeweler's box. Snapping it open, she gazed at a magnificent pendant, sparkling diamonds encircling a perfect round sapphire, paler than the usual deep blue, a color that reminded her poignantly of Jeremy's eyes. It had been a present from her bridegroom, though she hadn't wanted or expected it. In fact, she had sent word through Don Andrés that the only wedding gift she desired was a new houseman—the slave Claude, who belonged to one René LeClerc.

It had been her last act of rebellion, and the one thing she had done since she got home that seemed to surprise Papa. His eyebrows had gone up, but he hadn't said anything, and the message had been duly relayed. What her fiancé had thought, she had no idea, but no reply had come back. And in the morning, the necklace had been there.

She looked down at it again. She had, in truth, been struck breathless when she first opened the box. It was the most exquisite piece of jewelry she had ever seen. Jean-Baptiste Cavarelle, she had to admit grudgingly, had excellent taste. If Jeremy had given her something like this . . .

But Jeremy hadn't given it to her. She took it out impulsively, setting the empty box on the table. Jeremy hadn't given it to her, and Jeremy wasn't going to meet her at the altar today.

She held the exquisite gem for a moment on the palm of her hand. She had thought, before, that she wouldn't wear it, that she'd leave her neck defiantly bare when she walked down the aisle. But Papa was right. This marriage was awkward enough without antagonizing her new husband by spurning his gift.

She had just finished clasping it around her neck when she turned to find Don Andrés looking exceptionally handsome in black velvet in the doorway. His eyes were shining with pride, and enough love to quell whatever last resentment she might have felt at this wedding that was being forced on her.

"Papa . . . ?"

"It's time, daughter. We must go."

The sky outside was crystal bright, cloudless as a sultry summer day. A warm breeze drifted, water-scented, from the river, and new leaves rustled faintly on young maples lining the wrought-iron fence around the Place d'Armes.

The square was more crowded than usual for a weekday late afternoon. Bankers and merchants strolled past, prolonging their midday break, and every housewife seemed to be taking the long way round to the market by the levee. Curiosity was in the air, with much glancing over shoulders, and an occasional indiscreet hand pointing directly at the house where the Santana girl was rumored to be changing for her marriage to the most eligible bachelor in the Creole community. It was a lovely day for a wedding, Monday, of course—for Saturdays were considered vulgar, and Friday was the day of public hangings, which took place on the gallows in the center of the Place.

All pretense at discretion vanished as the door opened and Lili appeared on her father's arm. Not a watching eye was disappointed. Her gown was exquisite, flattering enough to intrigue the men, and so wonderfully *au courant*, the women were sure it must have come from Paris. The long train was white imperial satin, edged with sprays of roses embroidered in shimmering silver, a delicate motif charmingly picked up on satin caps that extended over the short puffed sleeves. By contrast, the high-waisted underdress was almost daringly simple, its rounded neck trimmed with white crepe ruching and silver lace. More lace showed in the wedding fan, silver again, which she carried with dainty white roses in place of a more traditional orange-blossom bouquet.

Lili lingered for a moment on the stoop, acutely aware of all the attention. Knowing it was expected, she managed a vaguely dreamy smile as she started slowly around the periphery of the square, her train supported by faithful retainers, some of whom had come out of retirement for the occasion.

If only they knew, she thought, those watching mamas with tears of nostalgia and envy on their lashes. If only they knew how miserable she was. And how desperately she wished she were almost anyplace else!

Or perhaps they did know. She paused, waiting as a cloth was laid out for her to cross the road without damaging dainty satin slippers. In a city where many a bride did not love, or even know, her bridegroom, wedding-day qualms were hardly unusual. And few mamas, and even fewer papas, were inclined to take them seriously.

A small group was waiting when they reached the steps of the cathedral. Lili's stomach contracted as she caught sight of Simone, who naturally had been chosen to stand beside her during the ceremony. If there were any way she could have hurried past, she would have. But the girl, seemingly oblivious of a week of tension and snubs, was already detaching herself from the others.

"Oh, Lili . . ." Her little heart-shaped face was pink with excitement as she hurried forward. Dark eyes glowed almost unnaturally bright. "You look so . . . *elegant*. I knew you'd be pretty—brides are always pretty—but you must be the loveliest that ever was."

Lili tried to draw back, but the girl had caught hold of her hands, and it was impossible to free herself without causing a scene.

"You're exaggerating, Simone. I'm probably the only bride you've ever seen. You've never been to a wedding before."

"No, but . . ." Simone flushed shyly. "I used to come to the square sometimes on Mondays when I was a little girl. I liked to watch the brides as they went into the cathedral. And you *are* the prettiest."

"Thank you." Lili forced a smile, sensing that the girl meant what she was saying. "You look very pretty too. That gown becomes you."

In fact, Simone did look pretty. Much prettier than Lili had ever seen her, though the dress she was wearing, oddly, was almost a copy of her own. The extravagantly rich satin had been tinted pale blue, and the roses that edged the modified train were white instead of silver, but the effect was startlingly similar. She even had a blue veil, spun through with strands of gossamer white that glittered like mist in the sunlight.

As if she were a bride herself, Lili thought, shocked, and wondered if the resemblance had occurred to Simone. Was she daydreaming even now that it was she and not her cousin who would walk down the aisle in a few minutes to wed the man she truly wanted?

It took all her effort to force herself to concentrate on what the girl was saying.

". . . a perfect day for a wedding. Everything is just right. You're going to be so happy . . . the happiest bride in the world!" She paused, blushing again. "Well . . . *one* of the happiest."

"Do you think so?" Lili couldn't control the bitterness in her voice as she searched her cousin's face, but not so much as a trace of jealousy showed. What had he done to her, this man? What had he said to convince her? Had he really made her believe two women could share one man, and both be deliriously happy?

"I *know* it," she said. "And I am happy for you. I love you so much, Lili. You're my cousin—my *sister*—and I'll always love you. I want everything to be right for you."

And she did. Lili pulled her hands back, terrified for an instant that she was going to burst into tears. In spite of everything, the child really did love her. Her heart felt as if it were breaking, though whether for herself or Simone, she did not know. Then suddenly everyone was moving, and she was being ushered into the darkened vestibule of the cathedral. A bulky form materialized out of nowhere, coming toward her. M'mère, so resplendent in mauve silk instead of her usual gray, Lili didn't recognize her at first.

In spite of herself she had to smile. M'mère had surprised her by choosing to remain with the Ursulines, not even coming back for a short visit when Lili had returned home. Now, eager to make up for lost time, she plainly longed to crush the young bride against her ample bosom— but, ever practical, she couldn't muss the expensive gown! So she contented herself instead with rearranging the ruffles at Lili's neck, and pretending the curls on her forehead were not already perfect.

"You are the most beautiful of all my girls . . . *la plus belle de mes enfants*. Even your dear Maman was not so beautiful on her wedding day. But then, her heart was heavy with grief."

"And mine, of course, is still untouched." Somehow Lili managed to keep her tone light. She could hardly blame M'mère for not understanding. Only Papa knew that her heart—and body—had been given to another man. And he wasn't likely to have said anything about it. "I'm just a silly, frivolous child."

"Not so much a child anymore. You are *la plus belle*, yes . . . but *la plus brave aussi*. There is a strength inside you, you do not yet know. This life you go to will be happy, I promise you . . . *very* happy."

Happy, again. Lili tried not to let her desperation show. Why was it that everyone thought—Don Andrés, M'mère, even foolish little Simone, who ought to have known better—that all a woman needed was a man, *any* man, beside her at the altar, and she would automatically be happy?

"You should have married, M'mère," she said gently, "and had a dozen children of your own. You fuss too much over me."

"I almost did marry . . . once," the woman said unexpectedly. "But that was a long time ago, and . . . things happened. Don't look at me in such a stricken way. I have never been sorry. You are a good girl, *p'tite*, even if you do have a will of your own. Now you are doing as your papa says. And trust me, you will not have the littlest *soupçon* of regret."

The start of the wedding was delayed for several minutes as the old woman was escorted to her seat. Sounds echoed back from somewhere deep in the cathedral. The musicians her father had hired, playing somber, sacred music . . . a low murmur of conversation, hushed as always when people spoke in church . . . but here in the vestibule it was so quiet Lili almost imagined she could hear the pounding of her own heart.

This is it, she thought with a dull sense of unreality as Papa led her to the aisle. This is really it. I am going to marry this man. I am going to join him at the altar, and say the words . . . and take the ring . . . and I will be his wife.

And what would he expect of her then? What would happen when he took her to his bed, anticipating the same enthusiasm he obviously received from Simone? How was his ego going to take the fact that she could never respond to him?

The great cavern of a cathedral was dim, even with the glow of hundreds of candles, and a cloying odor of incense hung in the air. The garish brightness of the painted walls, the sensuous greens and purples that never failed to shock visitors to the city, were so muted they could hardly be distinguished. Lili was intensely conscious of a slender figure standing at the end of the long aisle, impeccably attired in dark colors, as befitted the solemnity of the occasion.

A second man stood beside him, half turned away, tall and broad-shouldered. Lili's pulse quickened when she saw him. Jeremy . . . he was so like Jeremy.

Angrily she forced her eyes down, hating herself for the thrill that ran through her veins. Was this always going to happen? Was her heart forever doomed to flutter at the sight of someone who merely resembled him? Even on the day of her wedding to another man?

She lowered her head, letting the veil fall forward, partially obscuring her vision. Everything was hazy now, impossible to make out through a shimmer of white lace. Even those two dark figures remained indistinct as she approached the altar.

She did not see the face of the slender man in front, or she would have been aware of a faint smile forming on his lips. She did not even see as he stepped aside, and the other took his place. Then a hand was gripping hers, warm and strong, tightening around her fingers.

Funny, she hadn't expected his hand to feel strong.

Looking up, she found herself staring into eyes as blue as the pendant around her neck.

36

The wrong man. Lili had the strangest feeling as she stood there, her hand still in his, too startled to move, that she was marrying the wrong man. It was as if she had somehow stumbled into the wrong church and gotten into the middle of the wrong ceremony!

Just for an instant she thought giddily that she was making it up. That she wanted Jeremy to be there so badly, hungered for him so deeply, she was imagining his rugged face gazing down at her, his sapphire eyes filling with lights of laughter.

But then she looked again, and it *was* Jeremy's face. And the amusement in his eyes was distinctly real.

She would never know how she got through that interminable ceremony without fainting. The cathedral suddenly seemed excruciatingly hot, and beads of sweat dotted her hairline as she tried desperately to force her mind to work. What was he doing here? How had he managed to take the place of the man she was supposed to marry?

And why wasn't Papa jumping up from his seat, bellowing with rage?

Somehow she managed to concentrate enough to hear what the priest was saying, to make all the appropriate answers in all the appropriate places . . . and Jeremy was answering too. Only he wasn't answering as Jeremy Blaze, or Jérème Blaise, or anything of the sort. He was making his responses in the name Jean-Baptiste Cavarelle!

Stunned, she listened as the priest pronounced them man and wife. Then that same strong hand was guiding her gently to the side, and Simone was stepping forward— with the man Lili had expected to marry herself! A few minutes later, they had spoken the same vows, though without the elaborate religious service around them, and suddenly her cousin was married to someone who apparently called himself Julien Lafourchette.

An intense sense of betrayal surged through her as the two couples started down the aisle, Lili and her bridegroom in the lead, Simone following with her new husband. She knew she was being childish. She had just left the altar with the only man she would ever love. She ought to be thrilled, no matter what the reason. She ought to be on her knees thanking the saints that her life was not over after all.

Instead, she was trembling with fury.

He had deceived her! The whole thing was clear now, as it should have been the instant she saw him. Deceived and manipulated, he and Papa too—for Don Andrés must have had a hand in this! And no doubt he was pleased as punch at how clever he'd been!

"I hate you!" she hissed under her breath as they reached the still-empty vestibule.

His teeth flashed white in the shadows. "I'm sure you do, *petite*."

"And you think it's funny! Damn you, Jeremy! You're . . . you're a despicable cad!"

"Jean-Baptiste," he said, not bothering to contradict anything else. "The name is Jean-Baptiste. You might as well get used to it." Bending toward her, he whispered in her ear, "You're beautiful when you're angry."

The retort that comment so richly deserved was lost in a sudden rush of people gathering around. Swept along with the crowd, Lili felt herself being drawn out into the sunlight. Everyone was talking at once, clamoring for an introduction to her husband, whom no one seemed to have met, and asking a thousand questions. Her wedding, of course, had been anticipated for weeks, but Simone's had come as a complete surprise. It was all Lili could do to keep anybody from guessing that she'd been as shocked as they when her cousin stepped up to the priest.

Out of the corner of her eye she could see Papa, looking smugly pleased as he shook hands with this old friend or that. And keeping safely away from me! she thought, seething inside. She could hardly wait to get at him and tell him exactly how she felt!

She finally had her chance when he put her into the open carriage, festooned with satin and white roses, that

would carry the Cavarelles at the head of a long wedding
procession to their new home.

"You tricked me!" she accused hotly. "Don't try to
deny it, Papa! Everything you told me was a lie. You had
this planned all along. You sent me into the parlor that
afternoon knowing full well the man I was going to meet
wasn't my future husband!"

"Wasn't that the same afternoon you asked if I had
picked someone 'horrid' and 'hateful' for you?" Don
Andrés was chuckling unrepentantly as he helped her
into the carriage. "Well, daughter, what do you think of
my selection now?"

Lili slid to the front of the seat, leaning forward so
only he could hear.

"I think, Papa, you might have asked my opinion
before going to so much trouble. It's just possible I
would have said yes and saved you this elaborate charade."

"Oh, I doubt that. At any rate, it wasn't a chance I
was prepared to take. Ever since you were a little girl,
your head has been filled with dreams of the 'Fleurie
curse.' The only man you thought you could love was a
man beyond the pale of convention."

Lili gasped, beginning to catch on. "But those were
childish fantasies, Papa!"

"Perhaps, but any suitably arranged marriage would
have filled you with bodings of disaster. And dutiful
obedience, as I recall, has never been one of your many
delightful qualities. Now, be honest. Would you have
given any choice of mine a fair chance? Or would you
have decided, sight unseen, that you wanted no part of
him? It does seem to me the words 'horrid' and 'hateful'
were thrown out before you even met him."

"Well . . ." Lili squirmed. She *had* been determined to
dislike the man, even after she'd peered into the parlor
and seen that he was young and quite exceptionally handsome. But still . . . "You were wrong to play with my
feelings like that. And there wasn't any point to it! You're
my father. Even if I objected, you'd have won in the end.
You didn't have to trick me. You could have forced me
to marry him."

"*Forced* you? Without love? Or any hope for love in
the future? No, daughter, I didn't want that kind of life
for you. Question my methods, if you will . . . but not
the results."

He was still laughing as Jean-Baptiste Cavarelle came up and joined them. Seeing him, Lili felt her temper flare, and forgetting about Papa, she prepared to give this arrogant, impossible man a piece of her mind!

But before she could even open her mouth, he forestalled her with a maddening grin.

"Shhhh, sweet. Before you utter the charming endearments I see on your lips, I beg you to recall that there are well-wishers all around. Smile nicely . . . and blush if you're still capable of it. And for pity's sake, keep your voice down. You wouldn't want to besmirch your reputation."

"My *reputation*?" Lili looked, exasperated, from one man to the other. "Were you thinking of my reputation, either of you, when you plotted all this? If word had gotten out that I spent weeks in the bayous with a man to whom I was not married, my reputation would have been 'besmirched' forever. Even if he did later decide to make an honest woman of me!"

"Hush, love . . . remember those dulcet tones."

"And no one did find out," Papa added, keeping his own voice down. "I took great care to make sure nothing leaked out. I even sent M'mère to the Ursulines for fear she'd let something slip and set the servants' tongues wagging."

"Yes—and kept her there until the wedding!" Lili replied tartly. "Just in case she took pity and decided to tell me the truth." And that, of course, was why he'd been worried that she might be in the "family way." Because a baby in eight months instead of nine or ten would set even more tongues wagging! Choice barbs rose to her lips, but Jean-Baptiste was already in the carriage beside her, and it was beginning to move, leaving Papa behind on the steps of the cathedral.

There was plenty of opportunity for questions and answers on the long ride to the new house, which Lili had not yet seen, though Simone had tried several times to coax her to drive by. All she knew was that it was past the Faubourg Ste. Marie, or St. Mary, as the Americans were calling it, in what had been plantation fields a short time before.

She was riding forward, and Jeremy—no, Jean-Baptiste; why was she having such a hard time with that name? —was opposite her. She was so furious she longed to ignore him, keeping her face in a set smile as she nodded right and left to all the people who had gathered to watch them pass. But there were too many things she was dying to know.

"I understand about Papa. He's always had a compulsion to manage my life. But what on earth possessed *you* to do something so crazy?"

"Ah, well, I fell in love. Love has a way of doing that to a man. Smile, *petite*, and wave prettily. See, people are looking down from that window over there. I saw you one day on the levee, thrashing some poor lout who'd dared to abuse a puppy, and I knew I had to have you."

Of course! That day on the levee. She had thought someone was watching, then and later, when she'd gone back for the roses.

"But that still doesn't explain things. If you wanted me, why didn't you come to Papa and ask for my hand? A normal, decent man brings his own flowers. He doesn't arrange for a lady to get them herself so he can stand in the shadows and leer."

"That wasn't my choice," he said dryly. "I would have preferred, as you put it, to bring my own roses. I had just come back from France, fully prepared to settle down at last. But no sooner had I stepped off the ship than I found myself involved in certain political activities, which kept me from mingling with proper Creole society. And then I saw you, and I realized it wasn't a proper Creole lady I wanted at all. I wanted a highly improper hussy, with fire in her hair and a tongue that would burn through solid oak! In short, I wanted you. And the only way I could have you was to play along with your father."

"I suppose you agreed with him. You thought I'd automatically reject you because of some silly curse?"

"No. Actually I thought you'd be wild about me. I'm not inexperienced with women, love, and there is an attraction between us. Don Andrés, however, didn't see it that way. A strong-willed man, your father. Even the lure of the Cavarelle name couldn't sway him."

"And I don't imagine you tried very hard!" Her eyes flashed as she faced him, completely forgetting that people might still be watching. "It must have amused you. Sending your friend in your place. Were you so sure he wouldn't win me over? This Julien La . . . La . . ."

"Julien Lafourchette. My friend and half-brother. His

father, Lorenzo Lafourchette, was married to my mother. After they died, I sent for him to join me in France, which is why no one knows either of us here. And no, I wasn't worried. Your papa assured me you'd approach him with about as much warmth as an iceberg . . . and he's a very resourceful fellow. When he was afraid you might be wavering, he made a point of flirting with your cousin. And making sure you'd seen from the window."

"Oh." Lili turned away. They were just passing "neutral ground," the broad open space that separated the American and Creole sections of town. "He's very loyal, your brother. He didn't have any qualms about this?"

"A few. But as you say, he's loyal. And, of course, there was a reward in it for him."

"A reward?" In spite of herself, Lili looked back, curious.

"The hand of the fair Simone. Don Andrés had agreed to the marriage in exchange for Julien's cooperation. It was also, as I'm sure the wily old scoundrel knew, the best arrangement he could make for the girl. My brother may not have money of his own—his father spent every cent that came his way—but I've seen to it that he's comfortably situated. And naturally, Don Andrés provided a generous dowry for his ward."

"Naturally." Lili feigned interest in the bridal roses she was still clutching in her hand. Of course Papa had provided for Simone! In all the fussing over her cousin's future, she had forgotten how generous he was, and how seriously he took family responsibilities. Hadn't he even arranged a dowry for Chartreuse's daughter? "That's why Julien did it, then. So the son of Lorenzo Lafourchette could marry into a proud, if impoverished lineage."

"It was an excellent match, from his point of view, based on convenience, of course, rather than affection, but most Creole marriages are. I don't think he was too enthusiastic at first, though he seems to have warmed to the girl in recent weeks." He leaned forward, his voice teasing her to glance up again. "I wouldn't be surprised if they presented me with a niece or nephew a little ahead of schedule."

Lili looked him right in the eye.

"You could have told me, Jer . . . Jean-Baptiste. Not at first, maybe, but later, when you knew I was growing to care for you."

"I could have," he agreed, settling back in his seat and looking amused. "But I didn't."

Lili barely managed to hold her temper. He looked just like Papa, so smug and self-satisfied, she could gladly have hit him! The road was empty now, so she didn't have to keep up pretenses, but it would hardly do to stand up in the carriage and whack her new husband over the head with her wedding bouquet. When she had him alone, however . . .

"This was all Papa's idea, I suppose," she said evenly. "Or did you add some embellishments of your own?"

"A few here and there, but mostly the credit goes to Don Andrés. He wanted to follow the legend as closely as possible, and circumstances played into his hands. The physical resemblance, for example. I'm fair-haired and blue-eyed, like that first treacherous lover on a lane somewhere in Normandy. And, of course, Mardi Gras was coming up, so it could be arranged for you to see me first in a mask."

"They were in Brittany by that time. Lili-Ange and her 'treacherous lover.' And how could you be so sure I'd go to the quadroon ball? I didn't tell anyone—I didn't even know myself! I decided at the last minute on impulse."

His lips twitched faintly. "We slipped up a little there. Your papa assumed you'd be attending one of the private *bals*. He was so sure he knew which one, I even left my coach there, with the costume inside. Fortunately, I persuaded a young man on Condé Street to part with his mask for an exorbitant sum. And even more fortunately, by the purest coincidence, Chartreuse was enjoying the dancing that evening. She knew what was going on, of course, and while she didn't approve, she sent her man for the carriage."

"And from then on, everything went exactly as you had planned." It was all falling into place. The dress she had worn on the levee, obviously cut to his taste . . . the way he had pretended to be a highwayman, spreading rumors weeks before he appeared . . . even the roses that had been on the table that first morning at Bellefleur. He had known she would respond to roses because there were roses in the legend.

"Exactly. How could it fail? It was a perfect trap, baited, of course, with irresistible charm . . . and my natural animal magnetism. You were bound to fall into it."

Bound to? Damn the man's arrogance. Lili bit her lip
to keep from answering back. He was needling her. Just
waiting until she couldn't resist lashing out—then he was
going to laugh and tell her to be careful because servants
would be peering through the windows as they approached
the house! Her precious reputation again! She wasn't
sure she cared anymore.

She barely noticed the exquisitely proportioned building, set in a grove of magnolias and young fruit trees, as
they drove through an elaborately ornamented wrought-
iron gate onto a circular drive. Any other time, she
would have been entranced, gawking like a schoolgirl at
the massive central structure, stuccoed brick, with its
generous pillared veranda and wings that swept out gracefully on either side. It was a truly magnificent house, at
its best in the spring sunlight, glittering white against a
spacious backdrop of green-velvet lawn. Not even the
great plantations along the river—including Bellefleur
itself—were so imposing. Or so beautiful.

But right now, all she could think was that the other
carriages seemed to have fallen behind, and they would
have a moment alone when they arrived. In a parlor
somewhere perhaps, a little room off to the side, away
from prying eyes.

And the way she was feeling, a moment would be
enough!

When they reached the door, however, it was thrown
open by a smiling Claude, who was so profuse in his
congratulations, Lili didn't have the heart to cut him
short. Apparently her request for a wedding gift hadn't
fallen on deaf ears. He seemed genuinely happy to see
her, and much relieved when she assured him she had
not been hurt.

"Help arrived just in time, Claude. Thanks to you. I
managed to protect myself well enough, but if you hadn't
found Barnaby—and he hadn't gone to Chartreuse—I
don't know what would have happened. I trust Monsieur
Cavarelle has rewarded you well."

"Very well, *madame*," he replied in the modulated
tones of an excellent house servant. It looked like her act
of kindness might turn out to be a good bargain. "The
monsieur sent someone to buy my freedom that same
afternoon, and promised there would be a position for
me, if I chose. It was later I learned that you wanted me

to work for you here or at Bellefleur. I was most pleased, *madame*. It will be an honor to serve you."

Lili had a feeling the honor was hers. He had risked a great deal to help her.

"I am most pleased too, Claude," she said, eyeing the broad staircase that curved up from the spacious entry hall. So Jean-Baptiste had been ahead of her again, even when it came to taking care of the man who saved her. "We will speak later of where you're needed most, here or at the plantation. But it's quite breezy, and we took an open carriage from the cathedral. If you'll just direct me, I'd like to freshen up."

She was racking her brain as she started up the stairs, trying to figure out a way to get Jean-Baptiste to herself for a minute. But she needn't have worried. Waving the servant aside, he took it upon himself to follow directly behind her. Lili had no doubt what he was after! She had caught him looking at her that way several times in the carriage.

Well, good. Let him think what he wanted. He'd find out soon enough that she had something quite different in mind!

She barely had time to take in the sunny corner room, tastefully furnished in shades of beige and rose, with a satin canopy over the mosquito netting on the bed and dozens of delicate bottles—probably filled with his favorite perfumes!—strewn across a gilt-legged vanity. Her eye lit on just the thing she had been looking for. A porcelain water pitcher on a table by the bed.

She had just picked it up and was turning when Jeremy came through the door. Hurling it against the lintel, she watched as a torrent of water and broken shards descended on his head.

37

The look on his face was worth everything she had ever put up with from him. Astonishment blended into disbelief, followed rapidly by alarm as her hands found one of the perfume bottles on the vanity.

That would show him! Delicate crystal shattered against the door, releasing a cloying aroma of jasmine, just as he managed to pull it shut. And that! Another bottle bounced off the newly painted jamb, chipping the finish and toppling, surprisingly intact, onto the rug. Jean-Baptiste ducked instinctively, but not wisely, for his head ended up in exactly the same place as a little china vial with roses all over it.

Shocked, he straightened, staring at her with widening eyes. Lili stopped where she was, the latest bottle still in her hand as she watched a thin line of blood trickle down from his temple. She hadn't intended to hit him. She had only wanted to express—in a way he couldn't possibly misunderstand—what she thought of his disgusting behavior. If he hadn't ducked, the missive would have landed right where she intended, on the wall beside the door.

Before she could say anything, he had covered the ground between them in a single long stride. Trembling, Lili was sure he was going to strike her, which he no doubt thought she deserved after the way she had attacked him. But he only caught her wrists, twisting until she could no longer hold on to the bottle. Pinning her arms behind her, he brought his mouth down hard on hers.

Her gasp of surprise and indignation was lost in the force of that sudden masculine assault. Wildly furious,

Lili struggled to work free, hating him for the way he was claiming her mouth, as if he thought he *owned* it—hating herself even more for the little tremors of response that stirred inside her. Did he think all he had to do was *kiss* her and she would melt into a puddle of quivering compliance? Did he think one show of virility wiped out everything else?

Yet even as she tried to pull back, she knew it was a battle she was going to lose. His lips were too persuasive, hers too eager to remember the sweetness they had shared. Drained by that potent kiss, she felt the last of her strength sapping away, and, knees going weak, she swayed against him, no longer resisting, no longer even wanting to resist.

At least, she thought as he released her at last, he didn't look angry. Only determined—and wildly intense. It seemed he had missed her as much as she missed him. On one level anyhow.

"Is this your way of solving things?" she said sarcastically. "One quick kiss, and all's forgiven?"

"Why not?" His hands let go, but smoldering blue eyes held her in thrall. "It's as good a way to end a quarrel as any. And in this case"—he reached up, touching tentative fingers to the red gash on his forehead—"it may have been necessary to save my life."

Lili noticed that the blood had stopped flowing.

"I wouldn't have hit you if you hadn't ducked."

"And I wouldn't have ducked if you hadn't been throwing those bottles. Do you have any idea what French perfume costs? Ah, but here we are, bickering again . . . and there's such a delightful alternative. Take off your dress."

"What?" Lili gaped at him.

He grinned, enjoying her reaction. "I thought I enunciated quite clearly. Take . . . off . . . your . . . dress."

"But, Jer . . . Jean-Baptiste, you must be insane! What are you saying? That's *our* wedding reception downstairs. People will be arriving any minute." In fact, they were already arriving. Carriages could be heard pulling into the drive, and the sound of voices drifted up, muffled by heavy satin draperies at the windows. "What will they think if we're not there to receive them?"

"They'll think a randy bridegroom decided to start the wedding night a little early. It's happened before, *petite,* and it will happen again. There's plenty of champagne, and servants will circulate with trays of food to keep everyone occupied until the dancing begins. Now, about that dress . . ."

He reached out, gripping the rounded neck firmly with one hand.

"It really is a pity . . . such a pretty thing . . ."

"You wouldn't . . ."

"Oh, but I would."

He meant it. Shivering a little, Lili forced her fingers to find the fastenings, which had been hidden under one arm so they wouldn't mar the lines of the gown. However long she might know this man, she had the feeling he would always be able to catch her off guard, leaving her reeling, as if somehow it were the first time all over again.

The gown came loose, floating to the floor, and she was left in a gauzy silk chemise. It had seemed perfectly adequate earlier, when she had hotly refused to be bound into a corset, which her slender waist did not require. Now, the way his eyes were raking over her, it might not have been there at all.

"I think *that* is expendable." He caught the lacy neckline, as he had earlier with her dress, ripping it rakishly down the front. Then his arms were around her, and somehow they were on the bed, she as impatient as he to pull off the jacket that got in their way, the fine marseilles waistcoat, and both their hands were opening the front of his trousers, not even bothering to remove them.

Oh, God. It *was* the first time. Lili sensed that as she felt him penetrate her, felt the hardness, the strength of him filling her as never before. The first time they had come together not merely with desire, but deep, acknowledged love, and commitments for the future. The first time she had known, as he had all along, that they belonged to each other, that they would never in this life be parted . . . that she was his, and he always and truly hers. Fiercely sweet, possessive instincts consumed her, echoed in the hoarse moan that seemed to be torn out of his throat as their bodies surged and joined for one perfect moment in a completeness neither had ever felt before.

"Ummmm, love . . . I believe I needed that," he murmured as he rolled off her, one hand still tangled in her hair, the other idly caressing her breast. "It's been seven days and fourteen hours, almost to the minute. Lord, I never want to go that long without a woman again."

"A woman?" she teased, sure of him now, and unable to recapture her previous anger. "Or me?"

"You, dammit . . . you have ruined me for anyone else. In all those days, I didn't even *think* about going to another woman. Emasculating bitch! I probably couldn't have done anything if I'd tried."

"I hope not," she said, propping the pillows up behind him and snuggling into his arms. "But I still don't forgive you, Jean-Baptiste. It was a terrible thing, tricking me like that."

"I suppose so . . . but it was fun."

"*Fun?* How can you say that?"

"How can I not say it?" He grinned at the look of mock horror on her face. "You were glorious in your red dress at the quadroon ball, though I had been looking forward to that silver-spangled waterfall. Still, it was an unexpected treat, and very exciting. Any other female would have fainted dead away after being assaulted. But you remained conscious enough to respond to my kiss with astonishing fervor."

"And you tried to take advantage of it! Later, in the carriage, after you had abducted me!"

"Hmmm . . . well, yes." He had the good grace to look sheepish. "I must admit that kiss set my blood boiling. And you did give the impression of being some-what more, uh . . . experienced than you were."

"You mean"—Lili stared at him, intrigued—"you thought I'd been with another man."

"The possibility did occur to me."

"And you didn't mind, considering the fact that you planned to make me your bride."

"It did give me pause," he confessed. "But only for a minute. I was so blasted eager to have you, I didn't think of anything else. Later, when it became clear I was wrong, I felt like a damned boor. I suppose sooner or later I'm going to have to beg your forgiveness for that."

"Sooner or later." Lili smiled enigmatically. It was getting dark, and she noticed for the first time that candles had been lighted on several of the tables. Her new husband, apparently, had a knack for careful prepara-tion. "Was that why you were so reluctant to make love to me later? Because you were afraid of pushing me again?"

He shook his head gently. "I wanted everything to be right between us. We needed time to get to know each other, to become close in other ways too. I did truly want love to come before passion. And I didn't want to rob you of the sweet enchantment of a wedding night."

Lili, thinking of all the wedding nights she had heard about, wrinkled her nose. It seemed to her a barbaric ritual. A young bride, led away from the dancing by her mother—or the groom's sharp-eyed mama, if she was unlucky—dressed in a lacy gown and placed in the middle of an enormous four-poster to wait, no doubt quivering down to her toes, for a man she barely knew. That was an "enchantment" she could do without.

Jean-Baptiste saw the look on her face and laughed.

"Not the kind of wedding night you are obviously imagining. Innocence deflowered is one thing—ignorance is another. I wanted you to be ready and eager for the lovemaking we would share. What do you think I was doing that night you crawled so temptingly into my bed? I thought I could tantalize you, just a little, and keep my masculine impulses under control. Obviously," he added wryly, "I'm not as strong as I thought."

"Thank heaven," Lili said, thinking how angry she had been before, and how much harder it would have been to reconcile if they hadn't had a deeply caring relationship to draw on. "I only wish you'd given in sooner. It would have been a lovely way to pass those rainy afternoons at Bellefleur."

"There'll be plenty of other afternoons," he promised. "We'll be living at Bellefleur a good part of the year. The men I left behind are already planting this season's cane. That's why I took you there, so you could learn to love the place before we moved in." He paused, a funny expression coming over his face. "I picked the room downstairs for your reception because it was the most impressive. I had no idea you'd seen your father there. I had to scramble to get the sitting room across the hall ready for you in the morning."

Lili smiled as she recalled the fire on the hearth, and the cheerful calico table cover. There was bluster to this man, and arrogance enough for a dozen Cavarelles, but he could be sensitive, too, in ways she was just beginning to discover.

"Why didn't we stay there?" she asked. "At Bellefleur. Why did you take me away?"

"Pure selfishness on my part. I wanted to share with you the things that were important to me. The bayous . . . and my friends. I had already acquainted you with your own heritage. I thought you ought to know mine as well."

Selfishness? Lili stared at her wedding dress, in a crumpled heap on the floor. Sensitivity was only one aspect of this man's character. There was a kind of bravado about him too, a reckless disregard of danger that she kept forgetting.

"And you think that was sufficient justification for risking my neck? I know we were in an isolated area, but I can't believe the evils of Grande-Terre are so easily confined."

"Good God—Grande-Terre?" To her amazement, he threw back his head and roared with laughter. "I'd never dream of taking you there. Lafitte is trying to clean the place up, but it's still one of the worst hellholes on earth."

"But you said . . ."

"I did not. *You* said it. You took one look at the place and decided it was Grande-Terre—and the poor, incompetent actors I had hired were ruffians who'd 'cut your throat' if I asked them! Believe me, I had a hard time keeping a straight face when you came out with that. If your imagination hadn't been working so hard, you'd have seen how hopelessly unconvincing they were."

Lili tried not to laugh, but she couldn't help it. She really had been silly. Hadn't she thought, when he took her there, that they were going around in circles, passing the same landmarks over and over? They were probably a few miles from Bellefleur all the time! And when he took her out again—after she had gotten to know the bayous—he had had to blindfold her.

"And all those crates you were bringing in empty every morning and sneaking out at night—"

"Were strictly for your benefit." He looked down at her tenderly, fascinated by the intimacy of her hair splashed across his pillow. It was something he had seen before, but never with the sweet, surprising realization that she was his wife. "There were no pirates in the area. Just fishermen and farmers, for whom I'd been building a schoolhouse—which came in handy to bunk my actors! I had already made the acquaintance of Lafitte, and I *was* trying to win him over, but I think he would have been astonished rather than impressed by that motley crew."

"Then why did you—?"

"Because you caught me red-handed, love, and I had to come up with something. Quickly. I think, under the circumstances, I did rather well."

He had just lowered his head, planning to lead the conversation into more interesting lines with a kiss or two, when a sudden clamor rose from outside, sounding like every pot and metal utensil in the city was being banged together.

Lili sat bolt upright, too startled even to cry out in alarm. Harsh shouts rose above the din, strident, but difficult to make out. Jean-Baptiste tensed for a moment, then settled back on the pillows, half-smiling.

"Ah, I had forgotten. The time-honored custom of the charivari." It seemed that that first impression had been right. Every pot and spoon in the city probably *was* outside their window. "It looks like we're being singularly honored."

Lili giggled. Now that she was getting used to it, she began to distinguish the traditional cry of "Charivari! Charivari!" mingling with an occasional "Santana!" or "Cavarelle! Cavarelle!" Raucous wedding serenades, with burlesque processions and impromptu dancing, were as much a part of the New Orleans spirit as the elaborate *bals masques* or Mardi Gras parades in the days when street masking was still allowed.

"But we're so far out of town, Jean-Baptiste. It hadn't occurred to me anyone would come here."

"I think we'd have to be miles farther upstream before the citizenry would be cheated out of their fun," he replied, chuckling. "I suspect they'd have followed us all the way to Bellefleur." He was beginning to enjoy the bawdy good humor, though not the inappropriate timing, which he suspected had been cued by someone within the house. Ordinarily charivaris were reserved for the remarriage of widows and widowers, or when there was a considerable disparity in age. But given the prominence of the families involved, he supposed the noisy interruption had been inevitable.

A sudden howl went up, a lone wail like the cry of a mad beast, followed by renewed shrieking and much banging of pans. Lili found herself giggling again.

"How long do you think this is going to go on?"

"Hours, all night—I don't know. The more it torments us, the more I suspect they'll keep it up. When Almonaster's young widow remarried, ten years ago, they say the charivari lasted three days."

"Three *days*?"

Jean-Baptiste laughed. "Maybe they'll show mercy if we put in an appearance." Coaxing her out of bed, he reached down and picked up her dress. "We could promise a feast under the trees in the yard . . . and pray to God someone's had the good sense to alert the kitchen. Here, love, put this on. It wouldn't do to show yourself at the window in a dressing gown. Besides, who'll believe you're the bride if you don't look like one?"

Lili slipped into the dress, and even managed to pat her hair into some semblance of order, but it was impossible to work the fastenings without help, and Jean-Baptiste was already at the window, drawing back the draperies. Holding the gown tentatively to both shoulders—and aware of a distinct draft on her back—she went over and joined him. A deafening roar rose from the revelers.

Lili gasped as she saw the size of the crowd that thronged the street and spilled boisterously onto the lawn. A charivari was one of the rare occasions when all classes mingled, and she knew that guests from their own elegant soiree would be rubbing elbows with curious schoolboys and shopkeepers' assistants and laborers from the docks. Some were on horseback, others on foot, some in grotesque disguises or leftover Mardi Gras masks, but all seemed to have found a metal utensil of some kind, an old kettle, a shovel and tongs, a frying pan, a horseshoe, a rusty length of God-knows-what. And they were all banging for all they were worth.

Jean-Baptiste flung the window open, and Lili leaned out, smiling an acknowledgment to the cheers and bawdy good wishes, though she didn't dare wave. She was finding she needed both hands to hold her gown in place. Her new husband was no help, for no sooner had she stepped forward than she felt fingers on her bare back, sliding down to the cleft of her buttocks.

"Jean-Baptiste!" she hissed warningly.

"What, love?" he teased, his hand continuing exactly what it had been doing before—while with the other he had the audacity to wave to the crowd! "If you didn't want to tempt me, why did you leave your dress open?"

"You know perfectly well why. I couldn't get it fastened without help."

"Just as well." He bent over slyly, whispering in her ear, "You'd only have to undo it again."

Lili felt her cheeks flame crimson. The crowd bellowed with delight, redoubling their assault on the pots and kettles. Plainly, they had a good idea what he had just said, though they didn't know, she prayed, that his fingers were sliding forward, touching her in places that evoked very definite responses.

"Stop that right now," she threatened, trying not to let him see he was provoking more than her temper. "Or I'll . . . I'll swoon in your arms—face forward!—and that mob'll have the sight of their lives. The whole town will be talking about my backside for months."

Jean-Baptiste grinned, and she had the unpleasant feeling he was going to call her bluff and she'd have to go through with it! Then he relented, raising both hands as he called out to the crowd, parrying their ribald comments. Fortunately, someone had had the foresight to leave a wooden tub of paper-wrapped candies by the window, and he began to distribute them, a few at a time at first. Then, when that was too slow, he dumped the whole thing, vat and all, into the cheering, churning crowd.

Lili didn't know whether to laugh or throw a fit when, the masses mollified at last, he drew the window shut and closed the curtains. But she didn't have time for either, for Jean-Baptiste was making it very clear that he intended to pursue the diversion he had begun before. And Lili, remembering the feel of those wickedly tantalizing fingers, was not averse to the idea.

They spent several hours alone in the room they would be sharing, during the season at least, for the rest of their lives. Music floated up the curving staircase, sometimes rollicking, sometimes the sweet, haunting strains of a waltz, and they sat together on the bed, long after the lovemaking was over, talking as they never had before. Midnight had come and gone, the *ambigu*, the night meal, had been served downstairs, and Jean-Baptiste sent for fresh fruit and oyster-and-truffle pâté, with imported biscuits, which they devoured greedily, scattering crumbs all over the bed.

"I still don't see why you had to keep me in the dark," Lili said, finding to her delight that he had included several of the little ginger cakes he knew she loved. "A melodramatic kidnapping is one thing—but all those weeks we spent together? Why didn't you tell me then?"

"I couldn't—at first. I had given my word to your father. And I was enjoying myself, love. I liked teaching you about Bellefleur, and the bayous, and life in the city. And you were enjoying the kind of freedom you'll never know again. There didn't seem to be any harm. Later . . . well, later, I was afraid."

"Afraid?" That was the last thing she'd expected. "Of what?"

"That you'd be so angry you'd refuse to marry me. I almost did tell you—that morning I dropped you off at your father's house. The words were right there, on the tip of my tongue. But I decided to play it safe and make sure you were at the altar first."

"That doesn't sound like you. Playing it safe."

"It doesn't, does it?" He poured a glass of Madeira and held it to the light. "I doubt I've done three cautious things in my life—though maybe I should have. If I'd returned you sooner, as your father expected, you wouldn't have overheard an innocent conversation and felt you had to run away. Oh, God, Lili. If anything had happened to you—"

He broke off as he recalled the excruciating torture of that long night and the even longer day that had followed. He had blocked it out of his mind, not allowing himself to think about it—but it came back sometimes in dreams, and he woke to find himself trembling. He could have lost her. They might have taken her someplace he could never have found her. They might have hurt her so badly her mind would have snapped. He had heard of cases like that. And it would have been his own damn stupid, clumsy fault!

Lili saw the pain he couldn't put into words. Taking the glass from his hand, she set it on the table and kissed him slowly, gently on the lips.

"Nothing did happen to me, darling. I'm here and I'm safe . . . and I love you very much. I just hope it's over now, and I won't have to worry about your challenging that pig LeClerc to a duel."

"Nothing would have given me greater pleasure." He grinned ruefully, seeing that she was trying to distract him, and adoring her for it. The enchanting girl who had caught his eye that day on the levee was turning into a beautiful, tactful woman. "But I couldn't risk causing a scandal. Your father doesn't know what happened—or anyone else, for that matter. I had to content myself with giving the son of a bitch twenty-four hours to sell everything and get out of town. I don't think he'll trouble you again. But things might not have worked out so well, dammit!"

"Well, then," she said softly, "if you're feeling guilty . . . you'll have to make it up to me."

"Now?" He raised one brow.

"Not that way." She laughed. "You have such a predictable mind, Jean-Baptiste. I was thinking that we have to go downstairs soon and face all those guests, who've no doubt been having a wonderful time chatting about our absence. If you really want to make it up to me, you'll figure out how we can make an entrance without every woman in the place blushing and every man giving you a bawdy wink!"

38

After careful deliberation, and another helping of oyster-and-truffle pâté, it was decided that Jean-Baptiste should go downstairs first, alone. Stopping briefly in his dressing room for a fresh shirt—and a chance to rinse off the slight wound on his forehead and brush a lock of hair over it—he made his way to the ballroom, where the dancing had recommenced. A rather sulky maid, Marie-Louise, was sent upstairs to see what she could do with Lili's hair.

Pausing in the doorway, Jean-Baptiste enjoyed the reaction as one after another of the guests spotted him and hurried over, ostensibly to offer congratulations—though he noticed they all managed to get in a none-too-discreet question or two about his bride, and where she was at the moment.

Lying down, he told them, with a straight face. Or so he understood . . . though he hadn't seen her himself since she'd gone upstairs. It had been a long day, and naturally, after the warmth of the cathedral, she was feeling somewhat faint.

He suppressed a grin as he thought of the way she had looked when he left her, seated in front of her mirror in a dressing gown that did nothing to hide her charms, staring at pearl-twined braids that were in total disarray after their recent passion. There wasn't a way in the world anyone was going to think she'd been anyplace other than where she was, but he admired her spunk for trying.

It surprised him a little, his need to protect this woman, even from the affectionate gossip of friends who wanted nothing more than to rejoice in her happiness. He hadn't realized marriage would be like this. He had always thought of it as a convenience, a way to have the things a man wanted. A home, children, companionship if it worked out that way, a certain warm appreciation in his bed. He hadn't known the closeness would be so intense, the beating of her heart palpable in his own strong chest, even when they were apart. He hadn't known there would be such a difference, thinking of her upstairs in front of the mirror, and knowing she was his wife. His sweet, glorious, sensual, infinitely precious wife.

"Well, brother, I see you're your usual impetuous self . . . or do you expect me to believe that cock-and-bull story about a fragile bride languishing on her pillows upstairs?"

Julien had appeared beside him, looking carelessly elegant in his wedding garb.

"Easy for you to say. You've been getting *your* impetuosity out of the way, if even half the complaints I've heard from Don Andrés are true. And you haven't been separated from your lady for seven days."

"Touché." Julien, who never blushed, turned a ruddy hue. "But she is a little beauty, don't you think? . . . Oh, I know she's not elegant and glamorous, like your bride. But glamour's always been your thing, brother—and feisty high spirits. Me, I wanted someone sweet and plump to cuddle up and coo in my arms. And damned if I wasn't lucky enough to get her."

Jean-Baptiste glanced at Simone, who had been cornered by an elderly dowager with the most extraordinary coffee-tinted hair. She *was* turning into a little beauty, in her own quiet, very surprising way.

"I think we're both luckier than a pair of scoundrels like us deserves."

Julien agreed, laughing good-naturedly, and they chatted for a few minutes before he drifted away to greet an acquaintance across the hall. Jean-Baptiste had just turned, thinking he might send one of the maids up to see how Lili was getting on, when he noticed Don Andrés coming toward him.

Catching the stern expression on the old gentleman's face, he braced himself. Parental prerogatives, it seemed, died hard.

"Don't tell me you're going to berate me too," he said

with a deliberately rakish look. "For my 'impetuous' manner. I've just been hearing about it from my brother."

"Yes, well . . . the lad is right. You might have waited a decent interval before taking my daughter upstairs. If you can't consider her sensibilities, at least keep up appearances. There are certain conventions that must be observed."

"If you had wanted a 'conventional' marriage for your daughter, Don Andrés, you wouldn't have arranged to begin it by having her kidnapped! And if you had been looking for a proper, conventional suitor, you wouldn't have considered me."

"I suppose not, but . . . Dammit, man!" Gray-black eyes snapped beneath bushy brows. "You took advantage of her! That wasn't part of the bargain. I had a hard time keeping control when she insisted on telling me what happened. I really must protest—"

"No, sir, you must not. You are my father-in-law, and I respect you. I would never willing cause you grief. But Lili is my wife now, and you are a guest in my home. I ask you to remember that."

The old don's mouth tightened; then a faint twitch showed at the corners.

"I seem to have made a good choice. Not only have you learned to handle my strong-willed daughter, you're doing an excellent job with her papa as well."

Chuckling to himself, he turned, and with a jaunty step went out into the hall. Jean-Baptiste noticed that he paused for a moment to speak with Claude, who, to his surprise, had been quietly organizing things all evening. No doubt that was how the candies had made their way into the bedroom. And since the noisy charivari hadn't started up again, he'd probably arranged adequate refreshments under the trees as well.

Now he was listening attentively to Don Andrés, and pointing vaguely toward something at the rear of the house. The place where the revelers were enjoying their repast, Jean-Baptiste thought with a twinge. There was a lady who had almost certainly come with the others, curious and full of fun, and eager to share in her lover's big night. And because of the color of her skin, she wouldn't be coming inside.

It was fully an hour before Lili appeared downstairs.

The music had just broken off; one quadrille was ending and another beginning to form as she hesitated on the threshold. No longer garbed in her bridal gown, she had changed to a simpler outfit, a pale yellow silk underdress, interwoven with gold threads and covered by a floating film of gossamer muslin. The only trim was a bold Greco-Roman motif around the hem, deep blue to pick up the diamond-circled sapphire at her throat. Instead of redoing her hair, she had twined ribbons in various shades of blue and metallic gold among the pearl-studded braids and, tying them together, let them hang in one thick strand down her back.

The minx. It was all Jean-Baptiste could do to keep from whistling with admiration as he turned and saw her. She was going to get away with it. If she had come in, skirt rumpled, coiffure patched together, everyone would have known exactly what she'd been up to. This way they could only guess, and whisper—which he had a feeling she was going to enjoy.

She stepped forward with the most sweetly innocent smile he had ever seen on her lips.

"I do hope you'll all forgive me," she said to the roomful of people, who had suddenly turned and were staring her way. "I couldn't bear to come down in that heavy satin gown. The train is so cumbersome, I could hardly move . . . and I intend to dance with my husband all night."

It was her cue to him, and Jean-Baptiste, picking it up, came and took her in his arms. Showing just enough restraint to hold her decorously, he whirled her, without music, out into the center of the floor. The orchestra was confused for a moment—obviously they hadn't expected this—but Claude, who had been circulating among the guests with a tray of champagne, went over and whispered something to the leader; and belatedly, the slow three-quarters rhythm of a waltz filled the air.

Lili let herself go, forgetting everything else as she swayed to the sensual lure of the dance. It seemed so long ago, yet only yesterday, when a mysterious man in a mask had taught her how to waltz . . . and changed her life forever. Later, when they had been married longer and guests came to balls in their home, she would have little time for such indulgence. She'd be much too busy with her duties as hostess. But tonight all the rules were broken. Tonight she was a bride, and the music and the sweet enchantment were hers.

People swirled by, a montage of ever-changing colors, but Lili was so absorbed with the newness of being a married lady, she barely noticed. Only occasionally did one stand out. A girl she had known in convent school . . . a former beau, who kept throwing reproachful glances in her direction . . . a contemporary of Don Andrés', rigidly stuffy when he came to call, but kicking up his heels now with the best of them. And, of course, Simone, who, following Lili's lead, had slipped upstairs and put on something more sensible.

"I hope you don't mind," she said when they found themselves side by side as sets were forming for a new quadrille. "It was so clever of you, I couldn't resist copying. How did you ever think of such a thing?"

Lili grinned. Simone was probably the only person in the ballroom who hadn't an inkling why she had done it. "What a horrid child you are," she whispered, adroitly changing the subject. "You knew about this all along . . . and you didn't breathe a word."

"But I didn't!" Simone protested. "I just found out a little while ago because . . . well, there were reasons I had to know. But I swore to Julien I wouldn't tell. So of course I couldn't."

Of course. Lili grinned again as the set began and they were separated. Simone was obviously besotted with the man. She would do anything he asked. Just as she herself would do anything Jean-Baptiste wanted—though she prayed to heaven he didn't know it. She was used to twisting men around her little finger, and she rather liked the idea of keeping it up.

Everyone she knew seemed to be there, people she hadn't seen since she was a child, some of whom had traveled great distances to attend, and new friends, just met. All the men who could be spared from the plantation had come, and their wives, for Jean-Baptiste was fiercely democratic and refused to invite just the *crème* of society. Vava was there, of course, with her new husband, married just in time, if the roundness of her waist was any indication. And the three generations of Étiennes, the old man with hair as white as Don Andrés', and

Stevie and Dédé, and Tin-Tin, looking so dashing in a superbly tailored suit that the daughters of well-to-do men were fluttering their eyelashes and flaunting their dowries in front of him.

Lili couldn't resist a smile. It looked as if Tin-Tin was going to get himself settled into some staid old family—who wouldn't know what hit them when his relatives came to call!

Even M'mère was dancing. Her arthritis seemed to have declared a truce, and she bounced her heft with considerable verve through quadrille after galop after waltz, partnered by the elder Étienne, who, it turned out, was the man she had jilted years ago to tend to a succession of Fleurie daughters. There didn't seem to be any hard feelings, as far as Lili could make out. In fact, the recently widowed Étienne appeared quite smitten with his old flame. Watching out of the corner of her eye, Lili couldn't help wondering if fate was giving the generous nursemaid a second chance at romance.

Not that it was likely. Lili forced her concentration back on her feet so she wouldn't disgrace Jean-Baptiste as he spun her deftly around the floor. M'mère had already found several occasions to hint that she expected to be invited to Bellefleur in nine or ten months. Taking care of other women's babies had become a habit, and at her age, she wasn't inclined to change.

Still, when it came to matters of the heart, anything was possible. And they did make a good-looking couple.

Lili left the dancing only once, to go out into the garden. She had been vaguely surprised when Jean-Baptiste mentioned where her father was, and why. In her happiness, she had completely forgotten Chartreuse. She couldn't invite the woman to join them, of course. Such a social gaffe would clear the house in a matter of minutes. But she could go out and spend some time with her.

Light from the open French windows sprawled across the veranda, where dancers were enjoying the coolness, and pretty girls drifted off to stroll with their beaux through the shadows, eluding sharp-eyed chaperones. Behind the house, well past the formal gardens, tables had been set up under strings of colored lanterns that swayed in the breeze. Here the rowdy serenaders, pots and tongs forgotten, were stuffing themselves with gumbo, and *étoufée* so spicy that guests were sneaking out from the ballroom to enjoy a taste. Boisterous laughs and shouts rose above the music, and an open field provided space for energetic and wonderfully comical burlesques of the dancing within.

The lanterns cast more colored shadow than light, and Lili, in her simple ball dress, was able to wander among the tables unrecognized. She spotted Papa first, his white hair standing out against the elegant velvet *chaqueta* he always wore on formal occasions. Then she saw the woman beside him, slim and stately in a dark mantle, the hood thrown back to reveal startlingly aristocratic features.

Lili had almost reached them when Chartreuse looked up, flashing a warning glance. Belatedly Lili recalled that Don Andrés knew nothing about the slave auction, and therefore had no idea she'd even met his mistress.

Impulsively she thrust out her hands.

"You and I have never been friends, Chartreuse . . . but we are not enemies. I hope you realize that."

The other woman smiled, recognizing and enjoying the ploy of her own words twisted around to suit the occasion. "Yes, I realize. I'm glad you do too."

The few words that followed were suitably vague, and pointedly directed to Chartreuse, for Lili was still miffed with her father. Taking her leave a short time later, she assured the woman she'd be welcome anytime she felt comfortable visiting. There were, after all, many hours when no one was around, and Lili could entertain whom she chose in her parlor.

And of course, she added mischievously, they'd be hosting *many* masquerades.

She was aware, as she drifted off again, that the last look her father had given her was one of gratitude, and she was glad for his sake that she had made the effort. He had treated her abominably, of course! In that imperious way of his, he had simply decided what was best and set about it, without asking her opinion. But he *had* done it out of love. And she couldn't argue with the way things had turned out.

"I think you've finally laid your ghosts to rest," Jean-Baptiste said later as they walked alone through the beautiful rose garden, some distance from the house. Music seemed to float on the moonlight, faint and far away, and the air was sweet with perfume.

"Ghosts?"

"Lili-Ange and her Roger, and the others that came after. And your own tragically unhappy mother."

"What a funny way to put it, Jean-Baptiste. They aren't *ghosts*. They're just poor, sad people I loved . . . though I never really knew them. Not even Mama."

"Aren't they, *petite*?" He took her in his arms and began to whirl her down the long curved paths that wound through newly planted beds of roses. The orchestra was playing a quadrille, but he was holding her as if it were a waltz, creating steps of his own. "You couldn't see or feel them or hear them groaning in the night. But ghosts—real ghosts—aren't eerie visions. They're spirits you can't let go of. Parts of the past that haunt your heart."

The music sighed to a stop, and Lili left his arms, drifting deeper into the garden. There were no lanterns here, but the moonlight was bright, and roses seemed to glow blue-red everywhere she looked.

"I suppose I haven't been able to let go," she admitted softly. "I should have, long ago, but there's something of the little girl in me, who still believes in fairy tales."

"But you're not a little girl anymore, love. You're a woman."

"Yes, I think I am . . . thanks to you."

Jean-Baptiste reached out, picking the prettiest of the roses, a bud just coming to maturity.

"Here, let it end as it began. A single rose in the mud-dappled snows of France, offered by a man who wanted one night's pleasure . . . And a rose in the hand of a man who asks for a lifetime of love. And commitment."

Lili took it. "I do love you, Jean-Baptiste."

"Then it is ended, once and for all? The Fleurie curse? Not just in reality, but in your heart?"

Lili felt the velvet smoothness of the petals against her fingers.

"It is ended . . . once and for all."

"Good." He held out his arms. "The musicians have started again, a waltz this time. The night is warm, love . . . the moonlight soft on the roses."

"I don't know . . ." Lili glanced back at the house, windows dazzling with brightness. "It's our party, and everything is so gay. Maybe we should go back."

"There'll be other parties."

"And other moonlit nights," she reminded him.

"Yes, but not like this."

"No . . ." Lili smiled as she tucked the rose in her bosom, careful of the thorns. "Not like this." Letting go of the last of her inhibitions, she went into his arms. The music beckoned, the moonlight was waiting . . . and it seemed a shame to waste them.

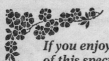

If you enjoyed this book, take advantage of this special offer. Subscribe now and . . .

GET A *FREE* HISTORICAL ROMANCE
—— NO OBLIGATION(a $3.95 value) ——

Each month the editors of True Value will select the four best historical romance novels from America's leading publishers. Preview them in your home Free for 10 days. And we'll send you a FREE book as our introductory gift. No obligation. If for any reason you decide not to keep them, just return them and owe nothing. But if you like them you'll pay *just* $3.50 each and save at least $.45 each off the cover price. (Your savings are a minimum of $1.80 a month.) There is no shipping and handling or other hidden charges. There are no minimum number of books to buy and you may cancel at any time.

send in the coupon below